MACHIR BAY

Alasdair Wham

Greenan Publishing

Machir Bay

First published in Great Britain in 2017 by Greenan Publishing, Ayr.

ISBN 978-0-9933400-1-7
Copyright 2017

A catalogue record for this book is available from the British Library.

For further information please contact info@greenanpublishing.co.uk

This book is dedicated to Ian Gemmell, born 1917, son of Christina MacMillan, Duich Lots. His love of family, life and Islay continues to be a great inspiration.

1

The contours of the land were familiar, the cooling breeze off the sea expected, the smell of wild flowers evocative, stirring distant memories. However, this was not the time for sentimentality; there was a task to be completed. He didn't want to think about what might come after; for now, he felt no fear, only a steely determination.

Through the binoculars he scanned the landscape. Below him, in a hollow beneath the cliff, was the old manse, a fine house, his father had told him, although he had never received an invite, never wanted to go. Now tourists booked it and the row of cottages beside it for holidays. Beyond the former manse was the church, perched on a hill, a former place of worship for locals, now a ruin, the roof having collapsed, the roof timbers fallen into the pews, looking like oversized wooden crosses. The once gleaming, white church building, closed for many years, was now scoured of its paint by the storms off the Atlantic, surrounded by gravestones, some of which had toppled over, others with their inscriptions now indecipherable. All remnants of a former age when the area had been more populated. Only bird life now flourished around the ruin, including the distinctive choughs, crow-like, but with red beaks and legs, and countless starlings.

There was a cottage by the church, and a new graveyard, beyond the self-catering cottages. To the seaward side of the church he could see the tall cross in the military graveyard, with its large bronze commemorative sword fastened to the stonework of the cross, towering over the rows of headstones, all within a low stone wall. He flashed a brief smile of satisfaction when he thought of the opportunities that the war had offered. The unexpected harvest from the sea had changed everything – not always for the good, he was now forced to realise. But this was not the time for regrets and, anyway, today would balance matters once and for all.

He could see the beach and the sea beyond the sand dunes, white capped waves indicating that conditions were rough. He knew well the fierce tides that haunted the west coast of Islay. Today was not a day for sailing, not with strong south-westerly winds blowing across the North Channel, which separated Islay from Ireland. The number of shipwrecks along the coast bore testimony to the folly of not checking the conditions before setting sail. Later, perhaps – if he still read the weather runes correctly – the weather would improve.

He manoeuvred his body, trying to get comfortable, his limbs aching with the long wait on the wet ground, the sun having not yet penetrated the ridge he lay on. Without taking his eyes off the scene below he fumbled for his hip flask and swallowed a mouthful of whisky, the fiery peaty liquid burning his throat, its warmth soothing his body and mind.

Memories of Kilchoman beach flooded back, engulfing him, like one of the winter storms which battered the coastline. Fragments of memories, like strands of DNA, swirled in his mind; family, fortunes, opportunities, all came to mind and were put firmly aside to concentrate on the task in hand.

Machir Bay. It would begin and end here. How appropriate,

6

he mused. Of the many bays along the indented coastline of the Rhinns of Islay, it was wider than most, at nearly a mile and a quarter, with high sand dunes, the southern half broken up by a stream which wound its way into the bay through the sand dunes, passing close to a car park before finally merging with another burn which emptied into the sea. At the southern end, where he lay, the bay was bound by a row of hills, which started as grassy slopes near sea level, above the rocky interface with the sea, but were crowned by steep cliff faces. The remains of an old military radar building, along with the more recent modern microwave communication towers that relayed information to and from other islands to the north-west, were perched atop the cliffs. North of the stream which spilled out onto the beach the dunes were much lower, almost at the level of the sands. A wire fence separated the beach from grassy fields, with cows and sheep grazing on the fertile grass. At the northern end, the sandy beach gave way to a rocky shore and, past the fence, a rolling grassy slope and low hills, which in season were populated with clumps of wild flowers, adding a rich tapestry of colour. This was true machir: grass-covered sand dunes, a unique natural environment, although he had never been much interested in the detail.

Just to the south of the stream, a tame trickle today, easily forded by those walking on the beach, the outline of a shipwreck could be seen at low tide, its metal structure coated in seaweed and slimy to touch. The bay was popular with surfers, who ignored the warning signs at the car park: strong undercurrents made entering the waters in the bay hazardous, with the danger of being dragged out to sea. It was a beautiful stretch of coastline, popular with those wanting fresh air and a walk, but he was familiar with the underlying dangers.

In his day there had been few tourists. Kilchoman and it scattering of houses were remote, a long journey by pony and trap from Bowmore or Port Charlotte, along a narrow road which crossed the hill from Loch Indaal. Beyond the road was Loch Gorm, an inland loch, a gleaming blue colour reflecting the sun, and beyond that Saligo Bay, further round the coast and even more exposed to the Atlantic breakers. Closer he could see the new distillery, peat smoke rising from the pagoda. In the past he had heard tales of others, more discreetly operated. Surrounding the loch and distillery were fields of ripening barley, a future harvest for the island's distilleries.

The gulp of whisky had done the trick, temporarily heightening his senses. With renewed focus he peered through the binoculars, locating the coastguard houses at a sharp corner in the single track road which wound up a hill to stop in front of the church. He could remember when the coastguard station and houses had not been built and the road up to the church was but a dirt track. The houses were also next to the start of the rough track leading down to the car park at the beach. Now he zoomed in on the bungalow on the hillside beyond the coastguard houses. It was as he remembered, although there had been changes and additions: a porch, a hut in the garden, a stone wall enclosing the house and garden extending down the access track, separating it from the farmer's field. His binoculars stayed on the house, studying the people who now and again appeared briefly in the windows as they moved about. He would be patient.

His mind wandered back to days on the beach. He had rarely been there for pleasure, but to search for salvage or gather seaweed for fertiliser. Hard days, long days, which he doubted whether the present occupants of the cottage could ever comprehend. Even on a day when the waves were not being driven by the wind or tide, wave after wave would break onto the beach before withdrawing. Nature's tidal display of incessant probing energy was impressive, particularly on stormy days when the roar of the sea, always present to some degree, was deafening. Today, as he had predicted, the wind was beginning to slacken off, no storm threatening. On windy days, however, the breaking edge of the waves would be flicked up by the wind, flecks of spray cast high as the waves tumbled over one another in their charge for the beach. This was the contested land, the narrow margin between sea and land, where the churning sea cascaded over the sand, spreading out, tentacles of water spilling far and fast as waves broke before retreating, leaving a slurry of soft sand. Today, as the tide line receded, several sanderlings scurried around the soft sand, stopping momentarily to stab the surface with their beaks, searching for small creatures lurking under the surface.

Time dragged. A sea fog, a haar, rolled in, covering the beach, sinking into the hollows, which would make his task easier, he hoped. It was then that he saw movement by the bungalow and preparations for a picnic on the sand dunes. Surely now he would have his opportunity: he steadied himself with another dram of whisky.

Other picnickers retreated to the tops of the dunes where the sea fog had already dispersed, still enjoying the day. A few people were walking along the beach, some exercising dogs; mostly they were heading towards the north end where the conditions were brighter. Even on a good day the beach was never busy. After all, this was Islay.

• • •

Through the haar a small boy, aged around four, ran playing with a plastic sword, slashing it through the air as imaginary pirates retreated before him, searching for a pot of gold, his tracksuit bottoms already splashed with sea water and flecked with wet sand, as were his red wellingtons. He was followed by a Border

9

Collie, who constantly circled him before jinking in to tempt him with strands of seaweed to be thrown, her long lean body mounted on long legs, ideally suited to running fast. The boy was wrapped up in his own imagination and ignored the dog's persistent attempts to engage him. On the beach, below the sand dunes, the temperature was cooler, the swirling mist lingering, trapped by the higher ground. It was becoming an unpleasant coolness, a dampness which penetrated the body and seemed to enhance the tang of salt sea air. It seemed the boy had wandered far from his parents, who were still atop the sand dunes.

Out in the bay a gannet dropped from the sky, its black-tipped wings appearing to merge in a vee shape as it plunged into the sea only to emerge seconds later, triumphant, water draining from its feathers, with a small fish, plucked from the security of the shoal, in its beak.

It was a cough which alerted the boy to the fact that someone was close. Startled he stopped, his sword poised in mid-air, and looked around half expecting to see his dad ready to play games. Through the swirling mist, however, the boy saw someone quite different; a man squatting on his haunches looking at him, shivering in the cool atmosphere. Startled, he stopped, his game forgotten. Again there was a cough, as if the man was clearing his throat. It wasn't a pleasant sound. The dog circled the man, tail wagging, but stopped a few feet away and lay down with her head turned away but with her eyes still on him, mouth open, panting after all the exertion of running along the beach, her black and white markings blending into the scene.

'I know your mum and dad very well,' the man whispered, finally breaking the silence, but there was no warmth in his tone. His voice was brittle, thin with a rasp. His mind seemed to be elsewhere, his eyes seemingly unfocussed.

The boy looked back, the sword held diagonally across his

chest, almost in defiance, but without any conviction, wide eyes staring. Had he met a real pirate? He had been warned about strangers and regretted getting so far away from his parents. He anxiously glanced along the beach in the direction from which he had come, feeling vulnerable. The sand dunes seemed far away and he shivered.

'I know your parents. It's okay, don't be frightened.' The man spoke again without any conviction. Even the boy sensed the insincerity, as he felt increasingly uneasy. The man didn't move but remained squatting. 'Come here,' he said. 'Come here.' The second command was given with more force, more passion, but still no warmth. He slowly held out a hand and shuffled slightly, as if he had been unbalanced by the move. A narrow, forced smile played fleetingly on his narrow lips, his gaze fixed on the boy, as if he was trying to hypnotise him, a snake ready to strike, a gannet ready to plunge. The dog went to pick up seaweed that lay in front of her, as if trying to break the spell, but stopped and lay down, her game forgotten. Alert to the new situation, her mouth opened and closed, as if she was gulping.

Imperceptibly the man edged forward, inch by inch, the impression of his feet leaving a twin trail behind him in the wet sand. The boy's eyes were now wide open, his lips tightly pressed together. Words failed, his mouth opening and shutting without sound, suppressed by fear. Another glance along the beach, more desperate this time.

'Come with me and I'll take you back to your parents. They'll be worried about you. I want to talk to them anyway.'

The boy stood rooted. The plastic sword fell to the ground but he did not try to retrieve it. A new small patch of damp spread on his tracksuit bottoms, and with that he seemed more agitated, losing control. He tried to speak but couldn't and a tear ran down his cheek, his face flushed. The dog, its tail now between its legs, edged into the space between them, emitting a low growl.

'We need to go,' the man said, and suddenly through the mist he launched himself at the boy, covering the short distance between them with surprising speed. The dog yelped and started to bark. The man aimed a kick at her and as a result staggered, losing balance. The boy turned to run, letting out a scream, but was transfixed to the spot, and it was now too late as the man grabbed him by the arm. Both fell to the sand, with the man clinging stubbornly to the boy. With an effort he clambered to his feet and plucked the boy from the sand, grasping him firmly under one arm with the boy's feet dangling in the air behind him.

'Got you,' he said, any pretence of friendliness gone, holding the boy under his arm, his feet dragging on the sand. He started to walk along the beach in the opposite direction from which the boy came, a hand now clasped firmly over the boy's mouth. The dog ran around, starting to bark, yelping louder and louder, ever more frantic.

The waves continued to crash onto the shore, but were now more distant as the tide continued to retreat, exposing more of the outline of the old shipwreck. From further along the beach voices could be heard shouting hysterically. On the track, which led over from Kilchiaran Bay, a group of people could be seen running down towards the bay. Danger had always been part of Machir Bay, it seemed, and safety on its shores could be elusive, as many sailors had discovered. Through storm and calm many a tragedy had been enacted. Today was no different.

2

Sunday - looking back

I awoke almost before I woke, if that makes sense, desperate to know if yesterday had been a bad dream, a surreal experience. Briefly, I remembered a soap where an actor had agreed to return to a long running series after a contractual dispute, all the events of the previous series undone by his sudden reappearance. Incidents from the last series were just removed, life's script rewritten, births, affairs and deaths undone, by the stroke of a scriptwriter's pen. If only it were that simple. The new reality rushed in like a tsunami swamping a beach, overpowering all in its surge and then dragging back the debris of peoples' lives into the ocean as it retreated, leaving a mess, everything totally changed.

I lay in bed, hardly having slept, my body still aching, the sun shining through the crack at the edge of the bedroom door to let me that know that a new day had begun. The empty space beside me only increased my sense of dread. What would Jenny think, when I couldn't even give myself a coherent answer? The duvet cover was twisted around me, its floral pattern smeared with my blood. At least, I believed it was my own.

Let me think. Friday was normal, but sometime between then and Saturday morning everything had changed. But how? There was a blank, as if my brain had stopped recording, stopped

13

inputting images, experiences, stopped creating memories. A complete breakdown. I, a cognisant human, had been placed on pause. Something had happened to my body. Had it been shut down, placed in suspended animation for a few hours? Was that possible?

When I slowly became conscious on that Saturday morning, when someone or something had pressed the play button again and my life had resumed, I had awoken with my head pressed against the corduroy pattern of our blue couch, my body resting partly on the couch, partly on the floor. The metallic smell and taste of blood and the stain on the couch alarmed me. I felt my cheek. It was scratched and there was a throbbing, stabbing pain on the side of my head, increasing by the second as I tried to move, leaving no doubt that I had been injured.

I tried to raise my top half so that I was perched on my knees but my head spun and I started to retch. I slumped down again. Gradually, I was becoming more aware of my body. My clothes were wet, one of my shoes was missing, and my shirt was ripped, one sleeve hanging by a few threads. The waves of nausea continued, threatening to overwhelm me, even as I lay head down on the couch. I closed my eyes and fought hard not to pass out. Sometime later, I don't know how long, I came around again and this time, using the couch for support, I edged my way towards the bathroom. More muscles were aching now and I rubbed them to try and ease the pain. The pain came in spasms, but this time, crawling along the floor, I reached the bathroom.

I lay on the cold tiles on the bathroom floor, gathering my strength, waiting until the urge to retch had passed, and then sat up slowly. I looked around. At least all was familiar, but my eyes were struggling to focus. The mirror above the hand basin seemed particularly blurred.

I started to examine myself, working down from my head.

That sounds systematic, but I really wasn't capable of that: it was more random probing at the sore bits as they transmitted signals to my brain. I struggled to stand up, knocking over the pale blue washing basket, fumbling to put the spilled clothes back in it, and hanging onto the toilet bowl to steady myself, but eventually I managed it. I splashed some cold water on my face and rubbed it with a towel I grabbed from the heated towel rail. The towel was soon smeared in blood, but is softness was comforting and I held it against my face, its warmth helping. Feeling, for the first time, a little strength returning, I dropped the towel and looked at the mirror above the basin.

I retched into the sink, an instinctive response. On the mirror was a message, written with gaudy pink lipstick in big bold letters.

Listen – don't go down to the beach

Listen was underlined several times. What the hell did that mean and why was it there? And as an afterthought, who wrote it? It was too much for my brain to take in. I grabbed the towel, using it as I had seen my son Ben use a blanket, as a comforter.

I waited a few minutes, stealing myself, the towel draped like a veil over my head. I lifted it and looked again, this time focussing on myself. My eyes were bloodshot, my mop of brown hair was matted with blood and entangled. Down my bloodied right cheek were several long scratch marks and on my neck was what looked like a love bite. Panic hit me like an electric shock, both gripping and painful. What had I done? Then another wave of panic surged through me. Where were Jenny and Ben? An animal like cry rose from within and I screamed out loud, my head pounding, blood pulsing strongly in the arteries of my neck and my body shaking. I calmed only when I remembered that they were away for a few days.

I stripped off my clothes, searching for the sources of pain. Some bruises had emerged already, others were still developing, just tender points. I washed myself then, still not feeling clean, slumped in the shower cubicle and turned on the water. The cold water jolted me but it quickly became warm and I sat motionless, letting the water wash over me. It teased at the cuts and bruises but added warmth to my body, the chill I felt gradually receding.

Eventually I stood up and towelled myself dry. In the bedroom I searched for clothes to wear. At least they were where I expected; a sense of normality briefly returning. I didn't have the strength to shut the drawers and still barefoot I went to the kitchen. I flicked the switch on the kettle and waited until I could hear the water approaching boiling before grabbing a white mug from the mug tree and fumbling for the coffee jar beside it. I sat down at the chair beside the kitchen table, added coffee to the mug and water and stirred. Then I stretched for the sugar bowl and added two spoonfuls. I stirred the contents for a while. It was therapeutic. I sipped the hot liquid slowly. Like the cranking up of an engine, stuttering, then purring, life slowly returned

I walked around the house, almost hoping that the walls would shout out what had happened. I noticed that the front door was open. Had it ever been shut? Had someone forced entry or had I let them in. I pulled up the blind, stopping when the light began to dazzle me.

I was relieved that, at least, I seemed to recognise the view. Over the garden wall and the grassy field beyond were sand dunes and then the sea. I knew where I was for certain. My house had not been transported to another site.

I walked around, looking at the mirror again. I didn't understand what the message meant – it was a total puzzle. Was it even a message for me? I had a sudden thought – take a photo with my phone. It would give me something to do, but despite searching the house I couldn't find it. I felt anger surge and I swore out loud, but felt no different. Can you see why I was so

16

nervous about waking up on Sunday morning? Nothing made sense, nothing at all. My whole bloody world had been scrambled like a jigsaw and I did not have the ability or the cover picture on the jigsaw box to piece it together again.

I sat down. Memories of what had happened on Friday were returning. I could remember most of Friday. A quiet day, a day off work, a walk along the beach, talking to some tourists at the car park beside the beach, and an evening meal, one of the portions of stew prepared by Jenny before she left. The thought of her made my stomach leap, I had to be able to explain all this to her. Late night cup of coffee and then... it started to blur. Had I gone out for another walk?

I tried to rationalise. Something had occurred. No idea what, but later I had found myself injured in my own house, with no recollection of how it had happened, the door opened, a shoe missing, a strange scrawled message on my bathroom mirror. What was I to do? Should I call the police, or Jenny, or no one until I could make sense of it? I must have sat for hours, my capacity to make any decision diminished by tiredness, exhaustion, pain.

The sun was now shining through the small window on the western side; the day was now well advanced. I finally made up my mind and decided to have another shower and go to bed. The shower was good but my legs and arms were now very tender, with ugly coloured bruising emerging. I cleaned my teeth and walked to the bedroom. I lifted the pillow and automatically reached for my pyjamas. Neatly folded, I was a creature of habit and Jenny did not like untidiness. I picked up the pyjama top and put it on, fastening the buttons. I reached for the bottoms but realised that something was in them. I grasped the pyjama bottoms and recognised the outline of my phone. There was a smudge of blood on the screen but it looked intact. Why would the phone be there? I always switched it off and left it in the lounge, something about

17

electromagnetic waves, Jenny said. So why would someone go to the bother of wrapping my phone in my pyjama bottoms? And then there was an old Pringle V-shaped jumper, with a diamond pattern, neatly folded under the duvet. Who would have put it there? I hadn't worn it in years; it had been a present from my mother, whose taste on that occasion had failed her.

Today was the present, however, and all the trauma and pain was still real. So up until… whatever happened, I could remember the day's events, and after… whatever had happened, my brain was functioning again. But there was a gap, a section of memory files erased.

3

Sunday

Being married to an artist can be challenging. 'Got to catch the light,' Jenny would say, and we would find ourselves alone on one of Islay's many beaches, shivering in the cold, at some unearthly hour. The garden hut or artist's studio, as she called it, was too small for the number of paintings that she was working on. That is why we removed the ceiling tiles in the lounge, dated and faded as they were, and exposed the roof trusses. Needs must, and the space provided a practical storage solution for an artist living in a confined space. I had checked yesterday that none of the sketches or framed pictures had been removed. Several paintings were bound in bubble wrap, for protection, almost ready to be posted to clients around Britain, as Jenny's reputation grew. A roll of bubble wrap and a roll of brown paper were balanced over the rafters, out of Ben's reach.

I tried to imagine how Jenny would react to the events of Friday night. Sympathy, concern, of course, but also questions – and I couldn't give her any answers. I sat down on the couch, the area of the blood stain still showing faintly. I had managed to remove most of the stain, and I would make another attempt later. That was the least of my concerns. As far as I could tell, looking around the lounge, nothing had been touched. It looked as if I had simply been dumped near the couch. It did leave an uneasy feeling that others, unknown, had been in my house, able to rummage around, while I was slumped on the floor and out of it.

Eventually, having sat in a numbed silence for some time, I realised there were no easy explanations, I got up slowly, my body reminding me of the damage inflicted on it, went across to the window and drew up the blind. The view over the field, the sand dunes, the hills, at the end of the bay, was all so familiar that it was hard to believe that something so dramatic had happened. I wandered outside, through the small wooden porch with its row of coat hooks, two set at a child's height, Ben's coats missing and that, at the moment, was a relief, and sat on the step barefoot, enjoying the warmth from the morning sun. The heat perked me up, but still failed to jog any memories, which seemed to be hidden behind an impenetrable curtain, shielded from examination.

I went back into the house, put on socks and shoes, hoping that a walk along the sand dunes and beach would jog some memories. I left the house and unbolted the low wooden gate at the end of the path. The gate swung on its hinges, revealing the blue wooden 'Mable's Cottage' sign and, screwed underneath the name plate, a 'Keep Shut – children' sign, which was mainly Jenny's idea. The low stone wall which surrounded our property, with a single strand wire fence on top, was our 'children only' area – Ben's domain. While there was little or no traffic or people around we still didn't want him wandering down to the beach by himself, not at four years old. In front of the gate was a wide grassy area, where the car was parked. An earthen driveway led down a hundred yards to the rough track to Machir Bay, with a metal sheet covering a deep hole, dug by the plumber about a month ago when he was repairing a field drain which had been a problem since the farmer built the wall. I reminded myself to contact, Jack, the plumber in the next week, but it was low on my list of priorities.

I reached the road to the car park. It was potholed and bumpy, but visitors didn't seem to care. Having reached the turn-off, by using the C15, one of the last C-class roads in Britain, a little extra wear-and-tear on their suspension to reach the beach was a small price to visit the shoreline.

There were two cars in the car park, both on the grassy verges beside the track, probably belonging to dog walkers or bird watchers. I looked around but didn't see anyone. I passed the council sign warning of dangerous undercurrents off shore and deciding to go left, crossing a burn, over a wooden bridge, and followed a sandy path up onto the sand dunes which looked down over Machir Bay. The sea was fairly calm, but the waves were still toppling over each other as they approached the shore, just not with the energy or enthusiasm they showed when the wind was blowing into the bay, from the south-west. The tide was out, exposing a metal section of an old wreck embedded in the sand, covered in seaweed and slime.

I looked back, across the fields to my low bungalow, to the windows on either side of the wooden porch. My rather old, reddish Volkswagen Golf, the colour faded, sat in front of the stone perimeter wall of the house. In the garden, positioned to overlook the sea, was Jenny's studio, a glorified wooden shed, held down by two ropes stretched over it, fixed at each end. At least, with the protection provided by the ropes, the hut was less likely to blow away in winter storms, something that had almost happened during a storm several years ago. The hut door was ajar and I made a mental note to shut it on my return.

The fresh air was helping me, clearing my head. I took my normal route, walking towards the cliffs at the south end, where I could see choughs, using the warm thermals to rise up the cliff

21

side, beyond the ruined church.

Between the church and the shore, reached on a path, which started beside the cottage next to the church, was the military cemetery, its prominent cross towering over the cemetery which contained neat rows of the graves of sailors, buried close to where their bodies had been washed up on the shore during the war.

By now I had reached a familiar depression at the top of the dunes, a place where I often stopped. There were a couple of empty beer bottles lying on the sand. I reached down to pick them up, intending to deposit them, on my return, in the bin in the car park, when I spotted my missing shoe. I had no idea how it had got there. Had I been drinking, watching the sunset, on Friday night? Or something else?

This all made such little sense it was surreal, but it helped me to reach a decision. I would phone the police when I got home. I took out my phone and photographed the shoe where it lay. I wasn't sure why, but it gave me a sense of doing something, getting back some control over my life.

I searched the area thoroughly, not knowing what to expect, but found nothing else. I grabbed the shoe, which was soaking, and began to retrace my steps first to the car park, dropping the beer bottles in the bin, and then headed back up to my house. Inside, I decided to photograph the mirror, with its message, and the couch with the remnants of the blood stain. I even took a selfie. I had cleaned up, but the scratches were still evident on my right cheek. Most of the blood had come from a cut above my hair line.

I noticed that the house phone, which we'd kept because mobiles don't always work around here, was bleeping. Someone had left a message, when I was out. I'm sure that I would have noticed the flashing green arrow on it earlier so it must be new – maybe it was Jenny, although I wasn't expecting her to phone

22

until tomorrow. That created a new problem – what did I say to her, when she phoned me?

The phone rang before I could pick up the receiver, giving me a jolt.

'Malcolm here,' said a familiar voice, a friend from schooldays, and I relaxed. How could he know anything about the last thirty-six hours?

'Are you okay?' he continued. He was not known for his sensitivity, but I could do with any sympathy at the minute. I wandered through to the kitchen, the receiver held to my ear, intending to make myself a cup of coffee.

'Are you okay?' he repeated.

'Why?' I responded now slightly puzzled by the show of concern.

'I phoned earlier, but you weren't in.'

'I was down at the beach,' I explained.

Malcolm's tone changed, a nervous edge emerging.

'I think we should talk and quite soon,' he said, speaking more quickly than normal. 'I was talking to Andy Johnstone last night, over a few whiskies, in the Lochside Hotel. I think he let slip something he didn't mean to.'

'Which is why he will always be a beat cop,' I said, again wondering where this was going. I didn't need to explain my dislike of Johnstone to Malcolm.

I could sense that he was about to say something that I wouldn't like, but I remained relaxed, as I couldn't see any connection to Friday night's events, whatever they were.

'Peter,' he said, finally blurting it out, having stopped trying to figure out how gently to break the message. 'The police are going to ask you about events that took place on Friday night.'

Bile caught in my throat, I couldn't help it and I coughed and gagged as I attempted to keep my breakfast down. I felt dizzy, lightheaded, overwhelmed by this unexpected turn.

'Catherine Robinson has made a complaint about you.'

It was as if Malcolm had punched me hard in the face, and I recoiled, speechless for a few seconds.

'Catherine Robinson? I haven't seen in her years,' I eventually responded, hoping that the conversation could be terminated there and then.

Catherine Robinson. Why had she returned to the island and what had she, of all people, got to do with Friday night? If events were bad before, they were now much, much worse. I was glad that Jenny hadn't phoned today. I wasn't sure she would be able to cope. I wasn't sure I could cope.

'She's saying that you attacked her and she wants you charged.'

'With what?'

'I think it is rape.' He knew it was rape, but was again trying to soften the blow.

I was speechless. My composure was crumbling fast. My hand ran down the scratch marks on my cheek, searched for the love bite. It was impossible wasn't it? But then I couldn't remember anything, could I?

'Meet me tomorrow after you finish work, at my flat. See you about five. I'll try to find out more. Oh, by the way, a few others overheard the conversation.'

It no longer appeared a good idea to contact the police. Instead, I would have to wait and hope that I had answers available, convincing answers, when they arrived.

4

May 1944

Captain Neil Whiteman was standing on the bridge of the *Empire Constellation*, looking south, unaware that the fingers of his left hand were tapping softly on the rail. His white hair was ruffled by the gusty wind blowing, from the south-west, over the Rhins of Galloway. The sky told him a familiar story; dark clouds were gathering, and with the wind intensifying they were in for a challenging journey. He turned and walked to the port side and looked north, observing that the stars over Arran were becoming obscured by clouds. His problem was that he did not know when that journey could even begin.

'The storm front is coming in faster than I thought, John,' he said, turning to his Chief Officer, John Ferguson, who though younger than the Captain, had a thin weathered face and looked older than he was. Both were experienced officers; they didn't need to say anything more. Whiteman was five years older and nearing retirement, but that would have to wait until the war ended. Both had joined the merchant navy from school and had served on North Atlantic convoys for three years. Whiteman's ship had been ordered, at the last minute, to make the journey across from Belfast that morning, where they had been expecting to join with other ships to form a convoy to cross the Atlantic.

Crossing the Irish Sea, from Belfast to Scotland to reach the sheltered waters of Loch Ryan and the Cairnryan Military Port on the eastern side of the loch, had only taken a couple of hours. The ship had been instructed to go the port, await further instructions, and then sail that night to rejoin the convoy it had originally been planned to be part of, destined for Halifax, Nova Scotia. Last minute changes to orders did not bother Whiteman; the weather did.

The *Empire Constellation* was a ten-thousand-ton Liberty Ship, built as part of a huge programme to replace the tonnage already sunk in the war. Mass produced, with prefabricated sections welded together, the ships were churned out in large numbers. With the rigidity created by the construction method making them more liable to roll in heavy seas, and the structural integrity dependent on the quality of the welding, they were not ideal, but they were functional and essential to the war effort.

Capable of eleven knots, the ship carried cargo in five holds, fore and aft, and had three masts supporting booms for cargo handling. Its weaponry consisted of light machine guns, with a four inch gun towards the stern and a three inch gun at the bow, intended for self-defence. Four large lifeboats were positioned on the deck. Crew accommodation was centrally located below the command and control section, and above the engines. She presently carried a crew of six officers and sixty other ratings, which was generally considered a full complement. Since taking charge of the ship, four months ago, Whiteman had worked hard to maintain crew morale and improve operational efficiency. He was more respected than loved and that suited him, given the difficult decisions he often had to make.

He retraced his steps and looked out over the empty wharves, the multiple railway sidings, many with empty wagons lined up in rows. Cranes, their jibs pointing to the south-west in the direction of the prevailing wind, stood idle. They had been ordered to berth beside an empty engine shed but in reality there were no other ships; the quays were deserted.

He turned to Ferguson and pointed over the empty wharves:

'It tells a story, John, all the equipment and troops have been moved south. I wonder when the invasion will be?'

'We'll discover some morning when we turn on the radio, but I suspect with good luck, we may be in Canada,' replied the Chief Officer.

'What is causing the delay? said Whiteman, returning to his major concern. The Chief Officer noted the Captain's fingers drumming more quickly on the bridge rail, with rising impatience.

'A signalling problem at Newton Stewart, I believe, Captain, but it has been fixed and the train should arrive soon.'

Twenty minutes past. Ferguson glanced again at his gold watch, attached to a chain. The *Empire Constellation*, tied to the quay, was rising and falling, the ropes straining, as the wind from the south-west increased. They needed to move soon before conditions deteriorated further.

'Tell Jeff to make sure that we are ready to leave as soon as...' His voice trailed away, as he didn't need to complete the sentence. Both men heard the sound of an approaching steam train. Looking south across the dockyard they could see it, manoeuvring its way slowly across the maze of railway lines, past a now dimly lit signal box, which he had not noticed earlier when blackout restrictions were in place.

Ferguson crossed to the voice pipe and shouted instructions. A muffled response was heard and the Chief Officer smiled.

'Was he happy as usual?'

'You could say, Captain. Probably relieved like the rest of us.'

27

'Thank God,' said Whiteman, adding, 'Let's get busy. The sooner we leave the better. The convoy sailed from Liverpool several hours ago, and will probably have rendezvoused already with the ships from Belfast.' He grabbed his cap, turned up the collar of his coat against the blustery wind, and ignored the rain that had started to sweep in, pleased to be able to get going.

Minutes later the steam engine and its two carriages had stopped inside the engine shed, wisps of smoke dissipating around the locomotive wheels. Whiteman remembered his orders and the need for secrecy, and understood why this berth had been chosen.

An officer and six men, including a sergeant, disembarked and scrutinised the scene around them in every direction, weapons raised. The officer shouted something to the sergeant and then hurried up the gangplank, and was immediately brought up to the bridge.

'Lieutenant Mitchell, Captain, sorry for the delay.'

'So am I,' Whiteford replied, but his tone quickly softened. 'But I don't believe that it was your fault,' he added, noting the youthfulness of the soldier. Most seemed that way, he thought, no doubt a sign of age. He swept his hand towards the sea. 'It's going to get rough, so I want your cargo on board without delay. The forward boom is being readied. The cargo will go in the forward hold number 1. I am sorry that I have only basic accommodation for your men. I hope that they are good sailors,' he added.

The Lieutenant gave an understanding nod, glad that he was not making the journey. 'Sergeant Harris and Private Lawrence will have that pleasure, sir,' he said.

Half an hour later the cargo, a dozen waterproof containers, had been installed in forward hold one and fastened down. Ferguson was intrigued, especially by the unexpected passengers, and so, he suspected, were the rest of the crew. But the Captain was, as usual, the soul of discretion. The containers were the only cargo being carried. The rest of the load was ballast: water filling the deep tanks. On arrival in Halifax the ship's ballast would be discharged, the cargo handed over and the *Empire Constellation* would then carry back valuable cargo for the war effort in Europe.

As part of a convoy there was nothing to mark out the *Empire Constellation* as being different, and that was the intention.

'Send a valuable item by special courier and it might attract attention and be intercepted. Send the item by post and it would probably arrive safely,' thought Ferguson, but in war everything carried a risk. He was only too aware that first they had to catch up with the other ships in the convoy, to ensure their anonymity, to merge with the crowd.

The *Empire Constellation* slipped its moorings, heading north out of Loch Ryan.

'Plot a course well north of Corsewall lighthouse, I don't want us too close to the shore in this weather.' The finger-tapping had stopped; the Captain looked more relaxed, more in control. 'What type of locomotive was that, John?' he asked once the ship was edging away from the wharf.

'Not sure,' the Chief Officer replied and, anticipating the Captain's next question, he added, 'I don't think that my father ever worked on one like that.' The Captain laughed; they were on their way.

Beyond the confines of Loch Ryan the water became choppier, the wind increasing. The dark hilly Ayrshire shore to the east could only be sensed rather than seen, as clouds driven in by the wind masked the coast. The navigator steered the ship some distance south and west of Ailsa Craig, the distinctive volcanic plug almost ten miles from the Ayrshire coast that marked the approaches to the Firth of Clyde, and headed south of the Mull of Kintyre, a rocky headland at the southern end of the Kintyre peninsula. Further to the south was Rathlin Island and the Northern Ireland coastline. This was the narrowest section of the North Channel, only thirteen miles between Northern Ireland and Scotland. In nautical terms it was a fairly confined space, and U-boat commanders would be familiar with the narrow channel and the possibilities it presented.

The weather was holding them back, the ship struggling as it attempted to traverse the pounding waves that were preventing them from catching up with the convoy. They needed to be far out in the Atlantic by morning light, the vastness of the Atlantic Ocean, their friend, to avoid enemy U-boats.

Whiteman was anxious. Everything depended on joining the other ships and the weather was hampering them. Only three months ago he had narrowly avoided being torpedoed on a similar trip. The thought brought back raw fear; his fingers were no longer tapping – they were shaking and he gripped the work surface firmly so that no one would notice.

He calculated that he was already behind schedule, in danger of being left behind. A signal indicated that the convoy was six miles away, a few miles east of Rathlin Island. Too far away for Whiteman's liking, who knew the dangers of lurking U-boats, ready to pick off stragglers. The escort ships probably did not know why they were joining the convoy late and had not prioritised them. The River class frigate, HMS *Mourne*, indicated that it would linger for as long as possible, and escort the *Empire Constellation*, but it was three miles away.

South of the Mull of Kintyre conditions deteriorated rapidly. The tidal currents on this stretch added to the ferocity of the waves, whipped up by the storm. The ship ploughed through a heaving sea that seemed to clutch at the ship, lifting it up one minute before releasing its grip the next and plunging the ship into a deep trough, which shook it, testing its construction and shaking its occupants. The ship groaned like a caged primeval animal, its bumpy journey inducing sickness in several sailors with two ratings injured, one with a broken arm after a bulkhead door slammed shut on his arm as the ship unexpectedly lurched. It was like a crane lifting and then dropping a metal box, filled with people, without warning. Men and any loose fittings flew around, crashing into one another.

A further message was received: the escort frigate was now only two miles away. Here was another factor for Whiteman to factor in – being thrown about at will was one thing, but if another boat was too close the sea room reduced, then a collision was possible in this weather. The bridge crew were alert, but high waves could block the line of vision until it was too late. By now more than one of the bridge crew had thrown up, splattering surfaces with vomit. Towels were being used to wipe surfaces, but the pungent smell did not help conditions. He pitied the two soldiers below, rattling about in an almost empty hold, and hoped that the cargo was still secure.

'Turn port thirty degrees, Cunningham,' Whiteman shouted, hoping to be heard above the noise of wind and rain battering the windows of the bridge, but that was difficult when the waves were rising all around, making the decision of direction to steer difficult if not impossible. Did they have enough power to continue to force the ship to turn into the waves? he wondered. While only in ballast, he knew that the ship was vulnerable to side roll. It was imperative to steer into the waves or risk a massive wave rolling the ship over.

The ship shuddered and plunged to a new depth, water flooding the decks, pulling the ship down under its weight, the bulkheads groaning, water seeping in around the edges of several hatches. But the *Empire Constellation* rose proudly, shaking off the water as it poured off the deck. Whiteman prayed that they were still watertight, that the gods of the ocean depths were favourably disposed. A minute passed; he glanced at Ferguson and nodded. Both men were relieved. No messages of despair from within the ship. They were coping, but the strains being placed on the ship were immense. One could only be lucky for so long.

Over the roaring sound of the wind, the finely tuned hearing of the Captain heard a message being passed up the voice pipe, and waited for it to be relayed to him. He glanced at Ferguson, impatiently as the Chief Officer asked for the message to be repeated.

Turning towards the Captain, he had to shout to be heard, 'Chief engineer says we are losing power. Not sure of the reason yet.' Whiteman nodded. The reason could wait, but if there was a problem he needed to avoid the shores of the North Channel. Without power, he could drift and the ship would be wrecked. He was well aware of the dangerous currents off the island of Islay.

'Update our position, John,' he ordered, keeping his voice, with difficulty, deliberately calm.

'A few miles south-west of Islay,' Ferguson stated. He shook his head, it was hard to be more precise. The Captain took this in and considered the information for a minute, mindful of others looking at him. The finger-tapping had stopped; it was time to display confident leadership. Such leadership, however, did not always guarantee success.

'Chief Officer, keep updating me. Jones, head down to the engine room and find out what is going on. We need more information.'

Already Whiteman could sense an additional vibration in the engine noise that he didn't like and a power loss that was worrying. There was no chance of keeping up with the rest of the convoy, who were probably, by now, scattered across the North Channel, each ship fighting its own duel with the elements.

There was no time to react as another towering wave hit the *Empire Constellation* and the ship suddenly heaved to the side, rolling thirty degrees one way and then almost the same in the other direction.. The disorientating effect was dramatic: the crew fought to re-establish their bearings, hanging onto fittings, instruments, anything that was to hand. The Captain was thrown against the sharp edge of a table, banging his head. Ignoring the pain and the trickle of blood, he shook himself and asked, 'Everyone okay?' There were nods, mostly, but also many worried expressions.

'Weather update,' he demanded.

'I believe that the storm will start to ease, Captain.'

The Captain was grateful for that. While the weather was causing them major problems, it also made the task of the U-boat captains difficult. As one problem eased, the next one would emerge.

Grabbing Ferguson by the arm, partly to give him stability against the ship's rolling, he pulled him closer and shouted in his ear.

'My orders, John, are to ensure that the containers survive, at all costs.' And he emphasised the three final words, gripping Ferguson's arm more tightly for extra emphasis. 'Take a couple of men and go to the forward hold. Check on these poor bastards, who will probably be in a bad state, and prepare for any eventuality. Get the boxes into one of the life boats and secure them firmly. Stay with them and await my further instructions. Try to do it without alerting the crew, and while it is still dark. The weather will ease in the next few hours.' He didn't need to add that, with limited power and daylight, they would be vulnerable to enemy attack, sitting ducks.

With a confident smile he sent the Chief Officer on his way. He turned to the bridge crew: 'Get the Chief Engineer to update me. We need more power. We are very exposed out here.'

To the west a few stars were appearing briefly, only to be quickly obscured by further clouds scurrying across the sky. The great dark mass of water continued to bubble like a vat of boiling oil, swilling in all directions. Whiteman held the binoculars firmly to his eyes, scouring the horizon for clues to their location. He swivelled the binoculars quickly round when a rating shouted: 'Sir, there is land to the north. Cliffs, looks like a lighthouse on top,' he added, puzzled.

Whiteman had been through the North Channel many times. He immediately grasped the danger.

'That's the American Monument on the Mull of Oa, Islay, not a lighthouse. Get us away from these cliffs, now. We are too close to the shore.' The crew detected the tremor in his voice, despite his best efforts. The monument had been built to commemorate the loss of the troop ships Otranto, lost in a collision off Machir Bay and the Tuscania sunk by a U-boat in these very waters during the First World War, a bad omen, he felt. They needed to get back into open waters away from Islay. They were much further north than he wanted to be.

Ferguson found the two soldiers soiled and frozen, but they still turned their weapons towards the sailors as they entered the hold.

'Sergeant Harris and Private Lawrence, sir,' the sergeant said standing to attention, the clunk of his rifle butt hitting the floor, echoing around the almost empty hold.

'Who are they?' said one rating, who had not realised that they were on board.

'Never mind', Ferguson said, and turning to the soldiers he motioned for them to put down their weapons. 'I'm the Chief Officer. You have gathered that we hit bad weather and our engines are struggling to cope. We will need to move you and your cargo.'

A weary Sergeant Harris, with a bruise above his left eyebrow, the result of being thrown against the bulkhead, reminded Ferguson: 'We must stay with the cargo. Our orders, sir.'

'Agreed but we need to get the cargo off loaded.'

Turning to the crew he said, 'We can't use the loading boom in the bad weather so we have to use the ladders.' Ferguson pointed to the stairs visible through the hold door to help the soldiers understand. He offered the soldiers some tobacco from a small tin. He did not smoke himself – gin was his vice – but found the offer of tobacco helped improve relations.

The ratings groaned as they realised they were expected to haul what looked like heavy boxes up ladders in these conditions.

'Get started but keep the boxes inside the bulkhead until we have them all on the top deck level', Ferguson ordered. He ignored the grunting and swearing as the boxes were hauled up the ladders, requiring two ratings to handle each box. The unpredictable movement of the ship making the task harder as the boxes were slowly manoeuvred up, step by step.

• • •

'Captain, we have lost contact with HMS Mourne.'

The escort had probably abandoned them. Whiteman's fingers were tapping again. The storm had by now moved north-east, leaving a heavy swell but nothing as dramatic as the previous few hours – a rolling, pitching sea, without the breaking rollers. Whiteman began to hope. 'If only,' he thought, 'we can avoid detection.' The steward brought a mug of tea, which he gripped, restoring heat to his hands, the hot sweet liquid also helping to revive him, to restore concentration.

• • •

Meanwhile, Ferguson and his men had struggled to bring the crates to the top deck and stack them, two high, behind a bulkhead door. He was impressed that the two soldiers could maintain scrutiny of the process. The unmarked crates were a source of many whispered conversations by the ratings.

'Too bloody heavy and no markings, what do they hold?'

Ferguson ignored all attempts to involve him in speculation, while he waited for the storm to abate. If he judged it wrong the crates would be swept overboard when he attempted to load them into the lifeboat.

Finally, he decided it was time to load the forward starboard lifeboat. He sent two men out to untie the rope holding the tarpaulin in place, and when an opening had been made he ordered the men to load the containers into the lifeboat. He hoped that no one would observe the scene, especially U-boat commanders. The task took longer than he would have liked but he had to ensure that the containers were secure and the tarpaulin fixed in place again.

The lifeboat was one of two that had an engine and he checked that it had fuel. The ratings moved inside but the soldiers remained until Ferguson suggested that they waited inside the bulkhead door. He offered them tea and blankets, and more tobacco.

• • •

Captain Ernst Rahe, of commander of U929, had kept his boat well under the surface, where the waters were not so turbulent as the storm raged above. He was aware of the convoy and wanted to avoid detection by the escort ships. With a storm like this he calculated that the convoy would be spread out and some ships vulnerable. He was waiting to select his prey.

The *Empire Constellation* was quickly detected by passive sonar and by periscope, its slow progress alerting Rahe, that it might be in trouble. Neither the dim light of the dawn, nor the grey rolling sea, could mask the ship edging its way across their horizon, limping along the Islay coast.

'Prepare forward tubes to launch the Zaunkoning and dive to sixty metres.' After four hundred metres, the Zaunkoning torpedo activated and homed in on the loudest object. He did not want it to be his own boat. One of the bow torpedoes was launched in an explosion of compressed air, surging forward, while the U-boat immediately did an emergency dive. The torpedo kicked on, picking up the sound of the stricken ship, closing quickly, an arrow of death in a restless sea.

In the dim light and heavy swell the torpedo was not noticed until it was close to the ship. Whiteman immediately ordered the ship, 'Hard to starboard,' to reduce the ship's target profile and sounded action stations, the crew racing to man their defences. There was not a lot the crew could do but wait and that was not for long.

The torpedo impacted near the stern, rupturing the metal plating and exploding in a ballast tank. The explosive wave shook the ship, throwing crew into the air and shaking the steel structure, which magnified the sound of the explosion like a clanging bell. The crew picked themselves up, clutching at their ears, but within a few seconds the shock wave had ruptured internal bulkheads, allowing water to cascade in, weighing the ship down. The bow rose from the surface. More water flooded in, the damage escalating as the engine room bulkhead was breached. Steam and smoke spewed out of the funnel as the engine room was flooded. Any crew trapped in the engine room were lost.

The general call, six short blasts followed by one long blast to abandon ship was sounded, although there was not sufficient steam left to power the final long blast, a truncated lament to a doomed ship. The crew scrambled towards the lifeboats. The four boats were swung out from their positions, by ratings who had often practised such drills and the process of lowering them started. Ferguson reached the two soldiers and grabbed the private who was closest and shouting at both of them to follow him. Opening the bulkhead door, he reached the lifeboat, which was now dangling at a crazy angle as the ship slipped down into the sea. Motioning to other crew, who had reached the deck, he issued orders as he ripped back the tarpaulin and forced the now terrified soldiers in. He ordered several crew to join them, struggling to be heard above the surrounding chaos, knowing that only those he selected might survive, as room in the lifeboat was limited with its cargo. Several others surged forward but he grabbed the rifle from the private and pointed it at the crew and ordered them to use the other boats. The threat worked as they quickly turned towards the other lifeboats in their desperation to abandon ship.

Within two minutes the lifeboat was free from the ship. A rating cranked its engine into life. The engine noise was masked by the dying groans of the ship; fuel pulsed out like blood from the stricken vessel. Sailors were jumping off the ship, frantically trying to reach the lifeboats. Ferguson was glad to note all the boats had been launched, and were circling the *Empire Constellation* in its death throes, crew calling to their mates, encouraging them, clutching at them, striving to bring them onboard. A few sailors hauled off their life jackets as they jumped, hoping that they could swim under the oil. The Chief Officer scanned the bridge looking for the Captain, and thought he briefly saw a figure in the bridge house. The end was swift. The sea boiled as air was expelled from the bowels of the *Empire Constellation*, and then she was no more.

An eerie silence descended punctuated only by the shouts

of crew looking for their mates, encouraging them to reach the lifeboats. Ferguson judged that about a quarter of the crew had perished along with the captain. He assumed command, shouting to the crews of the other lifeboats, and as the oars were brought out he stood up and indicated towards Islay, a few miles away. All would depend on the tide. He doubted if the U-boat would bother them and anyway they had only the soldier's rifles to defend themselves if it did attack. The U-boat commander would be anxious to get away, he reckoned, before any naval vessels or flying boats reached the area.

Ferguson switched off the engine to conserve fuel and so began the long row to the shore for the exhausted men. The last position that he knew was that they had been traversing the west coast of Islay, and he hoped that there were accessible beaches. Through binoculars he scanned the shore line, of what he assumed was Islay. The two soldiers sat mute, traumatised by their ordeal. The sergeant eventually motioned to the private. 'Arthur, do you have a smoke?' The private shook his head. He doubted if they would ever want to set foot in another boat.

There were four other crew who had clambered aboard the lifeboat. They were rowing steadily, but the extra weight they were carrying and the swell was draining their energy, countering their efforts and progress was slow. To keep up with the others and to give some rest to the crew Ferguson found that he had to keep using the engine.

'I imagine that we will get picked up soon,' said Ferguson calmly. 'Better to be sunk here than further out in the Atlantic,' he added, as consolation. He assessed that three of the crew, who he barely knew, were shocked and traumatised. The fourth, Cowan, a new recruit to the ship – his first voyage, Ferguson remembered – was more agitated. Eventually he could contain his frustration no more, blurting out:

'Why did we use up space with these boxes and not save more men?' He tried to stand up to add more force to his rage, but his mate pulled him down. Ferguson acknowledged the quick act of restraint.

'Captain Whiteman gave me strict orders to save the cargo. Don't know why, but I obey orders. So do you,' he added firmly. 'Duty is bigger than any of us.'

Another voice added, 'The Captain was a fine man and he went down with the ship.' Was there an implied criticism there? Ferguson did not want to think so, but the tiredness and cold was making him tetchy. He had to live with the thought that he had survived and the Captain did not. Such was war, such events had the power to haunt for a long time.

Ferguson turned away searching for the other lifeboats, trying to work out who had survived. The four boats were, at least, pulling in the same direction. The tide seemed favourable and beyond a headland, on which he could see what looked like a communication station, there seemed to be a bay.

5

Islay - May 1944

The crofter had been awakened early by the sound of an explosion out to sea. He waited, but there was no aftershock, so the incident had happened far out in the North Channel. He turned over, realising that he was cold, and saw that the peat fire had gone out. Only the distinctive smell of peat smoke lingered, tainting the room. He shifted the blanket that he shared with his wife and tried to sleep.

The next morning, he woke with the memory of the explosion during the night. *Probably a ship or hopefully even a U-boat*, he mused. He struggled into his clothes, trying not to disturb the family, who were sleeping on pallets of straw, a rough woollen blanket covering them. He knew little different, but was sad that he couldn't improve their conditions. His life as a crofter was hard: he possessed only a few sheep, one cow and a small patch of land carved out of the machir, fertilised with seaweed dragged from the beach. He left his wife and children sleeping and, grabbing his telescope from beside the door, left the rough-hewn stone cottage, with its thatched roof and pair of oars leaning against the outside wall beside his small, upturned boat. Blinking in the sunshine, he crossed a field, waded through a stream and headed up the sand dunes which overlooked the bay. The machir was a mass of small flowers, their colours glistening after the overnight storm.

He threw himself down on the marram grass, propped the telescope on a rock and steadied himself focussing the telescope with one hand and scanned the horizon, wondering what the tide might bring in. The sea was still rough, with a heavy swell, the waves breaking with a roar on the shore and then retreating, the wet sand glistening where the tide had toyed with it. With his free hand he rubbed his stubble, touching his moustache, pulled at his long nose, as he studied the scene. His narrow mouth was drawn tight with concentration, his lips pale and translucent.

'What will the tide bring in?' he wondered, waiting patiently. He was aware of someone approaching and turned to see his eldest son dropping down beside him, wearing a shirt and patched dark cotton trousers, but no boots.

'There was an explosion out to sea last night,' he grunted. 'Just checking if I could see anything.'

His son said nothing in response. Conversations between them were usually brief, the boy wary of his father's moods. A casual comment could provoke a strong, sometimes physical, response.

So like me thirty years ago, but with a good head of hair, he thought, but no smile of pride played on his lips. He felt the passing of time and resented it, but was pleased by the boy's interest. You had to look out for yourself, and the boy showed promise. He would have to cope without him, which would be difficult, when he left for the army in just a few weeks, despite being underage. More than ever he needed young hands around the croft; to do the work he now found difficult.

The boy nudged him and the crofter realised that he had not been looking out to sea, lost in his thoughts. A small speck on the horizon was drifting towards the shore. It looked like a lifeboat. A few minutes later he was sure... and behind it at least two more bobbed into view. The tide might bring them in. He hoped so, anyway, but it was turning. If the heavy swell persisted; they could be swamped. He nodded to his son: they had a mutual understanding.

Twenty minutes later a fourth lifeboat appeared. He could now make out several men on each and a couple of soldiers, which surprised him as it was slightly unusual. The men had seen the shore and were rowing desperately to try to reach it. The front of one lifeboat reared up suddenly and then plunged into the swell.

Poor bastards. The boat disappeared, only to emerge upturned and empty. Several men were splashing about in the water, but the strong undercurrents were dragging them out to sea. Even at this distance he could hear the screams of despair, and watched as one pulled off his lifejacket.

All the quicker to drown, thought the crofter, believing that he would have done the same. None of the other boats were making an attempt to rescue them. The occupants were slumped over the oars, exhausted by their ordeal. Gradually the currents separated the boats and the one with the soldiers, which sat lower in the water, was turned south by some vagary of the tidal ebb and flow, in a direction where he knew they would eventually hit rocks. In time his prediction was borne out. The boat jolted as it hit an underwater rock and rolled over in seconds, scattering the occupants, the lifeboat sinking without trace. He saw a face appear briefly above the water, only to be sucked down.

The other two boats got closer to the shore, in this game of chance where the odds of survival were decided by nature's roulette. The crew realised that they might be better to fight the elements together and roused themselves from their exhaustion. With a final surge of adrenaline they resumed rowing, now towards each other, the hundred yards between them narrowing slowly. The men were waving and shouting to each other. A gannet plunged into the water, its bubbly, milky trail would only have revived recent trauma in the minds of the sailors.

Despite their best efforts the swell cast them apart, and even the crofter had to turn away as the remaining lifeboats were also swamped. A sudden thought made the crofter scan the radar installations on the southern cliff edge of Machir Bay, but he could see no one on the cliff side.

Good, he thought. *They haven't noticed the tragedy.* He saw his son noting the location where the boat with the soldiers had sunk. The crofter was pleased that the boy had not been fazed by the sight they had just witnessed. He would do all right in the army, he considered, where he'd probably see a lot worse. Maybe even learn to make a new life away from this miserable existence, trapped in a beautiful location, but without the means to do anything but struggle to survive. 'Hell comes in different forms,' he remembered an old minister saying, on one of his rare encounters with a man of God.

Father and son walked back together to the low croft building, the crofter pausing to visit a hut made out of salvaged wood, screened with an old blanket, which passed as an outside toilet. When he returned to the dwelling his wife had prepared some bannocks for breakfast on a griddle over a small fire. With several mouths to feed he further cursed his existence as he sat and ate first, impervious to the faces looking at him, each hoping that something would be left for them.

By mid-morning an army jeep bounced over the rough track, stopping short of the beach where the stream, swollen by the previous night's storm, was now too difficult to cross. Undeterred, the officer and a sergeant waded through and walked up the dunes, scanning the horizon, as the crofter had done earlier. The sergeant pointed out something to sea. The crofter observed them, pulling on a pipe that was empty, his last tobacco finished days ago.

The two military personnel reversed the jeep and turned to reach the croft. The crofter was waiting by the only door, leaning against the stone wall. A small girl's head appeared briefly, intrigued by the visitors, and then quickly disappeared. There were not many visitors around here these days.

It was the officer who spoke. 'Sorry to disturb you, but one of our ships was torpedoed by a damn U-boat last night. Sunk without trace, but we hope that if lifeboats were launched they might drift in. Have you seen anything down at the beach today?'

The crofter nodded, making a play of fishing in his pocket for tobacco for his pipe. The officer turned to the sergeant, who rummaged in his own pocket, produced some tobacco and handed it over.

'Aye, I saw some lifeboats this morning, three of them. I couldn't help though. They were all swamped by the heavy swell a few hundred yards off shore. I think that the tides will eventually bring in some bodies. Maybe they will appear after the next rough storm. Poor bastards, so close.'

The officer thanked him and added, 'The police sergeant will be here soon and will ask you for a statement. Please don't discuss this with anyone other than the police. Morale and all that.'

The crofter, of course, had no intention of doing so. As he started to stuff some of the tobacco into his pipe, not moving from the door, the two soldiers abruptly turned and left. He walked inside to light his pipe from the fire. He was disappointed with his morning's work: he had hoped for more, but he would check out the lifeboat that hit the rocks and capsized so quickly. There was something unusual about that, he thought, as the tobacco in his pipe started to glow and he inhaled the smoke, savouring the moment.

• • •

When darkness fell the crofter and his son pushed the small boat away from the shore, the son digging the oars into the sand to provide the final purchase, then they were floating. The father held a lantern, its flickering light shielded by a blanket from any observers on the cliff tops. The son rowed in silence, pausing to turn and check his bearing, conscious that sound could travel a long distance in these conditions. Neither had a watch, but time was not important. Eventually they arrived off the rocks that the son had noted that morning, where the lifeboat had turned over so quickly. Father and son shared a quick glance as the son brought in the oars and stripped off. The boy dived in. The cold water sucked away his breath but he pushed down, fumbling about in the dark, until he felt something hard and solid. He traced the outline, recognising the shape of a boat. He rose quickly to the surface to draw breath and smiled at his father. On the next dive he extended his search, but was forced to return to the surface several times, before he felt the shape of a box.

In the light of the lantern the father could see that the boy was cold and shivering and hauled him into the boat and wrapped him in a rough blanket. His son pulled it close around him. Trying to control his shivering, he described what he had felt. The father was pleased, smiling at the son, a rare sign of approval, and indicated that he should row back. The effort would restore his body temperature, he said.

On the way back they saw a body floating on the surface. The crofter pointed it out and they changed course towards it. The body was that of a naval officer. The father searched the pockets of the dead officer for anything of interest, pleased when he found a tin of tobacco and a gold watch on a chain, which he quickly pocketed. The son then resumed rowing towards the shore, with the father dragging the dead body behind, the officer's dull eyes reflecting palely in the light of the lantern, before releasing him a short distance from the shore, well away from the area that they had explored. That would divert attention from where they had been, he felt.

His wife waited anxiously by the door as they returned, a tartan shawl protecting her from the cold. She watched as her son, still draped in the blanket, sat down by the fire. The crofter ordered his wife to put another piece of peat on the fire, a reward for his son's efforts.

6

Monday am

Catherine Robinson, she was the past, wasn't she? I was now happily married, with every reason to forget her. But now it seemed she had come back to haunt me. I definitely couldn't go to the police; I had form with her, according to them. My mind still refused to reveal, even give a hint, of what had occurred on Friday night. Had she scratched me, given me a love bite? What about the other bruises? I stood under the shower again, hoping that the hot water could wash away my problems. I had to go to work, it was Monday, but what if the police came to arrest me there? I could lose my job. Permeating all of this, bubbling under the surface, was the thought of Jenny's reaction. 'I couldn't remember,' did not sound like a good defence. I finished showering, still feeling bruised and sore, conscious of the scratches on my face; they weren't so angry looking now, but were still clearly visible.

My mind was preoccupied as I left the house, the car rattling over the metal plate in the driveway. I turned onto Highway 15, as Jenny and I called it, since the road had once been classified as the C15. Ben always laughed, as I usually made revving noises when we reached the road, but I sure that the irony was lost on him. Just thinking about him and Jenny was difficult. They were now my life and, I hoped, my future. The ten-year-old Golf diesel belched its usual clouds of smoke, adding considerable pollution to the crystal clear air of Machir Bay, but fortunately we didn't have many neighbours to complain.

In a few hundred yards I had reached Loch Gorm, the largest freshwater loch on the island and less than a mile from the beach at Machir Bay. Before the loch there was a road to the left, which eventually circled the loch, joining up again three miles on. For many years after Catherine left, I took the long detour around Loch Gorm, not wanting to pass her home, but after I married Jenny I became bolder, although in truth it was probably because I did not want to confess to her the reason for the detour.

Today, I continued straight on, curious to what I might see at the Robinson's farm. The single-track road, with passing places, was typical of the more remote parts of Islay, a source of frustration, particularly in the summer, when there were many visitors. Then you had to pull over to let other cars pass, but for most it was a chance to pause, waiting for the other car, to appreciate the ever-changing moods of the island. Islay-time as many locals called it.

The Ileachs, as the Islay folk were known, usually acknowledged other drivers with a friendly wave of the hand, a conditioned response to travelling on the minor roads, but one that looked strange on the mainland, where the habit was quickly abandoned.

The road was deserted. I drove pass the newest distillery on Islay, Kilchoman, a small farm distillery built on ground at Rockside farm to my right, its modest pagoda-style kiln showing some signs of activity, with wisps of blue peat smoke rising indolently. An outcrop of trees surrounded the distillery and farm, partially masking low hills to the rear. If I worked there, I often mused, I could walk to work, but I was grateful for the job at Islay Distillery, Bowmore. A job meant that I could continue to live on the island, which I desperately wanted to do, given that Islay was a continuing source of inspiration for Jenny's paintings, and a great place for Ben to grow up.

The loch fascinated me, with its ever-changing moods and its bracken-clad shores, which provided such a rich variety of hues as the seasons changed. The name Gorm meant blue in Gaelic, and with every passing cloud, every change of weather, and that was frequent on Islay, the blue colour could change, a steely blue one moment and a rich blue the next, as the clouds were swept away and the sun came out. At other times rain squalls could obscure the loch, driving rain turning the loch grey. I noticed a lone fisherman rowing towards the rushes at the shore in a small blue rowing boat, ripples from his oars spreading out on the placid surface, his hunt for brown trout over.

I still hadn't met another car before I reached the imposing farmhouse of Robinson's farm, set back from the road, at an angle. It was a long single-storey building, which many considered rather vulgar, its size dominating the two small outbuildings. Stone clad, with red roof tiles, the farmhouse, stood out, the two small green corrugated steel barns further from the road and at right angles to the farmhouse were modest by comparison. I could also see above the farmhouse the top of the hill which overlooked the farmyard: it always stirred up emotions in me, a mixture of frustration, love and hate, now reignited.

This morning, as I drove past the entrance, I glanced into the farmyard, or as far as I could see, the view partially blocked by a low breeze block wall which ran alongside the road. There was no sign of life, no faces lurking at the window, hiding behind curtains, no car or tractor sitting in the farmyard and the doors into the storage area built into the hillside, part of a cave that had been extended, which overlooked the farmyard, were shut and bolted as usual. It was ten years since Catherine had left the island so abruptly, and I still found it hard at times. I wondered what I would have said if I had seen her. Maybe I did speak to her the other night? My attempt to control the memories of the last two days was already under considerable pressure – perhaps I should have gone around the long way around Loch Gorm. On the other hand, possibly I should have gone in and asked if she was there, but with little hesitation I accelerated past the farm.

After the junction with the road that wound around Loch Gorm, the road twisted and climbed, not much by Highland standards, but enough when you got to the summit: the view over Loch Indaal to Bowmore was both dramatic and breathtaking. The tidal expanse of Loch Indaal and on its far side the village of Bowmore, appearing so close across the loch, but was in fact quite a journey by the road, which wound around the loch's shoreline. From this distance I could just about make out the distillery name: Islay. A bold statement by a famous distillery. Not many people have such a clear signpost to their place of work. I drove down past a wooded estate to reach the road that ran down the shoreline of the Rhinns, a two-lane road, a motorway by Islay standards, linking Bruichladdich, Port Charlotte and Portnahaven, the only public road that linked the Rhinns to the rest of the island.

I turned towards the head of the loch, grassy covered sandy dunes to my left, taking care as cattle and sheep were scattered over the beach, the road and fields, wandering at will. Healthy looking cattle and sheep, thriving on the island's rich pasture, which attracted farmers from the mainland, willing to pay a premium for Islay-bred farm stock. As I approached the wooded estate surrounding Islay House, I saw the small cattle market, its metal stalls empty, and turned right, passing through Bridgend, a small hamlet with a store and an hotel, where the River Sorn reached Loch Indaal.

I then kept to the coast, ignoring the signposted road to Port

Ellen, my heart pounding as I spotted an approaching police car, but the policeman, and it wasn't Andy Johnstone, drove past me, giving only the traditional Islay wave. I found myself breathing fast, my alarm taking a couple of minutes to subside. I then passed both the Columba Centre and the Scottish and Southern Energy Depot, to reach Shore Road, in Bowmore, flanked by houses, shops and hotels on both sides, none of which had been built with modern traffic in mind; parked cars and vans often hindered progress.

I finally reached Main Street, the broad road that runs down the centre of Bowmore, from the Round Church, perched at the top of the hill, until it joined the road I was on, at a corner. The circular, white church, with a tower, built facing down the street, was almost as well-known as the distilleries on the island, a landmark for visitors looking for a different type of spirit. South of the junction of Main Street with the Shore Road, the broad street continued, now known as the Square, down to a small harbour on the shores of Loch Indaal, providing handy spaces for cars to park on both sides of the street and in the middle. I was fortunate to find a vacant parking bay.

Every morning I rejoiced in the wonderful island that was my home. Machir Bay, the journey to Bowmore, Bowmore itself, all wonderful places to live, bring up a family. Today, however, my appreciation, was blighted by the recent events, dark clouds swamping my enthusiasm. Catherine Robinson had much to explain. As of the weekend I now had two questions I wanted to ask her, preferably face-to-face, if she was indeed on the island.

As I walked into the distillery I felt the smart phone in my pocket vibrate. I stopped to read the message, which I knew would be from Jenny:

Doing well, Ben enjoying himself, home Friday. Not able to phone tonight – at a meeting, much love Jenny xxxxxx

Jenny knew when I arrived at work, and whenever she was away, a message was waiting for me in Bowmore, where I could receive a signal. I replied in kind, guiltily relieved that I wouldn't have to speak to her, or attempt to conceal anything. At least I now knew the deadline for resolving my issues; I just didn't know what the outcome might be.

All distilleries on Islay are prosperous. The reputation for distinctive peaty whisky, abhorred by some, but loved by many, the romantic island image and the friendliness of welcome were a marketing executive's dream. Whisky lovers flooded in from all over the world, many as knowledgeable about whisky as the Ileachs themselves. With the Feis Ile, the Islay Festival of Music and Malt starting next week, the island was about to receive its usual big influx of visitors that it would struggle to cope with. Beds were booked up from year to year, campsites full of tents and campervans. Every morning a roving group of enthusiasts would migrate to a different distillery, as each distillery held a day of special events. The enthusiasts were desperate to purchase special bottlings, comparing each year's distillery bottling with the last and also comparing the different distilleries offerings, arguing over which were better, defending their favourite tipple, which if they did not want, could be sold on the internet for double or triple the price, instantly. A week in paradise for many, a toxic workout for livers for some. Somehow, I knew what the Rev Alan Walker of the Round Church would think. He had, too often, seen the downside.

Despite it being just after ten o'clock, the Islay Distillery shop was already busy. People were studying the range of whiskies on offer, from standard bottlings to special distillery only bottlings, and an exclusive range of whisky themed gifts and clothes. Tours were being booked as I entered. I was pleased: that kept me in a job. The ladies behind the reception were smiling, trying to help.

The sound of foreign tongues were interacting with their softer island tones, the common language of whisky lovers helping to overcome any translational difficulties.

Julie, a lady in her forties who was in charge of the shop, called me over. 'Peter, we still have a problem with the blocked drain, so continue to use the alternative route between the still room and the warehouse. Pence doesn't want the drain opened up until the silent season, if possible. Doesn't want to lose any production, if the problem is found to be bigger than it appears.' I saw her glance at my face but she didn't comment, the scratches not as obvious, I hoped, as I imagined. Jenny's make-up did its job and hid the worst.

Pence Gifford was the distillery manager and he reckoned the drains were so old that there could be anything down there, including bodies, he usually added with a smile, but more likely bungs for barrels, barrel staves and whatever else the distillery used. The small detour required was not a problem.

Today's visitors were the usual mix. There was a group of Swedes, a party of Chinese and a German couple – the wife coping with the husband's pilgrimage to the land of his favourite dram – and three Americans, by the sound of their accents. Whisky was an international business and the rise of the single malt from the eighties onwards had brought much-needed prosperity to the island.

By now I could recognise most European languages. I made my way past the Swedish group, pressed in the code on the door marked for staff only, and entered. I took off my anorak, hung it in my locker and put on my tartan waistcoat, adjusting my name badge: Peter Meldrum, Tour Guide, Islay Distillery. I was ready to start.

I shouted out, in the now crowded shop, that the ten thirty tour was ready to leave and asked people to follow me through to another room. I watched as they entered and were stunned by the expansive view over Loch Indaal. You don't have to sell Islay's natural beauty, just let them view it. Some looked longingly at the whisky bottles lined up behind the bar, which formed one half of the room, noting drams that they would like to sample later.

I stood to the side of a table, which had a tray on it with ten empty glasses, each later to be filled with a dram. The German couple looked at each other, the wife smiling; it was the husband's turn to be indulged. Increasingly, however, women were also becoming passionate about whisky, and their knowledge was often impressive.

I introduced myself, confirming that the tour would last about an hour, would finish back here with a dram and that they should be free to ask any questions or take any photographs.

I asked them their names and why they had come, a standard opening to help them relax and me to find out a bit more about the group. A Dutch couple, who had joined the party at the last minute, were touring the Scottish islands and were in Islay for a few days; the party of Chinese were more focussed on whisky and were travelling on to have lunch at Ardbeg, another distillery. The three Americans, an American girl of mixed race, called Sally, wearing a very bright colourful printed dress, with her two male companions, Jonathon and Brian, seemed to be caught out by the question about the reason for their trip, and I quickly interjected 'discovering whisky', to which they smiled and nodded.

Also on the table was a jug of water, and a glass bottle filled with barley. The water would be used later for their drams but was useful for making another point.

'Whisky is made using only water, barley and yeast,' I started, pointing at the water jug. 'No other ingredients are used by us, although some distilleries smuggle in some caramel colouring. We, of course, do not. Our product does not require it,' I added.

'Our water is also very pure and comes from a local river.'

The German, a large rotund man, immediately jumped in. 'Distilleries make a big play of the water,' he said, his flushed cheeks suggesting that he had sampled many different whiskies. 'How important is the water to the final whisky?'

'A good question.' Is there any other type for a tour guide? 'The water source is very important but the influence on the final dram is not very significant, once the water has been filtered and boiled. We just have a lot of water in Scotland and a good supply. Our water on the island can be very peaty, brown and dirty in appearance. You may have noticed it, if you are having a bath,' I added, 'but the peaty flavours of our whisky don't come from the water supply, but is added later, as you will see.'

I led them out of the room up some stairs, now labelled with a profusion of health and safety signs, a necessary evil if you wish to show visitors around, and onto the malting floor, with its fairly low ceiling supported by poles at regular intervals. There were rows of windows on two sides, which ensured ventilation, and wire grills which stopped birds flying in. Other than that it was fairly basic. Spread out on the floor was a six-inch covering of damp barley, twenty-one tonnes in total, which had already been steeped in water. It was being turned every few hours, and would be for six or seven days, depending on the time of year. In the corner one of the workers was turning over the barley using an electric machine, a much-welcomed innovation. Turning over tonnes of barley by hand was very hard work, but it had to be done to ensure that the barley was kept at a constant temperature.

My job was a lot harder in the 'silent season' when the floor was bare, but today, especially with the whisky festival so close, we were keen to show our art. I lifted up a handful of barley and held it out.

'The first stage in producing whisky is to produce malted

barley, that is, barley which has undergone conversion into malt. The malting floor is where this happens. If we are going to make whisky we need to release the starch trapped in the barley. To do this,' I explained, 'we wet the barley and let it germinate it on the floor, turning it over to ensure that its temperature remains constant. We are tricking the barley grains into thinking that it is warm, winter is over and it is time to come out of hibernation, and to start sprouting. Enzymes in the grain begin to convert starch to sugar, to provide food for the growing plant but instead we will use the sugar to produce alcohol.'

I let the group feel the damp barley and pointed out white wisps, signs of growth, on a few barley grains.

'When we see these we know that the barley is beginning to sprout and use up its store of starch, turning it into sugars. Having liberated the starch, we stop the process by heating the malted barley in the kilns. The malted barley, from the malting floor, is put in the kiln behind me.' I opened the kiln doors and a blast of hot air full of pungent peat smoke escaped. I shut the doors before the smoke became irritating, but the smell of peat persisted, hanging in the air.

'We spread the barley over the perforated metal surface in the kiln and heat it from below, first with peat and then with hot air until it is dry.' I turned towards the German, who had asked me earlier about the source of the peaty flavour. 'Do you smell the peat?'

He nodded.

'This is where the peat flavour in the whisky is added. We measure the level of peat in parts per million of phenol. We peat to a level of around 25ppm; some other distilleries on the island have much higher levels of peat, some less. Islay is famous for its peated whiskies. It is what we do best.

'We use peat partly because we have an endless supply on

the island, to dry our barley, enough for a few thousand years. A lot of distilleries, in other parts of Scotland, used coal in the past to dry the barley, but coal was expensive to bring to the island, although we did use it in the past to heat our stills. You will have seen peat stacks around the island. People still cut the peat and stack it, leaving it to dry over the summer before using it as fuel on their fire.'

By now those who had come to view the process were absorbed but some were startled at the industrial process, some concerned about the cleanliness, especially if people were tramping over the malting floor, and others couldn't link what they had seen so far to the final product. After all, there is not a lot of romance in damp barley and pungent peat smoke.

'Having dried the malted barley, we grind it up in a mill to produce grist,' I explained. 'We use a Porteous Mill,' the sort of detail that the enthusiasts crave.

'We now need to extract the sugars from the barley and we do this in a large tub, known as a mash tun, a large stainless-steel container. Hot water is added, which draws out the sugars to produce a hot sweet liquid, known as worts. The process is repeated at higher and higher temperatures to ensure that we get all the starch out. The leftover solid is known as the draff, and is fed to cattle, which helps explain why we have such happy cattle on the island.'

Smiles and nods indicated that they were still with me.

As I took them through another door I explained that the hot sweet malty liquid produced in the wash tun, the worts, was then cooled and piped into a receiving tank, called an underback, before being used to fill large wooden washbacks. In the room we had entered were six Oregon pine washbacks, large wooden tubs, capped with wooden lids. We were standing on a metal lattice floor, with only the top part of the washback showing above the floor. I opened a hatch on one of the washbacks and let them see the frothing, bubbling cauldron.

'Now that the worts have been cooled we can start the fermentation by adding yeast, which converts the sugar into alcohol and carbon dioxide. So far it is like making beer. If we hadn't cooled the worts then the yeast would have been destroyed by the high temperature.

'The bubbles are carbon dioxide, which some distillers trap and use to add the fizz to your fizzy drinks. Don't breathe too deeply or you will hurt your nose,' I added, ever mindful of health and safety.

The washbacks were like icebergs, showing only so much above the metal lattice floor. Underneath the true size of the washbacks could be glimpsed. 'Carbon dioxide is poisonous and plenty is being generated, but fortunately it is heavier than air and so sinks to the bottom of a room. If you were down at the base of the washbacks you would need breathing apparatus to survive. The holes in the lattice flooring also allows the carbon dioxide to sink through it.'

I produced a sample of the frothing wort and let any who wanted to sip it, with the warning that it was a good cure for constipation. A few volunteered, mainly the Chinese on this occasion. 'The fermentation continues for forty-eight hours. Fermentation times do vary from distillery to distillery.' I noticed that the wife of the German couple looked lost. I smiled at her: 'A lot of strange smells.'

She shuddered and grimaced.

'Wait until you try the final product,' I reassured her. 'That will put life back into you.'

The American girl, Sally if I remembered her name correctly, had barely paid any attention, looking around and checking her smart phone, presumably dragged along by her friends. I noticed her staring at me when she thought I was not looking. If I had been a teacher, like my father, I would have probably confiscated the phone. Her two friends, Jonathon and Brian, appeared more interested. She reminded me of someone, although I was probably confusing her with a celebrity from an American TV series. Her black hair was worn in an Afro style, and she seemed warm, friendly, but obviously just not interested in whisky; she was embarrassed when I caught her looking at her iPhone. Her two friends accompanying her were both quite burly, muscular and squat, with the one called Jonathon sporting a crew cut, and the other, Brian, a long straggly black beard decorated with tiny coloured bands of beads around the longest strands, and gelled black hair. Muscle bound they struck me as ex-army or fitness fanatics, not the sort I would like to encounter on a dark night.

I finished my time with the washbacks and ushered the party through to the distillation room.

When people enter the distillation room and see our four gleaming lacquered copper, pear-shaped stills, perched on painted brick bases, with lots of tubes making connections they don't understand, then something of the alchemy of the process always gets to them. People always enjoy this part, although maybe it is because some realise that they are closer to the promised dram.

I started the next part of my spiel,

'So far we have produced a fairly strong beer, about seven per cent in alcoholic strength, known as the wash, and we are now going to do what distilleries do best and distil the beer.'

I explained that the wash was fed into a receiving tank and then into the wash still, one of two types of still in the room, the other being the spirit still, but that both did the same type of job: they heat up and separate the different substances in them. Our distillation occurs in two stages with the first distillation occurring in the wash still. Water and alcohol boil at different temperatures, with the alcohol boiling first at a lower temperature. So the alcohol vapour passes more quickly to the top of the still and if it has enough energy it continues over the neck of the still to reach the condenser. It is like boiling water in a kettle: the steam passes out of the spout and will condense against a cold surface such as a tiled kitchen wall. In this case the condenser, which has cold water circulating in an outer tube, condenses the alcohol. The alcohol that doesn't have enough energy to escape drops back into the still, where the remaining contents are frothing and bubbling, refluxing, as it is known until they gain the energy to escape. In time we get most of the alcohol out and along with it comes lots of other substances, known as congeners, some of which we want and some we don't. The congeners are vital; they add flavour, make the malt whisky distinctive. What is collected after the first distillation is then distilled again this time in the spirit still along with any leftovers from previous distillations in the spirit still. Nothing is wasted. I then explained what happens in the spirit still and how the contents are separated. I talk about the foreshots, middle-cut and feints. Whisky has a language of its own. It is the middle-cut which is important to the distillery as it becomes the new make spirit and eventually whisky.

Some visitors look worried when they learn that some of the substances in the still are poisonous until I showed then how they are separated. The spirit safe, a copper-framed glass box, allows the nature of the spirit run to be tested, by turning knobs from the outside, the task of the stillman. In the past only the custom officer had the keys to the spirit safe, so that no one could steal the new make spirit, but that is no longer required. By turning the knobs the spirit can be diverted into the different receivers. The test is to add water and if the spirit does not go cloudy then the spirit is safe to use as new make spirit. The stillman's experience is vital. The visitors look relieved and thirsty. The distillation room is hot. There is so much I could have added: the type of yeast matters, the length of fermentation, and distillation, the size and shape of the stills, the angle of the lyme arm. It all matters in the alchemy which is whisky production. Each distillery has its own secrets, which they claim makes their whisky unique, and, of course, the best in Scotland. Chemists are still unravelling the secrets of whisky production.

I was hopeful that the distillery would, at some point, train me up to be a brand ambassador, but I knew I had to be put forward for extra training and like all things in a distillery, everything takes time and experience. Whisky matures slowly, and so does gathering knowledge about its ways; a lifetime of learning.

I then showed the group how the new-make spirit, the middle cut, is filled into whisky barrels and how these are rolled out of the distillation room and stored in a warehouse, to begin the long process of maturation. Many visitors are surprised that the new make-spirit is so clear, unlike the whisky they see in their bottles, and also a lot more alcoholic, around 63.5% on average.

Now was the time for the warehouse and the angel's share. At Islay Distillery, we had a historic warehouse down by the sea and I led them down to it, making a great play of unlocking the doors.

'This a dunnage warehouse, a traditional warehouse for maturing whisky. As you can see, it has low ceilings and an earthen floor, and is quite damp and dark. The waves battering the distillery walls also add to the whisky matured here. You can taste the salt in the air. In here the magic happens. Time, temperature, but especially the type and quality of barrels, all play their part. No two barrels turn out the same whisky even if they are sitting side-by-side for many years. Some of the whisky evaporates every year, about 2%. This is what we call our contribution to the angels – the angels' share.

'The new spirit soaks into the oak casks, leaching out

substances which give flavour and colour to the whisky. The spirit in some barrels take a long time to mature: the contents of others mature more quickly. It is hard to predict and the head distiller has to check each cask many times. The contents are allowed to be called whisky after three years and a day stored in oak casks, a rule set during the First World War to avoid drunkenness, by delaying consumption and also improving quality.'

One of the Chinese party muttered, 'What a good job,' and others nodded their approval.

'Sorry to disappoint you,' I told him, 'but Pence Gifford, our distillery manager, uses his nose more than anything.'

The tour was over. I led them back to the room we had started in, and saw them smile as they saw that their promised dram poured and waiting.

The group mingled, their mood relaxing as the whisky was sipped and savoured. The Dutch couple left early, the husband eager to buy some special bottlings in our shop. The Chinese party hung around asking questions, wanting to try other drams in our range. I was pleased with their interest, but hoping that they had a designated driver or were using a taxi to reach Ardbeg.

The Americans talked among themselves, sipping their dram, but I noticed that they left most of it.

'Did you enjoy your tour?' I asked as I joined them. They had hung around, being some of the last to depart, which surprised me given how little interest they had shown.

'Oh, yes,' said Jonathon, but it was said politely, I sensed, without any real conviction.

'Do you live on the island?' he asked, in return.

'Yes, on the west coast.'

'Which part?' asked Sally, showing more curiosity than she had up to now, suddenly being very interested and alert.

'Near Machir Bay,' I replied.

'Is that where the HMS *Otranto* was sunk?' she enquired.

I nodded and explained that the collision with another ship had occurred out at sea. The beach at Machir Bay had been littered with their dead bodies.

'But many sailors are buried in the military cemetery at Kilchoman, which overlooks Machir Bay,' I told her, pleased that I had now remembered something about the ships lost off Islay.

'I believe my great-grandfather was on board, a soldier being transported to England to fight in the First World War,' said Jonathon, whose drawl stretched out every word.

I expressed sympathy and added, 'You should go along and check the graves, although I think the Americans bodies were exhumed and returned to America or go to the Islay Folk Museum in Port Charlotte, who may be able to help with names.'

I glanced at the clock above the bar. Taking my cue they muttered thanks and turned to go, but not before Brian the third member of the party asked:

'Was there not also a ship sunk during the Second World War, near Machir Bay – a British ship?'

'There are numerous wrecks all around the shore of Islay, but I think you are right. It was the *Empire*... something...' But on this occasion my memory failed me.

'The *Empire Constellation*,' said Sally, quickly, studying my face for a reaction.

'You could be right, I'm not sure,' I replied, and I ushered them back to the shop. The Americans seemed almost more interested in me than the whisky, but that might just be paranoia, induced by my nightmare weekend. I was just glad that the tour was over, realising that I was tired, still recovering I found myself touching the scratches on my face, anxious to meet up with Malcolm, hoping he might provide some answers before Jenny and Ben returned.

7

January 1984

Islay Airport

As I sat in the Cessna 172 Skyhawk light aircraft, waiting for permission to taxi onto the runway I struggled as usual to get my long legs comfortable into the tight space beneath the bank of dials and the control wheel. Despite the discomfort I allowed myself a quiet smile; after all, I had hit the jackpot. Once I got back to the States, I knew what I had to do, and who to approach for support, although, of course, I would keep some details to myself. One thing experience had taught me was never to trust anyone completely, to keep some cards up my sleeve.

It had all gone so well, despite the awful weather of the last few days, which had not endeared me to Islay; a powdering of snow now covered the hills and fields, like an artist smearing white paint over a canvas, using broad strokes, not totally covering the whole scene. Rarely, I heard in a bar, does Islay get a deep fall of snow. The mists, the single-track roads, pulling over to allow cars to pass: I was not used to any of this in the States. Mackenzie's car hire were also none too happy when I returned their car: they spotted a scratch down the passenger side of it, the result of an encounter with a wall as I swerved to miss a sheep that had strayed onto the road. Unfortunate, but the insurance, would cover it.

It all started at a party in Southampton, when a woman, probably in her fifties, well-preserved, her hair obviously dyed, had started to bore people with stories about what her husband had done in the war. Her husband, a good few years older than her, was slumped drunk in a corner, a sherry glass empty by his side, sleeping it off. Normally, I run a mile from a woman like that, but this one was different, bored and wanting attention, and the drink was certainly cruising through her veins. As the few people around her went for drinks or a smoke I was left alone with her, near the kitchen door. The smells of supper wafting from the oven, pizza I remember, was making me hungry. However, something she said about her husband interested me and I forgot about my hunger. New projects often arise from careless talk, especially under the influence of drink. Her husband had apparently worked in the navy during the war escorting Atlantic convoys, ensuring that they got out into the Atlantic, through the North Channel, which the woman said was between Ireland and Scotland, so well north of Southampton, then. I had never been to either country and would need to check a map.

Not all the shipping made it, due to attacks from marauding U-boats, which was a sad, but an inevitable consequence of war. It was after the war, however, in the sixties, that the story picked up. This was after I had fed another glass of white wine to the woman, whose name turned out to be Ruth. Her husband had been contacted because his frigate had been dispatched from Derry to protect a stricken liberty ship whose engines weren't working as a result of damage caused by a storm. They were too late, and the ship had been torpedoed, near Islay. A patch of oil and a few pieces of wood and other detritus were all that they found on the surface, but it did allow them to mark the spot with a buoy. A team from London had arrived, quizzing him very closely when he returned. There was obviously more going on that he was not being told, but it was wartime and that was not unusual.

In the sixties divers, part of a salvage team, found the wreck, but failed to locate the cargo which they had expected to find in the hold. They noticed that the lifeboats had been launched. The Captain of the stricken ship had been given orders to protect the cargo at all costs, and some wondered if the cargo had been taken ashore by lifeboat – it wasn't that bulky – probably to the nearby island of Islay, given that many of the crew were eventually washed up there.

Despite having studied the police records of the time, describing the state of the bodies washed ashore, and the salvage gathered, they had made little progress. An area on the west coast called Machir Bay, where a few bodies had been washed ashore, had been searched, but by this time there was little evidence left. We are talking twenty years later. The investigation on Islay raised suspicions that some locals knew more than they were admitting to, something that had been suggested in police records of the time, but ultimately the investigation was abandoned. Ruth's husband had been interviewed, several times, to discover if he had any additional information.

Ruth was happy to talk and I encouraged her – smiling, making eye contact and moving closer to her. She seemed flattered and was disappointed when I left the party soon after, without leaving her a telephone number. She shouted after me.

'Ryan, it was good to talk. How long are you staying around here?'

'I'm afraid I am going back to the States tomorrow.'

I must be going soft, but it did not seem fair to have her hanging around the phone for the next few weeks, waiting for a phone call that would never happen. I smiled at her husband, who was yawning and looking around, not aware of what had been said, his best days long gone.

I was due back in the States in a few days, so time was short. A few phone calls to friends in London, and I had got some more nuggets of information. This project was looking promising. With a full pilot's licence and a credit card, I hired the Cessna 172 Skyhawk, high wing, single-engined plane and headed north to Islay. It was sunny in the south, but the weather worsened as I flew north. It was snowing and foggy as I approached the island, and I was lucky to be allowed to land. The Cessna skidded on the tarmac runway and after that the airport closed due to bad weather. I was the last flight in.

A fog had descended on the island, spreading in from the Atlantic, making it difficult as I drove around the narrow roads to get a sense of where I was. Machir Bay was fog bound, and so was Kilchiaran Bay at the end of a long, seemingly endless journey, full of tight corners, the gradient changing, rising and falling as the road clung to the hilly contours of the land, not to mention the additional hazard of sheep straying onto the roads. The roar of the sea was heard, but rarely glimpsed, due to the fog. A damp, heavy sea smell permeated the car, making me turn up the heater. I cursed that there was no air conditioning. Burial grounds yielded some information, and I even visited a few local farms, claiming that I was researching my family ancestry as an excuse for my visit, pointing to a notebook, hoping that no one would ask to read it, because it was full of jottings about the sunk ship, the *Empire Constellation*.

It was on my last night, when I was starting to feel despondent, with little progress, that I unexpectedly hit pay dirt. In the public bar of the hotel I was staying in, at a place called Bridgend, I recognised a woman who had been helping out on Loch Gorm, one of the farms, milking cows when I visited it. She was not unattractive, but struck me as very browbeaten and lacking in education or confidence, and I thought I might as well ask her a few questions. Anyway, I was lonely. She was shy, her head dipped, a fringe almost covering her eyes, reluctant to make eye contact. I used my American accent to good effect and gradually she smiled, her head lifting, not believing that I could be interested in her. She did not say much and normally I wouldn't have gone near her, but a few whiskies later she returned my gaze with a smile, and soon we were sitting side-by-side. She was drinking blended whisky, Bells, I think, and I hated it. It was bitter and difficult to swallow: give me a good bourbon any time. Why did the locals not drink their own whisky, given the number of distilleries on the island? I didn't intend to stay around long enough to find out.

I had learnt not to drink too quickly in situations like this, to keep a clear head. Iris, that was her name, was not too bright and she did not realise the significance of what she had told me. She wanted male company and I gave her that, inviting her up to my room, to which she readily agreed. I noticed that the barman watched us leave, but he wouldn't mind with the tip I had left. I was just a lonely tourist doing what tourists like to do on holiday. Later, I sent her home by taxi, probably dreaming of the tall American who had given her unexpected pleasure, a night to remember. I had no intention of seeing her again. I immediately phoned Jack in the States, from my hotel room, the smell of Iris' cheap perfume still lingering in the air as I waited for him to pick up the phone. I poured the remaining whisky down the sink, the stench of it overpowering, until I washed it away by turning on the tap. I had to use one of the hotel's telephone lines; it cost me a fortune. I was careful of what I said, telling him a few things, but keeping a few nuggets to myself, as was my way.

The next day, the weather improving, I drove down from

Bowmore to the airport and handed in the hired car, arguing over the damage, and then went across the road to the airport, a small rural affair, which I believe had been originally built as part of the war effort but now provided a lifeline for the island.

My Cessna was still parked in the corner, near the road, and having reported in, I settled the account for fuel and storage and I was escorted out to the plane.

And now here I am ready to get away. Campbell and two others, all dressed in overalls, helped me through the pre-flight checks. I was anxious to get away, but you do need to complete the checks. Campbell, a tall man in his thirties, made a comment about how awkward it was to fly a Cessna if you were above average height. He seemed very thorough and I slipped him a tip, after all I don't think that they would get many rich tourists like me, and he appeared competent enough to complete the pre-flight checks for me.

With permission to taxi onto the runway, I edged the Cessna forward and lined the plane up with the end of the airstrip. I saw Campbell waving with both arms, indicating that I should stop. He ran forward and checked something near the tail of the plane, and then with a broad smile, he waved me on. The tip had worked, he was thorough.

I was going to climb up over Loch Indaal and, now that the weather had lifted, I also wanted to overfly the island so that I could get the terrain clear in my mind, in preparation for my return.

Permission to take off having been granted from the small control tower, the Cessna sped down the runway, lifting off well before the end of the airstrip and gaining height quickly, turning over Loch Indaal towards Bowmore. I was high enough to see the narrow strip of sea that separated Islay from the neighbouring island of Jura. The hills on Jura were still snow-capped. Ranges of hills continued into the distance, peeking out from the low cloud base, further north.

From studying the maps before I left, I could identify Loch Gruinart, the tide having retreated to expose sand, almost to the mouth of the sea loch, and the narrow strip of land between it and Loch Indaal. The two lochs, separated by only a couple of miles, almost split the island in two. There was a big white house, Islay House, which I used as a marker to change direction, and then I was flying above the low hills of the Rhinns, heading south, flying over Loch Gorm to reach Machir Bay, the narrow strip of sand, at the head of the bay, gleaming in the sun. It was beautiful, and I was excited by the thought of coming back and what I might find, my impression of the island changing by the moment.

As I headed south, flying over the light house at Portnahaven, I banked slightly so that I could see the airport, the Mull of Oa, a peninsula to the south-west of the airport, with a monument on the cliff top, and a tall building, the Maltings they called it, where they treated barley before turning it into whisky, on the outskirts of Port Ellen. Ahead the coast of Northern Ireland was in sight

It was then that the engine started to stutter and then cut out completely. I didn't panic, I checked the engine temperature and it was okay. It was probably fuel starvation, but with the high wings, gravity should draw the fuel down. I reduced my height, trying to restart the engine, but the propeller blade had stopped turning. I tried tilting the plane from side to side to see if that would help, rocking the plane's wings to free any air blockage in the fuel vent.

I checked the air speed, which was in the sixties. Lights were now flashing on the control panel. I pushed in the fuel shutoff valve and both the fuel selector valves, and switched on the auxiliary fuel pump, and set the fuel mix to rich, but when I pressed the start switch the engine did not restart. No power, so I needed to make an emergency landing.

I ensured that my seat was upright and seat belt was fastened, and grabbed a bag from the seat beside me to place between me and the control wheel, to cushion any impact.

I got on the radio and calmly notified air traffic control, that I was suffering engine problems and losing altitude quickly.

I got their attention. 'Keep calm, sir,' the air traffic controller replied, in a patronising tone.

I set the transponder code to emergency 7700. 77 go to heaven, that didn't make me feel any better.

I needed to land at Islay Airport promptly. I would let Campbell and his colleagues know exactly what I thought of them. But I couldn't let anger cloud my judgement. I had to stay calm, but as the plane dropped and I struggled to line its path up with the airstrip, I finally cursed and swore.

The airstrip was looming up too quickly. I cut the idle, pulled out the fuel shutoff valve, and reached for the ignition switch, but it was all happening too fast, the airstrip too close. Had I done that in the correct sequence? I was fumbling, looking for the correct switches, trying to adjust the wing flaps, forgetting the emergency sequence. Where was the master switch?

Curse the incompetent bastards, but I should have checked the fuel vents were clear for myself; it was the pilot's responsibility. Damn the islanders and the island.

'Mayday, Mayday,' I repeated, more and more urgently, feeling cold, my hands clammy. I wasn't going to make it. Below, I could see a fire engine heading onto the tarmac, lights flashing, as I tried to make my approach, having been given emergency permission to land.

I left a final cryptic message, angry that I might not benefit personally, but sure that I didn't want the islanders to get away with murder.

The sea below me was getting closer, the plane was skimming the waves, a startled seagull splattered on the windscreen. With a final effort, I attempted to bring the plane up, as the shore rapidly approached. The plane lifted over the shoreline, but then dipped.

I braced myself as the front wheel hit the ground, too hard. Far too hard.

8

Monday pm

By the time I had completed my second tour I was quite hungry. No two tours are the same, and the second party of visitors were more involved, warmer, interested in what I was saying. Maybe it was just me. Every group gets the same spiel but I can add in a few extra stories, if I judge it will help. I showed the second group a whisky barrel which we keep on display, which shows how some of the workers, in the past, would try to get some of the new make spirit by removing the bung that sealed the barrel, dipping a container inside, filling it with spirit and resealing the barrel so that no one would notice. The sales of Heinz salad cream bottles in the local Co-op were the highest by head of population in Scotland, I explained, and an investigation led to the discovery that the bottles were the right shape for slipping into a whisky barrel easily. The distillery workers were emptying and cleaning the bottles, attaching a string to the neck and dangling or doonkering the salad cream bottle into the barrel and filling the bottles with new make spirit, when no one was looking. Given that they already received a generous daily allowance, and the high potency of the brew, they can hardly have ever been sober. Changed days: all I get is a monthly allowance of discounted whisky.

I noticed that Pence Gifford was around and about today, looking as if he had something on his mind. He joined the second group briefly, his usual professional self, before departing muttering something about missing whisky, which caused some of the party to smile.

With two more tours in the afternoon and a visit to Malcolm later, I needed a coffee and something to eat. With no Jenny to prepare a sandwich I headed down School Road, across the Main Street to the Celtic House, which had a cafe upstairs, searching for a coffee to take away and a slice of home-made cake. Bowmore was busier now than usual, especially with the festival approaching, with a lot of people about in Morrison's Square, an open area with benches, next to the Tourist Board and overlooked by a bank, enjoying the sunshine on a mild May day. The Co-op across the road was also busy, cars double parked, not unusual, as customers loaded up with groceries.

The wide Main Street in Bowmore rises steeply to Kilarrow Parish Church of Scotland or simply the Round Church, as it was popularly known, at the top of the hill. This was all planned by a previous landowner, who had based his vision for the new village of Bowmore on an Italian village he had encountered on his travels. The church overlooked the village and from there it was easy to see how streets criss-crossed the Main Street at regular intervals. The only differences between Bowmore and the village that had inspired it were the weather, and the production of whisky rather than wine.

The Celtic House stood on the corner of Main Street, where the main road through Bowmore tuned at right angles, along Shore Road, where I had driven this morning to reach work. The wide road continued down to the harbour.

Focussed on food, I didn't look at the wide range of Scottish books and gifts on display downstairs, but headed upstairs and ordered my lunch at the cafe. I was well known and the young assistant, Carol, soon rustled up my order as I waited at the counter. I could go back to the distillery to eat, but as it was a pleasant day, I decided to go down to the harbour. I still needed space to decide what I was going to do. I glanced at my phone but there was no further message from Jenny, only a text from Ronnie, a friend from Jura, who reminded me that he wanted to go out fishing with me on his rigid inflatable boat.

I collected my cardboard coffee container and slice of chocolate cake in a brown bag, and turned around. The cafe was busy, with all the tables occupied and that's probably why I had not noticed Donald Robinson sitting at a table, near the window, with another man. He was examining the screen of a laptop, taking advantage of the free Wi-Fi. At the next table, with her iPhone laid on the table in front of her, sipping a coffee, was Sally, her companions nowhere to be seen. I smiled, acknowledging her quickly, trying not to alert Donald Robinson, but he had seen me and stared at me, a scowl immediately apparent on his face. Like all the male Robinsons there was more than a passing resemblance to Field Marshall Montgomery, which had led to the father being nicknamed Monty, especially after his time in the army. He hated the nickname and it was a brave man who used it in front of any of them. A long nose dominated his face, jutting beyond his dimpled chin. On his top lip his moustache helped to soften his habitual severe expression. Donald still had his full head of sandy coloured hair, although I could see that it was starting to thin. I had really seen very little of him since that day many years ago, but my memory of his angry expression, seething with rage was still vivid, with Catherine cowering in the background, screaming. I hadn't wanted another flashback but I got one, an automatic reflex.

Our eyes locked briefly and trying to ignore recent events I did not flinch. I had nothing to hide, I assured myself. His blues eyes stared, narrowing as his expression intensified, a mixture of hate and anger, I thought. I was an unwanted intruder, 'don't complicate things for me,' was the message conveyed. He picked up his coffee while maintaining the gaze, ensuring I got the message, and then abruptly turned away as his companion, a stocky thickset man, a bit older than Donald, who by now must have been in his late thirties, nudged him and spoke something in his ear, stabbing with a stubby finger at the screen. Donald replied and the man looked up. I liked the look of him even less. My courage drained, and I froze. If Donald was known as a fearsome character, embodying his father's worst traits, then this man with his cold eyes and stocky appearance was in a different league. For a moment I thought he was going to rise up and come over to me, as he fixed me with an unwavering stare. I broke his gaze and reached the top of the stairs, noticing that Sally was closely observing the scene, and walked down to the lower shop, willing myself to walk slowly.

Outside I drew a deep breath. There was no point in kidding myself: that encounter had not gone well. No Robinson would acknowledge me since the night that Catherine left the island. It wasn't a surprise I suppose. I wondered what his involvement was, if any, last Friday. From his reaction to me, he obviously knew something had happened.

I reached the broad concrete concourse of Bowmore's small harbour. A thick concrete wall protected the small harbour and the pontoon from the worst that Loch Indaal could muster, although I had seen winter storms completely overwhelm these defences. As usual, the powerboat for the Islay Airport Rescue sat there, along with a few small boats. A low breakwater partially encircled the pontoon.

I sat down on one of the benches and immediately sipped my

coffee, trying to restore my energy levels, my hands still shaking. My only positive thought was it was not Donald's younger brother, Dylan, who I had met in the cafe. Since his accident he was rarely seen away from the farm, which the two brothers ran together. He had great difficulty in controlling his temper and had been arrested on several occasions for drunken brawling. Once, after one particularly boozy night, he had been fined for assaulting a tourist in the Main Street. He had been fortunate to avoid a custodial sentence, said the magistrate at the conclusion of his trial.

That apart, nothing was getting any better and my Pavlovian response to the encounter in the cafe didn't help. My chocolate cake was now unappealing, my appetite gone. I summoned up the energy to pick at it, the food lingering in my mouth, my stomach turning sour. Maybe the meeting with Malcolm this evening would throw more light on the situation, I dared to hope.

To my right, beyond the concrete wall, were the main distillery buildings. The harbour was a good vantage point from which to photograph the iconic distillery front with its bold lettering and beyond that, and higher up, Battery Point. I had many memories of meeting friends there after school, mostly good. To the left the clouds had cleared the Paps of Jura, their stark outline now prominent on the horizon. Nearer to me the backs of the hotels, bars and houses of Shore Street formed the sea front, a jumble of extensions and small gardens reaching down to the shore line. The area was littered with seaweed and plastic rubbish, with a few seagulls pecking for scraps of food.

I glanced at my watch and stood up, deposited most of my lunch in a litter bin and walked slowly back to the distillery. The distillery shop was still busy as I prepared for the next tour. The afternoon tours were busier, visitors keener to linger and talk and try a few different drams. I loved this part of the job, not that I was allowed to drink. Sniff and appear excited, but don't sip was Pence Gifford's motto. I manufactured what enthusiasm I could muster and smiled, but I was both tired and worried.

By four o'clock I was finished for the day, glad that the police had not shown up, and even lingered for a few minutes, deciding what to do in the hour before I could talk to Malcolm. I chatted to Julie behind the reception desk, asking how her family were doing when Mrs Hall, the distillery manager's PA, a smartly dressed lady in her fifties, opened the door from the admin office and spotted me talking by the reception counter.

'Mr Meldrum,' she was always very formal, especially in public and everyone respected that, 'I'm glad that I caught you before you left. Mr Gifford would like a word tomorrow.'

'Any particular time, Mrs Hall?'

'The morning, before or after a tour will be fine, Peter.' I was thrown by her using my first name, as she stepped closer to me peering at my cheek: 'How did you get that scratch on your face, Peter?'

'A cat,' I said.

'I thought it was a dog that you had?' She wasn't the PA for nothing.

'That's right. It was a neighbour's cat.' I hoped that I sounded credible. Of course everyone in the shop was now looking at me. I rubbed the scratch and smiled. 'You should see the state of the cat.'

I hoped that I sounded more convincing than I felt. It could have been a cat after all, couldn't it? Maybe Mr Gifford was going to offer me more training. On another week that would have been the first thing that sprang to mind, but not now.

With these final moments of the day causing my stomach more turmoil than I had expected I headed back to the Square, crossing over the outline map of Islay embedded in the paving slabs of Morrison Square, intending to kill time in the Co-op. But by now I was too agitated and I changed direction and headed along Shore Road to reach the Lochside Hotel.

I pushed through the door and into the whisky bar. One wall of the bar was lined with stone with a featured wooden bar counter, with racks of some of Islay's finest and some of its rarest whiskies lining the wall behind the counter. A whisky menu was on offer – it was Islay after all – with some eye-watering prices. Older whiskies and especially those from Port Ellen, which was now sadly closed for all time, were becoming rarer by the year and attracted those desperate to sample the whisky before it finally disappeared. I had, for a special birthday, bought my father a bottle of Port Ellen, which was rare even then, but now the same special release cost thirty times as much. Most people who bought Port Ellen these days were collectors, hoarding their investment for the long term. Ours had been finished long ago, but the pleasant memory of a lovely dram lingered, especially since it had been shared with Dad. In the corner of the bar was a Bunnahabhain whisky mirror, the one with the face of an old sailor and 'Westering Home' printed underneath, tilted so that the barman could observe the bar.

I knew the barman slightly and, having regained my composure, I asked for a pint of soda water and lime with ice. This was no time for alcohol and anyway I had to drive home. I took the drink and wandered out onto the patio overlooking the harbour. The bar was almost empty, but as I went to sit on one of the metal framed seats outside I noticed a man coming in. He had greying hair, was probably in his forties, not very tall, and was wearing a green T-shirt and jeans. The green T-shirt was emblazoned with the Ardbeg Celtic symbol. He was probably one of the first arrivals for the start of the festival, early for the party that was about to kick off on the island. As I sat staring out over

80

Loch Indaal I watched the waves sparkling in the sun, breaking meekly a few feet away, using nature's metronome to try to relax. This was how life should be. Sadly, it wasn't, at least not today.

By the time I left, the group of Chinese visitors I had shown around the distillery this morning had arrived in the bar. They had obviously enjoyed their visit to Ardbeg and were busy studying the whisky menu. One of them saw me and called over.

'Hi Peter, time for a drink now? Ardbeg is also pretty good, indeed they are all good but I do like the sherried Islay 15-year-old you let me try. But I'll have to try a few to make up my mind.' He laughed, a laugh which suggested that the sampling process was well under way. The rest were also getting into the spirit of the occasion, raising their glasses to me, and there was a lot of banter and shouting between them; little of it, however, was in English, so I was none the wiser. I saw the guy in the Ardbeg T-shirt sitting on a bar stool close to the mirror, smiling at the joviality. He was still supping his pint, which he had hardly started.

I stepped out into the soft spring evening, a few shadows already appearing in the narrow street, and ran into the Rev Walker, who was passing the hotel entrance. Islay is a small place, with a population of around three thousand souls and only a few villages, so such encounters are common and almost expected by the Ileachs. The minister often went for walks around the village, probably checking up on his flock. I liked him a lot; he was known for not just 'talking the talk', but also 'walking the walk'. In other words he did a lot of good, most of it quietly, and he had been a great support when my mother died, and when Jenny and I were getting married, in the Round Church. I stopped and smiled. If I was a few minutes late it wouldn't matter.

'How is your wife?' I asked, remembering that she hadn't been well.

'A lot better, thanks. They flew her to Glasgow for treatment and she's almost back to herself.' Medical treatment in Islay often meant plane journeys to one of the major Glasgow hospitals.

With his blue clerical shirt, dog collar and a tweed jacket he was instantly recognisable. The minister must be pushing sixty, I thought. His face seemed a little more lined than I remembered, but his hair a little darker. Even ministers can have a touch of vanity.

'How is Jenny?' he enquired.

'Away in England on business, with Ben. It's the last time she will be able to take him away with her before he starts school.'

The Rev Walker smiled. 'Time passes quickly and he is a wonderful wee boy, always smiling. Still fascinated by pirates?' The minister rarely forgot anything about his flock.

'Yes.'

'How is Jenny's business doing?'

She is trying to get a company in Leicester to produce prints of her works. Being a stickler for perfection, I don't know how it will go.'

'And the job at the distillery?'

'I'm enjoying it and hoping to progress.' At least I am if I don't get arrested, I thought to myself.

'It was good to meet you, Peter. I am on my way to see Mrs McGiffen, who is sick. I hope that we will see you soon.' And with a smile the minister left me.

'You will,' I replied and I meant it. We would need to get back to church. Especially right now: I needed to reaffirm that there was a deeper meaning to life.

We parted just as the guy with Ardbeg T-shirt left the hotel and quickly went into the Islay Whisky shop, a few doors away.

Feeling more positive, I walked back to Morrison Square and up School Street to Malcolm's flat overlooking the school. The only school in Scotland which could pass for a distillery, with its pagoda adornments on the roof.

Malcolm's small garden was looking good with some vegetables, probably carrots, starting to emerge in straight drilled lines. I hurried up the steps and was about to press the bell underneath the 'Baxter' nameplate when the door opened, and I was greeted by Alison, Malcolm's wife, who must have seen me coming.

'Hi, Peter. In you come. Malcolm will be out in a minute.' Alison, a small petite blonde, was drying her hands on a towel. 'The meal will be ready soon, just some potatoes and stew. Is that okay?'

I hadn't expected a meal but nodded my approval. Both were good friends from school days. They had moved to Glasgow when Malcolm was doing his journalism course and Alison worked as nurse to help make ends meet. The local paper had encouraged Malcolm to gain work experience by returning to the island, but I feared that if they did not move back to the mainland soon he would struggle to progress in his chosen career. Alison worked at the local hospital, a small holding facility, located to the rear of Bowmore. Minor injuries could be treated there, and patients could also stay there to recuperate after operations.

Malcolm emerged from the bedroom and sat down. He looked at me anxiously through his wire-framed glasses. I saw Alison cast him a worried glance: they had obviously discussed my plight. Who would bring up the topic first, I wondered. Nothing was said until the dirty dishes had been cleared away and Alison disappeared into the kitchen, although she was still within earshot.

'How are you, now?' he asked tentatively.

'Still a bit sore. No recollection of late Friday night or early Saturday morning.' I filled him in as best I could.

'Does Jenny know?'

I shook my head. 'I can't begin to think how to explain it to her. She would be too hurt.'

'Catherine Robinson. Who would have thought that she would reappear,' Malcolm muttered, shaking his head. We had all been at secondary school together and he knew the history between us: it had often spilled out over a few pints.

'I know, but seemingly she has.' I stopped. I could hear Alison clattering about as she cleared up in the kitchen.

'Have you heard anything else?' I enquired, not sure what I wanted to hear in reply. 'Did you get a chance to speak with Andy Johnstone again?' Naively, I hoped for some fantastic response that would resolve everything and end the nightmare.

Malcolm only shook his head. Alison came and sat beside him on the couch.

'So,' said Malcolm trying to lighten the mood, 'it just shows that you should always go down to the pub. You can always pick up something interesting.'

I smiled lamely and it was Alison who spoke next.

'You are innocent, Peter?' I was shocked by her comment but tried not to show it.

'I believe so, but when you can't remember and others are saying something different, you begin to doubt.'

'How do you explain the love bite?'

I hadn't expected this line of questioning. Perhaps I should have: Alison was very close to Jenny and protective of her. Maybe I should have said that Jenny and I made passionate love on the night before she left, but we hadn't; she had been too tired.

I shrugged. 'I know it doesn't look good.'

'Could you have been drugged?'

'Yes, possibly, but I have no knowledge of how a drug could do that or why it would happen at Machir Bay.'

'When people are raped, a drug is often slipped in their drink

84

beforehand. They have very little recollection. Worth exploring, Peter.' Did she think that I might have been raped? It had crossed my mind, but I had no unusual bruising.

'Will it not be out of my system?

'Depends on the drug. This happened on Friday night. GHB or ketamine would be gone by now, but there are others which linger in your system for up to seventy-two hours.'

Malcolm looked uncomfortable. I wondered if they had discussed this, before I arrived.

Alison looked thoughtful. 'Get me a sample of urine, Peter and I'll do what I can. No time like the present.'

Alison went into the bedroom and emerged with a case, which she opened and produced a sample tube for urine.

'Go into the bathroom now,' she instructed as I took the sample tube from her, unscrewing the top, as I closed the bathroom door behind me.

'I'll do what I can,' said Alison on my return with the sample. 'But it might not be easy. I understand the importance. Things like this do happen even on Islay. I'm sure Dr Khalid will help me out. I'll let you know the result if I get one.'

I felt better. It was a long shot, but at least something was being done.

Malcolm's serious face broke into a wide smile.

'Alison must like you.' He paused for effect. 'She wouldn't take any piss from me!'

We laughed. It helped to break the tension.

Malcolm had not encountered Andy Johnstone again, I discovered, but he was able to add a nugget of information that he had overlooked when he spoke to me on Sunday.

'I think Johnstone also said something about you walking your dog when you met Catherine.'

I pounced on the statement. 'Think, Malcolm. That couldn't

have happened.'

He saw the logic immediately. That cheered me up. The story couldn't all be true. Someone had embellished the tale, even if only in a small way.

'How are Susie and, of course, Jodie?'

'Susie is having a hard time,' replied Alison. 'Men aren't her favourite species at the moment. Jodie is doing as well as can be expected,' she added.

We talked for a lot longer, but kept running over the same ground. We all eventually concluded that Catherine would have to be interviewed and checked out physically. Maybe she had just phoned the police and they were waiting for her to turn up at a police station. Hopefully, she was having second thoughts.

I bade Malcolm and Alison farewell, grateful for their company, and walked back down to the distillery to collect my car. The square was almost empty now; there was just a few boys larking about. I drove up Main Street and turned left onto Jamieson Street and drove past the small police station. There was no sign of life. I turned the car around, realising that I had made the detour on the very small chance that Catherine might be around. I turned right, heading down the narrow and steep Hawthorne Lane. At the bottom, as I again turned right to head towards home, the phone vibrated in my pocket. Outside the power depot I stopped at the side of the road. It was a message from Jenny.

> How did your visit to the Alison and
> Malcolm go? Hope you had a good
> meal. The Leicester firm were no use –
> poor quality. Off to a firm in Doncaster
> tomorrow. Ben sends his love. So do I.
> Jenny xxxxx

My stomach lurched and I retched, quickly re-swallowing

the bitter contents of my stomach, praying that Alison had not disclosed anything to Jenny, not thinking that Alison and Jenny would have been in touch. This was tough, very tough and her return on Friday was getting ever closer. At least we hadn't spoken by phone Jenny would have known something was wrong and I didn't yet have a good explanation for her. A love bite from Catherine would be difficult to explain away, given the past history between the two of us and I suppose at the back of my mind I wondered how I had responded to what Catherine had done to me. I hoped that I had moved on and spurned any advances, but rumours spoke differently.

I drove home, taking the long way around Loch Gorm, my ability to cope with passing the Robinson's farm gone. For once, I hardly paid any attention to the sunset. As I drove the car past the farm gate at Saligo, close to the beach, even the deepening red sky and the bright sun, low in the sky, still dazzling, painting its reflection on the waves, were only a passing distraction – almost an irritant as they half-blinded me.

I parked the car, walked to the house and unlocked the door. Often I wouldn't have bothered locking the house, but now I checked the front and back doors. I was tired and decided against a coffee, stripping off and heading for the bathroom. An early night was required.

I had a shower the steam misting the mirror and I was disappointed to still be able to make out the faintest outline of the message.

Listen – don't go down to the beach

'Why 'listen'?' I pondered, and why was listen underlined? No sudden insight came to me. As the mirror cleared I saw the dirty clothes basket. Sticking out of the pale blue wicker basket was the clip end of one of Jenny's bras. I went over to the basket. No way had I left the basket like that. I remembered putting my

T-shirt in the basket in the morning. I lifted the lid and the bra slipped into the basket. I looked for my T-shirt and found it at the bottom, under some of Jenny's clothes. It should have been at the top. Someone had been rummaging in the basket while I was away. I put the lid back on as if that would blank out the memory. Someone must have been in the house. I walked thorough to the lounge and checked the front door. The key was in the lock and nothing looked unusual. I went into the kitchen and examined the Yale lock. I had not deadlocked it, I never did. I opened the door and studied the lock. There was a scratch on the metal latch and an indentation on the wood of the door. They matched; someone had forced an entry. Dusk was now falling, the intense redness of the setting sun over Machir Bay finally fading as the sun dipped behind Coul Point. I grabbed the torch hanging on a hook by the back door and went into the garden. To get in the intruder must have jumped the wall. I went over and shone the torch on the other side of the wall. The ground was soggy – I really did need to get the plumber to repair the blocked field drain. I shone the torch on the muddy surface on the far side and walked slowly along the perimeter. Soon I saw several muddy footprints, the tread of a boot. My fears were confirmed. Learning from my experience on Sunday, I went into the house, collected my phone and photographed the footprints, using the torch to illuminate them.

Inside the house I deadlocked the back door and made myself a cup of coffee. I sipped the coffee, ignoring the ache in my stomach, the need for a caffeine fix greater than a little local pain. I examined the photographs that I had taken and the imprint made by the boots. To a detective this would be important evidence, but my brain was slowing down. A set of footprints made by a boot – a male boot by the size of it. So no return visit from Catherine. The tread had small square blocks in the middle with wide channels leading to the edges. The heel had two semi-circular grooves, with one more worn than the other. A pattern which could be identified but probably the information was of limited value, as I couldn't go around asking people to show me the soles of their boots.

As I continued to sip the coffee the kitchen got darker the longer I sat. I could not for the life of me work out why someone would want to examine our dirty washing, unless they were looking for a sample of my DNA.

9

My father was from the west end of Glasgow, a product of the post-war baby boom. His father, my grandfather, John had served in the army with distinction, winning the Military Medal, in Germany, in the final days of the war, by saving several soldiers hiding in a shell hole, trapped by machine gun fire. As the pieces of lead zipped through the air inches above his head, he jumped out of the shell hole, startling the Germans, firing his sten gun from the hip. Unnerved, they broke, and a well-aimed grenade took most of them out. My father never told me if there had been any survivors. Years later he did show me the box containing the medal, but the handwritten letter from the King was missing. My grandfather never liked to make a fuss.

He had been housed in a prefab, in the west end of Glasgow, a scant reward for his sacrifice. Still, it was better than many received, and he settled back to work in the Glasgow Corporation bus depot, near Anniesland, where he was a mechanic. His first son, Peter, was born in 1946, three years before my father, Thomas. The two brothers were very close and enjoyed football and exploring the area with their friends, playing about in bomb sites, which were common in the area. In 1960 the family moved to a semi-detached council house in Knightswood, a few miles away. There was great excitement when the first small black and white television appeared. Dad also clearly remembered standing to attention at the Boy's Brigade, at the local church, when it was announced that President Kennedy had been assassinated. He returned home with Peter, who by this time had become a corporal in the Boy's Brigade, to find to their disappointment that all the television programmes had been cancelled and the screen was only showing a caption declaring that President Kennedy had been assassinated, with sombre mood music playing in the background.

A physics teacher, at the local Knightswood Secondary school, a Mr Hutchison, unlocked the potential in my uncle, creating an enthusiasm for experimenting with gadgets and how they worked. Some would have described it as an obsession. The street lost power one evening, when a circuit built by him fused the supply. I think that my grandfather was quite proud and my uncle promised to take more care.

During all the years that they were growing up a family tradition developed whereby the two boys would be sent through to their Aunt Mable, their mum's only sibling, in Edinburgh, while my grandparents could have a few days away together in the summer. The arrangement suited everyone. The grandparents had time to themselves and the boys were spoilt by their aunt, who doted on them. She lived in a big city centre flat, with high ceilings and a bay window that offered views of Edinburgh Castle. Mable loved to take the boys to see the attractions of the city, the castle, the zoo on Corstorphine Hill, museums and the many art galleries. Her love of art was indulged by the boys, who were savvy enough to know that feigned interest was rewarded by afternoon teas, usually at Jenner's department store. Mable appeared to live on her own and it was only many years later that Dad discovered that she had been briefly married to one of

91

the city's top investment bankers, who had been found with his mistress, and that my aunt had received a very good settlement.

Peter studied all hours to get his Highers, and got six at band 'A' in his fifth year. Entrance to Glasgow University was assured, to study physics, and a grant awarded, crucial to the family, which allowed him to go. Peter had to stay at home while completing his degree in physics, such were the state of the family finances. He got a first class degree in physics and was accepted for a PhD in optics at Glasgow and settled down to research life. I think that his father hoped that he would eventually get work at the nearby Barr and Stroud engineering works, who produced optical equipment, like periscopes for submarines and binoculars for the armed forces. Dad joined Peter at Glasgow University three years later, but chose to study history.

Peter surprised everyone by becoming a member of the Research Club in University Garden, which was open to postgraduates, and just across the road from the Physics Department, and this allowed him to stay away from home for longer, able to get a meal cheaply and relax. Amy, a postgraduate student in Zoology appeared on the scene and the two were inseparable. Dad saw them frequently walking hand in hand along University Avenue, the street that ran through the university campus. Several times the three of them had a coffee in one of the many cafes in Byres Road, frequented by students. Peter and Amy helped each other, understanding the pressure of postgraduate work, the long hours, the struggle to get results from experiments and the many frustrations of research. I don't know whether they would have got married or not. Events did not give them that opportunity.

By now Dad had met Mum – Margaret, a nursing student from Islay who was staying at the nurse's accommodation at the Southern General. Dad asked her up for a Gay Gordon, during a dance at the Highlander's Institute, in Berkeley Street, a meeting place for those living in the city, whose roots lay in the Highlands and islands and those like Dad, who with his friends discovered it was a good place to meet girls. They met up a week later at Glasgow Central station and went to the pictures, a James Bond film, Diamonds are Forever, starring Sean Connery.

One night, several months later, they were walking up from a dance at the Men's Union, at the bottom of University Avenue, over the hill past the university library and the main university buildings and down towards the science buildings, near Byres Road. They were level with University Gardens, where the Research Club was located, to discover police cars and an ambulance outside the Research Club. Dad thought nothing of it and watched as the ambulance, blue lights flashing sped past, heading the short distance to the Western Infirmary.

Mum and Dad said good bye as Mum got the Glasgow underground train home and Dad waited for a bus in Highburgh Road. My grandparents were in bed when he returned and Dad was making himself a cup of tea when the doorbell rang. He always remembers spilling the milk and trying to mop it up with a dishcloth, before hurrying to the door. It was a police sergeant, who asked if anyone else was at home and Dad immediately knew something was very wrong. He ushered the policeman in to the lounge and switched on the lights. My grandfather appeared, quickly tying the belt on his dressing gown, his anxious wife behind him, both fearing the worst.

The sergeant asked them to sit down as he broke the news that Peter had fallen from the balcony at the front of the Research Club. He had suffered severe injuries to his head and was declared dead by the time he reached the Infirmary. It was devastating for everyone. My grandfather, who normally could always control his emotions, broke down howling in grief. My Dad put his arms around him and held him tightly. For someone who had witnessed so much during the war, this was a crisis too far. My grandmother appeared to cope better, rushing about making tea, phoning the minister, trying to be practical.

I read all about it later, in a newspaper report in Glasgow's Mitchell Library. Peter Meldrum, a brilliant postgraduate, had fallen from the small balcony at the front of the Research Club and died as a result of his injuries, at the scene. An accident inquiry concluded that there was alcohol in his blood, but this would have been unlikely to be the main cause. It appeared, according to witnesses, that he had been arguing with his girlfriend and that she had left the Research Club moments before. I never discovered what happened to her. Did he jump in despair at breaking up or topple over the low stone balustrade as he shouted after her? Life does not always give clear answers; much can be left to puzzle over or fester in the minds of those left behind. Amy did not come to the funeral and when my Dad went to the Zoology Department, she had gone, her studies abandoned. Two ruined lives, probably a consequence of a minute's disagreement.

My grandfather never recovered, and dropped dead in the street with a heart attack a year later. My grandmother succumbed to a stroke shortly after. Within eighteen months of Peter's death, both were dead. Both should have had 'broken heart' written on their death certificate. My father was left to pick up the pieces.

He and my Mum were married at the university chapel a year later, in 1978, a proper grieving time observed. They stayed on in his parents' house. Mum had qualified as a nurse and got a job in Gartnavel General Hospital, on Great Western Road, so she did not have far to travel. Her job paid the rent and allowed Dad to complete his degree. My now he had decided to go into teaching and completed his postgraduate year, at Jordanhill College of Education. Armed with his teaching parchment he found a job at Woodside Secondary in the centre of Glasgow. He enjoyed it but my parents wanted something different. The city was fine but Margaret, in particular, felt the call of the islands and when a vacancy came up at Islay High School, Dad was tempted and Mum needed little persuasion.

They moved over during the summer and stayed with an aunt and her family, while they looked for a house. That's when they spotted the house at Machir Bay, a former croft with the original house demolished and a modern two-bedroom bungalow replacing it. It was vacant and up for sale, but when they enquired they couldn't afford the size of mortgage. But then fate played a part, when Dad visited Aunt Mable in Edinburgh. He was alarmed to see that she had lost weight and urged her to go to her GP. My aunt would not hear of it and by the time she collapsed in the street and was rushed into hospital and diagnosed, it was too late. Dad was by her side as she passed away.

Dad got a call from Anderson, Stewart, Drummond and Rankin, a firm of Edinburgh lawyers and travelled through to the city with Mum. They sat in a large office with floor to ceiling windows and a massive desk. Legal documents lined a suitably large table. Mr Rankin welcomed them and immediately dashed their hopes.

The flat that Aunt Mable lived in was not owned by her, but as part of the divorce settlement she could live rent free in the property until she died. The lawyer must have seen the expression on their faces as they glanced at each other and quickly added, 'But there is a sizeable sum left in shares, which have done very well in recent years. This, your aunt has bequeathed to you, Mr Meldrum.'

Stunned by the news they went for a celebration coffee at Jenner's. Aunt Mable had come up trumps and they arrived back at Glasgow's Queen Street Station very grateful and determined to put in an offer on the house. They spoke to Mr McCall, a lawyer in Campbeltown, and instructed him to put in an offer. Later that week the lawyer got back to them: 'Mr Charles Robinson declined your offer and asked for a further ten thousand pounds. Having spoken to Mr Robinson's lawyer I don't think that it is anything personal. He is desperate to sell but needs more money and he won't sell you any of the former crofting land, only enough land for a garden.'

This was before so many homes on Islay were snapped up as holiday homes, which forced prices even higher.

My parents discussed the situation and decided to go for it. The new price almost exhausted their reserves of money, but they instructed the lawyer to resubmit a bid, with a twenty-four hour deadline.

Anxiously they waited for the lawyer to get back to them and the four o'clock deadline slipped by. The next morning the phone rang in my aunt's farmhouse kitchen and my aunt quickly passed the phone to Dad.

'Mr McColl here, sorry for the delay. Mr Robinson was off the island on business but has accepted your offer. The house is yours.'

A month later they were living in paradise, according to Mum. I presume it was still summer and that they hadn't experienced the winter storms. They named the cottage Mable's Cottage, after Dad's aunt.

I came along in 1984 and was named Peter after Dad's brother. If I had been a girl I am sure that I would have been called Mable. My earliest memories are all of Islay. We rarely left the island. I was an only child: I am sure that my parents would have wanted more children, but it never happened. One thing they never gave me, despite many pleas, was a dog. Mum, who was usually so accommodating, did not want a dog and with both

Mum and Dad working, it was difficult, I suppose, because the dog would have been left alone for long spells.

In August 1989, it was time to go primary school in Port Charlotte, on the eastern side of the Rhinns, on the shore of Loch Indaal. It was a sunny morning. I was dressed up in a light blue sweatshirt, with the school badge on it and black trousers. I waited nervously for the taxi to arrive. After what seemed an eternity, I saw a red Ford Sierra trundle up the driveway and stop. A man in his early sixties, with white hair and a bushy beard, got out of the car. I was bit spooked until he spoke. His voice was friendly and with a big warm smile, he said, 'I'm Beattie. Everyone calls me that.'

With a pat from Mum I climbed into the back of the taxi. A girl was sitting there already, also dressed in school uniform, the same as me. She had blond hair, held together at the back by a clasp, a small upturned nose and blue eyes. I hadn't met that many girls living where I did, and was probably transfixed. I didn't know what to say. She broke the ice.

'I'm Catherine Robinson,' she said. 'I live in the big farm along the road.'

That was the first time that I met Catherine. Little did I know what an impact she would have on my life.

10

Beattie arrived each morning in his taxi to pick me up, always smiling, one of those who saw each day as a joy; his bushy beard, now more white than grey, made him appear like a benign pirate. He had been sent to the island during the war to help shuffle pilots and crew out to the Sunderland flying boats in Loch Indaal, and had fallen in love with the island and Mary, a local girl. When he left the air force after the war he headed straight back to Islay, got married, and did many jobs around the island before setting up Kintra taxis, based near Port Ellen.

He enthralled Catherine and I, each day, with stories of fairies in Loch Gorm, shipwrecks around the coast of Islay and tales of heroic kings and queens. It was several years before I realised that the stories were the product of his fertile imagination. Beattie called Catherine his princess, because she lived in a big house and me Peter Pan, because I was always running around with swords and fighting pirates.

'Someday you will fly,' Beattie said, 'and stop the pirates.'

Both of us loved him, and he would join in with our spelling homework, which Catherine and I always did together in the back of his taxi, reminding us to speak loudly as he was slightly deaf. Catherine was a natural speller and Beattie loved trying to catch her out. I preferred numbers, but Catherine would not practise her sums with me in case she made a mistake. There is a competitive streak in the Robinson family. The following year Dylan, her younger brother, joined us on the daily journey.

There were few other young people living in our part of the Rhinns so Mum and Mrs Robinson would arrange for us to take turns for the two of us, and sometimes Dylan, to be dropped off at each other's house for a meal, and to play together. When it was our turn to have Catherine over we would often walk up to the old radar installations and sometimes over the track to Kilchiaran Bay, passing Granny's Rock, a cliff formation that was meant to look like an old lady. It was Catherine who first saw the resemblance; I was less convinced. Over the hill in Kilchiaran Bay her dad owned a small wooden barn and a few fields, close to a graveyard. If Catherine thought that her dad or her older brother Donald were working over there she would not go, so we would pause near the top and search first for his Land Rover, turning back if it was there. Other days we might head in the other direction towards Coul Point, a headland to the northern side of the bay, to look for a sunken U-boat. These were happy times.

My trips to the Robinson's farm house were different. Mum and Dad were good hosts, but Mr Robinson was rarely there and when he was he paid his family little attention.

One afternoon we were dropped by Beattie at the entrance to the farm. I am sure that I was in Primary 5 at the time. I have often thought on the events that day, and I am sure that time and reflection has altered some of my perceptions. Just not enough, I am afraid.

Beattie never drove into the Robinson's farm. He swung the taxi around on the wide entrance to the farm and stopped.

'Too muddy,' he said. 'I don't want to be having to wash my

taxi before the weekend.' I had seen the farmyard in a worse state.

I had clothes for playing with me, and quickly changed in a spare bedroom. Even with five people in it the bungalow seemed too large, with its wide central corridor and spacious bedrooms, all en-suite. There was a lounge with a large coal fire recessed in a stone wall, and a strangely patterned flock wallpaper. It made the room appear dark and cold. Both the kitchen and lounge dwarfed ours in size and the dining room, with its long rectangular rosewood table, with matching carver chairs, with side arms, was far bigger than our fold-away table. Catherine and I looked very small when we sat in the chairs, our feet dangling in the air.

We soon ran outside, eager to play, and Catherine grabbed me by my hand and led me passed metal doors set into the hillside, a storage area, over the fence, to the rear of the two barns, and onto the low hills behind. I remember there were a few sheep and cattle scattered about munching the grass, so I suspect it must have before school closed for the summer. Holding a finger over her mouth to silence any questions, we quietly climbed until we were overlooking the farm, and a short distance from the road that Beattie had brought us along.

'Keep down,' she said and we crawled towards a rocky escarpment. To the side of it she showed me a slab covered in moss.

'Look what I found,' she said and we started scraping some moss and dirt from the slab, which we eventually managed to prise up and push over, exposing a rusty grill screwed down onto a concrete base, fixed, in turn, onto a wide concrete pipe. Catherine produced a torch and shone it down the ventilation hole. The two-foot diameter concrete pipe was only a few feet in length, and then it stopped; we could see only darkness underneath. Below that must have been a cavern, but our view was obscured by cobwebs. We were both excited, speculating on what it might be, adventurers who had discovered a long-lost entrance into another world. We were aware of a musty smell, since the removal of the slab, which added to our sense of intrigue.

'There must be another way in,' I whispered, 'I wonder what is down there? Could be a treasure hoard.'

'Don't talk about it when we get back,' replied Catherine. 'Dad doesn't want me to go near this bit of the farm. Says that there are nasty weed killers stored behind the metal doors. He might get angry.' I promised to keep our secret, but remember feeling excited by Catherine's discovery, our youthful imaginations stirred up.

Looking around and keeping low we retraced our steps, startling a sheep, which scarpered away bleating.

We climbed the fence and re-entered the farmyard, passing between the two green corrugated metal barns on breeze block foundations, and crossed over to the house. I noticed that the two metal doors, were bolted and padlocked.

We cleaned up, completed our homework and went through to the dining room when called. At home we always ate around the kitchen table but the Robinsons brought their food through from the kitchen in casseroles and served it at the table. Mum brought plates of food to the table, already on the plates.

I had noticed Mr Robinson returning by Land Rover a few minutes earlier. He was a lot older than his wife, almost bald and stooped, his trademark moustache grey and bristling. He must have been in his fifties then, and, I thought, always looked worried. When Dylan noticed his father he became quieter, and stopped teasing his sister. Donald was the last to arrive, his face red from being out in the sun all day, glancing at the two of us, but saying nothing. Mrs Robinson, a tall lady her hair tied in a bun behind her, showing many strands of grey, wore a large floral apron, which she removed as she sat down, wiping her hands on it. She said nothing either. The mood around the table was gloomy, tense, not like home.

Catherine's father, who was served first, ignored us and started to eat the stew in front of him, eating fast, taking little time to chew. Dylan glanced at his sister, and she gave him a quick smile in response. Her younger brother played with his food, holding the piece of meat on his fork, but not eating it.

Donald was a good bit older than us and already working full time on the farm, having left school as soon as he could. He snatched his plate of food from his mother and started to scoff down the food, obviously hungry. I was watching the others and trying to eat at a slow pace, as I had been instructed by my parents.

Mrs Robinson smiled across at me.

'How was school today, Peter?'

'We practised our tables, and when we finished we got to work on our project,' I said.

'And what was that?'

'Islay during the war. I got to draw a flying boat,' I replied.

Mr Robinson looked up for the first time and broke into the conversation.

'What is your project, Catherine?'

'I am working on the Lord of the Isles and drew a castle at Finlaggan,' she answered, but with little enthusiasm, not seeming to want to continue the conversation. She kept her head down and glanced at her Mum for reassurance and I sensed that both were nervous.

It was Donald who spoke next, looking across the table at his father.

'I saw the two of them,' and he pointed to the two of us, 'up on the hill, where you told Catherine not to go.'

I was suddenly aware of the loud ticking of the grandfather clock, for the first time, as a deep silence descended. Donald started eating again. He had dropped his bombshell and didn't care about the consequences. Mrs Robinson began to wipe her hands on the apron again. Dylan looked down and started to eat. Catherine went quiet, not daring to look up.

I found the silence frightening. I can see now that there was a power play going on. Donald wanted to keep in with his father, his actions suggesting that he was going to be, in time, a clone. If he caused problems for the rest of his family, he did not care.

Mr Robinson wiped his hand slowly along his mouth and briefly looked at his hand, examining a piece of stew which had been stuck to his moustache. He lifted his head and pointed to Catherine. 'Go to your bedroom and stay there until I speak with you.'

He turned to his wife. 'Could you not have kept a better eye on them. I'm disappointed.'

And then he turned to me.

'You can go home,' he said, and the words were delivered sharply, his cheeks beginning to redden. He glared at his wife. 'Take him home now.'

Mrs Robinson rose, tears in her eyes, casting an angry glance at Donald, but not daring to speak. I had frozen in fear, but Catherine gently nudged me and I quickly stood up.

'Thank-you for the meal,' I said, as I had been trained to and I walked to the door, collecting my school clothes on the way.

Mrs Robinson grabbed me, anxious that I left quickly. She looked back and smiled at Catherine, trying to reassure her, as she left the room.

'Let's go, dear,' she said, and I was bundled into the Land Rover which sat outside the house. As I got in I heard a scream; it was Catherine. I froze and looked at Mrs Robinson.

'It will be okay,' she muttered, and said nothing more until we got to my house.

'I won't come in,' she said and as soon as I shut the door, she spun the Land Rover around and headed back towards her farm.

Dad asked why I was home early and I tried to explain. He just said that every family is different, but I saw him catching the eye of Mum.

The next morning Beattie arrived in the taxi alone.

'The Robinsons have had to go the mainland,' he said. 'Unexpected family bereavement,' he added. I saw Mum glancing at Dad, but nothing was said. 'Donald is staying behind to mind the farm. He was waiting for me when I reached the farm.'

So Beattie took me to school, went in and spoke to the teacher, and at the end of the day he was waiting for me by the school gates as usual. As we passed the Robinson's farm, I saw Donald, on a tractor, on a field, near Loch Gorm.

'Now, don't be missing your princess,' Beattie said with a smile I could see in the rear-view mirror. 'If your Mum is not back I'll take you up to the old church and the military graveyard.'

He knew I was always keen on his stories about the tragedy of the HMS *Otranto*. In a town there would have been many other places to explore but out here at Machir Bay the graveyard was one of the more interesting places, especially to a small boy with a big imagination.

There was no car at the house so we continued round the tarmacked road, down a steep hill and wound up to the old church. The church was surrounded by old graves and an important Celtic cross and to the left was a new graveyard. Beattie helped me onto the top of the stone wall of the new graveyard. Loch Gorm was sparkling blue, like one of those old coloured postcards, with their over bright colours. Rockside farm was ahead, Kilchoman distillery had not yet been built, and I could see several horses from the pony-trekking school winding their way up the hillside, behind the farm, the sun reflecting off their riders' hard hats and hi-viz jackets. The fields were ready for the first cutting of grass for silage. Beattie pointed out a small cave and the choughs, with their red legs and beaks, sitting on the walls of the ruined church.

We then walked to the ruined church. If I remember right the wooden roof had not totally collapsed at that point. Hundreds of starlings sat on the rafters, in rows, side-by-side. Turning towards the sea we bypassed the cottage beside the church, and headed over a field, towards the military graveyard. A large granite cross, with a large bronze metal sword pinned to each side, was positioned towards the seaward side of the cemetery. In the cemetery were rows of carefully attended graves, mostly of men from the HMS *Otranto*, which had collided with the HMS *Kashmir*, one foggy night at the end of the First World War. Beattie told me of the collision at sea, and how few survived the stormy seas. The beach had been littered with dead bodies. The way he told stories never bothered me; they were informative, not frightening.

Beattie was trying to cheer me up, thinking that I was just missing Catherine. He didn't realise that, even at my age, I was really concerned for her, sure that something was not right.

We started to walk back, and I pointed out a small cluster of graves by the wall, picked out by the afternoon sun.

'Tell me about these,' I said, gripping his hand. Beattie had never mentioned them before.

He turned to me, slightly hesitant, and then led me towards them.

'These graves are from the *Empire Constellation*,' he told me. 'We must have talked about them before.'

I shook my head, sure that we hadn't.

'The *Empire Constellation*, a merchant navy ship, was torpedoed just off the coast and several sailors were washed ashore in Machir Bay.'

'That's the Captain.' He pointed out the grave of 'D Whiteman'.

His pointing finger swivelled. 'And the Chief Officer, 'J Ferguson'. Many perished.'

Beattie was thoughtful, stroking his beard, and I waited.

He produced his gold watch, on a chain, from his top pocket. We had often been allowed to hold it while he drove his taxi. On that day he turned it over and on the back was an engraved name – J Ferguson.

'I often wonder if that watch is his,' said Beattie, pointing again to the grave of the Chief Officer. I got it from Catherine's grandfather, Torquil Robinson, who originally lived in a croft, where your house is today. He gave it to me as part payment for work I did on his farm. I think that he was glad to get rid of it.' He fell silent. He didn't explain his final remark.

As I examined the gold watch Beattie added, 'I don't think that we should tell Catherine about how I got it. Let's keep it a secret.'

I nodded agreement. I didn't want to share secrets with the Robinsons.

'You know,' Beattie went on, 'the watch is pirate's gold, Peter, pirate's gold,' he repeated, a serious expression on his face. I knew in my heart that this was not a nice pirate story, and I handed the watch back without either of us saying anything more.

11

Tuesday am

Despite the discovery that there had been intruders in my house, I slept well, exhaustion at last taking over. In the morning, as I washed I noticed that some of the scratches were beginning to fade and the love bite was now just a small multi-coloured bruise.

'With luck...' I thought, 'by Friday, they might not be so noticeable.'

I made a mental note to pick up some shopping in the Co-op before I came home. Before leaving, I checked that the back door was deadlocked. Using my phone, I photographed the contents of the washing basket. Paranoia was getting a grip. That photo would take some explaining if Jenny ever saw it.

The Golf started with its usual clouds of smoke. As I drove on to the road, I was faced with an immediate decision – long way or more direct route? Refreshed by my sleep, and feeling bolder, I decided to take the short route, stopping to let a car pass at the entrance to Kilchoman distillery.

The road rises slightly on the approach to Robinson's farm and I saw what looked like Dylan, Catherine's younger brother, with a tractor, pulling a muck spreader out from one of the barns. I instantly regretted my boldness and accelerated, hoping I would be past the farm by the time he reached the road. I was about two hundred yards away when I had to brake sharply as another car was coming towards me around a corner. I pulled over into the passing space, ready to wave and let him past. I recognised the driver, Joe, one of the workers from Kilchoman distillery. He slowed down when he saw me and wound down his window.

'Ready for next week, Peter? he said with enthusiasm, leaning out of the window.

'Of course,' I replied, not wanting to engage in conversation, noticing that Dylan's tractor and muck spreader were nearing the road. My hopes of avoiding Dylan were fading by the second.

'What's the special bottling at Islay Distillery going to be this year?' he asked, eager for insight.

'They don't tell people like me,' I answered. Dylan had stopped the tractor at the entrance to the farm and was looking both ways. He saw my car passing most days; he would know it was me.

'Our bottling is an eleven-year-old, port pipe finished. Very nice, but quite expensive. We have only three hundred bottles.'

This was information overkill, but I tried not to show it.

'Good luck, I'm sure that it will sell out,' I said, but I was really wishing luck to myself. Dylan had stopped the tractor and was now looking in my direction. He had definitely recognised me.

'Must be going, Joe, I am a bit late, lots of preparation going on.' I winked, trying to convey that I was very involved in the preparations.

'Very secretive these days, eh?'

What could I say? I just agreed, and edged the car forward. Joe took the hint and drove on. I thought of turning around and avoiding Dylan, but there was a ditch on the far side preventing me, and so instead I accelerated, hoping to get by, but he was waiting and deliberately turned the tractor onto the road, hauling the muck spreader behind, just as I approached. I braked hard and stopped a foot from the rear of it.

Before I could react, my worst fears were confirmed. The cabin door of the tractor was flung open and out jumped Dylan, in bark blue overhauls, shouting at me. I pressed the central locking button just in time, as he covered the distance between us surprisingly quickly. A large hand wrenched at the door handle. Thwarted, a large fist then slammed against the glass. The car shook.

'Get out!' he yelled. 'Play around with my sister? I'll teach you a lesson!'

He swore and banged the bonnet, ignoring the pain he must have felt in his adrenaline-fuelled rage, and then kicked the door in frustration as he couldn't get to me. I tried to reverse, but I was too quick with the clutch and the car stalled. Seeing my predicament, he raced to his tractor and started to reverse, hitting the front of my car with the muck spreader. He jumped out again and with a leer in my direction he turned on the spreader, the muck immediately covering the car with black syrupy sludge, spreading over my bonnet and seeping into the engine compartment, through the grill on the bonnet.

'You're a piece of shit, man,' he shouted, laughing at his choice of words.

I had now managed to get the car started, and as I attempted to reverse, I noticed Donald Robinson running down the track to the road, buttoning up his checked shirt, shouting at Dylan.

A few strong words were exchanged and I used the opportunity to reverse, but Donald saw what I was doing and ran to my car, his mouth narrowed, his moustache flecked with spittle from yelling at Dylan.

'Keep away, Meldrum, don't make matters worse. Get on your way. I'll let others deal with you, but I can't be responsible if you come this way again.'

He gave me no chance to respond, but spun around and shouted to Dylan.

He roughly pushed his younger brother into the cabin of the tractor, and Dylan manoeuvred to the side, giving me just enough room to pass. In a few seconds, and with little dignity, I edged past them, breathing fast and gulping down air. The stench in the car overpowering.

I didn't stop until I reached the road junction beside Loch Indaal, where I pulled over onto the grassy area by the beach and got out to inspect the damage. There was a dent in the door and also on the bonnet, where the spreader had hit it, but far worse was the stench. The sludge had penetrated the engine compartment, clinging to everything, the heat of the engine making it solidify.

I drove the few miles to Bridgend Stores, at the head of the loch, and bought a token for their car wash, and pressure washed the car. I opened the bonnet, the farmyard smell still strong, and power washed the engine compartment. The smell was difficult to remove and, worse, I could smell it clinging to my clothes. I went inside, bought a can of deodorant and sprayed my legs where the smell was strongest.

My first tour was now in half an hour, so I drove fast to the distillery.

As I parked, the vibration in my pocket told me that I had another message. It was Jenny sending her love and attached was a selfie of her and Ben, smiling for the camera. Jenny looked lovely, her black hair with its centre parting and layers of curls down each side, tumbling over her shoulders, her smile perfect... but then, I was smitten. How I loved her. Ben with his brown mop of hair, a young clone of his dad, was grinning and looked very happy, a plastic sword gripped in front of him. Their trip must be going well and here was I in all sorts of shit. It seemed appropriate to describe it like that. I sent a quick text in reply.

I left the front car windows partially open, absolutely certain no one would steal the car, hoping that the good sea air blowing in from Loch Indaal might purge the smell, and walked into the distillery. The girls behind the counter looked up and smiled; for once the shop was quiet, with only a few visitors. As I went into the changing room, I heard one of them cough.

The tour group was bigger than I thought it would be, a mixed group of enthusiasts and their hangers-on.

Fortunately the distillery smells seemed to mask my own odour, although I did get one or two people sniffing the air trying to place the odours.

Not long after it was time to visit the warehouse and then the reception area for the final dram which, as usual, was already poured. Some of the group wandered over to the large window overlooking Loch Indaal to admire the view and savour their dram.

'Look,' said the enthusiast, 'there is Bruichladdich Distillery across the loch, where we are going this afternoon. I didn't realise it was so close. What an island! So many distilleries!'

Eventually everyone left and, as I returned to the shop, Mrs Hall appeared. I noticed her glancing at my face again.

'Mr Gifford would like to see you now, Mr Meldrum.' I followed her up the stairs. Mrs Hall worked in a small annex next to the distillery manager's office. She motioned me to take a seat. The door to the office was open and I could hear that Pence Gifford was on the phone.

'Must be head office,' whispered Mrs Hall. 'He was expecting a call earlier,' she explained.

The other person was doing most of the talking, but after a couple of minutes Gifford spoke, impatience evident in his voice.

'Okay, Jim, but the barrels are being loaded here and being counted onto the trucks. I've gone to the warehouse and checked and examined the footage from the cameras. Everything is okay at this end. Get someone to follow the truck and you'll discover your culprit.'

There was a pause and finally Gifford said firmly, 'I need to go. I have an appointment with an employee, who needs to be back on a tour in twenty minutes.'

I heard the phone being put down and Gifford called out my name. Mrs Hall pointed to the office and I went in. The dark varnished wood panelled walls were a feature which I was sure went back many, many years. Along one wall were storage units with wood framed glass doors, the shelves inside lined with small 250ml flat labelled glass sample bottles, filled with samples of whisky. On the Formica-lined top surface were lines of tulip shaped glasses, with long stems and glass lids. Above the surface were more wall-mounted units, with more wood framed glass doors, with bottles of many different sizes. This was a working office, the domain of the distillery manager, responsible for the quality and quantity of the whisky produced, although much of the blending was done elsewhere. Gifford was sitting behind the chair, observing me through his large round wire-framed glasses. His first name was the source of much interest. Some suggested that it was because he had been a month overdue, or that the name was short for suspense, but that did not quite work. He certainly used it for effect, often proclaiming to distillery workers: 'Every pence counts.'

Gifford was a benign figurehead but very astute. Promoted into the post in his early forties from one of the company's mainland distilleries, his ten years in post had led to many acclaimed bottlings and gold and silver awards at international spirit festivals for the distillery.

Gifford welcomed me with a smile and indicated that I should sit down.

He launched forth right away.

'Sorry to keep you waiting. Head office onto me again about missing whisky.'

So the comment the other day wasn't just humour. I studied Gifford more carefully: there were lines round the eyes, exaggerated by the large glasses, and his high forehead was becoming more dominant, his fringe of hair swept further and further back, flecked with grey.

'I believe I know what is going on in my distillery from start to finish; no part of the job is unimportant. If you let quality slip then years down the line the final product suffers. I know my staff, and I've watched footage from the CCTV cameras. Barrels weighed, results logged; careful loading. The problem is not here,' he added defiantly. 'The days of walking the dog are gone.'

That was the practice I had described to one of my tour parties yesterday. Plunging a container – at Islay Distillery it was usually an empty Heinz salad cream container – into a cask and taking the contents home, dangling from a string inside your trousers.

'And the quantities are more substantial anyway.' He stopped. Gifford was worried. 'Anyway, Peter, thanks for coming to see me.' I could see him putting his distractions behind him, focussing instead on me.

'You've worked for three years at the distillery since returning from Glasgow where you got that fancy degree in marketing. We are delighted to have you and we need to think now of the future.'

This was, hopefully, what I wanted to hear.

'After the summer the company wants you to be at head office to learn more of the trade and see other distilleries. I know that you are fond of Islay, but a wee while away will do no harm. The company will help out with temporary accommodation costs.'

This was an inevitable part of island life, leaving but hopefully returning. Ileachs were used to this, and there was many a sad parting, many families realising that once gone their loved ones were unlikely to return, succumbing to the attractions of the mainland. Jenny and I had discussed this, but the reality was harder than I imagined, present issues aside.

'Before you go I want to use you more around the distillery, a general helper, to broaden your experience. Tomorrow, I want you to visit some of our southern neighbours. Jimmy, at Laphroaig, is pestering me for our contribution to this year's charity bottling. I have some samples ready for him. I also want you to pick up an empty sherry hogshead at Lagavulin. Stuart and I are doing a wee experiment. Take the van and they will help you load it. I am sure there will be time for lunch at Ardbeg.'

Gifford rose quickly from his seat and went to the whisky samples and held one up. He unscrewed the top and nosed it, handing it to me after a few seconds. This was the part of the job he enjoyed.

'It's from a sherry cask, but there is a strange coconut influence that I wouldn't expect. Can you detect it?'

I didn't think that I was being tested. I had already discovered that my nose was only average, no use for being a master blender, whose noses, it was claimed, could detect thousands of different smells.

'The power of suggestion,' I replied. 'I'm not sure.'

Gifford accepted my response. It must be lonely being a distillery manager, relying on your nose to give you the information about the suitability of the contents of a barrel; how it would blend with other whiskies, and once married together, how the final whisky would taste. Whether it was a standard bottling of a single malt, created from many different barrels, or a blended whisky created from a range of malt and grain whiskies, the distiller had to work out how the flavours would marry, and which ones would dominate. As part of a training day, I once made a blended whisky. On the day, everyone rated it highly. I had learnt the trick of not overwhelming the blend with smoky Islay whiskies, but a week later the blend was undrinkable. To predict the final flavour range of a blend, before the blend was even married together, over many months, was a hard job. Detecting and identifying aromas and off notes required a special olfactory system. No wonder Gifford's highly trained nose was insured for a large sum: he was not easy to replace.

Gifford smiled. 'I'm tempted to send this to Neil at Ardbeg, telling him that this is the future for our ten-year-old expression. That would get him thinking. In this job you never stop learning,' he added. 'There's always something new to consider, some influence from the cask that you need to consider. I think of the barrels as children, unruly at times, but they can eventually be turned into something worth all the effort you put in.'

There were few greater enthusiasts for whisky than Pence Gifford. He literally lived and breathed whisky. At last good news, a small respite from the last few days.

'Peter,' he said turning more serious, 'take care.' I wondered if he had heard any rumours about me. 'You will be a great help next week with the Feis Ile.'

I thanked him, but as I got up to leave, he suddenly laughed.

'Are the farmers' treating their fields on the Rhinns, Peter? If you were a whisky barrel I would have you broken up and the staves burned.'

I couldn't help smiling. I thanked him and left. As I went through the outer office Mrs Hall sniffed from behind her desk, and I hoped that she had just heard the final part of my conversation with the distillery manager. I had thought the smell had gone, but that's why I would never make a distiller.

12

Tuesday pm

I didn't want to go to the Celtic House again, in case I ran into Donald Robinson, so I decided that lunch would be a sandwich, and I hurried across Morrison Square to the Co-op. While there I took the chance to wander up and down the aisles with a hand basket to collect some bread and milk. I then stopped at the ready-made sandwiches section beside the daily newspapers and magazines, and studied the deals. The chicken barbecue sandwich, packet of crisps and a soft drink seemed a good choice and I added them to my hand basket. I was aware that someone had edged very close to me, inside my comfort zone, and I automatically stepped back to make space for the person, when I realised it was the American girl from yesterday's tour, Sally.

'Hi, Sally,' I said, pleased that I could remember her name but uncomfortable with her closeness. 'Been to any other distilleries?' It was pretty inane but it was all that I could think of to say.

'Peter,' she said, with a look of concern which stopped any further pleasantries. She glanced around the shop. 'We need to talk; you are in a lot of trouble. We've noticed that people are tailing you.' Her face was serious, with no sign of the smile that had lit up her face yesterday; her brow was slightly furrowed, adding emphasis to her message.

'Meet me in the square –' she pointed out the window and across the road '– once you have finished.'

I was puzzled. I couldn't imagine what she wanted, when I recollected that she had been sitting at the table next to Donald Robinson and that other, nasty looking guy, in the Celtic House yesterday.

I nodded and turned away quickly, unnerved, looking around checking for goodness knows what. I felt the by now familiar rapid breathing and my heart thumping. I paid up and strolled across the road to the square, trying to appear calm. Sally was sitting on a bench in front of the Royal Bank of Scotland building, When I sat down she ignored me until I turned to her. I took my pack of sandwiches, from my plastic bag, waiting for her to say something. I felt awkward biting into the sandwich, any anticipated pleasure from eating it now gone. My enjoyment of food had markedly decreased in the last few days. I was more concerned about what was going to be revealed.

'Peter,' she said softly, not wanting anyone to overhear, 'let me be quite clear. I am not interested in you, so don't get the wrong impression. We have, I believe, something in common, our paths are overlapping. We don't have a lot of time. People are following you - I don't know why.'

She reached into her handbag and produced her iPhone. 'Listen,' she demanded, ' to the start of the recording I made yesterday in the Celtic House, when you saw these two men, one of whom I suspect you know.'

I heard Donald Robinson's cold voice first. 'That's the man I told you about, Roy, from Friday night.'

Roy, as I now knew him, only said a few chilling words in reply. 'Why is he still alive? It must never happen again.'

The recording stopped abruptly as Sally pressed the screen on her phone.

'Do you believe me now, Peter? We don't have much time.' She turned briefly towards me, her eyes looking intently for an acknowledgement of what I had just heard.

I nodded, fighting to control my thoughts, as panic rose, sheer blind panic, burning acid rising in my gullet, the sandwich now dry and inedible in my mouth.

'We are going on this afternoon's ferry to Kennacraig, but we will be back Thursday evening on the six o'clock ferry. We have urgent business in Glasgow; it can't wait. I think that I can help you, so come to the cottage that we are staying in, beside the farmhouse – High Coullabus, after nine. Do you know where that is?' I nodded. 'I think that we can help each other, and I'll play the rest of the recording, which will help you with your difficulties. You seem to know a lot about the Robinsons, and we want to ask you some questions about them. It will be easy,' she added, reassuringly.

'Yes,' I said weakly, and then clearing my throat I repeated myself, 'Yes,' this time louder – not more confidently, but definitely clearer. 'But why wait until then? Can't you tell me now, help me, play the rest of the recording?' I realised that I was pleading with her, my voice getting louder.

'Take care,' she said and again I saw that warm, somehow, familiar smile, this time offering reassurance but no answers. 'I will explain everything to you on Thursday.' With that she quickly stood up and without looking around headed in the direction of the shop. As she reached the road, I saw Brian, with his by now familiar long straggly beard, dressed casually in denim, walk quickly to join her. He must have been lurking further up the street. Whatever their relationship, it was not intimate, more functional: a means to an end, I thought. Sally glanced at him and nodded. They looked up the road towards the Round Church and a minute later, a large black BMW, appeared, driven by Jonathon.

They both clambered in, and the car drove around the corner and away down Shore Street.

I sat in a daze, not even thinking to note the registration number, until I heard another, more familiar voice say: 'Are you okay, Peter?' and I looked up. It was Malcolm's sister, Susie, with two Border Collies straining on leads beside her, eager for their walk. I had not noticed her; she must have been using the cash dispenser, behind the bench. I hoped that she hadn't overhead the conversation.

'Who was that?' Susie continued, a puzzled expression on her face.

'Someone from one of the tour parties I led yesterday,' I said, relieved that I could, at least, answer truthfully. Susie had been a good friend of Jenny's for many years, and ran a boarding kennel on the shores of Loch Gruinart, on the Rhinns, only a few miles from us. 'It's my party trick, I try to learn their names.' I did not want to say more in case I was caught out. This was getting too hard. I was still struggling to calm down, regain control.

'You certainly didn't look or sound happy with her. Was she disappointed in the whisky you offered her at the end of the tour? Your face is scratched, Peter,' she added. 'Jenny and Ben are away for a few days and look what happens.' The comment was not softened with a smile. Susie was always defensive of Jenny, still angry and raw from a recent painful divorce, and did not particularly like men at the moment. Jenny said that she was very bitter at being left with two young children while her husband had moved to the mainland with his fancy woman. She was trying hard to make ends meet, trying to set up a business and survive without her estranged partner's help. Not that he was offering any, according to Malcolm.

'I texted her an hour ago. She said that she might manage home sooner. Doncaster had gone better than expected and she might not need to travel on to Durham. She'll probably phone you later.'

I put my sandwich uneaten in the waste bin and screwed the top off the soft drink bottle and drank, its fizzy contents refreshing my dry mouth.

'That's good news,' I replied, putting down the bottle on the bench, hoping that my expression showed suitable pleasure at her shock announcement.

Susie was staring at me. 'If you say so, Peter,' she said, but her expression told me that I had failed to convince her. 'And you haven't even asked about Jodie.'

Without adding anything further she let the two dogs lead her across the square and up School Road, probably taking them for a walk along the shore, from Battery Point.

I finished the soft drink, struggled with a few crisps, most of which ended up in the bin, collected my remaining shopping, and walked slowly back to the distillery. I swore to myself as I crunched up the soft drink bottle. I couldn't even have told you what the weather was like, other than I probably wouldn't have been sitting on the bench if it was raining.

Why is he still alive? It must never happen again. The coldly delivered words echoed through my mind, replaying on loop, my head pounding as I tried to grasp the enormity of what I had heard. Roy had expected me to be killed. But why? Who was Roy? Why was I being tailed? Who was Sally and her two goons and what did they want? Why did she have to go away now, of all times? I stopped off at the chemist shop to get some paracetamol and wished I hadn't finished my soft drink, as I attempted to swallow two of the tablets.

Sometimes when you are under pressure you can raise your game and I think that I managed that during the afternoon tours, but by five I was done. I was desperate to get away and hurried

120

through the shop and down School Street to my car, which was parked just around the corner, near the harbour.

I was responding to Jenny's latest text message – which made no mention of an early return – and only looked up as I got near the car. Standing beside my car was PC Andy Johnstone. He was watching me closely from under his flat policeman's cap. Between the cap and his bearded face his eyes looked shaded against the sun. He wore a standard short-sleeved vest and stab-proof jacket. He was much the same age as myself; I think he had been about two years ahead of me at school.

'Run into something, Mr Meldrum?' he asked, his voice unfriendly, pointing to the broken bonnet grill. 'You do know that you should report accidents on the public highway?' I glanced at the broken grill and the early evening sun reflecting off the bonnet of the car. Despite the power wash the faded red colour of the car still looked grubby, the muck still tainting the air.

He shook his head; whatever he was after, it wasn't my car.

'Have you seen Catherine recently?' Direct and to the point and wanting to gauge my reaction.

I was just hanging on, barely holding it together. He waited for my response, leaning forward slightly, eager to hear what I had to say.

'Not that I am aware of.' My voice was flat. I was beyond showing emotion.

'There was a phone call, Mr Meldrum.' Any familiarity had now gone; his tone was now clipped and impersonal. 'But we can't locate her. We think that she has left the island. She is certainly not at the farm.'

The seconds lengthened as he looked for my reaction. I stared blankly back.

'She mentioned you and said that she would file a report. If our enquiries lead us to believe that she is in any danger or has been attacked in any way, then we will need to talk again.'

Obviously she hadn't or we wouldn't be having the conversation.
A lifebuoy had just been thrown at a drowning man, but I still
found it hard to regain composure. If the police believed that I
had committed rape they wouldn't be sending Johnstone to talk
to me. I would be in the interview room at Bowmore police
station, being questioned by some heavy from Campbeltown or
Lochgilphead.

'I don't remember meeting her in the last four years, so I
don't understand why she would mention me. I wasn't even aware
that she was on the island.'

I lied. She had been there on Friday night: who else would
have left the phone where she did or leave that jumper in the bed
or the trainer where we often met? I simply remembered nothing
about it. It was my get-out clause.

PC Johnstone shook his head, slowly, almost for effect. "Have
it your way, Mr Meldrum, but you may well get a visit soon, if we
can't find her.'

This was strange. Either the police knew something more or
they were fishing and for some reason they didn't want to take
further action. This was no accidental meeting.

I opened the car door and got in. 'Go to Christie's hardware
shop or the garage and get some car wash,' he added as a parting
shot, his face twisted in a sneer.

I gave a thin smile and drove off. In the mirror I saw Johnstone
speaking on his phone, nodding as he spoke, as if he was agreeing
with the person at the other end. He was so keen to report our
meeting that he had not even waited until I got around the corner.

I drove home the long way around Loch Gorm, and when I
got in I slumped on the couch and, despite all my worries, I fell
asleep and dreamt that Catherine and I were walking along the
beach, just like old times. I was doing all the talking – that was

a change – and she didn't answer. I grabbed her, spun her round and screamed. Her face began to fade away, features dissolving and as I watched her body became wraith-like, dissipating in the mist that had descended on the beach, her presence evaporating in front of me.

I woke, aware that several hours had passed, the room now descending into darkness. Her face had gone; I couldn't focus on it. Oh, Catherine, what were you doing back at Machir Bay? Come to tease me, haunt me or love me again? Please God let it not be the last.

I noticed the light blinking on the base unit of the telephone. While I had slept I had missed a call from Jenny. There was no message left. I tried to reply, but her phone was switched off.

13

Catherine never talked about the aftermath of my truncated meal with the Robinsons. When she returned to the island, if she had ever been away, she said nothing. Even at ten years old, I was aware that she was holding something back, and there was always some caution in her eyes, if her family was mentioned. A 'don't go any further' look.

By the end of our primary school days I could see that Catherine was changing, part of growing up. Her body changed shape and sometimes her face was white and drawn, and she hinted that she was not feeling herself. Being brought up on a remote part of the island, in the days before access to the internet was available to me, I suppose I was naive, shielded from the big world.

We said farewell to Beattie, who retired as we finished primary school, and a mini-bus now collected us and others on the Rhinns, for the journey to secondary school. Catherine and I, however, were bonded, good friends who stuck by each other.

Our first year at the big school in Bowmore was an eye-opener, as we met other boys and girls from across Islay and Jura. We all mingled fairly easily, losing our primary school identity and starting a fresh journey of discovery, becoming part of a bigger group, although in Islay everything is relative. Our whole school roll could easily be absorbed into one year of a mainland secondary.

I encountered Dad as a teacher for the first time, and while the pupils knew that I was his son, the feedback was positive – he was respected and known as someone who could communicate with pupils of all ages. His enthusiasm for his subject came across as genuine, which was not the case with a few of the teachers.

First year drifted into second year and by the end of second year, our circle of friends had expanded. Malcolm, Alison, Susie and Ronnie were the core, but others joined us from time to time. At the end of the summer term we arranged to meet up for a picnic on the Big Strand, bordering Laggan Bay, south of Loch Indaal. The Big Strand was a seven-mile stretch of sand, backed by sand dunes, stretching from Laggan Point to the south-west of Bowmore, south past the airport to Kintra, where the Oa peninsula begins. To me it was an adventure, a start to exploring the rest of Islay. Catherine was equally enthusiastic and we got dropped off in Bowmore, where we headed for the Co-op to gather supplies – Irn-Bru and Quavers, our current favourite snacks.

We wandered along the narrow aisles, checking what we could afford. Catherine was wearing a lovely floral dress that stopped just above her knees. The fact that I noticed her appearance suggests that my hormones were also starting to change. We were laughing while we were making our selection, rejecting some of the more obscure flavourings on offer.

Along the aisle I noticed a girl that I recognised from school, a loner, dressed in a tartan skirt with a white T-shirt, which was greying, after many washes, and a black jacket. Her black hair, unlike Catherine's, was not layered, but roughly cut, probably by her mother. She was crouching down to examine an item on the bottom shelf, unaware of us.

'She just put a chocolate bar inside her jacket. I saw her do it!' shouted Catherine suddenly, startling those in the aisle, and myself, as other shoppers looked around to see who she was referring to.

The other girl looked alarmed and defensive, wrapping her arms around her, which made her appear guilty.

'I didn't!' she shouted back. 'Don't you accuse me of stealing!' She was becoming red in the face and angrier by the second.

'Dakota McDougall, you're a thief,' shouted Catherine. I was stunned I had never seen Catherine act like this. 'Someone get the police,' she added, loudly. By now a small crowd was gathering and a shop assistant was trying to reach the scene, pushing past the shoppers.

'Catherine,' I said, 'are you sure? I didn't seen anything.' But I was ignored and the other girl sprang at Catherine, slapping her hard across the face. Catherine kicked out and they grappled with one another, punching and scratching, Dakota grabbing Catherine's hair and trying to bite Catherine's arm, which by now held Dakota in a headlock. I couldn't get near them to separate them.

Billy, the flustered shop manager shouted, 'If you don't stop I'll get the police!' but he was also ignored. Catherine was pushed against the baskets of bread, and they toppled over as the two girls lost balance and landed on the floor, still scrabbling for supremacy, blows being landed rapidly and with no little force.

Billy and another assistant each tried to grab a different girl to force them apart. Billy lunged at Dakota and grabbed her by her arms but this just allowed Catherine to land a further blow to Dakota and she screamed, blood trickling down her chin.

I was standing frozen, not knowing what to do, when I was pushed aside and saw the Rev Walker intervene, telling them to stop immediately. The girls paused for a second and the shop manager and his assistant, sensing their opportunity, got between them, pushing them away from each other. I think they both realised that they couldn't take the fight any further. Dakota's lip was bleeding and she was rubbing her thigh. Catherine was feeling the side of her head, a tuft of hair coming away, the strands floating to the ground.

'I'm ashamed of both of you,' said the minister. 'This is no way to behave.'

Catherine was still defiant. 'Her mother's a whore, there are not many she hasn't slept with on Islay.' I was shocked by what she said. This was not the Catherine I knew.

Dakota tried to lunge at Catherine again but was stopped, her face smeared with blood and tears, her eyes bulging, full of hate.

The minster snapped at Catherine, 'Stop, behave yourself,' and the edge in his voice reminded Catherine of who he was. Two ladies who had witnessed the fight joined in the chorus. 'Disgraceful, shameful,' they exclaimed.

Billy ordered the two girls out and the Rev Walker turned to me. 'You and Billy keep Catherine here, while I take Dakota home. Turning to Catherine he spoke sharply. 'I will want to speak to you later.'

A shop assistant started to pick the loaves of bread which had been scattered on the floor and to rearrange the display.

Catherine slumped into my arms drained of emotion and fight. I put my arm around her and she simply whispered, 'Sorry.'

Billy was angry. 'You are both banned and I'll be contacting the school on Monday.' I didn't plead my innocence: this was a time to support Catherine not criticise her, and anyway the school had just closed for summer. Hopefully, the incident would have blown over by the time the holiday ended. She was my friend and I held her tight. Together we walked out of the shop and down towards the harbour, where we sat on one of the seats on the pier.

Catherine clung tightly to me, her tears wetting my shirt as she sobbed quietly. After a few minutes she said sorry again and sobbed even more uncontrollably, an emotional geyser. I offered to get her a drink but she shook her head. She allowed me to wipe her face with my handkerchief, wiping away the tear stains and dabbing at some scratches. I could feel a raised lump on the side of her head.

'I hate her, Peter. You must never mention her name, if my family is about. She and her mum almost destroyed us.' And then surprisingly she added pensively, 'Maybe it would have been better if she had.'

I couldn't make sense of any of this. I was only beginning to calm down myself, thrown by the unexpected turn of events. I didn't even know that Catherine knew Dakota let alone hated her or why there was such a mutual loathing between them.

Malcolm and Ronnie soon arrived with Alison and Susie, anxious to hear what had happened, having seen us leaving the shop.

'Catherine was attacked by Dakota McDougall,' I said, knowing that this was only partially true. Alison and Susie put their arms around Catherine, and I stood up, leaving them to console one another.

'Are you okay?' said Malcolm, looking at my damp and bloodstained shirt. Alison got up from the bench and hurried around the corner to the chemist shop and returned with cotton wool and antiseptic cream and proceeded to clean up Catherine's cuts and scrapes. Susie gave her a bottle of Fanta and she drank it, regaining some composure.

'To think,' said Malcolm, 'that Dakota was going to be called Cincinnati but her Mum couldn't spell it.'

'That's not funny, Malcolm,' I replied, but it made me think about Dakota's mother, a woman who looked older than her age, with poorly fitting clothes, an oddity around Bowmore, lurking in the shadows. Dakota had an older brother but of him I knew even less.

I saw the Rev Walker in the distance and he changed direction when he saw us. He approached Catherine with a serious expression and asked her to accompany him along the pier away from us. He stopped a few yards from us and turned his back so that we couldn't hear him speak. Whatever was said was spoken quietly and Catherine seemed consoled and even appeared to nod in agreement. With a warm smile the minister left her and came back to us.

'Peter, you did well. Now all of you don't make matters worse by talking about it. Support your friend and don't have a go at Dakota.'

We agreed and he left walking up Main Street towards the church, at the top of the hill.

'We still have time to get the bus,' said Malcolm, and we trooped up the street towards the bus stop.

From where the bus dropped us to the beach was about half-a-mile along a rough track, before we reached the top of the sand dunes. The beach was deserted and we soon found a sheltered spot and laid down our bits and pieces. Catherine was very quiet and chose to sit, while the others looked around. The other boys started kicking about a ball that Ronnie had brought with him and I joined them briefly before going back to the girls. Catherine made a space for me and I sat beside her. She snuggled in beside me and we shared a bottle of Irn-Bru, taking turns in drinking it. She smiled and muttered thanks before burying her head in my chest again. The two girls shouted at the boys and joined them, leaving us alone. My life changed that day.

Later, I spoke to Dad about Dakota but he said little.

'Troubled background,' he said, adding nothing else.

• • •

Over the summer Catherine and I got into the habit of cycling around the island, taking food and drinks with us. We got as far as the Mull of Oa and visited the American monument, built as a memorial to those killed in the sinking of both the *Tuscania* and *Otranto*. It was a wonderful viewpoint, sitting on the edge of inhospitable cliffs which cascaded down to the sea, but it was a demanding, long cycle up a twisty steep road to get there. Once, there had been many inhabitants on the isolated peninsula south-west of Port Ellen, but they had been forced off the land and most had emigrated to Canada. There were still a number of deserted ruins. I could never envisage how the land on the Mull of Oa once supported eight hundred people.

From the monument you could see the North Channel bounded by Rathlin Island, and the Northern Ireland mainland to the south, and to the east the jagged peaks of Arran peeking over the lower Kintyre peninsula. The Kintyre peninsula rose to its end at the Mull of Kintyre, another headland overlooking the North Channel. The monument was proof of how contested this stretch of water was, how vital in wartime. Looking west over the approaches to Loch Indaal were the low-lying land we called home, the Rhinns of Islay, partially obscured by drifting sea mist. The North Channel was flecked with waves, patches of white turbulence, where different tides met.

'Dad was telling me that it must have been hell for sailors out there and even worse if their ship was sunk. Imagine floundering in these waters, cold and drowning.'

Despite living on an island I was no sailor, had no wish to cross the oceans. To me the thought of what so many sailors experienced was horrific.

'It must have been hell,' she replied with surprising venom in her voice. I looked surprised and she went on, 'I hate my father.'

I saw no logical connection, but could sense that she was expressing some deep emotion.

That day in the Co-op a lid had been partially lifted on a troubled inner life, a Catherine that I didn't know but had long suspected existed. Even gentle probing about her inner turmoil was rebuffed, softly but firmly. There was a bit of her I couldn't reach, a part that I could not rationalise, but the comment that she had just made suggested that the lid on whatever she was suppressing was in danger of blowing off.

As we sat with our backs to the monument, our picnic finished, Catherine took my hand in hers and smiled as she leant into me. Over the summer I had come to realise how much I loved the company of girls and one in particular.

'Peter,' she said softly, 'you really help me. I can't thank you enough.' I knew that she would add nothing else: the enigma of Catherine's inner self remained unexplained. Since I appeared to help her I was for now content, if not becoming a little frustrated. I was changing too.

14

As we progressed through school the teachers encouraged us to think about our subjects and what we wanted to do with our lives. I hadn't a clue and was advised by the guidance staff and Dad to take a broad range of subjects, to cover all options. In the end I decided that I was not a scientist and swung more towards business subjects. Secondary school passes a lot quicker than primary, it seems, and it was not long before I was preparing for my Standard Grades examinations at the end of fourth year.

By now my circle of friends was long established – Malcolm, Ronnie and the girls – and we used to hang around the Battery Point after school, a low headland overlooking Bowmore, where guns had once been placed to protect the village from attack from the sea. Battery Point also overlooked the distillery buildings, Loch Indaal and the Rhinns of Islay across the water, with, today, the many white buildings in both Bruichladdich and Port Charlotte villages, clearly visible. The path, initially behind the distillery buildings and accessed from School Road, was a favourite of dog walkers, who followed the path past the point and then down to the shore, usually returning along the shore line.

Catherine was on holiday abroad with her family, a winter break, despite impending exams – the Robinsons always set their own rules – and Donald was left to look after the farm. I was killing time until the mini-bus left to take me home or, if I missed that, a trip home in the car with Dad, who always worked late. A small group of more senior boys had joined the group, one of them Joe smoking and mucking about, throwing stones onto the beach, attempting to hit an old tyre that had floated in from the sea, challenging the others to see if they could do better, the usual male competitive thing. The others joined in searching for small stones as missiles, shouting and making fun of each other's attempts.

Dakota came up the path from the distillery, getting closer to us an old black and white Border Collie trailing behind her, pecking. It was a few years since the fight in the Co-op and I had rarely seen her around Bowmore and very little of her at school. I think she was often in the school's support base, organised for those who were getting specialised support, as she didn't join all her regular classes.

I heard that she had become a Goth and so was not surprised at her appearance. Her eyes were outlined with heavy black mascara, her lips were painted black, matching her fingernails, and the whole ensemble was finished by a black gown and cowl, which she wore up, obscuring her face, ironically, not wanting to be noticed.

You couldn't help but notice her and Joe made a comment, trying to impress his friends. 'Are you going north or south, Dakota?' But Dakota showed no reaction, her dog following her at an increasing distance. The others smirked as Joe baited her.

'Look,' said Joe, 'it's a Goth dog, it has black patches around its eyes.' The others laughed, which only encouraged him, and he tossed one of the small stones in his hand at the dog, narrowly missing it. I hated seeing animals mistreated, especially dogs, probably more so because I had never been allowed one.

'Don't,' I shouted. 'Leave the dog alone, it's old and you could hurt it.'

'Didn't mean to, Meldrum,' he sneered, with a grin on his face, while, for effect, weighing up the remaining stone in his hand.

'I'll get it this time.' He lifted his hand to make to throw the stone.

'Don't!' I shouted again and I saw Malcolm glance at Ronnie with alarm. Their buddy was getting into a fight. I was getting angry at the injustice; the dog didn't deserve it.

'Why?' said Joe. 'What are you going to do? Call Saint Thomas for help? Daddy's boy, eh?' And he squared up to me, the lit cigarette in his left hand held between splayed fingers, crouching down ready to take me on.

'Leave the dog,' I said firmly, not flinching, as the dog trotted slowly passed him.

Joe sniggered, and that annoyed me. He lifted his foot as if to kick the dog and I jumped in, and he punched me hard in the stomach, doubling me up. I groaned as Ronnie moved in too. I had fallen for Joe's feint and felt foolish, but was also badly winded. Out of the corner of my eye, I saw Dakota glance behind her but keep walking.

Malcolm and Ronnie stepped forward and Joe's friends pulled him back.

Joe spat. 'Teach Saint Thomas to give me a punishment exercise,' he said. 'Well worth it,' he added and they left, heading down towards the distillery. I was doubled up in pain, crouched on the ground, trying not to give them the satisfaction of hearing me retch.

Ronnie said: 'Boy that looks sore,' and Malcolm muttered, 'Next time call the RSPCA first, Peter.' They helped me to my feet.

After a few minutes' recovery, they walked with me down to

School Street, some distance behind Joe and his friends. Dad gave me a lift home, obviously wondering what had happened, but he didn't probe. I was pleased. I needed to stand up for myself and take the consequences.

Next day, at school, I was walking past the support base when Dakota came out. She looked at me and simply said softly: 'Thanks.' I sensed that it required a big effort on her behalf.

'How's the dog?' I enquired not wanting to dwell on yesterday's events.

'California, you mean?'

'What?' I said, not believing that could be the dog's name. A look of incredulity must have been on my face and for the first time I saw her smile. There was a real person beneath the make-up; someone who was coping by presenting a persona that she could hid behind, that helped her to cope. She reminded me a lot of Catherine in many ways.

'Misty is fine, thanks to you,' she said. Her body was unsure of how to reinforce the message she had conveyed, and she turned away awkwardly before going back into the base. But she had attempted a joke. As the base door shut, I saw Mrs Oldfield, the head of the base, look up and smile at me, pleased to see Dakota socialising with others. I am sure it was not a chance encounter. I'm pretty sure that Mrs Oldfield had encouraged it to build her confidence.

• • •

The next summer, exams over, when the weather was good, Catherine and I spent several days continuing our cycle tours of Islay. As usual, we met up outside her farm. It was accepted that I never went in, an unspoken agreement of many years, and together, with our cycle helmets, wearing shorts, T-shirts and backpacks, we cycled down to Loch Indaal. There we turned right and headed towards Portnahaven, at the western tip of the Rhinns, the opposite direction from our usual route to Bowmore. We first passed through the village of Bruichladdich. The distillery there had just reopened after being silent for many years, and we saw a party of visitors in a mini-bus driving through the archway into the distillery. Now operating under new owners, it was already adding a fresh chapter to Islay's increasing whisky success story. We passed the small pier at Bruichladdich, where fuel oil was landed for the island, and continued to Port Charlotte, the Loch Indaal lighthouse prominent on our left hand side as we approached the picturesque small coastal village, with its attractive harbour. We passed the Islay Folk Museum, located in a converted church and still surrounded by many old gravestones. Once beyond a narrow road bridge and over a small river with a pedestrian footbridge beside it, we passed the former bonded warehouses of Port Charlotte distillery, which closed in the nineteen thirties. One of the former distillery buildings is now a youth hostel.

Port Charlotte held many pleasant memories for us from our primary school days. We wandered around, reminding ourselves of the places we used to hang out, walked down to the pier and the small rocky beach, and wondered how Beattie was doing in retirement. The lady in the Port Charlotte stores remembered us, not believing how many years it was since we had moved onto the big school, saying how much we had grown.

It was a seven-mile cycle from Port Charlotte along a twisty single-track road, up and down hills, before we arrived at Portnahaven, another scenic village, passing the former bus garage, with the faded MacBrayne's sign on the wall, on the outskirts. The village of Portnahaven was clustered around a small coastal inlet, beside its near neighbour Port Wemyss, the two communities cheek by jowl. Houses clung in tiers to the hillside around the inlet, with a small harbour nearer to the mouth of the inlet. Fishing boats still used the harbour, but many of the houses, only used as holiday homes in the summer, were empty.

Out to sea were the islands of Orsay, with its tall lighthouse, known as the Rhinns of Islay lighthouse, and Eilean Mhic Coinnich, both of which provided some protection from the often stormy seas. We cycled down the hill to the inlet and stopped at a turning place for vehicles, and waited patiently for the seals to appear. The local seals were a tourist attraction, and they did not disappoint as before too long we saw them, their heads bobbing above the surface of the water, or turning over to play about, aware that they were being watched. We sat enjoying the heat from the sun, watching the seals, comfortable in each other's company.

We headed back up the road, passing the church, and visited the village shop for drinks and some cakes. Catherine was looking radiant, with her blonde hair peeking out from under her cycle helmet, her snug T-shirt and her long, suntanned legs. I was I know increasingly attracted to her, aware that she was good looking, enjoying the attention that she received, glorying in the fact that I had a beautiful girlfriend. The lady in Port Charlotte stores had summed it up: 'Catherine you are a becoming a lovely girl.' To me she was already. It was one of those moments where life seemed good, the world at peace, alone with someone you loved. I realised as my feelings swirled about that I was more than content with that conclusion. It would be difficult to envisage life without her, yet there was so much I didn't know, especially about her family; all of that part of her was still a mystery.

Refreshed, we took the narrow winding single-track road north, along the west coast. Just to the north of the village was the site of a tidal wave project, an experiment to supply some of the island's energy, which we had heard about even in primary school, and we diverted off the road to find the site. It lay next to a sandy inlet called Currie Sands. The whoosh and roar of the water entering the concrete building could be heard as we approached over a pile of broken rocks.

Back on the route north we cycled until we reached Kilchiaran Bay and a ruined church. This stretch of coastline had seen many a ship dashed against the rocks and destroyed. This was where we intended to leave the road, which wound all the way back to Port Charlotte. Catherine and I were going to follow the access road to the telecoms installations and old radar stations at Machir Bay and work our way down to the sands at Machir Bay.

We passed a farm and then reached a cemetery surrounded by a low stone wall. A sign indicated, as it did so often on Islay, that it contained Commonwealth war graves. A few yards from the cemetery was a small wooden slatted barn. I decided it was a good place to stop and wanted to go down to the beach, but I saw Catherine hesitate, suddenly looking anxious.

'The barn belongs to our family and so do some of the surrounding fields. It's one of those places I am not allowed to visit,' she reminded me.

We both knew what that meant; even though she had never told me what the consequences had been, I knew that they had been unpleasant.

'You said that your dad was away and Donald was at the sheep sales, at Bridgend,' I replied, trying to look on the bright side. 'Come on; we will be okay. We can put our bikes down at the beach, where they won't be spotted.' Trust her family to blight a perfect day.

To make the point that I wasn't concerned, I wandered over to the barn and walked around it. The double doors were bolted and locked and there was only one window, on the landward side, which was screened off with hessian cloth, although there was a small gap at the bottom corner where the hessian had been torn.

I could see nothing inside, other than the top of what looked like some sort of machinery. There was nothing very remarkable about the machine or the barn, but neither was there about the ventilation grill in the ground, back at their farm.

'Let's look at the graves and then move on,' I offered as a compromise, and she brightened up, looking relieved. Beattie had talked about this cemetery and we were so close I wanted to have a quick look.

I opened the metal gate, which creaked on its hinges, and moved inside. Catherine followed after a few seconds. There were two rows of neatly tended graves, mostly of unknown sailors washed up nearby. There were no victims of the *Otranto* disaster, as they all had been removed to the Kilchoman Military Cemetery, with the bodies of Americans exhumed and sent back to the States.

'Spot the odd ones out,' I said, she looked up and down each row, responding, without much enthusiasm, to my attempt to lighten the atmosphere. She soon spotted the odd ones.

'Sergeant D Harris and Private A Lawrence are soldiers,' she suggested. 'The rest are sailors.'

'You are right,' I said, adding, 'I wonder why they are here?'

Catherine was quiet, as if she was remembering something from the past, and I noticed that the lightness of earlier had faded from her face, and with her left hand she was subconsciously twisting the bottom of her T-shirt. I felt bad for suggesting we stay. Inwardly, I cursed the Robinsons and the apparent fear and control they exerted over Catherine.

'Let's go,' I said, not wanting to upset her any further.

We moved towards the cemetery gate, which had swung shut behind us, the spring ensuring that no sheep could enter to chew the grass and disturb the final resting place of the fallen men.

Then I heard a vehicle on the road, coming from the Port

Charlotte direction, gears changing as it drove down the steep twisting road towards us, the first vehicle to approach, since we arrived. Catherine reacted quickly, dragging me down, and I immediately realised why: it was Donald in his Land Rover and he was already indicating to turn up the track. "Keep down, we will be okay," I said, more with hope than confidence. I held Catherine close. She was starting to tremble as we crouched behind the wall, and I cursed my selfishness for lingering at the spot. We heard the Land Rover rumble over a cattle grid and stop. Donald got out, slamming the door. We waited, wondering if he would wander over towards us, but he had not noticed us. Catherine was ashen.

We heard a lock being undone on the barn doors and a bolt being pulled back. The barn door nearest us hit the cemetery wall as it was pulled open, making us both jump. Catherine shook and I put a hand over her mouth to stop her screaming. I dared to look up and realised that Donald was now inside the barn.

'Let's go,' I whispered. Giving her no chance to refuse I grabbed her, dragged her up and ran, almost dumping her over the far wall in my haste before jumping over after her, pausing, waiting for a shout from Donald.

A minute later Donald reappeared, carrying a plastic bag, which he placed on the passenger seat of the Land Rover. We kept our heads down and heard the barn doors being bolted and locked. We held our breath but didn't hear him getting back into the Land Rover.

Seconds stretched as I strained to hear his next move and then I heard footsteps and realised he was walking around the outside of the cemetery wall. In a few seconds he would see us. Catherine looked paralysed with fear and I was sure that we would be discovered. Then I heard Donald stop and shortly after heard him pissing against the wall, the usual Robinson class act. It seemed to last forever and was followed by the sound of a zip being done up and the footsteps retreating to the Land Rover. The door slammed, the engine started up and he was away in the direction of Port Charlotte. I listened until I couldn't hear the sound of the vehicle anymore and then peeked over the wall, confirming that he was gone.

I held Catherine close, feeling her quiet sobbing against my chest, and as that eventually subsided, I offered her a drink. It reminded me of her reaction after her fight with Dakota that day in the Co-op.

'It's okay, he didn't see us,' I said, several times, also trying to reassure myself. Once again I cursed my actions, taking full responsibility for what had happened. The mood of the day had changed, the air seeming cool as the gentle breeze touched our sweat-covered T-shirts, cooling our bodies, drawing away heat from them.

Catherine had retreated into herself, fighting her demons, head between her knees, breathing erratically as she fought to calm her emotions. I felt bad for delaying our departure from the cemetery, and angry at the Robinsons. I closed my eyes, trying to blank out what had happened, and jumped when Catherine suddenly touched my hand, which I had clenched into a fist, a sign of impotent rage.

'Peter, I am so sorry about my family. They have ruined our day.'

'Are you being abused by them?' I asked.

She shook her head. 'I can't say more, believe me if I could you would be the person I would share with.' She cuddled me, deflecting my own emotions. So there was something that she could not share. Just a few moments ago we had never been closer, yet now we were so far apart: even so, despite the last few fraught moments, there was still a connection, a bond, an emotional glue.

'Peter, I know that you don't want to hear this, but I might be

141

leaving the island. I overheard my parents talking a few nights ago and they want to move to the mainland, a place called Douglas. It's somewhere in Lanarkshire.'

The words hit me like a big wave surging over me and then retreating, sucking the life out of me. I felt dizzy, disorientated, with tears filling my eyes.

'I'll follow you,' I said, with a touch of desperation.

'You can't, Peter.' She tightened her grip on me. 'I love you,' she said. 'You have done so much for me. This is not easy for either of us and it is not what I want,' she added firmly.

I felt slightly comforted by what she said, but it didn't change anything.

We clung tightly, neither wanting to pull back, frightened to face the future alone.

'I love you,' I replied, and she nodded and I kissed her cheek, tasting the salt from her tears.

'I know.' Simple, bold, emphatic, what I realise I wanted to hear for ages, but not in these circumstances, never under these circumstances.

A few minutes later we gathered our bikes from the beach where we had left them and headed up the access road. We climbed over a locked gate, dragging our bikes over after us, continuing along the track past Granny's Rock, the old radar stations and telecoms masts perched on the rocky hills high above us. The track then descended, looking over Machir Bay; the waves gently caressed the shore today, the remnants of the wrecked boat exposed by the retreating tide. It was a scene of tranquillity I struggled to connect with, the familiar no longer providing comfort.

We left the track and I helped Catherine down the rocky crags at the end of the beach and we dropped down to the beach. We shivered in a gap between rocks that had not been warmed by the sun. There was now a silence between us that neither could bridge. Maybe it was the aftermath of the emotion released at the cemetery that had made her tell me about her leaving. There would never have been a good time. Apart from my parents, she was the only person that I really knew, having grown up together in such a remote area, becoming a good friend and more.

'Peter, it could be a while before I go.' She knew that she had upset me and was trying to provide some consolation. 'Let's cycle to Finlaggan tomorrow and make it a special day and try to forget about all this, for a while.'

We walked along the beach, the sand too soft to cycle, the twin tracks left behind by our cycles in the sand never crossing, and reached the path that led to the car park. Once there we stood together, before Catherine turned and kissed me. I could feel the passion and wanted to respond, but it wasn't the time or place and the kiss just added to my anguish. I watched as she got on her bike and cycled up to the road, leaving me behind.

I couldn't settle that night, my chest feeling tight. My brain kept returning to the thought of her leaving. I was desperately searching for a solution which would allow us to stay together but, however, I looked at the problem, I couldn't find one.

• • •

The next morning she was waiting for me at the entrance to her farm, dressed in a red gingham top and wearing denims and looking more attractive than ever. We cycled together, initially without talking, first to a brief stop at Bridgend Stores and then along the road to Port Askaig. After passing through the small village of Ballygrant, we turned left down a minor road and then left over a rougher track to reach Loch Finlaggan.

Loch Finlaggan sparkled on this sunny day. It was an inland

loch, with three small islands, two of which were close to the north shore where we stopped. These islands had been the centre of administration for the Lords of the Isles, who ruled this part of Scotland from the twelfth century. It was here that their councils met and decisions debated and reached. They ruled a large area from Kintyre in the south to the island of Lewis in the north. The largest island still contains many ruins and a few ancient graves dating from that time.

A wooden bridge connected the island to the shore where we stood. We walked across, watching the rushes wafting in the breeze and small birds darting about. If this site had once been busy, crowded with people and probably sheep and cattle, now it was deserted. To the north, the scree-covered slopes of the Paps of Jura glistened in the sun, a dramatic backdrop looming over everything else, looking so much more imposing now that we were closer to the eastern coast and the Sound of Islay, that narrow strip of fast-flowing water that separated Islay from its near neighbour, Jura.

Catherine was cheerful, or at least making a big effort, and led me by the hand until we found a sheltered spot in the lee of a ruined building. Insects buzzed around, untroubled by our presence, and a sweet scent arose from the many small meadow flowers. She had a special place in her heart for Finlaggan, and I always remember her drawing pictures of it, as part of a project in primary school. This is where Catherine would have chosen to be crowned as a princess. After yesterday, the small island was a place to seek solace, to indulge in fantasy, to draw a veil over the troubles of the outside world.

She took off her backpack, placed it on the ground and pulled out a small rug and carefully spread it out. Always neat and tidy, she seemed to be taking extra care, straightening out a folded edge. She smiled and pulled me towards her. Suddenly I knew what was going to happen next. My heart started to pound, my face felt flushed, but Catherine was calm, with a determined look on her face. Nothing was going to spoil our time together. No further words were spoken, and she lay down, settling herself on the rug and slowly undid the top few buttons on her red gingham shirt, exposing the top of her black bra. She smiled, an open loving look on her face, happier than I could ever remember her being. Today was for living and experiencing. I understood. Oh, how I understood.

How could people ever say that I raped her on Friday night? She wanted me and I her. I loved her then and would have today, if she hadn't left.

15

Wednesday am

It is only when I woke up the next morning and was washing that I remembered to check the washing basket – it was untouched. At least I now knew, after yesterday, that the Robinsons were all aware of what ever occurred on Friday night and so did Roy, whoever he was. According to Roy, I should be dead. Had Catherine saved me? Certainly Donald and Dylan were very angry with me. Somehow, I had upset their plans.

Pence Gifford had given me a different day, one with potentially a little more freedom and I intended to use the time in preparation for the meeting with Sally and her friends later in the week.

A quick shower and a bowl of cornflakes and I was out the house. I examined the car and surveyed the damage from yesterday. The kick on the door could possibly be knocked out, the grill would need to be replaced, but the bonnet showed no damage. The smell, however, still lingered, the muck having congealed on the engine. Hopefully, a few more washes and it would be all right.

This morning I took the longer route by Saligo Bay, crossing a bridge over a burn and following the road right at a farm gate at the beach. The base of a wartime radar transmitter could be seen through the farm gate, an early morning dog walker shutting the gate. I was now travelling north of Loch Gorm, separated from it by fields and a marshy area, a straight stretch of road ahead, a farm to my left.

I reached the turn-off for Sanaigmore Bay, with its isolated red telephone box, close to the junction. I always thought this was surely a perfect location for a film, whether a romantic call being made to a lover or a scene in a spy thriller, a plea for help before the baddies got there. My mind gravitated towards the latter.

I didn't take that road to Sanaigmore, however, but drove over another minor bridge and turned left onto the road that leads to Loch Gruinart. It was very narrow, with few passing places, which could mean having to reverse a long way if another car was coming towards you. Near the highest point I could glimpse Bowmore in the distance, before the road dipped down to the head of the Loch Gruinart. A sign pointed to Ardnave, near the mouth of the loch on its western side. Along there was Susie's small holdings. I was sad that her marital problems had made her become so embittered with life. I remembered many happy times in her company.

I turned into the Loch Gruinart RSPB visitor centre and parked in front of it. The centre was familiar to me from many visits with Jenny and Ben and I was greeted warmly by Stacey Brown, the on-duty warden, standing at the door to the visitor centre, a pair of binoculars in her hands, her boots already muddy from tramping around some field, checking, no doubt, on her avian friends.

'Hi, Peter, what brings you here this morning? I was just going to study the birds that are around this morning, do you want to join me?'

I quickly explained why I was there.

'I was driving along the road past the Centre yesterday

evening and I thought I saw a blue winged teal, near the road in the marshy area, dabbing for food in the water. I know that there were a couple a few years ago and when I checked the bird book, it seemed possible – the same colourings. Probably a male; a greyish blue head with a white crescent, light brown body and another white patch near the rear. When I stopped I heard it make a call,' I paused. 'It was like a short whistle.' I had tried hard not to sound too glib.

Stacey looked interested, as I had hoped, inviting me into the visitor's centre, putting down the binoculars and taking down a book off a shelf, flicking through the pages until she reached a picture of the bird I had described.

'That sure looks like it. I'll show you where it was.' And we walked up the stairs onto the observation gallery, its wide glass window fronting the Gruinart Flats, a big stretch of drained land famous for being the roosting spot, in winter, for thousands of barnacle and white fronted geese, wintering visitors from Greenland. At his time of year, there were few birds but no geese. I took the large telescope and zoomed in on a spot on the loch side of the road. I focussed in and then let Stacey look.

'I can't see it today, but that is where I think the bird was.'

Stacey studied the scene but couldn't see any birds.

'Keep an eye on the spot?' I said

'I'll write it on the white board as a possible sighting and keep looking.'

'I can't resist looking through the telescope, it's so powerful.'

'Be my guest,' Stacey replied. 'Do you want a coffee?'

'Not today, thanks. I just wanted to let you know what I had seen, but I must go in a few minutes.'

I turned back to the telescope and when Stacey had descended the steps, I turned it towards High Coullabus farm, which was about two miles away, on high ground beyond the flats. I zoomed in. I could see a small cottage beside the farm buildings. That had to be where Sally and her friends were staying. There was no black BMW parked outside, and no sign of life, so they must be away. At least that part of the story was correct. What did they want to know about the Robinsons? My feeling was that they had joined the distillery tour to get to know me... or was that just paranoia talking? They had certainly shown little interest in whisky and they had raised the topic of the sinking of the *Otranto* and the *Empire Constellation*. I needed to get a copy of the whole recording, hopefully to answer many questions – help me get out of trouble. I would do my homework in preparation for the meeting.

I turned the telescope back to the roadside spot I had shown Stacey earlier and joined her on the floor of the centre, privately thanking Dad, for his book on *Birds of the World*.

'Keep me informed,' I said and she nodded. She was a dedicated bird watcher. I felt bad about misleading her, but it gave me an excuse to look at High Coullabus, safely, from a distance.

Leaving the Centre, I joined the long stretch of single track road I had seen through the telescope. It was partly fringed by trees to the left, with moorland and the flats to the right. After nearly two miles the road curved sharply to the right, and eventually came out onto the Bridgend to Bruichladdich road, close to a farm and a bridge. At the bend, there was a junction with a minor road, which led to High Coullabus and several other farms.

I headed towards Bridgend, passing Blackrock, where there is a memorial to a plane crash. A Sunderland flying boat, based at Bowmore, had crashed in January 1943, returning from a long patrol over the North Atlantic, still with depth charges on board. It crash landed at Blackrock, the Captain having misjudged the height of the plane as he approached Loch Indaal. Of the twelve crew, eight of the crew got out unharmed, while three were injured and moved to the shoreline. Realising that the rear gunner was still trapped, the uninjured returned to try to free him, but the plane blew up, killing those who had returned, together with the trapped rear gunner. The force of the explosion broke windows across the loch in Bowmore and was heard over twenty miles away. The memory of that sad event helped me to get a sense of perspective: life was often unfair.

I received a text message from Jenny as I arrived in Bowmore. It said nothing about returning early and I was relieved. I sent a text in return, apologising for missing her call and informing her that I was going to be out this evening.

As I entered the shop, Julie, handed me the keys to one of the distillery vans, and a small box wrapped in brown paper.

'Just so you are not tempted to sample the whisky,' said Julie with a mischievous smile, 'we have packaged it for you. Tamper with it and we'll get an automatic text message. Pence has spoken to Laphroaig and Lagavulin and they are expecting you. Have a good day and don't think about us working hard back here.'

A few minutes later I was heading up Main Street and then along the road past the Round Church, on my way south, the package beside me on the seat. Two roads ran south to Port Ellen. I was on the Low Road, the other road was the High Road and ran further inland, almost parallel, with the two roads converging on the outskirts of Port Ellen. Both roads were straight, cutting across moorland, but both had lots of dips, making for a bouncy journey across peat bogs. On the Low Road, some of the bridges were slightly narrower than the road, which meant slowing down if another car was coming in the opposite direction. On the seaward side was Laggan Bay, with the Big Strand, a seven-mile long beach, separating it from sand dunes. Islay Airport was about half way down, at Glenegedale, next to the road on the sea side.

The main airport building consisted of a simple corrugated metal structure, with white and blue end panels facing the road. The control tower loomed over it to the rear; from there air personnel were able to observe arrivals and departures on the three runways which criss-crossed the airport. There was a small car park beside the air terminal. A regular daily service to Glasgow was a lifeline for the island and reduced the journey time considerably. By ferry and road the trip could easily take five hours.

South of the airport lay the Machrie Hotel and Golf Links, with many choosing to fly in for a game of golf on the famous golf links. It was a contrast to the many forgotten small communities, like the Duich Lots, slightly north of the airport and to the east of the road, where in the nineteenth century people had once been dumped in the middle of a peat bog, having been driven off the land by landowners. They survived by sharing a strong community spirit, eking out a life by reclaiming the peat bog to grow potatoes and other crops, tending to a few cattle and sheep. Eventually, about a century ago, they were able to move out to other accommodation.

I passed the entrance to the peat bogs owned by Laphroaig distillery, waterlogged tracks leading to freshly cut faces of peat, stacks of it drying in the wind off the sea. An abandoned tractor suggested that cutting the peat was not a high-tech task. Cleverly, the distillery had arranged a whisky experience that allowed visitors to cut the peat while being fortified by a dram.

People and whisky, both with their roots in peat bogs, it seemed, was a big part of the story of Islay. Indomitable spirit and peaty spirit made a potent, hardy combination.

After many miles, on the approach to Port Ellen, the road turned abruptly sharp left, and after a few hundred yards the High Road joined it, leading down past the Port Ellen Maltings, a tall grey corrugated metal building where the distilleries on the island got most of their barley malted, to their own specification. Only a few distilleries malted their barley at the distillery; Islay was one, but even they only malted a proportion. During primary school days at Port Charlotte, we spotted a tall tower – as it seemed to us – across Loch Indaal and Laggan Point and wondered what it was, until one of our teachers, Mrs White, told us it was the Maltings at Port Ellen. We were disappointed: we had thought it might be a castle.

One of the two ferry terminals on the island was located at Port Ellen, and next to it was a tall grain store, another local landmark. On the opposite side of the bay was a lighthouse, a more attractive sight.

Reaching the distilleries meant driving through Port Ellen, past the short road to the ferry terminal and around a small bay lined with houses and a few shops. The three distilleries at Laphroaig, Lagavulin and Ardbeg, on Islay's south coast, were a major draw for tourists, stretched out on a road running east out of Port Ellen, nearly three and a half miles of whisky heaven for enthusiasts. A pathway had been completed to link the three distilleries with Port Ellen, allowing visitors to walk to each distillery in turn, touring them, buying whisky in the distillery shops, sampling a dram or two, and not needing to use a car. A bus service helped those who wanted a faster mode of transport or were unsteady on their feet after their visit. It was wonderful marketing, on a par with our own distillery and a wonderful revenue earner for the tax authorities. For a time more tax was raised per head of population from the whisky produced on Islay than anywhere else in the United Kingdom outside of the square mile at the heart of the City of London's financial district.

I pulled into Laphroaig distillery and wandered down to the offices. Set in a small bay, Laphroaig was the closest of the three distilleries to Port Ellen; the setting was very photogenic, the welcome warm. A warehouse lined one side of the bay and the distillery name was printed large on its side. Islay distilleries were good at this form of advertising, which was even visible from the air. The main distillery buildings sprawled out from the bay, the familiar smell of peat smoke wafting over the area, seeping into every pore. Two visitors, from Scandinavia by their accents, were taking photographs beside a commemorative stone whisky barrel at the entrance, and others were milling about.

The shop was busy as this was before the Islay whisky festival. Tam, one of the distillery workers recognised me.

'In for a proper dram, Peter?' His overalls looked out of place among the smartly uniformed shop assistants, but people were attracted to the genuine article, someone who got their hands dirty, and I knew from the past that he could tell a good tale, having worked for over thirty years at the distillery.'

'Just bringing a superior dram to you,' I replied in kind. 'To improve the quality.'

Tam laughed and accepted the package. 'Hah, no doubt the boss will make up his own mind about that,' he said.

We talked for a couple of minutes, both looking forward to the festival, and then I bade him farewell and drove on to Lagavulin. I parked beside one of the warehouses. This was yet another Islay distillery, located in a picturesque bay, complete with a ruined castle. The shop was a bit more formal, wood panelled, touches of tartan, but the welcome was just as friendly.

The manager came out and again the talk was of the festival. He made a quick phone call and I returned to the van. Shortly afterwards two workers emerged, pushing a small barrel, and together we manoeuvred it into the van, securing it with rope. It was a two hundred and fifty litre sherry hogshead, half the size of a sherry butt.

'Maybe it's for another charity bottling,' the older of the two

153

workers said, 'or for one of Gifford's innovations.'

I thanked them and drove on to Ardbeg. I had no business there but wanted an early lunch and the Old Kiln restaurant was renowned for its food. I wandered down to the sea and walked up the steps to a low promontory that gave a view over the distillery and the warehouse, with Ardbeg written large, as expected, on the side exposed to the sea. There was a small pier, no longer used, where the puffers once tied up, discharging coal and collecting whisky barrels – at that time, usually for blending in Glasgow.

Ardbeg had been closed for a time in the nineties but was reborn before the new millennium and was now producing whisky again. About a hundred whisky barrels were sitting upright, close to the sea, awaiting filling, occupying the space next to another warehouse. The rims at their tops were filled with water from a recent shower of rain, darkly shimmering in the sunshine.

The cafe was located in the old peat kiln, under two redundant pagodas on the roof. The cafe shared the floor area with the distillery shop, and had a tall vaulted ceiling with exposed metal girders. I arrived in the cafe just as the morning tour ended and the tour party were gathering around a large table, with trays of empty glasses waiting to be filled.

I sat down in the corner of the cafe and was studying the menu and the specials board, half listening to what the tour guide was saying, always open to trying to improve my own performance, when a familiar voice rang out.

'Good to see you, Peter!' It was Ronnie and his young Polish wife, Maria.

I got up, delighted to see them, and gave Maria a kiss on each cheek as she brushed her long hair to the side to make space for them. Ronnie shook my hand warmly.

'What brings you here?' I asked.

'I might ask the same of you, Peter. Spying out the opposition?'

'On an errand for Gifford, and treating myself to lunch,' I replied

Maria was looking as attractive as ever, and her English was slowly improving. She was a good few years younger than Ronnie, probably in her early twenties and mature for her years. Ronnie was sporting a Mexican-style droopy moustache and, I noticed, his hair was beginning to thin on top, just like his father.

'Is he looking after you on that foreign island of Jura, Maria?'

She smiled. 'Sometimes, but he has to do something about the rain, it never stops.'

'It's a lot drier on Islay,' I joked.

We chatted while our order was taken and the food served. Ronnie owned a rigid inflatable boat, which he chartered out. He had brought over two guests who were staying at their bed and breakfast in Craighouse, the small village on Jura. Like many islanders he made ends meet by juggling several jobs.

'Our guests wanted to visit Islay's distilleries,' he explained, 'and we offered to bring them. They wanted to taste a few drams so need a taxi, which we can provide. At a cost,' he added.

Ronnie was always practical, generous to friends, and looked very content with life.

'When are you coming over to Jura with Jenny and Ben?'

'Soon,' I replied.

'Did you get my text?' asked Ronnie.

I had forgotten, not surprisingly.

'Unlikely to be this weekend.' Very unlikely, I thought to myself.

'A pity, I have no charters this weekend.'

We paid up and left. At the moment I envied Ronnie his tranquil life.

'You look tired,' was his final comment and Maria, who I had noticed glancing at me several times during the meal, echoed his thoughts. At least they didn't comment on the still visible scratches.

'Peter, take care,' she said and hugged me as we parted.

Good friends, that's what I needed.

• • •

I drove back through Port Ellen and turned at the road which led past the warehouses of the former Port Ellen distillery, now mostly filled with barrels of Lagavulin. On impulse, I had decided to drive up to the American Monument on the Mull of Oa. The road twisted as it rose, over several hundred feet, and threaded between a few green fields where the soil was fertile, with some patches of woodland, but mostly peat bog. I parked at the car park and walked up the path to the monument. The all-encompassing panorama from the top was familiar. My parents had brought me here but, most memorably, I had fond memories of cycling here with Catherine.

Now I knew what had stirred me to make the detour. It was here, as we sat identifying the different land masses and watching the power of the heaving ocean, that we understood why a monument was necessary, a memorial to conflict at sea. Something had stirred in Catherine and she had blurted out: 'I hate my father.'

So profound, yet unexpected, a revealing juxtaposition of tales of previous wars and current inner conflict, of someone who was hiding a secret. I wondered again what the connection was.

When I returned to the car park, another car, a later arrival, had parked on the opposite side with the occupants busy studying an open map. As I started the van's engine and reversed, I looked at the couple peering at what looked like an Ordnance Survey map. I recognised the man; he was the person who had been nursing a pint in the Lochside Hotel on Monday evening. Islay is a small island and you do bump into people, my unexpected lunch companions making the point, but I did think about what Sally had said: 'You are being watched.' I slipped the van into gear and headed back down to Port Ellen, glancing in my rear-view mirror from time to time.

So far the day had provided a welcome break, allowed me to draw breath, while I waited for the return of the mysterious Americans and the recording which might help me. I had to be prepared for meeting them and could only think of one person who might be able to help.

16

Wednesday evening

Around six o'clock I left the distillery, having earlier deposited the sherry hogshead in safe hands, and walked up Main Street, towards the Round Church, before turning left onto High Street. It was a quiet residential street, with a mixture of council owned and private houses. It was a while since I had done anything other than drive along here. Probably the last time I had walked along it was when I was leaving the church, after a funeral.

On the right were a row of single storey cottages, with a central door and a window to each side. Many of the houses had been recently painted white, but the one I approached was needing attention, its paintwork peeling.

I lifted the hinged door knocker and rapped it against its plate, and waited. After a few minutes, I heard shuffling as someone approached the door. A key was turned in the lock and the door knob turned. The door was opened a few inches and I saw an old lady peering out, her white hair thinning, her face drawn, a faded shawl wrapped tightly around her shoulders.

'Hello, Mary,' I said, and there was a flicker of recognition.

'Oh, Peter, it's good to see you. Beattie will be pleased.'

Her twisted hand, the knuckles gnarled and deformed, pulled the door fully open, and I waited as she shuffled slowly along the hall way. Then I followed, as she went to the room to the left, calling out, 'Beattie you have a visitor, young Peter.'

A familiar voice called out, 'Bring him in.'

Again, I waited until Mary slowly entered the room before following her in. I could see Beattie staring at the small fire, a trickle of smoke rising, a faint red glow coming from a few pieces of coal smouldering on the grate. He was sitting in a small upholstered chair which boasted faded linen arm covers with scalloped edges that did little to hide the fact that the original upholstery was threadbare.

He coughed several times, attempting to clear his throat, wiping his hand across his bushy beard. I noticed Mary looking on, concerned, and as he raised his hand she got his face mask fitting it gently on his face. He breathed deeply from an oxygen tank by his side. Slowly he settled and he at last could look at me, a smile emerging faintly, playing at the corner of his lips. As he caught my eye it became stronger, something of the old warmth taking hold, the blue eyes duller, but still full of life. I was sorry to see him in such poor health.

'It's good to see you, Peter,' he finally said. 'I'll be okay in a minute. Lungs not what they were. Sit down.' He motioned to the other chair. I glanced at Mary but she smiled and said:

'I'll make a cup of tea for you both. Do you take milk? And sugar?'

'Both, but please don't go to any bother.'

'It's no bother, Peter, your visit will cheer him up.'

The room was poorly furnished, with a sideboard along one wall and a small semi-circular dining table with two chairs tucked underneath. A few family photographs decorated the walls. There were also black specks of mould spreading from the ceiling down the outside wall, behind Beattie, and a damp smell in the room.

I had not realised how long it was since I had been there.

Such was the force of Beattie's personality, the magical world that he had created for Catherine and me, that I had not previously noticed the decline which was now so apparent. As if reading my mind he said, 'Ninety-one last month, not doing too badly, still here.' He coughed again, but less violently than before. 'And you,' he went on. 'How are Jenny and Ben?'

'Away at the moment, but due back on Friday. Business,' I added.

'She has done well, that girl of yours, and Ben will be starting school soon. I wonder who will be his taxi driver?'

I hadn't thought of that: the world was beginning to turn. I was conscious that I was now part of the cycle of life; I was doing things for Ben that my parents had once done for me.

'I wanted to talk with you, Beattie, mostly about the past.'

'Go on,' he said, but before I could start Mary brought in a cup of tea on a saucer for each of us, a digestive biscuit perched on my saucer. She shuffled out of the room, back to the kitchen.

'Age is not always pretty in what it does to you, Peter,' he explained, 'but we are happy. Best decision I ever made. Lovely girl, Mary, worked out so well. It doesn't always, does it? You took a long time to get over Catherine, but you're happy now.' It wasn't a question – or at least, I didn't interpret it that way.

'Catherine was back on the island last week,' Beattie said unexpectedly, and my stomach tensed. I knew that, but confirmation is different, removing any doubt.

'Tommy was here yesterday, after his shift on the taxi. He said that he saw her on Friday, coming off the afternoon ferry, at Port Askaig. By herself,' he added, knowing that I would probably be interested if I thought that she had found someone else.

'Andy Johnstone was there, grandstanding, doing his 'I'm the only cop on the island' routine, standing beside his police car. He spoke to her for a moment before Donald came and picked her up.'

Johnstone had always had a soft spot for Catherine, asked her out a few times, but she had more sense. He would be curious why she had returned after many years.

'Taxi drivers get to hear a lot. After a few minutes passengers often forget that we are there and talk among themselves. I could tell you a few interesting stories, but you have to be discreet.'

He slurped his tea and wiped his mouth with the back of his hand. I took the chance to sip my tea and eat my biscuit. I realised that I wasn't sure how to start.

Beattie broke the deadlock. 'You'll want to ask a few questions about the Robinsons, I suspect.'

'I do, Beattie, but take me back to when you first met them.'

'I arrived on the island in 1942 when 246 squadron had been reformed and they were trying to establish a base here, for Sunderland flying boats. A bad idea, if you ask me but it let me meet Mary. Loch Indaal was too rough, the swell made landing difficult. I was assigned as part of the team that operated the Bowmore taxi, as it was called, the wee boat that transferred crew from shore to plane. I was there the night the Sunderland crashed at Blackrock, on duty, on one of the flareboats. There was always a buoy with a flashing light positioned in Loch Indaal, to help landing. When a Sunderland was expected, three boats went out, one positioning itself near the buoy and the other two to each side, forming a lit path for about two hundred yards. The wind was strong from the south that night, I remember, and it was bloody cold out in the loch and one or two of the lads were being sea sick. The Sunderland should have flown to Oban where they could have landed without any difficulty, but being short of fuel after a long patrol it attempted a landing here, and the Captain misjudged the height. I think that you know the rest.'

I nodded.

'The shock wave from the explosion blew us out of the boat and I was ever so glad of my lifejacket. We scrambled back on board and made shore, frozen but alive. I was deafened by the explosion – my hearing eventually recovered, but was never quite the same. When we got back to the pier we changed our uniforms and had a cup of tea, fortified by a strong tot of rum and then we were driven around to Blackrock to help out. That was the first time I met Torquil Robinson. He came like the rest, from all over the island, to help. I never liked him, cold and uncaring. I saw him searching some of the dead crew for their private possessions, pocketing a cigarette case and a few other knick-knacks, but before I could do anything about it a sergeant saw what was happening and told him to stop and hand them over. He was lucky not to be charged.'

'He lived with his family, roughly where your house is today. It was a small croft and it must have been a struggle for him and his wife and family to survive. A few potatoes, a cow and some sheep. You rarely saw his wife. I never heard her speak and I was at the croft a few times. We were often sent to places like Machir Bay, to search for anything washed up, often dead bodies or to check reports of U-boat sightings. Waste of time, but it kept us busy and we would call in looking for a cup of tea, but we never got any. No island hospitality from him.'

'His oldest son was called Charles, Catherine's father. Just like his old man, cold and uncaring. He was called up to the army – I think it was in 1944, I can't quite remember – and he returned after a few years. Monty's double we used to call him, just like his father, but not to his face; he had a reputation as a violent man. Almost killed Seamus McNeil from Saligo in a dispute over a cow.'

'In the late forties there was a change of fortune and they built another house on the land, the one that you are living in. It would be the sixties before they bought out the Henderson's at

Loch Gorm farm and over a few years demolished most of the buildings, apart from a couple of old farm workers' houses, which they lived in while the farm was rebuilt. Caused a lot of talk. They used a company from the mainland, a right rough crew, but they had to employ some locals like me for tasks at the end, like painting. They had probably fallen out with the mainland lot. Poor payers, but John had just been born, so we needed the money. That's how I ended up with the gold watch, probably stolen from some poor bugger.'

'J Ferguson,' I said.

'Yes.' Beattie appeared briefly flustered, having forgotten that he had told me before.

'Pirate's gold,' I reminded him, but I was anxious not to interrupt his flow and smiled for him to continue.

After a short pause while he rubbed his mouth again with the back of his hand, he went on.

'There was a lot of talk about the Robinsons and how they could afford to buy and then improve the farm. Most of the improvements were to the buildings, I saw little evidence of them improving the land.

'I often drove farmers home from the market, and they always liked a dram or two, so I often overhead gossip. There was a lot of curiosity and I suppose jealousy about the Robinsons. No one believed that they were making any money out of the farm, but people were wary of them. Torquil died sometime in the sixties, and Charles took over.'

I nodded pleased that he was filling in the back picture. I knew some but not all of this.

'I mustn't forget,' said Beattie. 'During the sixties a team of government officials from the mainland arrived asking questions about a sunk ship. Nobody was very sure of who they were. They were very secretive, apart from once when they had a drink in

Bowmore on a Saturday, and I was taking them home to the cottages they were renting, near Port Ellen.

'It was obvious from the questions they were asking that they were fishing for information about a ship that was sunk off the coast during the war, the *Empire Constellation*. A year before a salvage team working out of Derry had reached the wreck and searched it thoroughly. Sometimes their boats came into Port Ellen to pick up supplies. That's when they realised that some people had probably escaped on the lifeboats. There were bodies washed up at the time, but little else.

'I was in Bowmore at the time it was sunk. Heard the explosion. That sort of thing happened quite a lot, sadly. The U-boats were a real menace.'

'Anyway they focussed their search on Machir Bay, looking for the lifeboats that had escaped the sinking. They checked police records from the time and were especially interested in the fate of the lifeboats. I think that they found a couple of bits of wood from the lifeboats, but little else. The sea can smash up boats into fragments very quickly.'

'Did you find out what they were looking for? It seemed a big operation unless there was something in particular they were looking for,' I said.

'I overhead two of them discussing what could have happened to the cargo of gold that the ship was carrying.'

My heart thumped. I knew it. It made sense and if the gold was missing, either it was at the bottom of the sea or it could have been removed from the ship as it sank. Precious cargo, the Captain must have wanted to keep it safe. If it had got as far as Machir Bay then the Robinsons could have salvaged it. It would help explain their sudden wealth.

As if reading my mind Beattie continued, 'They were very suspicious of the Robinsons, asked a lot of questions. One of them was sure that old Robinson was not telling them everything. They asked me what I thought of them and no doubt others too. They arrived at the farm one morning and searched it thoroughly, but they found nothing. They even searched that storage area formed out of an old cave. I think Charles Robinson had been tipped off; after all he must have known why they were on the island.'

'When they left Robinson was quiet for a while, waiting to see if they would return, I suppose. After a couple of years he demolished the farmhouse and rebuilt it. Later, in the eighties, some wags called it 'Islay's Southfork' after that TV programme, Dallas. The house was certainly grand, but it had no soul. It was like an empty box with fancy furnishings.

'In the seventies Charles surprised us all by marrying. No woman on the island would go near him. There were stories about how he treated women. I took one home late at night, in my taxi, from Robinson's farm and she was in a state, bruised and with a black eye. Catherine's mum, a beautiful girl called Linda, was a good bit younger than him. Came from somewhere in Lanarkshire, some poor mining village. Tall, long blonde hair, a bit of a looker the local women said, and I am sure the men agreed. I'm sure she saw this seemingly rich man and thought of a cushy life on a beautiful island.'

'He destroyed her. She soon realised that she was living in a prison. Linda couldn't cope, was crushed by his cruelty and indifference. He even had another woman on the go at the time.' He hesitated. 'They had a big argument over that, when she discovered what was going on. This was after Donald and Catherine were born.'

Beattie stopped, rubbing his beard, thinking about what to say next.

'Mary,' he called out. 'Could we have another cup of tea? And I am sure that Peter would like another biscuit.'

I heard the kettle being switched on and shortly afterwards fresh tea, and another biscuit for me, was brought through from the kitchen. I was aware that Beattie was looking at me, gauging my reaction so far, deciding how to continue.

'Catherine was feistier than her mum but it must have been hard for her,' he said.

I remembered only too well the fear at the dinner table that night, many years ago, as they dreaded an outburst from the father.

'There's more, Peter. In 1984, the year you were born, there was a terrible plane crash on Islay. A small plane had just taken off, with an American pilot, who was returning south.'

He stopped speaking for a few minutes, eyes unfocussed, deep in thought.

'Ryan Loudoun III, that was his name.'

Relieved that he could remember, he went on.

'The plane crashed landed on the airstrip and burst into flames. The tarmac melted in places and in the official report the fire crew were criticised for taking too long to tackle the crash. There was little of the plane left after a few minutes. The investigators were also critical that procedures were not followed during the clear up. You can read the report, if you look it up. They blamed the crash on fuel starvation, probably blocked air vents to the fuel tanks, unusual in that type of plane, I believe, but they found nothing else to explain the accident.

'The local paper described it as a tragedy and put the blame on the pilot; after all, the crew at the station had little experience, and the pilot is ultimately responsible for checking his plane prior to departure.

'Loudoun had only been on the island a few days, staying at Bridgend. I heard that he didn't like the island, and the weather while he was on the island had been poor. He didn't see it at its best. The impression I got was that no one liked him; he was arrogant, looked down on everyone. I did hear, however, that he had managed to impress some of the local lassies.'

'Anyway, a few weeks later I was running Jim Campbell and his wife to the airport. Jim was part of the crew that had serviced the plane and tried to douse the flames when it crashed. He is a cousin of Charles Robinson. He was very excited, they were both going on a holiday overseas, very expensive, very posh, quite out of their league. His wife struck me as very surprised and delighted, as if she had won the pools. I got the impression that she didn't know how they could afford the holiday. Campbell described it to me as a 'bonus' for services rendered, which I thought was odd.'

As he was talking his eyes had been fixed on the wall behind me, fixed on a spot to the right, but now he turned his gaze onto me again.

'Peter,' he said, 'I can't prove anything, only rumours, but I am sure,' and he emphasised the last four words by saying them slowly, 'that Robinson had something to do with the crash.'

'Campbell tampered with the air vents?

'Yes,' Beattie replied. He picked up his cup and took a swallow of the tea.

'There was a lot of speculation about the final message from the American. Very cryptic.' Beattie paused again trying to recollect the exact words:

'It's close to Arthur and Dominic. No one knew what he meant. You can check it out in the final accident report too.

'In the late eighties and nineties, when you and Catherine were young, Robinson spent a lot time off the island, on business. I used to run him to the airport and pick him up to take him home on his return. Said very little. I was always careful not to look at my watch, in case he wanted to claim it back.' Beattie smiled.

'You could never trust him. Sometimes I saw him on the ferry.

167

Never liked who he was with, and if he saw me, then he ignored me. One night I picked up Donald at the rank in Bowmore and gave him a lift home. Donald was very drunk. I took him into the farm and rang the doorbell, needing help, as he had passed out in the back of the taxi. His father was furious at the state he was in. He was sick over the back seat as Charles and I tried to help him out. We got him inside, his mother fretting over him, and I asked for a bucket of soapy water to clean the inside of the car. Charles blew up and told me to get lost. That wasn't quite the language he used, but Mary might hear. When I asked for the fare, he refused. He had lost his temper. Made me wonder what they all had to put up with. I vowed I would not enter the farm premises again. That's why I waited outside each day for Catherine. He called me a few times for lifts to the airport, but I always made out that I was too busy. He spent less and less time on the island in later years.

'Now,' said Beattie, 'we are at the point when you and Catherine took a shine to each other. I thought, even on the first day when I picked you up, that something would happen. I hate to cause you pain, but she was always so keen on you.'

It was interesting hearing his slant on us. So keen. I thought that I was the one keen on her. After all these years I could still experience an emotional response.

'Peter,' and Beattie leant forward, 'you tell me what happened next and I'll add in anything I can.'

17

It was the last Easter holidays of my school days. I was leaving at the end of the summer term, hopefully with good enough grades to get into university. I had applied for several courses in business management and marketing at Strathclyde University, in Glasgow. We were all moving on. Malcolm and Alison were now an item and preparing to leave to study in Glasgow. Ronnie was still searching for a girlfriend: 'It wasn't easy on Jura,' he told us, and was hoping that a move to the mainland would solve his problems. He intended to set up a charter business, with money left by a distant cousin, and was going to take a course in nautical studies and obtain his certificates to allow him to take passengers out on charter trips in the waters around Jura. Catherine didn't know what she wanted to do and didn't want to discuss her future. I had hopes of her moving to Glasgow, where we could live together, away from her family, but still at the back of my mind I remembered Catherine saying that they could be leaving the island, and I wouldn't be able to follow. That grim scenario was hanging over us and the uncertainty was beginning to eat me up inside.

Dad was approaching retirement and he and Mum had travelled to the island of Iona, further up the west coast, for a week's spiritual retreat. St Columba, the Christian missionary who arrived from Ireland in the sixth century to spread the Christian message, had established an abbey on the island. My parents were staying at the residential quarters beside the abbey, on a retreat organised by the Iona Community, which was based there.

Catherine and I were left alone at the house. Her mum still insisted that she came home each night, but we had a lot more freedom and given the poor weather that Easter we were glad for a roof over our heads. The westerly gales swept through Machir Bay, saturating the Rhinns with rain, flooding fields and generally making life miserable for farmers and others. It was a bonus only for the bird watchers; many birds, including some rare foreign visitors, arrived on the island, blown in by the gales. The RSPB visitor centre at Loch Gruinart was busy with visitors watching the geese starting to leave the island; vee shaped flights of geese could be heard overhead as they sailed over with their powerful beating wings and honking noises.

Catherine arrived about ten o'clock. We had a coffee and watched a DVD, a lazy morning, with little said between us; we were comfortable together. We had a laugh when she spotted a green diamond-patterned Pringle jumper in my room, something which I had got as a Christmas present.

'You're not wearing that, if you are going out with me,' she said, laughing, holding the jumper to the side as if she was going to drop it in disgust.

'It's incredible the bargains Mum can find when there is a sale at Bruichladdich Halls,' I replied, and I put it on for her amusement.

Later, when the weather improved, or at least it stopped raining, we walked down to the beach, crossing the wooden bridge over the burn swollen by all the rain. We turned south along the beach and when we saw further rain was likely we turned back to the house. After lunch we decided to risk a cycle trip and decided on a visit to Ardnave, at the head of Loch Gruinart, hoping that the freshening winds would provide a clear view to Colonsay and the hills of Mull beyond. Catherine prepared a small picnic and with shorts and our rain jackets we left the house. At the RSPB visitor centre we turned left, taking the single track road, which twisted up the west side of the loch. The tide was going out, exposing the sand flats on Loch Gruinart. We passed the ruined church and graveyard at Kilnave, sitting close to the loch and separated from the fields by a low stone wall.

At Ardnave we left our bikes by the loch, in front of Ardnave House. Several bird watchers with binoculars and fancy cameras on tripods were positioned around the loch: a swan was attracting most attention. We left them behind and walked between the house and the farm steading, taking the rough road beyond, to reach the sand dunes. About half-a-mile from the shore was Nave Island, a brick chimney, the only visible sign of previous life, although there was also meant to be a ruined chapel. We could see the low-lying island of Colonsay and the hills of Mull, with the peaks of the tallest hill beyond, Ben More, still obscured.

We sat on the top of the sand dunes, on the rough machir, which was riddled with rabbit burrows, and huddled together as the wind freshened. Down below was a concrete pool and a sluice gate, part of an old lobster farm, Dad had informed me. I thought it was something to do with the herring trade, which for a short time flourished on Ardnave, but that was on the other side of the promontory, before the herring was fished out.

It became too cold to sit about and we completed a circular walk around the headland, watching the waves breaking at the mouth of Loch Gruinart. On the eastern side stood the ruined farmhouse at Killinallan, with farm buildings and its tall concrete silo a short distance behind the farmhouse. We collected our bikes and headed back. We reached Kilnave Church and decided to cycle down to the ruin, a distance from the road. The church was a simple stone building, roofless for many generations, the walls covered in lichen, with a narrow window in the shape of a pointed arch overlooking the loch. We had a habit of looking at gravestones and we found a grave of someone connected with the Queen Mother's family. Then we wandered into the ruined church itself.

The scene is imprinted in my mind forever. As we stood Catherine slipped a hand around by back and snuggled her head against me.

'I always wanted to get married in a place like this,' she said, and I looked at her, wondering where this was going to lead.

She released her grip and we faced each other, holding hands.

'Peter, I love you,' she said firmly, tears welling up in her blue eyes as she struggled to contain her emotions. 'Do you love me?'

'Yes,' I replied, really strongly, determined to ensure that I didn't get misinterpreted. I knew this moment was special.

'Let's promise to look out for each other.'

I agreed, understanding that was the only offer available.

I sensed how important this was for her, as she examined my face, grasping my hands more firmly as she spoke.

'Neither of us knows what lies ahead,' she said, although on reflection I wonder if she did know something was about to happen. 'But our love will never die.'

We made our promises to the chorus of a pack of seals gathered on a sand spit, in the loch, making wailing noises. I don't know now if that was a romantic serenade or a portent of bitter times ahead.

Our passions aroused, we cycled down towards the RSPB visitor centre and stopped, abandoning our cycles and walking fast to the bird hide at the head of the loch. Much to our disappointment there were people there. We walked back slowly to find one of the wardens standing beside our bikes.

'A word in your ears, folks,' he said. 'Our hides are for observing birds only.' And having delivered his message he continued past us, heading for the hide.

We cycled home. It was early afternoon, and I bade her farewell at the entrance to her farm and arranged a time to collect her later. Our passion would wait. I kissed her on the cheek, not knowing it was for the last time.

18

I sensed that something was wrong as soon as I reached the farm entrance. I heard shouting and in the farmyard was another vehicle, a white van, its front facing me and its backdoors wide open. The Robinson's Land Rover was also there, its tailgate raised. Two men, dressed in black, scarves over their faces, were running around with baseball bats. I watched in horror as one swing a bat at Dylan, and while the first swing missed, the second caught Dylan on the head and he crumpled to the ground. The guy who hit him grabbed him by the arm and started to drag him towards the van. I could see that Dylan was unconscious, blood on his face.

I immediately thought of Catherine and ran towards the front of the house, startled to see that her parents were sitting meekly in the backseat of the Land Rover, no expression on their faces. I ran up the few steps as Donald ran out with a golf club, swinging it widely around his head. He shouted at me to go and then ran towards the man who was dragging Dylan away. I ran past him and saw Catherine screaming at me from the hallway to go away, tears streaming down her face.

I couldn't leave her; hadn't we just promised to look out for each other? I grabbed her, pulling her along the corridor away from the door. I had just got to her bedroom when I heard a roar and another man appeared out of the dining room, shouting and running towards us. I pulled her into her bedroom and quickly jammed a chair under the handle. Within seconds the door shook as the man charged at it, shaking the door frame.

'We've got to get away!' I was almost shouting. On her bed were two cases and I realised that she had packed her clothes; the wardrobe doors were open. Beside the cases was a framed photograph of us at a recent school dance, smiling, a world away. I knew what this meant, and the emotion added another level to the adrenaline surging through my body.

Catherine reacted quickly, turning the handle to the window and flinging the window wide open.

'Get out or you will be killed!' she screamed, and grabbing me by my cycling jacket she pulled me to the window, pushing at me desperately, trying to get me to go. The door frame shook again and this time the chair edged along the floor.

'There's nothing you can do. I love you but please, please go.'

I hesitated. The chair moved again.

'Go!' she screamed, and she was becoming hysterical.

I went to kiss her, but she pushed me away and as the door burst open I balanced on the window ledge and dropped to the ground. I slipped over in the flower bed, which saved me as the man who had hit Dylan swung a baseball bat near my head, shattering a flower pot beside me. He swung again, but I quickly ran around the back of the Land Rover. All he had to do was cut me off by running across the front of the Land Rover, a shorter distance, by a few yards, and block my exit from the farm. Fear gave me speed and I got around the Land Rover before he made the other side of the bonnet and I ran as fast as I could, sensing more than taking the time to look that he was on my tail. As I reached the gate, I scooped up my bike and ran onto the road.

Such was his speed that he slipped on the wet metal surface of the cattle grid, near the entrance, losing seconds, swearing as he lost balance, and I used the time to get on my bike and start pedalling.

I fumbled the gears but gradually picked up speed. There was a thump and my rear mudguard shattered as the baseball bat hit it. The bike wobbled and I thought that I was going to fall off, but I clung on. The forward momentum of the baseball bat cost him more seconds as the bat hit the ground and I pedalled as I never have before or since, putting vital yards between the two of us and making my escape. I listened for the sound of the van in pursuit, but only heard more shouts from the farmyard.

My legs were beginning to seize, the effort I had exerted catching up with me, but I kept cycling until I reached the turn-off for my house. Thinking that I didn't want them coming to the house after me I turned up the road towards the church, freewheeling down the hill and then as I tried to climb up the steep hill in front of me, I fell off the bike and was sick at the side of the road. I was gasping for breath between retches, my chest heaving, anger, desperation and despair raging through my body.

' I couldn't save her,' I kept repeating to myself, and I let out a roar of frustration.

I heard a car coming in my direction and threw the bike over a low wall and scrambled into a sandy depression on the seaward side of the road. I heard the car change gear and head towards the church. I glanced up, but it was Mr Clark from the cottage at the top of the hill, beside the ruined church, an elderly man. He drove on, not aware of me.

We had just promised to look out for each other and now we were apart, Catherine leaving with strangers. To have complied with them, she must have expected something like this to happen. The memory of her parents sitting quietly in the back of the Land Rover came back to me. I had never seen Charles Robinson act

176

like that and what would become of Dylan, injured? Would he be treated? Had Donald escaped?

Then it hit me that I was wasting time. If they were leaving then they had to get a ferry off the island. I ran back to the house and dialled 999. I was put through to someone who knew nothing of Islay and struggled to take in what I was saying, probably partly my fault for speaking too fast.

It was nearly five o'clock and the last ferry left Port Ellen in just over an hour. A supervisor came on the line and tried to calm me down, asking a few more questions. They promised to investigate. It seemed so inadequate: I don't think that they quite believed me. I put down the phone and slumped on the couch.

I was still there the next morning when Sergeant Muir, from Bowmore police station and a police constable rang the doorbell. I let them in and they saw the state I was in.

Muir sat down beside me, removing his police cap to reveal a fringe of grey hair. The police constable did not sit down but took his cue from the sergeant and stayed silent.

'We spoke to Mr and Mrs Robinson, and Catherine, before they left the island. Mr Robinson was driving. They couldn't understand the fuss, but said that they were leaving the island. Frankly, Peter, you were the main reason. They felt that you and Catherine were getting too close and they wanted her to have time away from you. They have bought another house and she will finish her schooling elsewhere. They don't want you trying to contact her again or they will have a lawyer obtain a court order restraining you from seeing her.'

I could not believe what I was hearing.

'I don't believe you,' I said, numbed by what he had just told me.

'If you take my advice and move on, I'll ensure that this is the end of the matter.' He smiled, but there was a hint of steel behind his expression.

'What about Dylan?' I said remembering his head injury.

'Donald took him to the hospital, after his fall, and he has been flown to the Southern General hospital for observation. His father went later to be with him, when he got back to the mainland.'

'And Donald?'

'At the farm, when we called in this morning. We did not find anything unusual.' By now I detected a slight edge of irritation in his voice.

'When are your parents back, Peter?

'Saturday.'

'I will have a word with them,' Muir said.

As they left I heard Muir say to the police constable, 'Lucky I know his father or he would have been in trouble with his cock-and-bull story.'

I had the wisdom to shut the door before I punched the wall and swore.

19

Beattie asked me to put a few pieces of coal on the fire, which was almost out. As I bent down to the fire, I noticed that his eyes were moist and he looked very thoughtful.

'You can understand why I can't go to the police, I said. 'I don't trust them.'

'Son,' he said, 'that was awful and the police chose to ignore you, dismiss your report.' I was glad that he didn't say story. Maybe the local police are corrupt. I often wondered why no one dug deeper into the Robinson's finances and their activities. You were very angry and upset.'

It was a statement of fact.

'I know it didn't excuse what I did...'

'...to Joe,' he finished the sentence for me.

A month after Catherine's departure I was in Bowmore, when I encountered Joe, outside a pub, smoking. He had been drinking and there was still that bit of bad blood between us, since that day at Battery Point.

'Still protecting Goths,' he said, courage coming from the drink and his two friends standing beside him on the pavement.

Malcolm, who was with me, put a restraining hand on my elbow, but I couldn't resist rising to the bait. I was simmering inside, angry with the world. Life was bloody unfair. Joe was just in the wrong place.

'It was the dog I was protecting, not the Goth, but you would have trouble knowing the difference,' I replied. Joe tossed away his cigarette and faced up to me.

'Come on,' said Malcolm, trying to pull me away, but I reacted too quickly, moving towards Joe and punching him hard on the face, while slipping my right foot behind his leg. Joe went flying and hit the ground. I was standing over him as he started to rise, groaning and looking a little stunned, and I kicked him hard in the stomach, doubling him up. His friends moved in to protect him and Malcolm grabbed me.

The barman must have been alerted because he came out and shouted, 'Get away or I'll call the police.'

Joe looked at me with more respect as he was helped to his feet, wiping a trickle of blood from his chin, the fight gone from him, his face ashen.

'We're quits,' I said. He nodded, and I walked away with Malcolm along Shore Street, rubbing the knuckles on my right hand, which were grazed and sore.

'Peter,' Malcolm said, after a few moments of silence, 'you need help. You have to get over Catherine.'

I nodded but the reality was I didn't know how to. I was hurting too much and missing her terribly.

Malcolm bade his farewell, with a glance back along Shore Street to check that Joe and his cronies were not following us.

'See you soon,' he said.

I was learning to drive, but had failed my test the first time, so I still needed to get a taxi home. I was lost in my thoughts when I heard a voice: 'Peter, can we talk?'

It was Dakota, wearing a red anorak over a simple floral dress. I was surprised; she had not been seen around school in

180

the last few months. No one knew where she had gone. But that wasn't the only surprise: gone was the Goth look. Her appearance transformed. No longer shy, she appeared confident, her black hair attractively centre parted, hair tumbling down over her cheeks, held back with two bangles. Her green eyes, and I hadn't noticed their colour before, added brightness to her smile. Her face narrowed attractively towards her chin, giving emphasis to her high cheekbones.

She noticed my expression and laughed.

'Don't call me Dakota, she said. 'I am now Jenny, after my grandmother from North Uist. They said that would be better.' She laughed. 'A lot better. So no old jokes or I will do to you what you just did to Joe.'

I was embarrassed, but she laughed again. 'He deserved it and thank-you again for your support that day.' Pointing at my hand, she added, 'Come home and I'll wash that for you.'

So I found myself walking down a narrow passageway off Shore Street, through a rotted wooden-framed door hanging on broken hinges at the entrance. I had never noticed the passageway before. There was what turned out to be a communal door on the left and Jenny entered it. Four names, written roughly on slips of paper, were in name holders at the side of the door. A narrow set of stairs led away from the small hall, which was dingy and in need of painting, There was a strong smell of damp and I could see rising damp, a blotched yellow stain, on the wall by the door.

She led me up a rickety flight of bare wooden stairs to a landing where two doors faced each other, and unlocked the door on the right. The small upstairs landing was no better in appearance than the entrance hall. Inside the flat there was a small living room and kitchen, and a single bedroom with an unmade double bed in it. I looked out of the window, through a dirty net curtain, and saw only an overgrown grassy slope with bare patches, topped by a high wooden fence, probably allowing the people who lived beyond to block out the sight of the flats. In the living room there was a couch that could be pulled down to make a bed, a sideboard that was scratched and scuffed and a small semi-circular table, end onto the wall.

Jenny did not seem bothered by her surroundings, having grown, I presumed, to accept them. She was filling a kettle with water at the sink.

'Where is your mum?' I asked, immediately regretting my question.

'Out,' is all she replied. 'Working as a cleaner,' she added quickly. She took off her anorak and threw it on the couch. 'Come to the sink,' she ordered.

Jenny ran the water until it was warm and held my hand under the water, using soap and a cloth to wipe my hand. I enjoyed her touch, but was suddenly guilty about Catherine. I don't think that Jenny noticed and in a minute she was drying my hand.

'Tea or coffee?'

'Coffee, please.' We sat down on the couch and looked at each other.

'I asked Dad where you had gone,' I said, 'but he wouldn't or more likely couldn't tell me.'

'He has been a great help, although it was another teacher, Mrs Scott, the art teacher, who has been most supportive. She reckoned that lurking underneath that Goth creation of mine was a person with artistic ability. Mrs Scott applied for a grant for a place on a residential art course, near Comrie, in Perthshire. She sent samples of my work and I was accepted. The teachers, organised by your dad, had a whip round and got me new clothes and a big supply of make-up remover.' Her laugh was most attractive, I thought.

'I didn't want to go but Mrs Scott drove me, and the rest is history – or maybe art. I loved it and the people I met. They really supported me.' I could see that Jenny was pleased to tell me her story and I was proud that Dad was a part of it.

I heard footsteps on the stairs outside and wondered if her mum was coming back. Instead, there was a loud impatient rap on the door on the opposite side of the small upstairs hall.

'Rent money,' said a familiar voice, and I heard a door being opened. Money must have been handed over, because I heard a muffled 'thanks'. It was the first time I had ever heard Donald Robinson say thanks.

I heard a few footsteps and then a loud rap on the door of Jenny's flat.

'Don't be late with the rent again. You had it easy too long and you must pay up.' Jenny sat silent but I could see her face was becoming flushed.

'Don't be bringing home clients, Mrs McDougall, or I'll report you to the police.' I only knew one Robinson who had tact and class, and she was gone. So I wasn't surprised when Donald added: 'Not that you'll be getting much trade now, I imagine.'

Jenny stood up and shouted back, 'That's because your father was such a lousy teacher and from what I heard you're not any better. You better watch out or you'll be lifted.'

There was silence for a moment followed by a thumping on the door and a few oaths.

'Be gone,' said Jenny, 'or I'll be reporting you.'

There were more oaths and further threats, but then I heard footsteps retreating down the stairs.

'Wow,' I said, and I placed my hand on her shoulder, full of admiration.

She didn't move away from me but simply said, 'He needed to be told that, bastard that he is.' It seemed that we had a lot in common.

Her mood lightened. 'You're the first boy to sit on my bed,' she said with a smile, and it took me a second to realise what she meant. She took my hand off her shoulder, but I did notice that it wasn't done too quickly.

I didn't know what to say next but Jenny, as I was quickly realising, was a step ahead of me. 'See you at school, Peter. I believe that we are both getting a prize next week.'

• • •

'Beattie, I left the building stunned by the turn of events, realising that there were also many questions I wanted to ask. I did, however, have a sense of pleasure in hearing someone standing up to Donald Robinson.'

Beattie coughed and began to splutter, holding up a hand to indicate that he was okay. 'I wish I had been there,' he said, once he had recovered. 'Not that I would have wanted to interrupt anything,' he added with a smile.

I grinned. 'But you know me; full of self-pity, I mucked everything up.' I paused then added. 'But maybe it wasn't the right time, but I only know that because I know how things worked out in the end.'

• • •

The small hall was full, the curtains drawn to stop the evening sun blinding people. Staff were sitting on a raised platform behind a long trestle table which had been draped in a muted tartan pattern cloth. Numerous certificates, shields and cups were organised in rows in front of the staff. It was also to be Dad's final prize giving before he retired, and he was awarding the prizes as guest of honour. His short speech was appreciated and his comments about always being an Ileach warmly applauded. I saw Mum sitting beside him, wiping away a tear. I duly went up for my certificate, a third-placed prize in Business Management, and smiled proudly at Dad. The first prize in Biology should have gone to Catherine, but tactfully her name had been withdrawn.

You know that you are getting towards the end of the prize giving when the table is clear and there are only a few big cups and shields left and Jenny had still not received anything. Eventually only one cup was left. It must be for Jenny. It looked impressive.

Dad cleared his throat. 'It is my great pleasure to present a prestigious award to one of our pupils, whose talent has been recognised at a national level. The Charles Steiner award is given, on the advice of a committee of prominent artists, to the young person who they believe has shown outstanding promise. The award comes with a scholarship to the Glasgow School of Art for three years. What an honour for someone in Islay to achieve this. It is given for her series of landscape paintings, including one of Machir Bay, which will from now on hang in our foyer. The judges note that her use of abstract expressionism brought them joy, not a word usually associated with artists.' People in the audience laughed. 'Her creative use of landscapes is both original and dynamic and shows great promise. 'It gives me great pleasure to award the prize to Jenny McDougall.'

There was thunderous applause and Jenny stood up and smiled at Dad, shook his hand and kissed him on the cheek. I noticed that Dad blushed.

She held the cup up for a few seconds and then sat down, but not before a few photographs had been taken, for the local newspaper. Later, each with a glass of orange juice, we stood side-by-side looking at her painting of Machir Bay, now hanging in the school foyer. I have to say that I recognised very little of Machir Bay, and I did ask her where my house was.

'Over there by the plunging gannet,' she replied, and I was

none the wiser, but kept my ignorance to myself.

Then she looked at me and said, 'I'm going away for a few weeks. Part of the prize is a trip to Paris, but would you like to meet up on Tuesday night, say about eight?'

'Yes,' I replied, remembering that I was already meeting up with Malcolm and Ronnie for a farewell to school night, and an introduction to some of Islay's whiskies that we were now legally allowed to imbibe. It shouldn't be a problem to mix business and pleasure.

On Tuesday evening we started at the Lochside, moved to the Bowmore Hotel and after that I wasn't sure. The trouble with whisky is that you can drink it too quickly; it's meant to be savoured, especially cask strength whiskies. We started early because Ronnie had to get back to Jura, on the last ferry. We were certainly enjoying ourselves, when the pub door swung open and in walked Jenny, looking radiant but with a scowl when she noticed me. I glanced at the clock above the whisky gantry and noticed the time. I was late.

Jenny saw us and walked across to our corner table. 'Jenny,' I said, 'I'm sorry,' attempting to rise to my feet.

Malcolm, and this was when I realised that he was slurring said, 'Jenny, it's my fault. He wanted to see you.' He stopped, his eyes suggesting a lack of focus, his lips no longer coordinated. 'He wanted to see you,' he repeated, but the words were getting elongated. 'I mean. Hey, that was a wonderful prize that you got.'

Jenny picked up the water jug on the table in front of him and threw it in his face. The barman immediately shouted out, 'Stop that young lady,' and she gave him a scornful, withering look.

Jenny turned to me, spotting the double Laphroaig I had in front of me and picked up the glass and threw it in my face. The stinging liquid burned my eyes, the reek of TCP filling my nostrils. The barman was out from behind the bar immediately.

'Peter,' she said, 'maybe someday, but at the moment you're too full of self-pity.' She turned away, brushing the barman aside, and walked out the door.

'You're all barred,' shouted the barman and we got up, but not before I rushed to the toilet to wash my face, my eyes filled with stinging tears. I remember thinking about what she said, noting that it wasn't a complete brush-off. Afterwards, I don't recollect very much else about the evening.

·   ·   ·

'Was the barman called Sam?' asked Beattie.

I shrugged and held up my hands.

'He told a funny story very like yours,' he added.

Mary offered us another cup of tea but we both declined. The fire was still struggling to barely heat the room.

'Thanks for coming,' he said. 'I know that I have more to hear,' and I nodded. 'There are many questions that you didn't ask.' He was correct. At the moment I had heard enough.

Beattie coughed again and Mary gave him his face mask, carefully positioning it on his face.

It was time to go.

'I'll visit you soon,' I said, preparing to leave, but between deep breaths Beattie motioned for me to stay a minute longer with one hand, while fumbling in the pocket of his shirt with the other.

He took out a gold watch and chain from his shirt pocket and pulled off the mask.

'Take this, Peter and give it back to the rightful owner,' he said, taking a deep breath. 'If you can find them. I never should have taken it,' he added. 'It's pirate's gold.' There was a grim intensity on his face. 'And it's time piracy was stopped.'

I wasn't sure how I was going to do that, but I accepted the challenge by taking the watch and chain from him, subconsciously rubbing it in my hand as Mary showed me out, maybe expecting a turbaned genie to appear in a puff of smoke to come to my aid. My chances of stopping piracy were just as farfetched, but I had learnt a lot that might be useful tomorrow night. I was now better prepared and had many of my suspicions about the Robinsons confirmed. If the Americans were interested in searching for the gold, they were looking in the right place. But was there any left?

20

Bowmore was quiet as I walked back to the car, passing Donald Caskie Square, named after a famous Islay minister, known as the Tartan Pimpernel, who remained in France after the Germans overran Paris, during the Second World War. He was a minister, at the Scot's Kirk in Paris and helped over five hundred military personnel to flee France and return home. His story of dedication and valour held in high regard, not just by Ileachs. Only the Co-op was open at this time, and there were few shoppers about. Morrison Square was empty, apart from a man getting money from the bank cash machine. I checked and replied to Jenny's message as I walked. She sent her love but didn't say where she and Ben were now.

My car was parked on School Street, so I went by the side of the distillery. A van was parked on the road beside the distillery building, a hose running from it, through a metal grill at ground level, into the distillery. *Still problems with the drainage*, I thought. I heard the van's engine running, powering what sounded like a pump, as I crossed the road. The 'Drain Clear' company was from Larkhall, which was somewhere in Lanarkshire, so it was an expensive option, but Gifford wanted to keep the distilling going until the silent season in a couple of months.

The road was quiet and I did a quick U-turn in the car and headed home, the long way by Saligo, pondering over what I now knew about the Robinsons. It seemed likely that they had somehow found the gold from the sunken *Empire Constellation*, and sold it on. Surely it must all be gone by now. The American pilot, however, thought that he had discovered something, and whatever it was had cost him his life, so as late as the eighties there must have been some left.

'It's close to Arthur and Dominic.' That short message kept coming to mind. What did it mean? Ryan Loudoun III had spoken to someone in the States, from the island, before departing, and the additional information he passed on in his final moments must have been important. Maybe he had been holding something back and, realising that he would die, he had wanted someone else to be able to act on what he found, without alerting the whole world. Catherine had never mentioned these names as people who were around the farm. Of course, they would probably have been around before she was born, which was the year that the plane crashed.

When I reached home, I made myself a cup of coffee and sat down on the couch, still thinking over what I had discovered. What would they do with the gold? They couldn't simply hand over gold bars or coins without a lot of questions being asked. I had a sudden thought which made me sit up, spilling some of my hot coffee over my trousers. They would probably melt the gold down before selling it on, so that it couldn't be traced. They would need a furnace to melt the gold and the store, under the hill, would be a good place to do that. They wouldn't want people poking about and looking down the old ventilation shaft. I had never seen inside it, which was suspicious on its own. We were forbidden from going near it. What were they hiding there? The aggressive reaction of Catherine's father, when he knew we had explored around the ventilation grill, now made sense – he wouldn't want anyone to discover his secret. Progress at last, and then I realised that the farm had been searched in the sixties, and nothing found. How would you hide or get rid of a furnace capable of melting gold? What size would it be? Charles Robinson knew that he had investigators on the island; he might have shifted it elsewhere. But where?

Then I remembered my cycle trip with Catherine to Kilchiaran Bay. The Robinsons could have moved the furnace there and hidden it from the investigators. I looked out the window and saw that the sun was setting and decided that I would walk over there tonight to have a look. I collected the torch from beside the back door, put on my anorak, and headed out. It was a chilly night, a cool breeze blowing in from the sea, the lights of Northern Ireland on the horizon flickering in the gathering darkness.

The car park was deserted as I took the path over the dunes and up to Granny's Rock. The tide was almost in, the remains of the wrecked ship submerged, the strip of sand narrow. I was out of breath by the time I crested the hill and looked down on the far side, and paused to recover. Looking north, I could still make out Saligo Bay and Loch Gorm. Ahead of me in the gloaming I could just make out the ruined church by the bay, the farm buildings and Robinson's barn beside the small military cemetery.

It's close to Arthur and Dominic, I wondered.

I walked quickly down the rough track and reached the cemetery. I flashed my torchlight on the gravestones looking for a clue. I thought back to that day when I played the game of 'I-spy' with Catherine. What was different? Two of the graves were of soldiers. I looked for their graves and photographed them. It just might be: Sergeant D Harris and Private A Lawrence, their graves side-by-side.

'It's close to Arthur and Dominic.' The cryptic phrase spun in my head. 'Close to…' I walked towards the barn, vaulting the low cemetery wall, and circling around the barn, the sights, sounds and smells of that day many years ago playing out in my mind.

The doors were still bolted and locked. I found the window on the far side, a hessian covering still blocking a view inside. The small gap that had offered me a glimpse of a machine inside, many years ago, had been covered up. On impulse I searched around, picked up a stone, and smashed the glass. The sound of the breaking glass seemed loud, reverberating off the hillside, making me hold my breath. I expected a light to go on in the nearby farmhouse. Instead a dog barked and I hid behind the barn, hoping that the dog would not be sent out to investigate. It was almost dark now, and after a few minutes of waiting, I pulled back the hessian covering and shone my torch in the window. The machine was still underneath the window. I lit it up, revealing a thick coat of dust and grim covering it. I reached in and grabbed some of the hessian cloth to rub the top of it. After a little effort I managed to make out 'Parker and Thomson', the writing upside down to me. I photographed it with my phone and then shone my torch further inside. The barn was otherwise empty.

I let the cloth fall over the window again and removed the few shards of glass from outside, depositing them behind a bush. Hopefully, no one would notice what I had done.

I hurried up the path, the sound of the dog barking again echoing in my ears. There was a full moon and a shaft of moonlight reflected in the waters of the bay as I climbed down towards Machir Bay and back to my house, the whereabouts of the Robinson's gold still a mystery.

21

Thursday

I arrived into work early and phoned Fiona at the Islay Folk Museum. A friend of my parents, she volunteered a few times in the week to work at the museum, which was situated in a former church in Port Charlotte. Although it was not opening time she was already in and listened to my requests.

'I'll see what I can do and get back to you as soon as I can.' There must have been an edge in my voice because I didn't request a quick reply; it was unlikely that the information was readily available, but she seemed to sense, without asking too many questions, that it was important to me.

I made myself a cup of coffee and settled down at the computer in the backroom of the distillery shop to search for information, online. It was worthwhile, but I was interrupted by Mrs Hall coming in to collect a gift box from a shelf, and I decided to abandon my search until later. I felt uneasy around her; she seemed very curious about me.

I checked my phone and there was no message from Jenny, which was unusual. I sent her a quick text.

The island was now getting busier, with many arriving early for the Feis Ile, the Islay festival of Music and Malt. The morning tour was full, with one Norwegian offering me fifty pounds if I could

193

keep him a bottle of our festival special. I declined. I had noticed that several boxes of whisky, marked 'Festival Special' had been placed in the back shop, but even I didn't know the final selection; only Gifford and a few people in Glasgow at the administration and bottling plant were privy to that information. Last year we had bottled from a port pipe cask, similar to Kilchoman this year, but every year was different and eagerly anticipated. At this rate we would need security to ensure it was kept safe.

Each distillery held a special open day which was always busy with a queue of enthusiasts. Some queued outside from early morning to ensure that they could purchase the distillery special and get in on the events organised for the day. We had arranged for a special tutored nosing of vintage Islay whiskies, and the tickets had sold out within minutes of going online. One of our brand ambassadors was coming across to lead it and give a talk on the history of the distillery. I hoped to be around to hear her and learn. Despite everything, I had my ambitions. I helped to unpack whisky glasses after the tour, in anticipation of the extra visitors, and to set up a display of distillery photographs taken over the years, showing the many changes in the distillery.

The day passed quickly and I did not receive a reply from Fiona. Nor was there a message from Jenny, and I wondered if her phone battery needed recharging.

I headed home to get ready for my evening visit to High Coullabus to meet the Americans.

• • •

Just after nine I drove round by Saligo and then down past the RSPB visitor centre, and along the straight section, beyond the centre, taking the turning for their farm cottage. I passed a couple of farms before turning onto the High Coullabus farm track and finally reaching the cottage. The black BMW was parked there now, and some of the windows in the cottage were open. They were back.

Sally opened the door, dressed in denims and a black roll-neck sweater. She smiled and welcomed me inside, into what was the kitchen area and lounge. There was a coal fire but it wasn't even set.

'Did anyone follow you?' she asked and I shook my head, not that I had looked that often in my rear view mirror, but you would notice; Islay roads are quiet.

Jonathon came through from one the bedrooms to the front and muttered, 'He wasn't followed,' barely acknowledging me. He sat down on an easy chair, rubbing his crew cut with one of his hands. Brian was sitting on the couch, pulling at the tiny coloured beaded bands on his beard, staring at me, making no attempt to engage or help me to settle. Both men were wearing almost matching camouflage trousers and dark green T-shirts, while Brian was also wearing an unzipped black jerkin. Not the sort of people that you would want to meet on a dark night.

'Thanks for coming,' Sally said.

'Did I have a choice?' I replied, and Sally laughed.

'This is certainly not how you expected to be spending your time with both Jenny and Ben away, and not having Jodie for company.' There was an underlying edge to her statement. She was letting me know that she knew all about me. Sally read my reaction as she sat down on the couch, beside Brian, and pointed to the other easy chair.

'We wish you no harm and we can help each other.'

'Can I hear the recording that you made?' I asked, as I sat down. 'It would help me ease my concerns.'

The other two glanced at each other. I was curious as to where the balance of power lay among them.

Jonathon was quite blunt: 'Are you going to tell us all you know about the Robinsons?'

That was easy. 'Yes.' *But maybe not everything tonight*, I added to myself, wondering what room I would have for manoeuvre.

'You might also have to offer more direct help to us, before you get home.'

'Like what?

'Show us around the Robinson's farm, or parts of it.'

'That could be dangerous.'

'Yes,' said Sally, interrupting and attempting to defuse the growing tension. Whoever the two men were, they were not diplomats, more like ex-army.

'But I would accompany you,' said Sally. 'And when you have shown Brian and Jonathon what they want to see, then I'll get you away. You won't have to go into the farmhouse. We need to check something out.'

I had an idea where this was heading.

Sally took out her phone and fiddled with it, repeatedly pressing the icons.

'Ready,' she said, and I nodded. The other two were silent, almost sullen; this part of the evening was just a means to an end to them.

I heard Donald's voice again. 'That is the man I told you about Roy, from Friday night.'

The response was still chilling: 'Why is he still alive? It mustn't happen again.'

Now I waited aware that my phone had just vibrated, leaving a message.

'He won't go to the police. Catherine ensured that he will remember nothing. When he woke up he'd have been worried about what he might have done. He's weak; he'll attempt to cover the matter up and hope that his wife doesn't find out.'

'You better be right, there can be no compromise on security,' replied the one I knew as Roy.

'We can't just go about knocking off locals; it would only bring attention to us and to the island, and we might be exposed,' Donald stated, but I could tell he was feeling the pressure, an anxious edge in his voice.

'No, but security is vital. If you think that I am ruthless wait until he arrives. You must deal with Catherine; she is becoming a liability.' That sounded like an order. As I struggled to take in what was being said, he added, 'Her heroin addiction is a problem. You know what to do.'

Donald replied, and I tried hard to glean any brotherly empathy, any kindness, any sympathy into what he said, but failed, 'I'll deal with it,' and the recording stopped. Sally fiddled with her phone again.

'Do you want me to repeat it?' Sally said.

'No.' I tried hard not to show emotion, conscious that the others were looking at me, trying to gauge my reaction. Poor Catherine, life had not gone well for her. Heroin addiction, that was awful, poor, poor Catherine. What might have been. It sounded as if she had tried to help me, but why? What had I been doing that night and what was she up to? I remembered the vow that day at Kilnave Church; we promised to look out for each other. I had failed, but she had succeeded in looking out for me, probably saved my life.

Sally looked sympathetic. 'I know that you were very close at one time, Peter. It must be difficult to find out that she is now a drug addict and keeping bad company. I'm sorry but you needed to know.'

'Very close,' I snapped angrily, 'before her bloody family took her away.'

'Want to help stuff the Robinsons, Peter?' Brian asked leaning

197

forward, impatient, breaking into my train of thought with a forced sympathetic look on his face which, I felt would disappear in an instant if I rejected his request. His callousness annoyed me and even Sally cast him a disapproving glance.

I took time to compose myself for a few seconds before replying. 'You have no idea how much I hate the Robinsons. They have destroyed a person that I loved, that I loved an awful lot.' I noted the past tense that I had used, and hoped that I could continue to agree with it: that I wouldn't experience an upsurge in buried emotion or guilt for Catherine.

I took my phone out of my pocket and checked it. There was good reception at the farm, probably because it was high on the hillside. There were now several messages from Malcolm. 'Phone me urgently,' was the first, followed by 'very urgent' and 'very, very urgent'.

'I have to phone a friend,' I said. 'Urgent, he has some test results for me.'

The three of them looked uncomfortable and Sally said, 'Just speak from here, we'll try not to listen.' I presumed that Malcolm was phoning about the drug test result.

In defiance I stood up and walked outside, noting that Brian and Jonathon did not look too pleased with my action, but I saw Sally motioning with a hand, trying to placate them.

Malcolm answered quickly.

'Where are you?' he said, sounding very agitated.

'Around and about. Do you have news for me about the drug test?' I replied. Brian was now standing by the door listening and I turned away from him, the phone pressed to my ear.

'No, but I have had the police at my door looking for you. A police inspector accompanied by Johnstone, a show of force, very official. They want to speak to you urgently and if they don't find you in the next few hours, they'll get a warrant for your arrest, they said. Very tight-lipped about the reasons, but it must be about last Friday.'

I closed my eyes and breathed deeply, disappointment and dread surging through me, competing with each other. I had hoped that the threat of the police contacting me would have gone away, but no: here it was right back in my face. I found myself subconsciously rubbing the fading scratch marks on my face. I knew now I could resolve the issue by getting hold of the recording, but that came at a cost and was also fraught with danger. I didn't trust Sally and her friends; they were too intense. Would they keep their part of the bargain?

'Thanks, Malcolm', I replied, trying to make my voice sound unemotional, and turning towards Brian and giving him a look that I hope conveyed something of the irritation that I felt about his lack of trust for me. I continued, 'I hope to be able to resolve matters very soon. When will the test results be in?'

'Alison's not sure, it should be soon.'

'That would be helpful,' I said, trying to sound calm as I ended the call, but hoping that I had conveyed the urgency of discovering the result.

It was now approaching dusk, with the fields and moor around the farm growing darker, the colour of the fields fading away to a monochrome grey. I was aware of cows munching grass and of the cold breeze blowing from the sea. High clouds were scurrying across the sky, intermittently blocking the light from the full moon. Not far away I saw the dark waters of Loch Gruinart. I shivered and walked back in, ignoring Brian, who was zipping up his jerkin.

'Okay, I'll help you', I said, when I re-entered the cottage. I was between a rock and a hard place, not much attracted by either.

The atmosphere immediately relaxed and Sally offered me a coffee, which I accepted. I sipped it and then put it down on the floor beside the chair. Brian looked more relaxed and crossed his legs, which given their thickness wasn't too easy. I saw the sole of his boot exposed, as he did this, and my eyes were immediately drawn to the tread of his boot. I recognised it instantly, and I am sure that the photograph on my phone would confirm it. It was very likely that Brian had been in my house looking around. What the hell did he want with our dirty washing and what else had he been up to in our house? My fragile stomach was churning again, my heart beating faster once more. I was going to be extremely careful in answering their questions.

'Right, Peter, tell us what you know about the Robinsons,' said Brian impatiently. 'And we do know some of the background,' he added, which I took as a warning that they were going to judge my contribution for completeness.

'We especially want to know about the *Empire Constellation*,' said Sally.

Plunging in, I said, 'And the gold cargo it was carrying.'

Jonathon and Brian were now alert.

'From what I gathered there was gold on board, a special shipment to help pay off war debts. The ship was delayed in joining a convoy bound for America, because it was diverted to Loch Ryan from Belfast, to pick up the cargo. Bad weather meant that it never caught up with the other ships, and engine problems left it floundering. With little power, it was helplessly drifting along the coast of Islay by morning, a sitting target for any U-boats in the area. The Captain realising the danger, thought he could get the gold ashore. His orders were to protect the cargo, at all cost. The gold was probably transferred to a lifeboat and, thereafter, at some point the ship was torpedoed. I am not sure of the exact sequence. The lifeboat was carried into Machir Bay by the tide and capsized and the Robinsons must have seen it happening. Later they discovered and salvaged the gold. They hit the jackpot. They were living in a poor croft at the time, hand to mouth existence, but on the son's return from the war the Robinsons soon bought Loch Gorm farm and did it up, probably on the proceeds of the gold that they sold.'

'Charles Robinson sold the gold to Janner and Jones, a London firm of bullion dealers,' Sally explained. 'An acquaintance found that out while he was in London'

'Was it the American pilot who crashed, Ryan Loudoun III by any chance?' I said, guessing, making a sudden connection and Sally nodded. The visit to Beattie was paying dividends. 'A lot of people on the island know about him,' I explained, before Sally continued,

'The firm were a bit disreputable, known for dodgy dealings, but Robinson got a good price. Drove a hard bargain'

Somehow I wasn't surprised.

'Then investigators got suspicious when they visited the island in the sixties, and the Robinsons lay low for a while,' I continued.

'Did they smelt the gold on the island?' Jonathon asked.

'That is the speculation.'

'Is there any left?' put in Brian.

'That's a good question, I said. 'But Sally, what about Ryan Loudoun III. Did he think that there was some left?'

'He told Jack Loweski, his friend in America, about it.'

'And what did he do?'

'Nothing. There was a lot of coverage in the States about the plane crash. Ryan had a bit of a reputation as an adventurer, but there was no public mention of why he was in Scotland. They probably assumed that it was to do with a woman. He had form.'

Brian butted in. 'I'm Brian Loweski, Jack's son. My father did nothing about it. I don't think that he believed Ryan. One phone call did not convince him. It was all a bit unreal. He only told me last year, before he died, about Islay and the gold. That's why I am here.'

'Me too,' said Sally, after a few seconds.

'I'm along for the ride,' said Jonathon. 'Brian and I are ex-marines'.

'We also know that even this year Janner and Jones received gold from the Robinsons. It came direct from Islay. They seem to need a lot of money,' Sally added.

'We think that there was an operating furnace on the farm, and while it might now be closed it is a good place to start looking for the gold. That's why we need your help. You know the farm from your time with Catherine. We hope that you can tell us where is the best place to look.'

So they wanted practical help - that was a lot more dangerous.

'I have a problem,' I said. 'Last Friday night I was drugged, probably by Catherine Robinson. You heard her brother Donald talking in the recording. Please don't tell me that these people, Roy and friends, are searching for gold.' Describing them as Roy and friends made them almost sound harmless, which I was sure they were not. 'They are involved with something a lot bigger and nastier. Drugs? Do you really want to get involved?'

'I don't know what they are doing but we are looking for the gold. I agree that we should not get involved with Roy and his friends. I don't think that we need to,' Brian replied.

'I know that we have to be careful', said Sally. 'We noticed that you were being followed. Ex-military personnel are trained to look out for trouble, after all it could be a terrorist following, a possible abduction attempt.'

'Cheer me up more. Why would I be followed?'

They shrugged. 'Maybe Catherine is keeping an eye out for you,' Sally said.

'Or more likely some of her friends who think that I should

be dead,' I added.

'Jonathon checked out the farm earlier and only Dylan was there, everyone else had gone, probably left the island. So it is a good time.' Brian got up and moved across to the kitchen table, producing a folded piece of paper and a pen from his inside pocket. Draw me a map of the farm,' he said, opening out the paper.

It wasn't difficult and I told them about the ventilation grill. I presumed that they wanted access into the storage area, built into the hill. They listened intently, and asked a few more questions. It seemed that an old Ordnance Survey map showed that there had been a cave underneath the area where I had positioned the ventilation grill. The Robinsons must have had the cave enlarged and had secure doors fitted at the front.

'Okay,' I said, 'We can approach the farm from the east, scrambling up the hill until we are looking over the farmyard. If I remember correctly, the ventilation grill was on the lee side from the farmyard and the top of the escarpment is rocky, which should provide some cover. You need to be aware that cars coming along the road might spot you, as you are not too far off the road. I'll take you there. I have only been there once. Sally comes along and she sends the recording as an attachment to these email addresses.' I gave her my email address and Malcolm's. 'Then I walk away.'

It would probably be a waste of time at the farm, but that wasn't my concern.

'One thing that you didn't mention,' said Sally. 'What about the message from the pilot before he was killed?'

'It's close to Arthur and Dominic,' I replied

'Yes, that message.'

I laughed. 'I was born the year the plane crashed, so I am not the person to ask,' I replied. 'It caused a lot of comment at the time, I believe, but it is still as cryptic today as it was then. Dad told me about it much later, when I was a boy and he hadn't a clue what it meant. I believe that it was the talk of Islay for many years, a standard question, 'Do you know Arthur and Dominic?' A joke line for cocktail parties. If they didn't know at the time, then I am unlikely to have figured it out.'

I was going to add that Bruichladdich would probably produce a valinch at their shop, for visitors to fill their own bottle, and call it: 'Arthur and Dominic's secret cask', but I felt that was going too far and showing disrespect to another Islay distillery. Okay, my response was still over the top, but it killed any further speculation.

Thankfully, Sally accepted my answer, and Brian and Jonathon started to pack small rucksacks. We were going to the Robinson's farm, I presumed, as soon as it was completely dark.

22

It was during one of my final lectures at university, a critique of some economic theory, a personal bête noir of our professor, that my phone, which was on mute, vibrated. Bored, I pulled it out of my pocket and glanced at the message. Missed call from Alison. I showed it to Eilidh, who was sitting beside me on the same uncomfortable wooden bench, an angled writing surface in front of us, where we were making notes on our Oxford student notepads. High tech we weren't and frequently I couldn't even read the notes that I made with my Bic pen. It was like being in a church, with serried ranks of wooden pews, but here, in what was a large lecture theatre, the rows of benches were tiered with only two students sitting near the front, the rest scattered around the echoing lecture theatre, the lecturer appearing as remote in reality as his lecture was from real life.

Eilidh smiled. She knew Alison, having met her and Malcolm a few times, and enjoyed their company. We had had them round for meals in the flat that we rented off Byres Road. I shrugged, not sure why she was contacting me.

'Maybe an invite,' I whispered, not wanting to draw the attention of the professor, who after all would be marking our final answers in a few weeks. Professor Bell, with his goatee beard and wire rimmed glasses, looked like the Russian revolutionary that he craved to be, was now in full flow.

I was still showing Eilidh the phone, when it vibrated again, this time a text message from Alison.

'Contact me urgently.'

I showed it to Eilidh.

'Doesn't sound like an invite for a meal,' she whispered as Professor Bell cleared his throat, an indication that he had noticed our lack of attention.

Eilidh pivoted to the front, with an apologetic look on her face and looked down at her notes, picking up her pen, writing on her notepad. Professor Bell continued his exposition and Eilidh showed me what she had written.

'Maybe you should phone her back when the lecture finishes in ten minutes,' and then she had added, 'The professor is a prick!!!' She gave me a mischievous smile, framed by her fizzy red hair.

Eilidh and I had soon become close in our first year, during accountancy classes, our backgrounds forging an immediate link, both of us being from remote parts of the country, thrown together in the big city. We needed each other for confidence and to interpret our new and strange surroundings. Together we enjoyed visiting the sights and sounds of Glasgow life. Eilidh liked art galleries and going to the theatre, and I had started going to Partick Thistle football matches on a Saturday afternoon. There was a novelty in seeing football matches live, with a pie and Bovril, and not Sky Sports on some large screen, in a pub in Bowmore. Eilidh even came along to a few matches: 'For the pies,' she said.

By the end of the session we were sharing a flat and living together. Despite being at Strathclyde University, with its campus located nearer the centre of the city, we had found a flat in Highburgh Road, almost on the Glasgow University campus, a short distance from where my uncle died. It was a traditional west-end flat with high ceilings and large bay windows. We were on the third floor, high above the street, able to look down on city life.

I met Eilidh's parents when they visited Glasgow, just before Christmas in our second year of study. They didn't approve of our living arrangements, but the father, Iain, seemed to accept that this was modern living and was pleased, with his love of single malts, to meet someone from Islay. A gift of a distillery only bottling of a fifteen-year-old sherry cask from Bruichladdich and we were good friends. This was the first time that either Eilidh or I had lived with someone else and it took time to adjust, and required compromises along the way. Eilidh was better at this than me. I suppose I was used to my mother looking after me and Eilidh, correctly, expected me to cook and share chores around the flat, something I was slow to accept.

Nights in the pubs on Byres Road and back to the flat together were enjoyable. Late night pizzas ordered and visits to the famous curry houses in the area made for a self-indulgent life, adding a few pounds to my frame.

I think, looking back, that our relationship met our mutual needs for companionship and intimacy, but never really connected at a deeper level. I was very, very fond of Eilidh, but never really loved her. By now, I suppose, the reason was obvious. I had never got over Catherine, traumatised by the way we had separated. Even with Eilidh I was waiting for something bad to happen, to pull us apart, and it was difficult to commit: unconsciously, perhaps, I was protecting myself from more hurt.

Catherine and I had known each other since primary one; we were very comfortable in each other's company; our lives entwined, often not having to say anything, each just knowing what the other was thinking. Although I accept that Catherine

207

kept a lot back from me, she didn't do it to exclude me, more to protect me. This was all unfair on Eilidh, who offered so much, an attractive girl, with distinctive red hair and a ready laugh, a personality which sparkled and drew admiring glances. I didn't know how lucky I was. For our relationship to work out, we should have met at a different time.

During our third year, I was feeling the pressure of endless lectures, essays and deadlines as our course intensified. We helped each other and spent long hours in the university library, looking up books for ideas and searching the internet. Looking back, I might have been slightly depressed, which was not unknown when you were working hard, with the end of the course not in sight. Lots of hurdles ahead, without the initial novelty or enthusiasm of being at university. Our studies had switched from the excitement of new ideas to a means to an end, a degree, a passport to a job.

One night, travelling home alone on the bus, I was looking out the window while the bus driver waited for the traffic lights to change. It was raining and the glass was steamed up. As I wiped it I saw Catherine walking on the other side of the street. It had to be her, the way the woman walked, her height. In a second I was at the bus door, pressing the emergency release – much to the annoyance of the driver – running across the street, a car beeping its horn, as I raced around it. I reached the far pavement and desperately searched for Catherine. Running, bumping into others, frantically searching. I dived into shops, looked down side streets, studied people across the road, scanning the crowds, but all to no avail. Was it Catherine? I don't know but within me a yearning had been reignited, and I had to find her.

On Saturdays, instead of going to the football, I walked around the city centre, sitting in the cafe in John Lewis's in the Buchanan Galleries, on the first floor overlooking the concourse, studying those scurrying by. I never did see her.

Once when I got home, Eilidh asked how the match had gone at Firhill, Partick Thistle's ground, and I said, 'It was a rubbish match.'

Eilidh looked at me, perplexed. 'It must have been,' she said, fixing me with a puzzling look. 'The floodlights failed and the game was abandoned.' Thereafter I sensed Eilidh cooling, no longer completely trusting me.

Outside the lecture theatre I phoned Alison, who was back on Islay at the time, working shifts at the small hospital in Bowmore. She answered quickly, her voice different, not her usual friendly banter, as if she was choosing her words carefully.

'I saw your mum here this morning. She collapsed outside the Co-op after taking a funny turn. People stopped to help her and Billy came out of the Co-op and quickly got an ambulance.

'I called your dad and he came immediately. Dr Khalid was called; he contacted Glasgow and an air ambulance was arranged. Your mum and dad flew to Glasgow and were taken to the Southern General hospital. Peter, I think that you should get there as soon as possible. I said that I knew how to contact you quickly.'

I sensed that there was more, but Alison was being careful in what she said.

'I'll get there right away. How's Dad taking it?'

'As you would expect, very calmly and reassuring to your mum, who was a bit confused, but he looked very worried.'

Eilidh was studying my reactions to the conversation, wondering what was happening.

'Mum has been taken unwell and she has been flown to the Southern General. I need to go,' I explained.

Eilidh nodded. 'Of course. Will I get you a taxi?'

I nodded. 'See you later.'

Dad was sitting, looking quite composed, as I arrived in the ward and pulled back the curtain that surrounded the bed. He looked up and smiled, the practice of being a father, always providing reassurance to your offspring, was there, but I could sense that it was a front. He was devastated. He waited until I had gone to the bed and brushed the hair from Mum's forehead, as I reached down to kiss her softly. There was no response; her eyes were closed, her mouth twisted.

I retrieved a plastic seat from a stack beside the ward doors and sat down beside Dad.

'What are the doctors saying?' I asked and at that his composure crumbled and we hugged for several minutes before, in a voice cracking with emotion, he tried to speak.

'She won't make it,' he said with a mighty effort, before emotion took hold again and he shook. I held him more tightly, trying to get a grip on my own emotions.

'They did a scan when she arrived. It has been a massive stroke and she won't recover. Nature will take its course.' His eyes filled with tears again. A kind nurse brought us a cup of tea and shortly after we were ushered into a small room, where a consultant tried to let us know what the prospects were, a nurse standing beside us in the room as we listened.

Dad seemed to absorb the information, or at least the news had been partially absorbed. He accepted what had occurred, while I broke in, arguing that they had to keep trying. The consultant was patient, and explained about the quality of life. I wasn't listening but Dad with dignity thanked him, and we went back to be with Mum. Mum was declared to have passed away a few hours later.

Standing on what was a fresh bright morning at Machir Bay, I watched as the coffin was lowered into the freshly dug grave, the comforting words of Rev Walker being carried away in the wind, which was gently lifting the the green cloth draped around the edges of the grave.

I looked around at the ruined church, towering over us, the starlings roosting on the rafters, the choughs watching from the gable wall of the church, sheep munching at the grass in the fields and Loch Gorm displaying a deep blue hue. Blue smoke was rising from the Kilchoman distillery and behind me I could hear the quiet roar of waves crashing on the beach. All familiar sights and sounds, but they paid no homage to Mum; they were just the incessant rhythms of life, not moved or changed by the scene being acted out in front of them.

The Rev Walker was still speaking.

'Think of death not as a full-stop but as a comma, as life carries on.'

His words were floating in and out of my consciousness, snatches of his eulogy being heard, but most of his words swept past me as I tried to cope with the raw emotion of the occasion. I felt as if I was adjusting a radio dial to improve the strength of the signal, but emotional interference kept blocking the message.

As we filed back down the road to the cottage, where friends had prepared food, I was trying to cope with the tides of emotion which rose suddenly, like those big waves on Machir Bay, breaking unexpectedly, leaving a foaming froth of bubbles, the sea appearing calmer but with much turbulence remaining beneath the surface. I looked around the mourners, who avoided direct contact, their eyes respectfully averted. I caught myself thinking about Catherine, hoping that she was there paying respects, that some good could come out of this, that there was meaning to life. But she wasn't, and I felt ashamed that my thoughts had drifted to her, when I should be grieving.

There and then I resolved to make this a turning point in my life, to respect Mum's memory. Life doesn't need to come to a full-stop, to paraphrase the minister: it carries on. However hard it would be I would move on, dwelling on the good that Mum had done, the happy memories of our time together. I resolved to shape the future and free myself from the past. Thoughts of Catherine would no longer control me, hold me in a past that no longer existed. Catherine had moved on, so must I.

Eilidh hadn't gone to the funeral. There was a good reason, with our final exams only a few days away, but both of us knew that when the exams ended we would go our own ways, without bitterness, but with our relationship ended.

It was very hard to leave Dad but he insisted, encouraging me to do my best in the forthcoming exams. I returned to Glasgow and tried to absorb myself in final preparations. Everything was a blur but somehow I coped and completed the exams.

Eilidh was now talking of returning home for the summer, before heading south to start an internship in Manchester. I had not been successful and wanted to return to Islay to be with Dad. Later, I would intensify my efforts to get a job.

The week before I gave up the lease on the flat an envelope was delivered to the house, an invitation to an art exhibition. I was going to leave it out for Eilidh, it was more her thing, then I read it more carefully and realised that it was addressed to me. It was an invite to attend an exhibition entitled 'Seascapes' by Jenny McDougall. I looked at the date. I would still be around, so I filled in the reply card and posted it back. I wondered how Jenny would have changed, recollecting the feisty girl that had emerged chrysalis-like from the suffocating cocoon that was her earlier life.

The gallery, near the Merchant City, was compact with off-white walls, their colour not distracting from the many framed pictures, that were hung on the walls, which in turn were illuminated by spot lights fixed to wires which ran round the gallery, suspended from the ceiling.

I handed in my invitation and examined the display of dramatic seascapes. I had not been trained, despite Eilidh's best efforts, to interpret abstract work. I did my best as I slowly made my way around the gallery, accepting a glass of chilled white wine from a lady who seemed very enthusiastic about the paintings.

I stopped before the last one, titled 'Catterline Bay 2008, a tribute to Joan Eardley'.

A voice from behind said, 'She's my hero,' and I turned to see Jenny standing there, in a lovely floral-patterned dress which stopped just above her knees. She was wearing a silver pendant around her neck and hair was parted so that it fell evenly to both sides of her face and over her shoulders.

'Abstract expressionism,' I stated, proud that I could remember the term.

'Don't believe that crap,' she replied, and laughed as a woman nearby looked shocked. 'Joan Eardley is now my inspiration, but maybe you haven't heard of her.' Her eyes widened, waiting for confirmation from me, before she continued. 'She painted, amongst other things, large seascapes at Catterline, on the northeast coast of Scotland, using huge canvases, standing on the seashore, in all weathers.'

'Sounds interesting, I would like to learn more,' I replied, captivated by her demeanour.

'So have you forgiven me?'

'I haven't drunk Laphroaig since. Drink can cause you to miss out.' Perhaps it was the wine, but I was flirting and being encouraged, I thought. I was surprised at our instant rapport.

I got a personal tour of her paintings and I noticed a few people watching us, wondering about us. They looked pleased.

'Peter,' she said, 'I am going to have to circulate. I am hoping to sell a few pictures. I am going to Islay in a few weeks.'

'Let me know. I would be pleased to see you.'

'Great, I have a VW campervan which I use for touring around.'

'Ban the bomb badges on it and floral transfers?'

She laughed. 'Mostly rust.'

I left shortly after, already looking forward to her visit.

A few weeks later, Dad came across for my graduation. We met up for a meal beforehand.

'I have an announcement, Peter. Before your mum died, we had applied to be wardens on Iona, at the abbey. We had been successful and I have decided still to go. The change will be good for me. I find it hard without your mum. Too many memories around Machir Bay. I was hoping that you could come back for the summer and look after the house, until you make up your mind as to what you are doing.'

It was a shock but it made sense. I was going to come back anyway, so I quickly agreed.

I graduated that afternoon. Eilidh was there and we talked briefly, still friendly. After the cap was placed on my head and some Latin incantation spoken over me by the Vice-Principal, I stood up, newly graduated, and looked at the gathering of proud family and friends there to celebrate success. I smiled. I was no longer scanning the crowd for Catherine. I was beginning to shape the future.

23

Jenny phoned me just a few weeks after we had met at her art exhibition. I was surprised at how pleased I was to hear her voice, and she sounded warm and friendly. She was coming over to Islay to look for scenes to paint. Inside I also hoped it was an excuse to see me again and I was delighted, excited about the thought of renewing acquaintance. It wasn't just that there were few girls of my age on Islay, and I already knew most of them from school, but I felt that we had made a connection, a rapport, a warmth; hopefully, the beginning of a mutual attraction. We got on well, we were relaxed in each other's company, and yes, she was also attractive and talented, good fun to be with. I couldn't stop thinking about Jenny, her long hair, with centre parting held back at the sides, her sparkling green eyes, with a hint of mischief, her attractively shaped face tapering to a sculptured chin which somehow reinforced her feisty personality, increasing the impact of her broad smile. I hoped that she could live up to my idealistic fantasy.

I watched as the light blue VW campervan turned off the road, trundling up the driveway and, yes, it was definitely rusty and the noise of the engine made me think that the exhaust was not long for the world. Jenny parked beside my Golf and as I came out to meet her the campervan door opened and a small bundle of black and white fur jumped onto the ground, racing around me, avoiding my touch with ease, followed by Jenny in tight jeans and an oversized blue fleece top with a few spots of paint on it; her working clothes, I guessed. Her appearance excited me and I was glad for the distraction created by the puppy or I might have appeared flustered; my fantasy was living up to my imagination. As it was I detected a certain nervousness in Jenny, which pleased me. This meeting also meant something to her.

'She's lovely,' I said. 'What's her name?' I had to spin round to see where the Border Collie puppy had gone.

'Jodie,' Jenny replied, flicking her hair, which had fallen over her face, to the side, and laughing at the dog's antics. 'I hope that you don't mind me bringing her. Jodie is only twelve weeks old, so this is one of her first outings. We'll stay in the campervan; she is not fully housetrained yet.'

'Hi, Jodie,' I said, trying to get her attention. Like most Border Collies you have to wait until they decide to come to you. I crouched and waited, pretending to ignore her and in a minute she flopped on the ground by my side and rolled on her back waiting for her tummy to be tickled.

'Beautiful markings,' I said. 'I love the white stripe on her head between her eyes, the white ruff around her neck. Her two front legs also look like they have been dipped in white paint.' And then I noticed her eyes. 'She has a blue eye.'

'Bred from working stock, the farmers' believe that the blue eye means that their eyesight is more acute, better for spotting sheep,' replied Jenny, 'and anyway I just fell in love with her.'

Given my love of dogs, I couldn't disagree. The attraction was instant and I sensed that Jenny was pleased with my reaction to the puppy.

'Well, welcome to my home. Come on in and I'll make the

coffee. Instant, I'm afraid,' I added. I noticed Jenny looking around slowly taking in Mable's Cottage and the surroundings.

'I love the views,' she said. 'Machir Bay is so beautiful. Islay has so many nice bays, plenty of potential for painting.'

'Painting, walking, whisky; there's plenty to do.'

'Sounds good,' she replied, following me into the house.

Typical Jenny, so far she had told me where she would be staying and that she was here to work, and she had only been here for five minutes. I was slightly disappointed, but my male ego had probably gone into overdrive imagining what could happen when we met.

Be patient, I instructed myself.

As it was a warm day we took our mugs of coffee outside and sat at the picnic bench, and talked about many things; the success of the exhibition that I had attended, where she had got Jodie and what she wanted to do on the island, and also about me. She was curious about what I was doing which, in reality, was not a lot. I was living in the house rent free while Dad was away in Iona, and I was working in a bar in Port Charlotte to help pay the bills. I had taken a few days off to be with Jenny. I told her that I was looking for a job and had sent in CVs to all the local businesses, which really meant distilleries. The time slipped by and we both started to unwind. Jenny had seemed nervous, quieter than usual and I also realised how much I had hyped her visit in my mind, longing for her company.

Jenny collected a Canon digital camera with a heavy, wide-angled lens from the campervan and we wandered down to the beach. Machir Bay was basking in summer sunshine, the sky blue, the sea calm, the tide receding, with only the faintest of breezes to tease the long grass on the sand dunes. We made our way down from the high dunes to the beach, skipped over the burn that split the beach, hardly getting our feet wet; the burn an anaemic trickle today. We walked to the north end, where low rocks separated the beach from a farmer's field, and scrabbled over them to sit down on a rock close to the fence, where we could look south, along the deserted beach. A chough was perched on a nearby fence post, observing us. It flew away as we sat down, its red legs and beak reflecting the sun, adding a daub of colour, like that from a painter's brush, as it climbed in the sky.

'It's not always as pleasant as this,' I said.

Jenny agreed. 'I have been here on wild days when the sea is whipped up and the beach pounded by Atlantic breakers,' she said. 'When it is safe to stand only on the higher sand dunes and even then the sea spray can drench you. A good storm is what I need for my paintings, more dramatic. I'll just have to remain until a storm arrives,' she added tantalisingly. Rarely did I hope for bad weather, but a storm could be helpful, I mused. I had never noticed Jenny in this part of Islay before. Without money or means of transport, it must have been difficult for her to get around the island.

By evening we were both even more relaxed, helped by a glass of Australian Shiraz at the picnic bench, looking over the bay, the sun starting to dip, throwing sharp shadows beyond the cottage. The breeze was picking up. Jenny collected a jacket from the campervan. Jodie was a constant source of fun, a tireless dynamo, a blur of fur, as she ran around, bringing us sticks, the instinctive desire to be busy already apparent. Jodie was good for us, if ever the conversation faltered, and it didn't often. She was a useful distraction, a source of laughter at her antics, comments on her behaviour enabling our conversation to pick up momentum again. The chat wasn't as bantering as at the art exhibition, little sign of flirting, a little more measured from Jenny, but she was probably tired after a long journey and ferry crossing.

As the sun set, Jenny showered in the house and thanked me

for a wonderful day, before heading out to the campervan. Jodie eventually flopped onto a small dog bed beside her in the back. The campervan was basic inside, but Jenny seemed to enjoy the life and freedom it offered, and it did after all compare favourably to what she had been used to previously in Islay.

I went to bed alone and even if the day had not met my wildest fantasies, I knew in myself that my feelings for Jenny were real, and had become, if anything, more established.

The next morning the weather was still bright, even if the wind had picked up in strength. We breakfasted inside, Jodie playing about, ever alert, and the two of us made our plans for the day.

'I have always wanted to visit Saligo again,' Jenny said. 'I have seen pictures on the internet of the beach and I think that it has the potential for my type of painting.'

I suggested that we prepare a picnic and spend the day there. I had no doubts that Jodie would love it.

We cleared up the few dirty dishes, made some sandwiches, a flask of hot water, packed the coffee and we were ready. I still felt a slight gulf between us, despite Jenny appearing less tired, but I fought with myself, tried not to over analyse.

The journey in the campervan only took five minutes and we parked on the verge just off the road, near a gate, at a sharp bend in the road. Jenny immediately started taking pictures of the narrow bridge we had just crossed and the cottages beyond, moving her head from side to side, looking for angles.

She turned to me, flicking her hair to the side, a new habit I had noticed since her arrival, and smiled broadly. 'I love this, looking around, trying to imagine what I can do. Oh,' she added excitedly, gazing over my head to the hills at the northern end of the beach. 'I had forgotten about the sleeping giant! It looks like the Sydney Opera House, with the sheer cliff edge facing the sea and the rest of the hill tapering away,' and she was quickly busy, taking more photographs, this time with a zoom lens.

'I'm not sure that the angle is right,' she muttered as she focussed on the task in hand. We passed through the gate, walked past the wartime remains of a radar mast, with sawn off metal legs projecting out of concrete casing. Ahead was the Atlantic; there was nothing between us and America but a few thousand miles of ocean. We reached the top of the sand dunes and Jenny became more energized, biting down on her lip and moving her head up and down as she surveyed the beach.

'I love Machir Bay because of you,' she said,' but there are not so many angles to paint there. Look at these jagged lichen-covered fingers of rock projecting into the sea, and the movement of the waves, even on a calm day. This is wonderful.'

I don't think Jenny had realised what she had just said; maybe it was just a slip of the tongue, but it cheered me up no end. She was now quite animated as she took in the scene, scanning from one end of the beach to the other.

We clambered down the sandy dunes, not another soul in sight, entranced by the powerful waves, which seemed to mount on the backs of each other in their haste to crash on the shore. Beside the fractured rocks, worn smooth in places, with seaweed trailing from their surfaces, were small pools of water draining back to the sea, leaving soft sand behind. Jenny took a number of close-ups, while still taking time to throw seaweed for Jodie. I was impressed by their energy.

I wandered about, avoiding getting in the way of her photos, taking my turn to play with Jodie. As I clambered over the rocks I noticed that someone had spelled out on small stones on one of the rocks: Calum loves Chloe.

I called Jenny over and showed the message.

'Can you incorporate that message in one of your paintings?'

I asked.

Jenny looked pensive for a moment. 'I could, but I would protect it, hide it in the picture, in a safe place. My paintings are vivid, look dramatic, as I focus on the power of nature. I do also like warmer aspects, but maybe it wouldn't work, too obvious.'

'Reflective of your upbringing?'

'Yes,' she replied without any hesitation and not even making eye contact. 'It was my tutor, Ben, who showed me how to release my emotions through art. Painting is my therapy. I can step away from the anger I still feel at times and leave it on the canvas, usually with great dollops of paint. That's the theory anyway,' she added with a smile, slightly embarrassed that she was appearing too serious. 'Enough introspection. This is a wonderful beach. I can already see several paintings emerging, taking shape in my mind. Peter, you are very patient. Just give me another hour and we can have lunch.'

Two hours later, we sat together on a slab of rock, eating our sandwiches, drinking coffee, feeding the dog some biscuits Jenny had brought. Islay continued to be benign, doing its best for us, the sun shining on us, helping us to enjoy the beach and each other's company.

We returned home in the late afternoon, and Jenny immediately began work on sketching her ideas, sitting on a canvas chair beside the campervan. I took Jodie for a walk and then on my return prepared the evening meal. It was interesting to watch Jenny so absorbed in her sketching. Every stroke was thought about; she often turned to another sketch pad as she worked on some small detail before moving back to the main sketch. I wondered if I would recognise where the message I had seen on the beach was hidden on the canvas, and given the abstract nature of her painting, if I would even recognise the message.

221

I had to call Jenny a couple of times before she emerged from her artistic trance and came into the cottage to sit down at the table.

'That's me for today,' she said. 'you need to get initial sketches done to see if there is enough to work with. I am trying to loosen up the structures, blur the image of the rocks, the waves, so that I can interpret them more meaningfully.'

'It's a lot of work, and I can begin to see why it is so absorbing, a passion for you,' I said and she looked at me for a minute, taking in what she had heard me say. She simply smiled at me, warmly.

'A glass of wine is called for.' I poured her a glass of chilled Marlborough Sauvignon Blanc.

Jenny sipped some and then took a bigger mouthful.

'Very good,' she said raising her glass, 'to the two of us.' We clinked our glasses together and I brought through the first course.

The meal completed, Jenny sat on the single seat, much to my frustration, leaving me still alone on the couch. We talked easily enough, Jenny telling me about her experiences at art school and the tutors, some of whom she respected, others she thought pretentious and out of touch. In turn, I described my course, trying to make it sound interesting, but largely failing. Some people get passionate about marketing, but I usually thought of it as a cynical exercise in boosting profits. Jenny had passion for her art, if not art school; I was glad that the lectures, essays and assignments were behind me. Jenny had a vocation, I had a job which paid the bills, or most of them. However, our conversation had become a lot easier, more wide-ranging; poor Jodie was neglected.

'I always meant to ask you how you got my address to send an invitation,' I asked as I opened another bottle of wine, no cork just a screw top, but still New Zealand, which we both seemed to enjoy.

Jenny paused for a second before replying, looking in the distance before turning her head towards me, flicking her hair away from her face.

'Catherine Robinson gave it to me.'

I quickly swallowed some wine to cover my surprise.

'But you two are sworn enemies,' I said, remembering the fight in the Co-op.

'I know,' replied Jenny, 'but she appeared one night at the exhibition, out of the blue, and praised me for my work, but it wasn't me she was interested in. Peter, she has aged a lot, I didn't recognise her as she came in. Very drawn, hair much shorter, her blue eyes dull, as if she was tired of life. I felt sorry for her and it was clear she wasn't angling to be snide or have a go at me. If anything the tables had turned; I was the one in the dominant position. She congratulated me, wished me well on the success of my portfolio.' Jenny laughed. 'Although she was a bit surprised by the price tags. She then started to talk about you.'

I was struggling to remain impassive, suddenly very aware of a facial tic that I was sure Jenny would notice. I was pleased, however, that my heart rate was steady; there was no Pavlovian overreaction in my body systems. I was still looking forward, not back.

'She had spotted you around town, alone, looking anxious. Observed you sitting in John Lewis, looking at the crowd below. She wanted more for you, felt that you were being too hard on yourself. There is nothing you could have done to change anything. Didn't think that Eilidh was right for you.' Jenny's eyebrow flickered. Facial tics were catching, it seemed.

Jenny was very aware of what she was saying. By now I had put my empty wine glass down and was listening intently. Catherine had not forgotten me, was still fulfilling her vow, and

Jenny was studying me for my reaction.

'When Mum died,' I said slowly, ' I decided to put the past behind me, move on, look to the future. It has not been long, and I would have had a different reaction if you had said this even a few months ago, but now, well I don't expect to meet Catherine, and she has no sway over me. I'm glad you told me. I mean, I feel sorry for her, will always have fond memories of her, but I can't influence the situation. Nor do I wish to,' I added, with what I hope was sufficient firmness.

'She wishes you all the best,' Jenny said. 'She thanks you for all you meant to her, and says that she has made a new life, one that you can't be part of. Nor, I suspect would you wish to be; there are issues.' Jenny didn't elaborate and I didn't ask, not wanting to appear too curious about Catherine.

Jenny came over and sat beside me, put her arm around me and nestled in beside me.

'I'm sorry that it didn't work out for the two of you, Peter.'

'Life can offer better opportunities,' I replied, and kissed her gently on the cheek. 'As we both know, Robinsons can be very hard work.' At that, she pressed her body closer into mine.

So ended our second night. I held Jenny close, enjoyed her warmth, the delicate perfume that I hadn't noticed before, the contented silence between us. A short time later, Jenny went out to her campervan and I went to bed, not so frustrated, and a bit more optimistic. We were resolving issues, hopefully, for better times ahead.

Islay had to let us down eventually. The weather the next morning was windy and wet. Jenny took an early trip down to the beach and was excited when she eventually came back to the house for breakfast, her hair wet, but her face beaming.

'I'll work on some sketches later, but I see how I can get a different angle on the bay, using the hard-layered rocks, at the south end for a close-up.' Satisfied she sat down to coffee and toast. 'Can you come with me to Sanaigmore this morning, Peter?' she asked. 'I have an appointment with an art gallery there, to try to sell some of my pictures.'

I knew the place and was happy to accompany her. Shortly after, we passed Saligo, where Jenny insisted on stopping for more pictures, and then around Loch Gorm, until we reached the turn-off for Sanaigmore, near the red phone box, and followed a winding road down to another sheltered bay. We passed the memorial to the victims of the sinking of the *Exmouth of Newcastle*, in 1847, a sailing boat crammed with those forced to seek a new life in Canada, which was driven onto nearby rocks by a raging storm and was destroyed.

The rain had abated by the time we reached the art gallery and coffee shop. I left Jenny to pitch her wares, while I took Jodie down to the nearby shore, returning later to have a coffee with her.

'I've to get back to her with more samples. Hopefully, she is interested. My bank balance can always do with a boost,' Jenny told me.

We returned to Saligo once again to watch the waves roar in, pummelling the shore, repeatedly, without pause, as the wind drove them in. What a contrast to yesterday's tranquil aquatic display, but after all, this was Islay, and today was a day for a dram by the fireside, some might say.

We toured the Rhinns, mainly staying in the campervan, but bravely venturing out near Portnahaven for Jenny to take more photos. Evening came around quickly and I put on the wood burner to take the damp chill out of the room. Jenny was happy to help prepare the meal and I found another bottle of wine and a half full bottle of Lagavulin. I closed the blinds to reduce the noise of the storm and lit a few candles to add atmosphere.

As we finished the meal the conversation again turned to her work.

'How long does it take you to complete one of your paintings,' I asked curiously.

'Some are finished quickly, but others,' and she rolled her eyes, 'I can never finish to my satisfaction. Those you find in my flat or crammed in the back of the campervan. Hopefully, I will return later to them with fresh inspiration. Generally it takes several weeks to finish a painting, but I will probably be working on several at the one time.'

Gusts of wind were now buffeting the gable end, raindrops creating a frenzied beat on the exposed windows. The dog had found solace next to the log burner, enjoying the heat. The wine, and now the Lagavulin, had taken their effect. Jenny was leaning against me, relaxed, the busyness of the last few days catching up with us both. The candles were flickering, responding to the whim of the convection currents set up by the belching heat of the log burner.

'Why did you call your dog Jodie? I asked innocently, having almost run out of things to say.

A simple question, but the answer was going to change my life, forever.

Jenny lifted her head from my shoulder.

'Do you really want to know?

Intrigued, I replied, 'Yes,' and Jenny got up from the couch and sat down beside Jodie on the floor, in front of the log burner.

'Did you ever see the film 'Taxi Driver'?' she asked.

'Starring Robert de Niro?'

Jenny nodded and added, 'and Jodie Foster.'

My knowledge of films was at best shaky, but Eilidh had once dragged me to a special showing of the film at a cinema in Byres Road. I smiled, proud of my knowledge, but the smile froze on

226

my face and Jenny saw my reaction.

'The child prostitute was called Iris,' I suddenly remembered.

'The same name as Mum's. De Niro tried to rescue Iris, but she didn't want to be rescued. I hated the film, found it boring, but it still made a big impact on me; I could relate to it. Why did Mum sleep around? She could never explain that to me. We never, to be honest, had that sort of conversation. No one in the film explained why Iris had left home to become a prostitute. Why did she behave the way that she did? Life is strange. Mum was good looking in her day, attractive to men, but she let the death of her husband – he wasn't my father, I never knew him, whoever he was – destroy her. With the help of Charles Robinson.'

By now Jenny's voice had risen in pitch, with an emotional edge; the outpouring was important to her, to explain herself, and she only paused to fortify herself with a sip of Lagavulin. Jodie was alarmed by the change in Jenny's tone. Jenny put down her whisky glass, held the puppy close to her, stroking her, letting her curl up on her lap, trying to calm both the puppy and herself.

'I became interested in Jodie Foster, not particularly for her role in Taxi Driver, but because she was a talented actress who had to fight for respect for her talent. She became a role model to me and that's why I called my puppy Jodie, to remind me to keep fighting, never give up, to always better myself.' She placed Jodie gently back on the floor.

'People ask why social work was not involved with my family, a child at risk, but Mum was clever. Robinson had influence and, for a price, she was protected. Not that many on Islay used her, too risky if word got out, and not much demand, but the tourists, especially inflamed by a dram, were keen on her.'

'I wanted security to be able to come home and not have to peek around the door to see if anyone was in. That's why I became a Goth, I suppose, to hide behind a mask, hoping that no one would bother with me, notice me. No chance. I just became thought of as a freak,' She laughed, embarrassed by the memory.

'The school was great when they discovered my artistic talent. They organised for me to go to an art school, in Perthshire, for gifted youngsters, and I'll never forget that your Dad was one of those who made it possible. One of the teachers there, Ben, was so patient, encouraging, gave me self-confidence. It changed my life.'

'It must have been so difficult,' I said. *And such a contrast to my own happy family upbringing.* 'But you have done so well. I'm proud of you.' That finally started Jenny's tears.

'You need to know this, Peter. You were one of the few pupils who showed any kindness. You stood up for Misty, that day, at Battery Point. No one else had done anything like that.'

I could still feel the impact of the punch as she spoke, but I hadn't expected this outcome, years later. I think now that I would have happily taken more blows.

'Peter, I feel that I have known you a long time, often only from a distance. I realise that you loved Catherine, but I can see that is behind you now. I would love to get closer, but I have never had a relationship, that's why I have been coy since I arrived. I still carry some scars from my upbringing, casual relationships frighten me. As a woman, I am the very opposite of what Mum was, probably a reaction to her lifestyle. I don't even know who my father is – is he from Islay, who knows? But I love you, please be patient, I so want...'

'Marry me,' I said, not impulsively, but with, I hope the love and conviction, that I felt. I had never been surer, more confident, more forward-looking.

Jenny looked stunned, and after what seemed a long few seconds she said, 'Yes,' and we met half way across the room, each reaching out to the other, words forgotten.

'And let's be quick,' I said. 'I don't want to wait to start a new life with you,'

Jodie, caught up in the emotion, started barking, grabbing a ball, bringing it to us.

'I come as a package with Jodie,' Jenny cautioned.

'I expected nothing else.'

That night, once the storm had died down, Jenny slept in the campervan. This time I wanted everything to be just right, to respect my new partner.

A month later we stood before the Rev Walker in the Round Church. Dad had island-hopped from Iona to be there, Malcolm was my best man. Ronnie led Jenny down the aisle and Alison and Susie were her bridesmaids. We honeymooned in Jura, at Ronnie's house, with Jodie. A year later Ben was born, and in the same week I was offered work at the Islay Distillery.

24

Thursday night

When it was completely dark we drove to Robinson's farm. Low cloud scurrying past overhead continued to intermittently block the moonlight. There were few visible stars; it was a good night for what was planned. We saw just a single light on at the farm, in one of the bedrooms. So far so good. I drove behind the BMW, Sally in the car beside me, and we stopped a few hundred yards beyond the farm, pulling over into a passing place next to Loch Gorm, being careful to leave enough room for someone to pass. The two of us then clambered into the back seat of the BMW and Brian drove to the entrance of the Kilchoman distillery, where he turned the car around and drove back and parked, beyond the farm and off the road. He reached behind the driver's seat and produced a rubber holder for a fishing rod, which he stuck on the bonnet, good cover for the presence of the car; fishermen out on Loch Gorm.

Brian and Jonathon took their rucksacks out of the booted section of the BMW and Brian handed me a torch. We climbed over a low fence and headed into the hills behind the farm, with me leading. I kept the beam of the torch low as we worked our way towards the hill overlooking the farm buildings, trying not to disturb any sheep. My thoughts naturally went back to that afternoon with Catherine, the innocence of our exploration. I had not been back since. The circumstances were so different now; no sense of innocence remained.

It took me a few minutes to find the rocky escarpment, several small bushes having taken root since my previous trip. At least they offered some additional cover, and I crouched down behind them, indicating to the two men that this was the area. The two metal barns and the low farmhouse dominated the scene, the farmhouse far too big for the size of farm. It was obvious to me now, but years ago I just accepted the size, not questioning. Outside the house was a Land Rover and as my eyes adjusted to the poor light I saw a tractor parked between the barns and a trailer unattached beside it. In a few minutes, I hoped, Sally and I would leave the two men and work our way behind the barns, up a gentle slope opposite and then head down to my car, job done. And I would get evidence to help me prove my innocence for last Friday night, when the police came calling.

Brian, keeping low, examined the ground and started scraping the soil away with a trowel, probing for the slab which concealed the disused ventilation grill. I could see my breath in the cold air as Brian worked away.

Loch Gorm was inky black, other than an area on the far side where the moonlight was reflecting off the surface of the water. Sally was waiting beside me, glancing at me occasionally, but otherwise watching the two men. Jonathon was examining the bushes that had grown on the top of the escarpment, pulling at them, presumably to find out if they were sturdy enough to have a rope attached to them that could take the weight of one of the men.

After twenty minutes, Brian motioned for me to come to him and he whispered, 'Are you sure that this is the area? I can't find the slab.'

'Yes,' I replied, and shuffling around on my bended knees I joined the search. The sooner this was over the better. Jonathon had now come over, having tied a rope around the sturdiest bush, and the two of them probed the soft ground, with trowels. It was not a big area, but we were not making much progress.

I watched the headlamp beams of a car approach from the Kilchoman direction, and we all ducked down until it passed, the beam lighting up the hills ahead. I watched it until the beams disappeared, as the car reached the crest in the hill and headed down to Loch Indaal. Sally had her hands pushed firmly down in her pockets, fighting the cold, not wanting to join in the physical effort.

In the farmhouse I noticed another light had gone on. Probably Dylan going to the bathroom, I imagined. On the far side of Loch Gorm a car was travelling around the loch, slowing down as it reached the bend at Saligo beach, its headlamps becoming brighter as it turned the corner.

Brian was now sweating and I could hear his laboured breathing in the still night air as he worked away, pulling back the grassy surface. Then I heard a scrapping sound, the trowel hitting something hard – a stone or a slab. Brian intensified his efforts and cleared away the soil to expose a concrete surface. He called out Jonathon's name, very quietly, and he came over. Within a few minutes the surface of the slab was exposed.

I could see Sally smiling with relief. Brian opened his ruck sack and produced a crowbar, digging it into the ground and prising up the slab. Jonathon grabbed the slab as it was raised and threw it to the side, and both men examined the hole in the ground, Jonathon shining his torch beam down into the hole. I could see the grill that I had first seen all those years ago, still fixed to a concrete frame by four rusty bolts, and watched as Jonathon collected a hacksaw and starting sawing away at the bolts, while

232

Brian shone his torch into the hole instead.

'Not long,' I said to Sally and turned away, looking down again at the farmhouse, lost in my thoughts. I suppose that is why I didn't see the beams of the headlamps, approaching from Loch Indaal. A vehicle was driving fast, its lights rising and falling on the contours of the hilly road. Sally nudged Brian and we all dropped to the ground as the beam of the headlamps briefly illuminated the hillside and then I watched in horror as the vehicle, which I could now see was a van, turned off the road into the farmyard.

Outside lights came on, making me shrink further into the ground. The van stopped in front of the house and three people quickly got out. I crawled to the edge and watched. Could one of them be Catherine? I was aware of Sally by my side.

'They are men,' she said, reading my thoughts. 'But what are they carrying into the house?' To me the long slim cases looked as if they could contain weapons, or was my imagination beginning to run riot? One of the men was tall, like Donald.

Dylan was at the door welcoming them in and after a few minutes the outside lights went off. I wondered where the men had come from. There was no late night ferry, so either they had been staying elsewhere on the island or they had been dropped off by a yacht or other small boat, somewhere along the coast.

Brian and Jonathon had increased their efforts, not letting the presence of the visitors distract them. Jonathon was by now on the last bolt, with the cutting noise now seeming very loud to me in the cold night air. Then the grill was free and the two of them lifted it off the concrete frame. Jonathon produced a rope ladder and attached it to the rope that was wound round the trunk of the biggest bush, and dropped the coiled rope ladder down into the space below. Brian put on a head torch, and after tugging at the rope ladder to check that it would bear his weight, he edged towards the hole and started to shimmy down, with

Jonathon grasping the rope ladder tightly to give extra support. I could see a light beam moving about as Brian twisted and turned in the cavern space. I heard a muffled voice and saw Jonathon relax his grip on the rope ladder and move to the edge of the hole. Brian was in.

Sally and I moved towards the hole and heard Brian saying that the cavern was quite large, with not very much in it, just a few wooden crates and some rusty tools.

'Not used very much, lots of cobwebs,' he said in a loud whisper.

The musty smell that rose from the hole triggered more painful memories for me. I wanted to go, but Sally was focussed on the what was going on in the cavern. After ten minutes, Jonathon called down to Brian, 'How are you getting on?'

'Sally,' I said impatiently, 'I've done my part, let's go.' The gold, and I seriously doubted if there was any there, was of no interest to me. The presence of the men in the farmhouse was a bigger concern.

'A few minutes more, we might be needed to haul Brian up,' she replied.

I moved away in disgust and looked down at the farmyard. I suddenly noticed that Brian's torch beam could be seen through a crack in the cavern doors and moved back to the hole to warn him, and as I did I saw the farmhouse door open and someone come out, hanging around the door; a brief flare of light and a cigarette was lit. I dropped to the edge of the hole warning Sally and Jonathon about the danger of Brian's torch beam being visible from the farmhouse and crawled back to the edge of the escarpment. The man was still smoking, the faint glow of the tip of the cigarette visible. I could also still see Brian's torch beam faintly through the doors, and crawled back, ever more alarmed.

'Come on,' I said, 'let's haul Brian up now.' My tone was

insistent. Jonathon ignored me, but Sally looked more alert, realising the danger.

'Hold the rope ladder. I'm coming up,' Brian said, much to my relief. Both Jonathon and myself braced ourselves and felt his weight as he started to climb the rope ladder. The bush was also taking some of the strain. We heaved and heaved, grunting, straining. Beads of sweat broke out on my forehead, immediately chilled by the cold air. The stem of the bush was bending – and then it cracked, freeing the end of the rope. Jonathon and I felt the extra strain, as we took Brian's full body weight, the rope ladder slipping down a few feet before we could secure our grip. We could hear Brian swearing and feel the rope ladder swaying about. Sally crept over to see if the man by the farmhouse door had noticed or heard anything.

We both pulled on the rope ladder and started hauling Brian up again. I could see the beam of his head torch, but he didn't have a free hand to switch it off. I could almost see him now and with our heels dug in, Jonathon and I edged back from the hole, using all our strength, my arm, leg and back muscles aching and cramping, my strength waning.

With an effort Brian's head and shoulders emerged from the hole and he released his grip on the ladder and planted his elbows on the ground, heaving himself up. Jonathon grabbed him and pulled him out of the hole. I switched off his torch and we all lay grasping for breath. Despite my aching limbs, I crawled to the edge overlooking the farm and looked down. The door was open but the man had gone inside. I was relieved and crawled back.

'Did you find anything?' I said and was surprised to see him nod his head.

'Let's put the slab back and then we can go,' he said, between deep breaths, and he produced a gold coin from his pocket. 'Lost in a corner and there was an old box, metal lined, could have been

235

one of the original boxes from the ship. They must have been put back there after the investigators left. Loudoun was correct – there was still gold after they left, but it must be somewhere else on the island.'

'Only one,' he said flicking the gold coin up in the air, the moonlight catching it. He was looking directly at me. 'But there must be more elsewhere. The coin wasn't that grimy, I noticed, so it can't have been there for too long.'

Suddenly, I heard a shout and crawled back to the edge to see the three men and Dylan emerge from the house with torches, running towards the doors to the cavern.

'They must have seen the torch beams,' Jonathon said. 'Let's go!' He rose and started to sprint down the hill side away from the farm, closely followed by Brian, leaving Sally and me alone.

'So much for standing together,' I said. I grabbed Sally and pulled her in the other direction, down the hillside, towards the back of the first barn. She followed me and we quickly made the safety of the back of the barn. On the hillside to the east of the farm I briefly saw somebody on the horizon, but they immediately dived down.

We hid behind the barn, hearing the sound of shouting and watching torch beams playing across the ground. They couldn't have seen us, because they ran up towards the top of the slope, where the hole was.

'When I say, Sally, we sprint across the space between the two barns, keeping low, and then let's keep going until we reach the car.' I briefly looked around the edge of the barn and saw Dylan unlocking the two doors into the cavern. One of the men was running up the hill side towards the hole that we had just left. I couldn't see the others.

This is not good. My bravery crumbling, I swore. I caught Sally looking at me, wondering what I was doing, but I quickly composed myself, glancing around the corner of the barn again. I nodded at her and we both ran as fast as we could.

We reached the other barn without incident. I indicated that we should keep low and we continued to run, reaching a wire fence. I was clambering over it, glad that we were escaping without detection, when there was a clunk, followed by a flash and the farmyard lit up, and we were bathed in light. There was a shout and I didn't even look back, both of us running across the marshy ground beyond the fence, until we reached the safety of some shadow. Both of us were out of breath, but there was no time to recover, and we ran on until we reached the road. I saw the car a hundred yards away and we sprinted towards it. I flung the door open, reached up for the keys behind the visor and fumbling, put the key in the ignition, and seconds later we were away. I kept the head lights off until we were some distance from the farm. Hopefully they had not identified me and the quicker we got away the better. We drove past Kilchoman distillery and I continued on up to the house. Where else was there to go?

25

The house was in darkness as I braked outside and stopped. We had managed to get away, but I suspect a long night lay ahead, while we waited to see if they had recognised us, and would follow. Already I was regretting getting involved, but then what choice did I have?

'Let's go inside,' I said and, still trying to compose myself, I opened the door, which wasn't locked. It should have been locked; it had been when I left earlier this evening. So I was tense when I entered, with Sally following me. I shut the door. Caution stopped me from putting on the light. I was aware that we were both breathing hard.

'Going straight to the bedroom, Peter?'

I jumped, just making out Jenny sitting on a chair in the darkness.

'I didn't think that you would be back until tomorrow.' I stopped, realising how bad that sounded. So that was why she had not texted me today, she had come home early.

'Susie phoned me,' Jenny said, her voice barely controlled, simmering with suppressed anger. 'Told me that Catherine was back and that you had problems with her.' She switched on a small lamp. I could see the anguish in her face as she studied me. Before

I could say anything she said, 'Quite a loving encounter, it would seem. And who are you? Of course, the girl from the square. Quite a collection, Peter. The two of you out of breath, panting with passion, I suppose.'

'Where's Ben?' I said, desperately thinking of how to begin my explanation, searching for a few seconds extra.'

'At Susie's, I didn't want him to see us falling out.' I saw that she had been crying. She was wearing a mid-length white dress and, despite the tears, or maybe because of them, she looked more attractive than ever. 'Why, oh why, Peter? I gave you everything, you know that.'

'I can explain everything.'

'Including the visit from the police, this evening? Why are they looking for you? They will have probably issued an arrest warrant for you by now. And look at the state of the two of you, muddy, wet and torn clothes. What have you been up to?'

'This is Sally,' I said.

'Go on.'

'She has a recording which will help to explain everything.' I turned to Sally.

Sally looked embarrassed. 'I don't have the phone with me. The boys did not trust you. I was made to leave it at the cottage. I did, however, send on the recording to you and Malcolm's email address before I left. I thought that only fair.'

'That's no use to me at the moment. Your two friends, who ran away at the first sign of trouble and left us to escape by ourselves, haven't come out of this very well,' I replied angrily.

Sally turned towards Jenny, who was sitting quietly; but I could read the signs. A storm was brewing.

'Peter did not rape Catherine Robinson. He was drugged and dumped here at the house. I saw it happening.' Sally looked at me: 'Brian, Jonathon and me were walking along the beach.

239

We noticed people picking up packages, dropped off by a rigid inflatable boat. I recognised Donald Robinson and of course, because of the connection with the gold, the boys were curious.'

'The gold?' said Jenny, incredulous.

'It's a long story, but let Sally finish,' I said. I was learning new facts.

'We watched as you came down from the cottage, unsuspecting, a late-night walk, gathering some of Jenny's drawings, when you were spotted. We could do nothing. When you realised that you were in danger, you ran, but were caught. Catherine argued with them, It looked as if they were going to kill you. Instead they forced something into your mouth and you were dragged back unconscious to the cottage, and dumped.'

'You could have told me this much earlier,' I said, with the emphasis on the much. Sally had explained, however, why I was out; collecting drawings, which must have been blown out of the hut, Jenny's studio.

'We needed your help.'

I looked at Jenny, who was struggling, not surprisingly, to make sense of what she had been told.

'Catherine saved your life,' she said, and Sally agreed. This almost seemed to help her.

'And the scratch marks and love bites?' she added. I wasn't out of the woods yet.

'I saw Catherine bend down and kiss Peter,' Sally said. 'She could have done it then. When you listen to the recording you'll discover that they hoped that it would prevent you, Peter, going to the police.'

Jenny wanted to believe; the storm was beginning to subside.

The phone rang and I looked at the number on the display screen; I didn't recognise it. The ringing tone echoed loudly around the room. Sally looked at the number and snatched up the receiver.

'Yes, Brian, where are you?' Her voice hinted at anger, but she stopped abruptly and then said, 'Are you sure?'

She put the receiver down quickly. 'It seems that we were identified. A Land Rover has just left the Robinson's farm and is heading this way. We need to go, now. Hurry, we don't have much time.'

I looked towards Jenny. 'Please believe me. Grab a coat, we have got to go.'

Sally said quite simply: 'If they find us here, they will kill us.'

I grabbed a jacket for myself and one for Jenny from the coat hooks in the porch, and shouted at her.

'Come on!' I was relieved when she got off the chair, but she refused my offer of a helping hand. Putting on her jacket she went towards the door almost in a trance.

'Sally, you drive. Don't put on any lights. Drive up the hill opposite, turn around and wait. I will flash a torch and you drive down, pick me up. I have thought of something that might delay them.'

Jenny was alarmed: 'This woman just said that they will kill you.'

'We need to delay them or they will kill us all. I know that all this sounds incredible, but please trust me. I think that I can delay them enough for us to get away.'

'Incredible,' Jenny repeated, and shook her head, but, importantly, she followed Sally out and got into the back of the car, looking shell-shocked. I watched Sally drive down the driveway and head up the hill opposite, lights off. I glanced anxiously along Highway 15, but as yet there were no headlights approaching.

I switched off the lamp in the lounge and, leaving the front door open, ran down the driveway. I didn't know if my plan was possible, but when I reached the metal plate covering the gap in the driveway I reached down and tried to lift it. It was heavy, and had been pushed into the ground by the car repeatedly driving over it. Crouching, I tried to prise it up, but it wouldn't budge. I tried pushing it to one side and it moved a few inches, leaving a gap. I wriggled down into the space, up to my ankles in mud and cold water, and obtained more leverage. I was now able to lift it free of the ground at one side, the plate making a squelching and sucking sound, and with a big effort I raised the plate up and flung it over. I repeated the effort and heaved it to the side of the driveway. There was a two-foot gap stretching across the driveway with a three feet drop. More than enough to cause damage if they drove in fast. For the first time I thanked Jack for the delay in repairing the field drain.

I looked along the road and could now see lights approaching, fast. Time to go. I ran into the house, locking the door behind me and ran out the back door, grabbing the torch hanging there and deadlocking the door behind me. The car was now very close, almost at the foot of the driveway, the headlights starting to illuminate the house. I ran to the back wall and vaulted it, crouching behind it, in the field.

I could hear the tyres rumbling on the driveway and then, as I ran down the far side of the perimeter wall, keeping low, I heard a loud bang, followed by a grinding sound and I briefly saw the rear end of the Land Rover rise and fall, its brake lights briefly illuminated. I reached the road and flashed the torch beam.

From the driveway, car doors opened and slammed, and I heard someone groaning, followed by swearing and shouting. It was quite dark, with the front end of the Land Rover embedded in the hole and its lights having gone out. They would be incredibly annoyed; an understatement. I looked up the road, but I couldn't yet see the Golf. I flashed the light again, then heard a shout. I had been spotted.

Several torch beams were playing about the scene as people got out of the Land Rover. it was difficult to avoid them.

'The bastard is over there! Get him!' I recognised Donald's voice. I looked back and saw briefly, in the light of a torch beam, that blood was streaming down his face from a gash on his forehead.

And I ran, sensing someone giving chase. Then I saw the Golf approaching, and I had to slow down, waiting for it to draw level, my pursuer getting ever closer to me. As the car reached me I flung open the door and jumped in. My pursuer clutched at the door, managing to hold on to it, but Sally accelerated rapidly, screeching around the corner and he lost his grip. I clutched at the door and managed to pull it shut. Jenny was screaming in the back; hysterical.

'Go left!' I shouted at Sally. 'Take the long road. They may have a back-up car coming along.' And Sally, still without using the car lights, turned the car to the left and accelerated.

'Jenny, are you okay?' I shouted, and then tried to control my voice to calm her down. She was sobbing.

'It's the shock,' Sally said. 'At least we had time to grasp some of the events. Jenny had none.'

'I'll be okay,' Jenny said, from the back as we sped along.

When I jumped into the car I had briefly seen the carnage at the house. The front of the Land Rover must be damaged, but it was high off the ground to begin with and I could see two men trying to rock the vehicle as the driver tried to reverse. They would be after us soon.

'Sharp corner up ahead and then a few curves,' I told Sally. 'And when you see two houses on the left, slow down, there's a narrow bridge and sharp right-hand corner'.

I looked across Loch Gorm towards the farm. The lights were blazing and I noticed lights separating from the farm, heading the opposite direction from Machir Bay, a vehicle speeding along, heading towards the junction with this road. The word had got out, and we needed to be quick if we were going to beat the vehicle to the turn-off to Loch Gruinart.

'There's another car and it will be trying to cut us off.'

Sally saw the cottages and bounced over the bridge, braking hard as she screeched around the corner.

'Hard left ahead,' I said.

'See it,' said Sally.

'Now it straight for some distance, watch out for narrow bridges.'

We tore along the road, still without lights.

'Road turns right,' I said and looked across the end of the loch. For a second the other vehicle's headlights flared brighter.

'They are at the road end. We might be slightly ahead of them.' Time would tell. We passed the isolated phone box and Sally had to break sharply to avoid hitting a sheep on the road, which cost us a few seconds.

'Drive past it on the verge.' The wheels squealed as we encountered soft mud, but the grip held and we were on our way again, bouncing over another narrow bridge.

'Left,' I said, but Sally knew this bit and was already turning the steering wheel, near to another house.

I could see the other vehicle's lights but they were still some distance away.

The road was very narrow between here and Loch Gruinart, It would be a disaster to meet another car, but we drove on, reaching the high point on the road and speeding up as we drove down the hill on the other side, passing the RSPB visitor centre and reaching the long straight stretch at the head of Loch Gruinart.

A startled bird rose in front of us, flapping its wings in fright, and narrowly missing us.

'Almost there,' I said, twisting around to look at Jenny. She was trying hard to compose herself, a handkerchief gripped tightly in her hand. She saw me looking and muttered, 'Sorry I doubted you.' It was the sweetest sound I had heard in a long time.

I smiled, and reached across, grasping her hand and squeezing it.

'I love you,' I said softly. 'We'll get through this somehow.' But that was said more in hope than expectation.

Sally had reached the junction. I looked in the side mirror and could see headlights near the RSPB visitor centre.

'Don't brake, just slow down, or they will spot our brake lights.'

We were about a mile ahead of them. We reached the farm and quickly drove up the driveway, parking behind the cottage. There was a light on and Brian came out, ushering us in. I looked across the road. A barn owl left the security of a ruined barn, appearing to float through the air, looking for prey, aware of our presence but choosing to ignore us. I couldn't imagine that the Robinsons would be so understanding. I put my arm around Jenny and hugged her as we entered the cottage.

Someone had lit the coal fire and the room was warm, which made me realise how cold I was. I led Jenny to one of the seats, sat on the floor beside her, and took off my trainers and socks and put them close to the fire to dry.

No one spoke, but Sally went to the sink, filled the kettle with water and switched the it on. There was tension. None of us were pleased with Brian and Jonathon.

Eventually I said: 'Jenny, this is Brian and Jonathon, who were with us earlier, although they left rather abruptly.' Looking at the two Americans, I introduced her.

Brian spoke up. 'When we heard the shouts, we were going to stay with you, until we noticed a few people on the horizon, a short distance to the east, and thought it was a trap. It was all so quick and I thought that you had seen them too. We were surprised that you didn't follow us.'

I had seen someone, so maybe there was some truth in his story, but they could have checked back.

'The people from the farm didn't follow us and we sat in our vehicle. I noticed the Land Rover leaving and we drove up the hill where there is a signal and phoned you.'

'How did you know my number?'

'It is in the phone book. I looked it up when we arrived,' replied Brian, pointing to a BT phone book lying conveniently on a small coffee table by the couch. 'And I have been trained to use my memory, as part of my military training.'

Sally seemed to accept their explanation, but she still was not happy.

'We are meant to be a team. It doesn't feel like it.'

I was more unsure, but there was little point in pursuing their explanation further at this point. There were more pressing issues to consider.

'So what do we do now? The Robinsons and friends won't go away.' I got up and wandered into one of the bedrooms at the front of the cottage, and carefully pulled back the curtain to look out the window. From the elevated position of the cottage, I could see as far as the RSPB visitor centre, and I immediately spotted two vehicles moving slowly around the roads, their headlamps giving away their position. One of the cars had only one working headlight. The hunt was on and we were the prey. It sounded dramatic, but after what I had seen at my house I was in no doubt that we would be in deep trouble if they found us.

I returned to the lounge. 'Let's make sure that the Golf is hidden. Can you hide it, Brian?' He went out and shortly after I heard the Golf being moved. When he came in again, he said that the car was well out of sight.

'Do we call the police?' asked Jenny.

I had strong reservations. Many years ago when I had called them, they had not believed me. I was stitched up by Robinson's contacts, which seemed to include the police. The local police were even less likely to believe us, with an arrest warrant having probably been issued for me by now, and I didn't trust Andy Johnstone. And if I was arrested Jenny and Ben would be left alone. Would they be safe? That was the clincher. I gave my views and no one demurred.

'Let Jenny hear the recording,' I said, and Sally openly went into the room that I think was Brian's and collected her phone, which I could see was lying on the bed. They said nothing, accepting her behaviour. Sally played the recording and Jenny listened open-eyed, turning to me in astonishment and reaching out for my hand.

'I'm sorry,' she said, sympathetically. 'Poor Catherine.'

'I'm okay,' I replied. 'I feel very sorry for her, nothing more.'

At least Jenny was on side and that must have been difficult for her, given the events that she had experienced in the last hour.

I started to think about the next steps. My mind was becoming clearer.

'These people around Robinson are very dangerous and we have stirred them up. I also have no idea who the people were near the farm earlier tonight, but they didn't want to be seen, so I don't know how to deal with them. Could be a rival drugs gang trying to muscle in, but that sounds more like an scenario belonging in a film, not Islay. Unlikely to be the police, since they seem to have made their decisions.'

I turned to Jenny, my mind made up. 'Jenny, we must collect Ben and leave the island until they have gone. It's the only way that you can both be safe. However, I think that it is too dangerous to collect Ben tonight'

Jenny agreed. 'Maybe Susie can bring him across early tomorrow.'

And then I had another thought. 'Sally, I have just remembered in the cafe in the Celtic House, they had a laptop in front of them. Any idea of what they were searching for?'

'Yes,' replied Sally, 'they were checking the BBC weather site for Sanaigmore, for this weekend.'

'That's as close as you get to Machir Bay on the BBC weather site. Jenny, I definitely think that we should leave until this is all over, and it sounds as if it will be soon.'

'We could go to Colin. My brother,' she added as an explanation to the others. 'He lives in Ayr. I haven't seen him for a long while but I am sure that he would put us up.'

'If you don't mind I'll come too. I am too easily recognisable on this island and Brian and Jonathon like to do their own thing,' said Sally, looking scornfully at them.

I checked with Jenny and she nodded her agreement, her opinion of Sally seemingly having changed since their initial encounter.

'Jonathon and I will stay, we have unfinished business here,' Brian stated.

'How are you going to get off the island, with the police and the Robinsons looking out for you?' Jonathon asked. 'The ferry terminals and airport will all be carefully watched.'

'I have a plan,' I said, 'but we will have to wait until the morning to see if it is feasible. In the meantime, let's get some rest. I doubt if we will sleep.'

Sally let Jenny and I use her room and she lay down on the couch. I washed and returned to the bedroom. I saw a light outside and carefully prised back the curtain a fraction and slowly let it fall back in place. Outside a Land Rover, with a very dented front end, and one working headlight, was slowly going along the road. I knew who they were looking for.

26

Friday am

I don't know if I slept for long, but I became aware of Jenny rubbing my back and realised that I must have dozed off. Immediately I was alert, but Jenny spoke softly:

'I'm glad that you got some sleep. You must be exhausted, you poor soul.' She nuzzled into me and hugged me. We lay for a few minutes together in silence, before reality kicked in and all the memories of the last week reawoke in my mind. The now familiar searching for solutions began straight away, to resolve some of the problems I faced; to bring my life back to some semblance of normality. At least, with Jenny, I felt that I had the support which I had lacked in the last few days and I felt her love oozing through me, giving me confidence. We talked about what had happened since she and Ben left for England. She didn't criticise me for not telling her earlier. Maybe she would later. Eventually Jenny stopped me and said, 'You talked of a plan, Peter. Tell me about it.'

Jenny was focussing on the next steps and our family's safety. That was the important thing now.

I shared my thoughts and she didn't raise any objections, although I could see that she was still mulling it over, looking for snags, which was good.

'It might work,' she said finally, her face relaxing. She

snuggled close again. 'Who would have thought we would have to deal with things like this?' I could sense her inner strength and knew that she had a steely resolve when her mind was made up, and I so needed that now. I gave her a great hug and told her that I loved her.

When I got out of bed I went to the window and carefully prised back the curtain. It was a pleasant day, blue sky and with the few high clouds appearing light orange as they reflected the early morning sun. All looked quiet, but I knew that a vehicle could be parked in a passing place waiting for us.

We joined the others in the lounge and made ourselves the first coffee of the day. Brian and Jonathon were more casually dressed and without their camouflage trousers they looked less threatening. Poor Sally hadn't had an opportunity to change, with her room having been given over to us, and with a nod to Jenny she disappeared into her bedroom.

'You guys are welcome to stay, but the longer you are here the more likely you are to be discovered. What are your plans, Peter?' asked Brian, always to the point, with the subtext being that they wanted to get on with their own plans.

With a reassuring nod from Jenny, I outlined the plans. Not much was said, and Brian and Jonathon seemed to accept their minimal role. With everyone's agreement I then went outside to make the first phone call. Ronnie was in, but surprised to hear from me so early in the day. I got to the point, asking for help, and he listened carefully.

'So you want me at the pier, once you have got Ben and for me to take you over to the mainland.'

'That's right,' I replied, 'and I'll pay your fuel.'

'That's not the problem,' replied Ronnie. 'It's the people who are looking for you. It might get messy. Would you not be better throwing yourself on the mercy of the police?'

I outlined my reasons and Ronnie cautioned me. 'You might be getting into a lot of trouble and you could even end up inside. It'll be a long way to go to visit you.' He paused, waiting for a reply, and when I didn't make one he said, 'It's your call. Let me know when I have to pick you up. The tides should be in our favour any time after eleven this morning.'

'Thanks, Ronnie, I owe you one.'

'You sure do.' He cut the call.

Then Jenny phoned Susie from the bedroom, and they had a long conversation. When she re-emerged she looked happier.'

'A big apology from Susie to you, Peter,' Jenny said. 'She says that she's sorry for any misunderstanding. Feeling a bit of a fool, I think. It seems her ex left an old van behind in his haste to leave the island. Susie will bring Ben across in that. I'll drive, as the one less likely to be recognised, with Peter and Sally in the back and Ben on the booster seat beside me.'

I turned to Brian. 'Brian, you take your vehicle and turn left at the at the bottom of the farm road, then head towards Loch Indaal. Check if anyone is looking out for us, then phone us once you're through Bridgend. We'll then leave, cut through the minor roads to Islay Square and then join the road towards Port Askaig, further east. This allows us to bypass Bridgend, where the only road out of the Rhinns meets the Port Askaig road. That junction is likely to be watched,' I explained.

'If we time it right, and we have to, then Ronnie will be waiting to take us off the island. For the moment,' and I glanced at my watch, 'it is just after ten o'clock. We won't leave for another hour. Susie will bring Ben here in forty minutes.' I looked around at our band of brothers and sisters, everyone seemed on board, even Brian and Jonathon.

We stayed indoors with the curtains closed over and waited, with little conversation. I imagine this was how soldiers felt before they went into battle. I glanced at our two soldiers of fortune, but they seemed relaxed. I wondered if they had ever seen action; somehow I doubted it.

While we were waiting, I felt my phone vibrate, and took it out to look at the message.

'Islay distillery,' it read, and I looked at the time, '10.15.' I had forgotten to phone to say I wouldn't be in.

I opened the message.

> *Please contact Mr Gifford asap to explain absence.*
> *We need you in. Are you okay? Police were talking*
> *to Mr Gifford this morning. Please reply. Mrs Hall.*
> *PA to the distillery manager.*

More complications. I shared the message with Jenny. She frowned: 'It will work out okay, when they know the full details.' There was nothing I could do but hope that she was right and they would be understanding.

The house phone rang three times, the signal that Susie was leaving her house. I reckoned that if she left her smallholdings on the shores of Loch Gruinart, she should be here in fifteen minutes. I was so looking forward to seeing Ben again.

I noticed Jenny and Sally talking away and Sally was offering some of her clothes to Jenny; a friendship was being forged. I took Brian's binoculars and went back to the bedroom window, scanning the area for suspicious vehicles. I kept looking until I saw Susie's white van coming down onto the Gruinart Flats road from the Ardnave road, and checked that no vehicles were following. Then I heard a police siren and through a gap in the small wood in front of us, I saw a blue flashing light, heading towards Loch Gruinart. I waited to see if it turned right onto the road in front of the farm and was coming for me. I lost it for a minute and then I saw it racing down the straight section, by the Gruinart Flats, lights flashing. I watched Susie's van pull over into a passing place, and held my breath, until the police car shot past the van. I watched as it took the Ardnave road.

'Susie is almost here!' I shouted, and we finished our preparations.

The van turned and parked behind the cottage, out of sight of the road. Jenny and I both went out and released Ben's seat belt and I lifted him off his booster seat. He was so delighted to see me, dropping the colouring book he was holding, his face wreathed in smiles, and he gave me a great big hug. He was a daddy's boy with his mop of brown hair, but he had Jenny's green eyes. Jenny also received a big hug and Ben quickly showed me the pictures that he had been colouring in.

'A dragon, that's super,' I said recognising that his colouring in was improving.

Susie got out, avoiding direct eye contact with me, until I smiled and thanked her. She said very little, still embarrassed.

'I thought that the police car was going to stop you,' I said.

'I wondered for a minute, but it continued straight on. Andy Johnstone was in the passenger seat and even gave me a wave.'

'How regal,' I replied with a touch of sarcasm.

We quickly loaded the back of the van with our few possessions and Susie went into the cottage with a small backpack: her lunch, she explained. 'And I have left some sandwiches for you in the van,' she added. 'Don't worry about the van, it's no use to me.'

Brian and Jonathon clambered into their BMW and muttered about being back in an hour and drove off. They would deliver Susie home when they returned. I went back to the window and scanned the moorland again. There was now an ambulance with a blue flashing light tearing down the road on the Gruinart Flats. That seemed better, a visitor must have fallen and hurt themselves, hopefully nothing too serious, and it did take away one of the few police cars on the island and meant that there was one less to look for us.

I watched the black BMW leave, turning left and heard it rumbling over a cattle grid. Ten minutes later, Brian phoned. 'No suspicious vehicles that we could see. Good luck.'

We thanked Susie for being a great help and we trooped out to the van. Ben was strapped in the front seat and Sally and I clambered into the back, lying down on the floor, gripping the inner wooden frame for stability.

'Behave yourself, you two,' Jenny said, laughing. 'Remember I have got a rear view mirror.' We shut the doors at the back and made ourselves comfortable. Jenny reversed the van, turned it around and drove down the driveway, and followed the route of the BMW. It was a twisty road, with Islay's usual undulations, passing through open fields, with cattle wandering freely. The van braked a few times, as cattle slowly cleared off the road. We reached the junction with the Bruichladdich road in good time and Jenny turned left. A car passed, with the driver giving the customary Islay wave, a local, and we followed the road around a sharp left hand bend, skirting a wood on the left with the loch to the right. Jenny quickly reached the junction at Whin Park, and turned left rattling over a cattle grid onto to a rough surface. There was no other car in sight, so far so good.

When you have been to the Islay show, held annually in fields around here, you knew that there were several small minor roads, part of the Islay Estate, which led through to Islay Square, the nearest that Islay has to a retail park, with old converted farm steadings, occupied by several local businesses. We didn't stop, but continued through, until we reached the Port Askaig road, and turned left.

It was frustrating for Sally and me. Other than forward, we could not see what was happening. Jenny needed more eyes to be alert for danger, yet if I was seen, then the danger would be magnified. The stretch of road led towards Port Askaig, where there was a ferry terminal at the foot of a steep curving road. Cyclists leaving the ferry usually ended up pushing their bikes up the steep incline. However, Port Askaig was not our destination.

We reached the small village of Ballygrant and passed through, keeping to the speed limit, not wanting to alert any police or draw attention to ourselves, and continued east towards the road end for Finlaggan. I tried not to dwell on my day there with Catherine. If that day marked the end of my childhood, goodness knows how I would look back on today, in future years. As we neared the junction, Jenny called back: 'A car waiting at the junction, two men in the front and another in the back seat. The driver is smoking, his window down and he is giving us a lot of attention. He has just thrown his cigarette out and is starting the engine. This is not looking good.'

I changed my position, straining to look out at the car, a black Audi. I saw instantly what Jenny meant.

'Not far to go, don't accelerate or they will be certain that we suspect them.'

Jenny agreed, but I could see her grip the steering wheel more tightly. We passed the road end and drove on.

'The car has pulled out,' Jenny said, 'and is following us.'

We passed the small village of Keills. Ahead the Paps of Jura loomed large, appearing to be directly at the end of the road. A few cyclists were using the cycle route on the other side of the road.

'Almost there,' she said. 'They are not speeding up, just tailing us. The front seat passenger is on his mobile. He is now speaking to the driver, issuing instructions. Here we go, the driver is accelerating, going to overtake. He is level, I am going to ignore him. He signalling for me to pull over.'

I kept my head down.

'Are you sure that they are not police?' I asked.

'Yes, the backseat passenger's window is going down and he has just produced a shotgun.'

'Acknowledge them and try to stop, before the turn-off to Bunnahabhain distillery.'

'Slowing down. The car has stopped and the guy in the back is jumping out.'

'Accelerate hard past them and take the road to Bunnahabhain distillery.'

The van picked up speed as the guy with the shotgun motioned to Jenny to stop, but had to jump back as the van sped past. Something metallic hit the van, probably the shotgun.

'He's getting back into the car,' said Jenny, her voice louder, surging with adrenaline.

'You're doing great,' shouted Sally. 'Don't slow down!' Sally and I were thrown against each other as Jenny turned off the main road and accelerated. Ahead was a sharp right bend, at a pottery shop, but we made it on two wheels, the tyres screeching.

'Is this exciting, Ben?' I asked, not wanting to scare him.

'I feel sick, Dad,' he replied, which was not the answer I wanted.

'Don't worry, not far to go,' I replied. *Only four miles* I added to myself. But it was going to be a long four miles on a very poor road. No wonder Bunnahabhain didn't get as many visitors as other distilleries. I let Jenny concentrate on driving, assuming that the Audi would be, by now, on our tail.

We passed Loch nam Ban on the left, the water supply for the nearby Coal Ila distillery. I wondered why my mind had churned up that information.

'They are behind us, a few bends away,' Jenny said.

'Ardnahoe Loch coming up on the left. We are making progress.' I had fished with Ronnie there one night and we were driven away by the midges. Hopefully Ronnie would be waiting for us.

'Campervan ahead. It's okay, he's pulling over, letting us through.'

Jenny drew level with the campervan, having to slow to a crawl to get past and suddenly wound down her window, catching the attention of the driver.

'You don't know how to drive on these roads! You're useless! I am going to report you,' Jenny shouted at him angrily.

'Keep cool,' I said, before I realised what Jenny was attempting. I could just see the driver, an innocent victim of our charade, his face reddening with anger, exploding with indignation. Jenny sounded her horn and angrily gesticulated at him and drove on fast. The campervan pulled away – and the Audi came around the bend and had to break hard. There was no space for it to pass. We heard horns sounding. Jenny had bought us some time. The road continued to twist and turn until we were above Bunnahabhain Bay, where it dropped down to the distillery, past some ruined former distillery workers' houses.

'Is Ronnie's boat there?' I asked.

'Can't see it,' Jenny replied, and Sally cast me a serious look.

'Daddy!' shouted Ben. 'I am going to be sick.'

'Hold on, Ben, we are almost there.' This time I wasn't lying.

'I can see his boat coming around the headland,' shouted Jenny, with relief.

We drove down fast into the distillery, past buildings on both sides and stopped on the pier, abandoning the van in the middle of the pier. A tour guide was startled as he escorted a tour party from the visitor lounge across to the main distillery buildings, shouting that we were going too fast.

Ronnie's boat was now almost at the pier, his head above the Perspex canopy, and Maria was holding out a wooden bargepole with a brass hook as the boat edged closer to wooden steps. She used it to pull the boat in the final few yards.

'Quick, out the van and take what we can.' We piled out, with Ben holding his stomach and starting to retch. I looked up at the road, which could be seen above the distillery buildings and saw the Audi racing down. It was going to be close.

Maria was now up on the pier, hooking a rope over a bollard.

'No time,' I shouted and pointed to the car. 'We must go!'

Ben had stopped retching: I picked him up and carried him to the edge of the pier. Sally was already down in the rigid inflatable boat, putting our few possessions in it. Jenny climbed down the steps, followed by Maria. I handed Ben over to Sally. I had started to follow when with a squeal of tyres the Audi turned the corner, passed the distillery buildings on the sea side and braked hard, swerving to avoid the van. The men jumped out, racing to stop us, as I scrambled into the boat. Ronnie saw what was happening throttled the engines as one of the men reached the edge of the pier, holding out a pistol with two hands, in front of him.

'Stop!' he shouted, but Sally reacted quickly, grabbing the bargepole and hooking him around the ankle and pulling hard. He wobbled for a minute, teetering on the edge, and then toppled into the frothing wake left by our engines as we roared away from the pier.

The other two were left helpless as we put distance between us and them.

'My God,' said Ronnie.' You were not joking. The bastards would have killed you. Us,' he corrected himself.

'Well done, lady,' he said, turning to Sally.

'I'm Sally,' she said. 'Pleased to meet you.'

Jenny was hugging Ben, calming him down.

'We got away from the bad men,' she said and looked across at me. 'For the moment.'

'I have a thermos flask of hot coffee,' said Maria, as she handed out lifejackets to us. 'Anyone interested?'

We all accepted her offer. That had all been too close and Jenny was right.

I went over to Jenny and Ben and put my arms around them. Ben was upset. 'Bad men,' he kept repeating.

Ronnie had now manoeuvred his boat past an old wrecked fishing boat on the southern edge of Bunnahabhain Bay, out into the middle of the Sound of Islay. With a strong racing current aiding us, we made rapid progress, soon passing the Caol Ila distillery, set in yet another cove and then, beyond the next headland, the Port Askaig ferry terminal. The Islay ferry had probably just left Kennacraig, on the mainland, and the CalMac jetty was empty. The company's buildings sat at the bottom of cliffs. We saw empty spaces where cars would soon start to queue for the next ferry, and the hotel, and the lifeboat which operated from there. The Jura ferry, which used a different ferry slip nearer to the Port Askaig Hotel, had just reached the island of Jura and we could hear its ramp going down with a clang on the concrete slip.

Ronnie kept the speed up, the deep V-shaped hull of his RIB hydroplaning, cresting waves and then crashing down, which didn't help Ben. Indeed, only Ronnie and Maria seemed immune to queasiness. We passed the McArthur's Head lighthouse, on Islay, perched on the cliff-edge, and started to turn towards Jura before heading across the open water to the mainland.

Ronnie let Maria take the wheel and came back to sit beside us.

'I can drop you off at Tayvallich, in Loch Sween, where the Jura passenger service terminates. There is a bus service from there to Lochgilphead.' He studied our reaction and saw that I was uncomfortable. He thought some more. 'But they might set up a reception party. I sometimes stop at a friend's, I don't think that you know him, Peter, who has a small jetty, just south of Tayvallich. I keep a car there for trips on the mainland, an old Ford Mondeo. Use it and get your business done. Be careful.' And without trying to alarm Ben further, he added, 'Not nice people. I won't ask your destination, in case someone questions me. In fact I think that we will try and stay at our friend's tonight.'

We entered Loch Sween, glad that the sea became calmer, helping to settle our stomachs, and shortly after moored at a small jetty at the bottom of a long garden which led up to a bungalow that had a conservatory built on the wall facing the sea.

An elderly couple came out to greet us and ushered us in. Ronnie must have contacted them while I had been trying to sleep during the last hour. They introduced themselves as Tim and Elizabeth. Elizabeth promptly took Ben into the house to clean him up and Tim made us hot drinks and we finally ate the sandwiches that Susie had made for us. Ronnie went away to take the tarpaulin off his car and get it started. Tim searched for, and found, a booster seat for Ben from the back of his garage.

Ronnie, by now, had driven the blue Mondeo to the front of the house. Ronnie hugged Jenny and then Sally, his serious face reflecting his deep concern. He shook my hand and then hugged me too.

'Good luck, old friend,' he said simply. As Jenny got into the driver's seat Maria ran and hugged her and then gave me a big kiss on the cheek. Ben was looking very sombre, not looking forward to another journey. Sally got into the back of the car beside him, and with final directions from Ronnie, we drove out of the driveway and headed north. My mood matched Ben's.

27

Friday pm

We left Tim and Elizabeth's house, watching them wave us goodbye as we drove away, and passed a nature reserve before continuing north, towards Tayvallich, a pretty village with a pontoon for visiting yachts, where I had imagined that we would have been getting off Ronnie's boat. However, Ronnie had felt that if there was someone looking out for us, this is where they would be waiting. Hopefully, Ronnie's caution was unnecessary but his offer of a car had been an unexpected bonus. The disadvantage of the Mondeo, however, was that the occupants could easily been seen; there was no tinted glass, so anyone looking for us would soon spot us. I sat in the front beside Jenny with Ben, on his booster seat, in the rear behind me and Sally behind Jenny.

Jenny was happy to drive, but there was a long journey ahead, three plus hours, so we would each take turns. All this was going through my head as we encountered the first houses of the Tayvallich and saw a corrugated metal coffee shop next to the pontoon.

'There is a police car beside that metal building,' said Jenny, but I immediately noticed that no one was in it. As we drove on Jenny smiled, as she looked in the rear view mirror. 'They were getting coffee,' she said, 'so no high alert.'

'Going to Colin's is the best idea,' Jenny proclaimed, a while later, as she drove. 'I tried to phone him when we were crossing to the mainland, while you were sleeping, but got no reply. I know roughly where he lives in Ayr. Mum and Colin lived on the Robinson's farm for many years, in a small farm worker's cottage, at the entrance to the farm, by the road. It's demolished now. He must remember a lot about the Robinsons.'

I recollected seeing the cottage on the old map that Brian had showed me last night. I had wondered where Jenny's mum had lived, before the flat in Bowmore; now I knew.

'I have a few other questions for him. Time to get some answers to my family's troubled past,' Jenny continued. 'I don't know who Colin's father was or even mine. Probably even Mum doesn't know,' reflected Jenny ruefully. I turned and checked that Ben was asleep, not that he would have been able to follow the conversation. His head was rolled to one side and his eyes closed, the colouring book still clutched firmly to his body.

'He might also be able to tell us how the Robinsons got caught up in the drug crowd or the situation that led to them being involved,' I said.

'Let's not get ahead of ourselves,' Jenny cautioned, 'but at least we should be out of trouble, where we are going.'

I saw Jenny glancing, at Sally in the rear view mirror, checking that she was asleep.

'Do you believe that there was gold on that ship?'

'Yes, I do,' I replied. 'I saw the gold coin that Brian found last night in the cavern. I also talked to Beattie, a few days ago, and he confirmed that the authorities knew about the gold and had searched for it on the island. They suspected the Robinsons, but couldn't find any even after searching their farm. Sally claimed there is a company in London still receiving gold from Islay, as recently as this year.'

'Interesting,' said Jenny. 'Another question for Colin. I hope that he is cooperative. For both our sakes we have to resolve all the issues caused by the Robinsons. They have blighted our lives for too long.'

We drove on, mostly in silence, reaching a road that ran parallel to the Crinan Canal, then drove into Lochgilphead and north to Inverary, with Loch Fyne to our right. The late afternoon sunshine was warming the car and I lowered the car window for some fresh air. Sally was still asleep in the back. We passed through Inverary, where we were stopped at traffic lights controlling the traffic over a narrow bridge as we left the small town. We continued north, eventually reaching the head of Loch Fyne. Cars pulling caravans were slowing down the traffic, heading away from Glasgow for the weekend.

We reached the Rest and be Thankful, a high pass from which we would drive down to Arrochar, and were getting closer to Loch Lomond and the main road south, the A82. Argyll's indented coastline certainly added to the length of the journey, which I would normally have enjoyed, with the scenic views over lochs and hills, but today I was just impatient and fretful. I kept looking behind to see if we were being followed, becoming anxious about a black Mazda, that appeared to be always just two or three cars back, but it took the road for Lochgoilhead, near to the Rest and be Thankful.

We stopped at Luss, a popular tourist stopping place on the banks of Loch Lomond, for a comfort stop, and took a walk to stretch our legs. Sally, who had woken up, offered to take Ben a little further and we accepted. The two were getting on well. Sally seemed anxious to be supportive, not wanting to intrude, giving Jenny and me space. She took Ben away, along the narrow beach towards a small pier, which gave us a chance to talk, in private.

'Any reply from Colin?' I enquired.

Jenny examined a message received on her phone. 'He is travelling back, been away on business, can't see us until tomorrow. Mandy, his wife, is at home, but he didn't offer us a bed or hospitality.' She shrugged and added, 'Colin can be difficult.'

'We'll need to find an hotel,' I said, but Jenny was ahead of me, using her phone as she spoke, and a couple of minutes later she said: 'I've booked us into the Horizon Hotel on the sea front, at Ayr. It is a couple of miles from where I believe Colin lives. I have another text from him, he'll see us tomorrow at ten. He's not over friendly,' warned Jenny again as we clutched our disposable cups of coffee, sipping at the hot sweet liquid. 'We were never that close, there were twelve years between us after all, and he was desperate to leave Islay. Amongst other things, he didn't want to share the make down bed with me, not surprisingly. Hated living in that hovel we called home and has never been back to the island. As you know Christmas cards, most years were all we had. It will be interesting to finally meet his wife. Even Mum wasn't at the wedding.'

'I'm not surprised he left,' I said.

Jenny agreed, but added, 'He is very introverted with a bit of a temper. It didn't make life easy.' It was a reminder of how tough life had been for Jenny and how proud I was of her for all that she had achieved subsequently.

I took over the driving after Luss, giving Jenny a rest. A short distance south of Luss, we reached Balloch and the open countryside was gradually replaced by houses and factories as we entered the industrial central belt of Scotland. We crossed from the north to the south side of the River Clyde over the Erskine Bridge, just after we had passed through Dumbarton, and then travelled towards the centre of Glasgow, passing Glasgow Airport, before joining the M77 which took us south to Ayrshire. The road was fast and we soon saw Ailsa Craig, that isolated lump of granite, off the Ayrshire coast, well known to those travelling by sea between Scotland and Ireland as Paddy's Milestone. The high, jagged peaks of the Island of Arran were also prominent to the west. I had never been to Ayr and looked around with interest as we followed the bypass round by Prestwick Airport, before turning into the town and reaching the sea front where our hotel was located, a modern building, just set back from the long concrete promenade.

We checked in and as Sally and Jenny wanted to rest, I took Ben out to give them peace. The beach was busy, packed with day visitors from Glasgow, by the sound of their accents. I took Ben along to a play park and watched him playing for an hour, getting him an ice cream on the way back to the hotel.

The four of us later had a meal in the hotel restaurant, watching the sun dip behind the peaks of Arran, turning the sea a glorious red colour. We turned in early and slept well, feeling safe for the first time in a while.

28

Saturday

Next day, we drove out to Doonfoot, a suburb of Ayr a short distance from where we had been staying, passing the entrance to Bellisle Park, and after crossing a bridge over the River Doon, we turned right to reach the sea front. Colin lived in a big house, right on the front, separated from the sea by only a road and grass-covered sand dunes. We looked at each other in surprise as we parked. How could he afford this?

Colin was waiting for us, a tall gaunt figure silhouetted in the doorway of his house, watching us as we parked in the driveway. I saw him note Sally's presence and he seemed to ignore Ben, which was surprising given that this was the first time he had seen him. Behind him, I could see someone I assumed must be Mandy, a slightly built lady, her hair prematurely streaked with grey, tense, I thought, at meeting us. Jenny and I shared a knowing glance and Jenny immediately started smiling, being friendly and making an effort to bridge the gap.

'Come in, I'm pleased to see you,' said Colin, but his face conveyed a different impression, his eyes avoiding mine. I only had a vague memory of Colin from school days. He had been invited to our wedding, but had not managed to attend, nor had he made his own mother's funeral, although that was less surprising.

'This is a lovely house,' said Jenny brightly, as she got out the car. 'And what wonderful views.' She paused, looking around, and then added, 'You even have your own ruined castle.' She pointed to a ruined castle on a nearby headland, which was already fascinating Ben.

'And this is Ben, your nephew,' said Jenny, freeing Ben's seatbelt and helping him out of the car. I noticed Mandy smiling, but there was little reaction from Colin.

We all walked into a large lounge which extended from the front to the back of the house. Through patio doors at the rear I could see an extensive garden, mostly grass. There were only a few stunted bushes, but I think that was down more to the sandy soil, and was not necessarily a lack of gardening expertise.

We all sat down, Ben sitting beside Sally, and Jenny opposite me.

The awkward silence continued for a few seconds before Colin said, 'Get them tea, Mandy,' with an sharp edge that we all immediately noticed. Mandy dutifully trooped out of the room and we heard noises from the kitchen as cups and saucers were gathered.

'Colin, thanks for seeing us,' started Jenny. 'I know that you are busy, but we are staying a couple of nights in the vicinity and we wanted to see you. This is Sally, a friend.'

Colin barely acknowledged Sally. The conversation was painful, like talking to a brick wall.

Questions about his job (he worked for a building company), how he liked living here (it was an attractive area), were parried with grunts and little in the way of a verbal response, the bare minimum. Mandy returned and placed the tray with the cups and saucers on a low table, and then brought through tea and biscuits, glancing at Colin, almost seeking permission, before she passed the plate of biscuits around. Jenny had told me to expect an uncomfortable occasion, but this was dreadful and I was riled at his treatment of Mandy.

Sally broke the ice by suggesting that she take Ben for a walk. She got up quickly and went out the front door and we saw her reach the grassy dunes across the road, holding hands with Ben.

'Well,' started Jenny, when Sally had gone. 'It's a long time since we had a chance to catch up, Colin, and Mandy. I am pleased to finally meet you,' she continued determinedly. 'It is too long since I have talked to my brother.'

'Half-brother,' Colin interjected.

Jenny replied directly. 'I am your only family. We might not know our fathers, but we shared a mum, who had lots of faults but....'

'If this a search for missing family history, then stop. I don't want to discuss it. Mandy knows how upset I get talking about my family. It is difficult for her to live with me because of my moods and temper.'

At least, he showed some self-awareness, I thought.

'Who is your father, Colin?' I asked quietly, not wanting to rouse him any further, but not willing for Jenny to be blocked from bringing the subject up.

Colin twisted towards me and spat out, 'Charles Robinson, of course.'

Jenny looked shocked, me less so. His behaviour was rude and domineering, and that was so Robinson-like. His appearance, even without the Robinson nose, suggested a link, the narrow face, the scrawny look. I had wondered as soon as I had stepped out of the car.

'You never told me that before,' Jenny replied, trying to remain calm.

'Long before you were born, I lived on the Robinson's farm with your mother,' – I thought that was a telling comment – 'in a tied cottage, by the entrance to the farm. It was demolished not long before you were born, and we were made homeless. Mother was Charles Robinson's bit on the side, when he was bored and he couldn't find anyone else, and few wanted him, I've heard. Mother's husband had died and she was on her own and he used her, took full advantage of her vulnerability. He visited several times a week. I was always put out, but I could hear them. She didn't put up much of a fight or show much interest in me.'

'She was helpless, on her own, vulnerable, had no money,' pleaded Jenny.

'Don't make excuses, she could have left the island. He never acknowledged me and when his wife came along, he didn't stop, even after his wife found out. Oh, Robinson and his wife certainly had big battles, as Mrs Robinson started to understand the mistake she had made.'

There was an increasingly angry edge to Colin's voice, his face becoming florid. Mandy sat quietly, looking down, not wanting to draw attention to herself, anxious, her hands clasped together.

'So you see why I don't want contact. Too many memories, nightmares, a story of control and manipulation and I could do nothing to stop it, with her weakly complying.' The final words were almost lost, as his voice cracked. So much pent-up emotion.

'Maybe she was trying to protect you but couldn't cope. It was an abusive relationship but such things were often swept under the carpet, not talked about, in the past,' Jenny said. 'And if you won't acknowledge Mum, then surely you can talk to me. I did you no wrong and I appreciated the support you gave me, the nights we had to move out for our safety. The night,' and Jenny hesitated, 'when you saved me from that man who wasn't just satisfied with our mother. Half-sister, or sister, which I would prefer, you mean a lot to me. I would like the opportunity to repay you.'

I looked at Colin. His tense facial expression eased, some of the high colour fading. Jenny's comments had connected, a link had been established.

'I understood why you left the island and why you didn't turn up for mother's funeral. You had had enough, but I am different now. Notice the name change, my husband, my wee boy? I am willing to share that with you, want to, love to, if you will let me. And I didn't know who your father was and I think I can, though we have to talk more, begin to understand the depth of your feelings.'

'We all hate the Robinsons,' I put in, 'for different reasons, but you know they mustn't control us. We have to move on or they will have won.' Given our present predicament, maybe I had gone too far in being so placatory, but I wanted to support Jenny, who must be finding this all very difficult.

I saw Mandy nodding, tentatively stretching a hand towards her husband, gently rubbing his back.

'Peter's right,' she said, and Colin turned quickly towards her. I thought he was going to tell her to shut up, but he didn't; instead he looked uncomfortable and he picked up his cup and drank some of his tea.

'Did you know who my father is? Is he still around?' asked Jenny, and I could sense how wound up she was, wanting an answer but preparing herself for a revelation that she might not like. I wanted to put my arm around her, comfort her, support her, realising how much this quest meant to her.

Colin thought carefully before replying, 'I think that he is dead, but I am not sure.' I felt that he was holding something back, for whatever reason. 'There was a big argument one morning when Charles Robinson almost broke down the door and screamed at her for meeting someone, some man, the previous night, demanding to know what she had told him. Robinson had received a phone call about it from a cousin who worked in a hotel. I believed that I had seen the worse of Robinson, but this was off the scale.'

'When was this?' I asked, curious.

'It must have been 1984, because it was the year that we left the farm, which was just before we found out that she was pregnant, with you. He ordered us both out of the cottage and off the island. She should have gone, it would have been easier, but she went to see the Rev Walker, looking for a place to stay, and he went to the farm. Brave man. Told Robinson what he was going to say from the pulpit the next Sunday, if Robinson didn't provide for them. We paid no rent, not that the flat was worth much, until you left school, Jenny, thanks to Rev Walker.'

Tears were now running down Jenny's face, whether it was because of the emotion or because, like me, she was starting to piece together the significance of the timings, I couldn't tell. Maybe both. I remembered my conversation with Beattie, which now seemed so long ago. Beattie had not suggested that the American was Jenny's father, but the implication had been there, the timing. I had just chosen not to probe further. I moved over to Jenny's seat and sat on the arm of it and put a protective arm around her.

I heard the front door open and shut and Sally appeared at the lounge door with Ben. I raised my hand, gesturing that this was not a good time and she moved away from the door and no one else noticed her presence or Ben's.

'I was the reason for us leaving the farm?' questioned Jenny.

'Yes,' said Colin.

'Robinson wasn't my father?'

'No,' said Colin firmly. 'No one could be certain, not even your mother, given that she slept around, but my money would be on the American pilot who was killed leaving the island. He called in at the farm; I can't remember the reasons he gave, but he tried to become our best friends. He asked lots of questions, some strange ones.'

'About gold?' I butted in.

'Yes, how did you know that?' But Colin's reaction was strange, crossing his arms, looking down, immediately becoming more defensive.

'Most people on Islay have heard the story of the *Empire Constellation* and the unexplained wealth of the Robinsons,' I replied, and added, 'What did you know about the gold?'

Colin became agitated again, Mandy quickly withdrew her hand, reading the runes.

'Is that why you are here. Oh, lovely house. How come you have done so well? It's too late the gold has been spent.'

There was silence for a minute, as the implications of that statement sank in.

'We are not after your gold. Keep it. Spend it as you like, it hasn't brought you much happiness, that I can see,' said Jenny.

'How did you get it, Colin?' I asked.

Colin shrugged. 'Okay,' he replied. 'I was a small boy. I had always been warned about not going into the cavern or storage area, or cave as we called it. Keep away, ghosts, stories about evil spirits destined to make Donald and me scared. One day I was alone on the farm and the cavern doors were left unlocked by mistake. I went in, curious, and found a pile of gold coins in the corner, hidden under a old blanket. Stupidly, I took quite a few of them.'

That sounded like quite a lot to me.

'And I hid them in our house. A few hours later I heard Robinson raging. Donald got most of the flak, which struck me as unfair. What a beating he gave Donald and then he came looking for me, but by this time I had hidden the coins across the road, underneath a bush, covering them with stones. I got thumped, but reckoned it would be worse if I owned up. He eventually left me and returned to start on Donald again.'

Which I felt helped to explain why Donald had been so keen to inform on Catherine, the day I had gone to play at their house and eat with the Robinsons.

'I never returned the gold coins. Eventually I hid them under the ruins of an old croft, at Duich Lots, off the High Road, where no one would find them. I took them with me when I went to Glasgow, and sold them to a dodgy dealer...'

'And that's how you got the money for the house?' Jenny asked.

'No, but enough to get us a small deposit.'

'Wonderful,' said Jenny. 'You screwed the bastards. Well done.'

'Good on you,' I added.

Colin looked surprised by our reactions.

'Anyone who upsets the Robinsons, gets our appreciation,' I explained.

'You enjoy the windfall, God knows you have suffered enough,' Jenny said. 'Good news, Peter,' she said to me, and I nodded in agreement.

'Was there a furnace for smelting gold in the cave?' I asked.

'Not by then, it had been removed to a barn, at Kilchiaran Bay, in the sixties. No one would have looked for it there.'

'Is there any gold left?' Jenny asked.

'There should be, but Robinson spent a lot of the money. I believe that he ran up large gambling debts. In the eighties, he also started holding stuff for people, using the storage area. There were always people arriving at strange times. He was sucked into working with harden criminals. I met Donald one night, in Bowmore, and he was very drunk and told me some things that were going on.'

274

So much made sense to me now. Why Catherine and I were warned not to go near the storage area, under the hill. How Charles Robinson was brought down by his own greed and lack of self-control.

'So many questions,' said Jenny. 'Can you answer this one for me. Why was I called Dakota when I was young?'

'I don't think that she ever knew the American's name, so she called you after the state he came from. Maybe it was her way of winding up Robinson. Robinson's wife never believed that the American was your father; she assumed that it was her husband, and it really soured relationships in the family. Hard to think that they could have been any worse.'

'North Dakota is where I come from,' said Sally, entering the room with Ben. 'And I think that Colin is right about the choice of name.'

'So, I am half-American,' said Jenny, barely managing to absorb the news.

'The things that you learn about your wife,' I said, a poor attempt at jocularity.

The briefest of smiles played on her face as she glanced at me, but she was finding all this hard to take in.

'I believe that the American was called Ryan Loudoun III, that's what Beattie knew him as.'

'Ryan Loudoun III,' repeated Jenny, her face blank, experiencing too many emotions for one to be dominant. She was silent for a minute before saying, 'I am so glad that we came, Colin. You have no idea how much you have helped me. I have a lot to think about. I am so sorry that you had such a hard time when you were younger and I am so pleased that you took the gold. You deserved that, for all that you went through. I couldn't have made it if it hadn't been for you.' She got up went to Colin and hugged him, and then went to Mandy and hugged her. Colin was still too tense to respond, but Mandy threw her arms around Jenny and warmly embraced her.

'So, how long have you lived here,' Jenny said brightly. 'It's such a beautiful location, not as nice as Machir Bay, of course,' she added with a smile, 'but very similar.'

'Are you staying at Machir Bay?' Colin asked.

''Yes, in my parents' old house,' I said.

'Your father was a good teacher. Helpful to me,' Colin replied.

'He's living in Iona, since Mum died,' I told him, and he seemed genuinely sorry to hear about Mum.

More tea was brought and an hour passed as the healing process began and we started to catch up on the events in our lives. Eventually, I could see Ben getting restless and I suggested that we leave and take him somewhere.

'Colin and Mandy, it has been so nice to meet you,' I said, 'and I would like to invite you both to Islay, very soon. We can show you the beautiful side of Islay.' Jenny agreed, pleased that I had suggested the visit.

They stood at the door, Mandy with her arm wrapped around Colin's waist, as we reversed out of the driveway.

'Where do we begin?' I said, as we drove away from the house, adding, 'Ben you were so well behaved. Like an ice cream?'

'I noticed that there is a coffee shop just over the bridge. I would love a coffee. Tea is not really my thing,' Jenny said.

'And I noticed that there was a sign for a play area in the park we passed. We could stop there and take a break and drink our coffee,' Sally suggested.

A few minutes later we were parked in front of an old mansion house that had become a hotel and was now being renovated, the building surrounded by security fencing. We sat on a black coated metal seat beside a large grassy area, fringed by mature trees. Ben heard chimes coming from the play area, which was partially obscured by the trees, and with ice cream in one hand and Sally holding the other, they went to look for it, leaving Jenny and me alone.

'How do you feel?' I said.

'There is so much to take in,' she replied. 'I'll need to look Ryan Loudoun III up on the internet.

'I already have,' I replied, and Jenny looked at me, surprised.

'I got the name from Beattie the other day and Googled him. He was a bit of an adventurer, flying to the island, having heard rumours about the gold, Beattie said. But here is the interesting fact: he was a very skilled artist. His paintings, particularly since his death, are sold for considerable sums of money. That could be where your artistic genes come from. Oh, and he also had your eye colouring.'

'This is a crazy day, Peter, and in time...' She ran out of words.

We held hands and sat quietly for a few minutes before I got up to put my crumpled coffee cup in the bin. A car had driven up beside us and I noticed a very tall man get out, releasing his collie dog from the back seat. The dog immediately circled him, waiting, and the man stooped, picked up a stick from the grass, and threw it for the dog.

'Just like Jodie, she has got a blue eye,' I said.

Jenny smiled. 'I am so looking forward to getting her back.

I laughed and Jenny looked puzzled.

'If we told that man what we have been through in the last week, he wouldn't believe us,' I said, by way of explanation. 'Which reminds me, I better check the phone for any messages.'

I turned on my phone; there were three messages. The first was from Alison.

> *There were traces of rohypnol in your urine. It is a date rape drug. One of its effects is complete or partial amnesia.*

277

I showed the message to Jenny and she looked relieved. 'That will be helpful, when we return to the island.'

The second message was from Malcolm

A woman's body was found near Loch Gruinart
yesterday. She was murdered.

I remembered the police car with its flashing lights and the ambulance. 'Who was it?' I wondered. But I think I had already guessed. My heart thumping fast; I felt dizzy. Before I showed Jenny the message I opened the last one, sent just an hour ago.

The woman is Catherine Robinson. Police looking
for you. Maybe we should talk? Malcolm.

Jenny, stood up, when she heard me groan in horror, and snatched the phone from my hand, quickly reading the last two messages.

'The curse of the Robinson's has struck again,' she said, her face drained of colour. 'Oh, Peter.' She hugged me tight, not capable of finding any other words.

As we stood there lost in our thoughts, I heard a siren in the distance coming closer, the pitch of the siren changing as it sped along the main road in our direction. Then I saw flashing blue lights through the fringe of trees. Briefly, I thought that they had travelled on, but then I saw the lights, now closer, through the trees from the approach road to the car park, the road we had driven in, and a police car appeared, bouncing over the speed bumps. It braked right beside us. From the other direction another police car approached and braked.

A senior policeman with braid on his cap got out of the first car and came up to me.

'Peter Meldrum?'

I nodded, my mouth too dry to speak.

'I am arresting you on suspicion of murdering Catherine Robinson. You do not have to say anything. But it may harm your defence if you do not mention when questioned something which you rely on later in court. Anything you do say may be given in evidence.'

Before I could react a police constable slipped handcuffs on me, and led me to the back seat of the waiting police car. It all happened so quickly. I turned to see a policewoman comforting Jenny, now slumped on the bench. In the distance, I saw Sally and Ben running towards me. The very tall man with his dog was looking, from the trees, at the edge of the lawn, incredulous at the scene unfolding in front of him. He could never understand what we had been through.

29

The next hour was a blur. Etched in my mind was the shocked look on Jenny's face and Ben who had started crying and shouting about: 'Bad men taking Daddy,' as I was bundled into the police car. I was whisked away and my handcuffs were removed once I reached Ayr Police Station, which was only a five-minute ride, a brick and concrete building, dating from the sixties, with a church behind it. The duty sergeant read me my rights and told me that I could be held for twenty-four hours without being charged. I was fingerprinted, a DNA swab taken, my possessions and phone removed. I was then placed in a cell and when the cell door was locked, I slumped on the simple waterproofed blue mattress, on a metal plinth, gagging at the foul smell from the open stainless-steel toilet. The cell walls covered in graffiti, the scribbling of previous occupants, most of whom seemed angry, sex crazed or on drugs. Little natural light filtered through the glazed brick window at the far end of the cell, but a bare bulb in the ceiling provided a harsher light, which flooded the area. There was a sliding glass portal in the heavy metal door which allowed me to be observed.

I had little option but to wait and see what was going to happen next. I couldn't believe that Catherine had been murdered.

I didn't even know that she was still on the island. I felt shocked and upset: for it was horrifying, and so sad, a tragic end.

I didn't have to wait long until I heard the key turn in the lock and the door opened. I looked up and immediately recognised the man who came in, even before he sat down at the other end of the bed. He was the guy from the Lochside Hotel, not wearing an Ardbeg T-shirt this time, but a tartan shirt hanging loose over his denims. He looked very tired, his face lined, his greying hair making him look older than I remembered, and that was not yet a week ago.

'Hello, Mr Meldrum,' he said, with no recognisable accent and a quite deep voice, croaky sounding, as if it had been damaged by smoking.

'I recognise you from the Lochside Hotel,' I said, 'and in the car, at the American monument.' But any slight sense of getting an advantage was soon squashed.

'Just the hotel? You are not very observant.' The voice sounded cold now, with a tone of contempt. Maybe he recognised that, for he changed tactic.

'Call me Nick. May I call you Peter?

'Are you a policeman?'

'Sort of.' He smiled, but the smile hardly spread across his face, a flicker, barely moving any facial muscles. He wasn't going to give much away.

'Do I not get a lawyer?'

'You can, but it will only make matters more complicated, delay your release. We need your cooperation, time is short, we need to speak, urgently. Catherine Robinson's actions in saving you and what you did by visiting the farm have caused havoc, and wrecked carefully laid plans, undone a lot of hard work. Due to you, we might miss out on a significant prize,' he added. I think that he regretted Catherine saving me. Nice guy.

'I'll cooperate.' What had I to lose? I was sitting forward on the edge of the mattress, my elbows resting on my knees, eyes fixed on the far wall. I wanted to be back with Jenny and Ben. I'd do anything. 'I want to know why you arrested me on the suspicion of murdering, Catherine.' I turned to confront Nick.

'As I said, you are here because of your stupidity and the damage you are doing to an operation that has been years in the planning, and for your own safety. Believe me, if they could get a hold of you, you would be dead, just like Catherine Robinson, bound and gagged, your throat slit and left to bleed to death in a peat bog.' The details of her death, added to make a point, to emphasise the seriousness of the situation.

'When her body was found by one of the wardens at the RSPB visitor centre, you were immediately a prime suspect to the local police. They told me that you have history with Catherine. Believe me they are not totally persuaded of your innocence. It has taken a lot to convince them otherwise, and for me to be able to speak like this to you. There will be angry exchanges but they will be held above my pay grade.

'One of the wardens remembers you acting suspiciously on Wednesday morning, around the time, we believe, that the victim was killed, talking about a rare bird you claimed to have sighted, maybe trying to establish an alibi, she thought, later. One of the policemen on the island...'

'PC Johnstone, you mean.'

He didn't deny it, but continued, '...had heard reports of an incident last Friday night, which he had not initially passed on, thinking that Catherine Robinson was drunk, knew about your relationship with Catherine, and he says that she phoned him later, to recant the accusation. He also claimed to have seen your car parked near the hide around the time that the murder occurred. It is also, I believe, a place where you and Catherine used to have intimate relations, many years ago.'

'That was a long time ago and Johnstone's lying about seeing my car near the hide,' I replied.

'Probably.'

'So why am I here?'

'As I said, for your safety. You have upset some very dangerous people and it is important that, if our plans are not to be totally ruined, we need those people to think that the spotlight is off them and that you are, indeed, the prime suspect. They will know that you have been arrested; that's why we made it so public. They might, just might, go ahead with their original plans. I need information from you,' he continued. 'What took place on Friday night?'

'I can't remember anything. Traces of rohypnol were found in my urine, which seemingly would wipe out any memories.'

'Very convenient, don't you think?'

'It was detected in my urine.'

'It could have been tampered with, but I did see the text and we are checking it out. So you remember nothing?'

'No.'

'But you suspected it was Catherine?'

'Yes. I found a jumper, a present from my mother, which neither of us liked and joked about, in my bed. No one else would do that.'

'Quite a steamy relationship. What about the scratches on your face and the love bite on your neck?

'I don't know what happened.'

'Really, do you expect me to believe that.'

'Well, I can't explain how the marks occurred.' I shrugged.

Nick's tone became more assertive with my repeated denials.

'Still harbour any feelings?'

'No, I'm happily married.'

'Once more just for old time sake?'

'No, definitely not.'

'Any other indications that it was Catherine?'

'I found my phone wrapped in my pyjamas, and a message scrawled in lipstick on the bathroom mirror. I recognised her writing.'

'What did it say?

'Listen, and the word was underlined several times, don't go down to the beach.'

Nick looked thoughtful and got up and left the cell. The door wasn't locked behind him, and he returned a few minutes later.

'We are checking something out. In the meantime continue.'

'Malcolm phoned me the next day; he's a friend from school.'

'The husband of Alison who did the urine test?' He was well-informed.

'Yes, told me that he heard Andy Johnstone talking about me in a pub, claiming that Catherine Robinson was going to make a complaint of rape. But he didn't report it, did he?'

'No, but a woman in the bar overheard him talking and informed the police at Lochgilphead. She didn't think that it was right that you were not questioned.'

'How did she know I wasn't?'

'I can't answer that, on grounds of confidentiality,' said Nick, passing on quickly, 'The police at Lochgilphead got involved, believing that their island colleagues were not following procedures and went looking for you.'

'That didn't please you, did it?' I suggested.

'No, we didn't believe the allegations and wanted them played down. We were too late to influence their decision. Tell me about your friends,' he said, changing tack again.

'Who...'

'The Americans.'

'They are not friends, although Sally has got close to Jenny. I met them when they joined me on a tour of the distillery last Monday morning. I then saw Sally in the Celtic House, a cafe near the distillery, when I went for a carryout lunch. She was sitting next to Donald Robinson and a mean-looking individual, called Roy. You'll have heard the recording?'

Nick nodded. 'It was on your phone, transferred by Sally. Did it not strike you as odd that she was sitting their recording their conversation?'

'Until I realised that they were interested in the Robinsons, then it made sense.'

'Why were they interested in the Robinsons?'

I explained about the gold.

Nick scoffed. 'I heard about that,' he said, dismissively, 'but continue.'

'Sally spoke to me the next day, played me part of the recording she had made in the Celtic House and invited me to the cottage where they were staying, a couple of days later. Said that she had to go to Glasgow on urgent business and wouldn't be back until then. I went, they played me the recording. I knew from Malcolm that the police were looking for me, probably going to arrest me. They offered to give me the recording, if I would help them.'

'Did that not sound suspicious?'

'Yes, it was blackmail, but I was desperate, my wife was coming back. Indeed, I didn't know this then, but she was already back on the island.'

'So you were blackmailed into burgling a farm,' he continued and there was a hint of sarcasm in his voice.

'I know what it sounds like, but to me it was a way of resolving the claims made against me,' I replied, getting angry at his manner.

'More like digging a hole for yourself,' Nick stated bluntly.

'What did they find in the cavern?'

'Brian said that he saw a part of a crate which he believed once held gold.'

'Did you see it?'

'No, but I did see the gold coin that he found.'

'Did you touch it?'

'No.'

'Probably chocolate.' There was a pause while he let me think how gullible I was.

'Sally told me later that they had seen what had taken place on Friday night.'

'Very convenient,' said Nick.

'She said that they saw packages being washed up on the shore, dropped off from a boat.'

Nick sat up and I thought he was going to say something, but he just motioned with his hands for me to continue.

'The three of them saw me out for a walk and being attacked. I must have stumbled on the smugglers at a bad time.'

'Sounds like it.' But he was non-committal and his manner was riling me. The problem was that everything I said sounded weak and Nick gave very little away in his reaction to what I was saying, other than trying to undermine me.

'Was it you on the moor?' I enquired, remembering how I had seen a figure briefly silhouetted on the horizon when I was running away.

Nick nodded.

'Were you alone?'

'Yes.'

'They said that they saw several people.'

'They were lying. They are not reliable,' he replied dismissively. 'Brian and Jonathon got booted out of the US army several years ago for smoking pot. They would have known what was being

286

washed up on the shore. They wanted some. Brian was probably trying to emulate his father, Jack Loweski, who was a big-time drug dealer in the States. Silly boys did not realise what they were playing with. Now tell me about Sally.'

'She is interested in the gold, was curious about a plane crash on the island, back in 1984. An American died, but there were rumours that he had discovered the whereabouts of the gold. I think that brought the three of them together – a common purpose.'

'Um,' said Nick, not sounding convinced. 'Have you heard of the Lorimar Clinic in Glasgow?'

I shook my head.

'Your friend Sally takes every opportunity to phone it; that's why she is so keen to take Ben away, so that she can phone them without you knowing.'

'What does the clinic specialise in?'

'A lot of things, unfortunately for us, and due to patient confidentiality we haven't found out her interest yet. She went there when the three of them went to Glasgow, leaving you to sweat. Sally also phones a number in North Dakota which, with help from our friends, we are investigating. We don't trust her and that's another reason we wanted you here, away from her, with our operation at such a delicate stage. Be careful,' he cautioned. 'She appears to be trying to cultivate a friendship with your wife, but we don't know why.'

I noted that, not sure how to react. Sally did seem different from the other two, but I was learning to trust no one.

'Who are the Robinsons involved with?' I asked, curious to find out.

'The biggest drug dealer in Ireland, Desmond McGrory. Well known, lives south of Limerick, controls the drug trade in the Republic. Donegal is not that far away across the North Channel

– twenty-odd miles. Sends regular shipments across to Scotland. Most arrive in Scotland, through the Robinson's farm, in Islay. Great cover, not exactly what Islay is known for.

'The Robinsons were compromised years ago when Charles Robinson rang up big gambling debts. Tried to pay the debts off by cultivating drugs in the storage area, under the hill, growing cannabis, and then tried to produce crack cocaine, the old ventilation shaft might have been useful then, a relic of the previous owners of the farm. But he wasn't very good at it. Only succeeded in running up more debts. Incidentally, you wouldn't have needed the ventilation shaft for smelting gold. You could smelt the gold in your kitchen.

'A visit from some hard men from Glasgow and the two sons were left to run the farm. They were used to smuggle drugs, delivered to the farm from Ireland, onto the mainland. Charles Robinson, his wife and Catherine were effectively kept prisoner on the mainland. It's a common tactic among druggies, ensures everyone will cooperate. They were allowed out, sometimes, but only to deliver the drugs that Donald brought over to them from the island. We have known about that arrangement for years. Better to know the supply route and where it leads to; we can always cut it off later. We were going to do so now, but...' And he looked at me, exasperated, not needing to add that their plans had been mucked up.

'We had hoped to tempt Desmond over to Islay, where we could apprehend him. He was carrying out a review of the drug chain, according to our sources, which would probably cost some people their lives.' Nick checked that I had absorbed that bit of information. Unlikely he'll come now, since Catherine intervened to save your life. He'll sniff out the danger and stay in the Republic. He is totally ruthless. Cross him and he will kill you. You will now be on his radar, so be very careful. He will also have ordered the killing of Catherine to make a point: that loyalty is always to him. He will be angry at losing her; she was once clever and dedicated, but drug abuse had got to her. She was unlikely to have lasted much longer,' he added, almost casually, and his indifference was another of his traits which angered me.

I found it difficult to think, the news was awful. I wiped my nose, tears not far away, but I didn't want to show a reaction in front of Nick.

'Once we know when the next drop off is, we'll close it down. So near...' Nick looked away, regretfully.

There was a knock on the cell door and another man, casually dressed like Nick, but younger, came in and asked Nick to follow him outside. I noticed my phone in his hand and even with the cell door shut I heard a message being played, but couldn't make it out.

Nick came back in with the phone, and without further explanation, he pressed an icon on the screen and I heard a familiar voice.

'Peter,' Catherine began, her voice immediately triggering so many memories, 'when this message pops up on your screen, whatever you do, stay away from Machir Bay. Don't go down to the beach. It will be extremely dangerous, you will be killed. I am sorry that our first meeting in many years ended like it did, but they wanted to kill you for stumbling on their activity. I couldn't let that happen.

'I couldn't face losing both you and our son. You didn't know that I was carrying your baby when I was forced to leave the island. I only discovered it a few days before, was not sure how to tell you, needed your support, so much. I am sure that I would have got it, Peter. I know that you loved me. I couldn't return or let you know, they wouldn't let me. Dad's fault for gambling. We had no choice but to help them or they would have killed Donald

289

and Dylan. Jason was very like you in appearance. All my love, Catherine.'

'What happened to Jason?' I demanded, shouting.

'I don't know.'

'Not good enough!' I shouted louder this time.

Nick stood up to leave.

'Hold on, Nick.' I spat out his name contemptuously. 'I find that I have a son, who's died, it seems, and you just shrug with indifference.'

'We knew of no one of that name or age that lived with them in the time we were aware of them. It's a mystery, so I can't help you. Sorry,' he said, and watched as I sat numbed.

'How did my son die?' I demanded again.

Nick continued to ignore my plea.

'Listen, you bastard, tell me.'

'Peter,' he replied, 'I will try to find out, but I am not promising anything. I see this all the time. Actions taken many years ago can have far-reaching consequences, out of proportion. Life isn't always fair.

'However, I must go. It was an embedded message that Catherine left on your phone,' Nick explained, 'which would only appear on a particular day. So we now know when the next drug run will be. It's tonight. I must get back to Islay immediately.'

Nick hesitated at the door of the cell. 'You will be released when it is safe,' he said. 'Meanwhile we have added an app to your phone, activated by going to your contacts list and searching for the name Alan Siviter and pressing call. It will link you to us and also give us your position. Swap contact lists with your wife and she will also be able to use it. It will transfer from phone to phone. If they come for you, use it. We'll do what we can, but you will need to be very careful, and don't let Ben out of your sight. Sadly, these are the consequences of joining in with the plans of the

Americans, the result of a moment's madness.'

As the implication of his message sank in, he left, and this time I heard the key turn in the lock. I was glad for the solitude, as I tried to piece all the events together. I sat with my knees drawn up on the bed, my arms wrapped around them, slowly rocking back and forward. Catherine had borne me a son, who I had never met, and I never would. And now Jenny and Ben were probable targets for a ruthless gang. Maybe Catherine should have left me to my fate, on the beach, a week ago.

30

Sunday

I have to say that the police were kindly; they were probably a bit uncomfortable that I was in one of their cells. There were obvious tensions between the police and whoever Nick worked for. Nick, had called in a big favour in asking the police to hold me. I was sure that there would be ructions later, but that was not my concern.

A police sergeant sat with me for half an hour after Nick left, doing no more than listening to me and providing a cup of coffee, a human touch that I appreciated. He arranged for a fish supper to be brought in to me and provided an extra blanket. I hardly slept, disturbed by the sound of drunks being brought in, and a brief fight in the corridor outside my cell. By the next morning I was restless, wanting out, and I banged on the door to get attention, fretting about what Jenny and Ben were going through. It was a different shift, and I got a grumpy response, told to be patient.

I was listening to the sound of a church organ wafting through the cell wall from the church next door, adding a surreal touch to my stay, presumably an intro to a morning service at the church I had seen yesterday, when the door swung open and a police inspector came in.

'We have orders,' – so he was covering himself – 'to release you. We can't guarantee your safety, but the person you spoke to yesterday has outlined the help available. Please follow it. Your wife is waiting for you.' He indicated that I should follow him.

I was asked to sign that I had received my phone and other possessions back and was led into the reception area, where Jenny was waiting. I could tell that she wanted out of the police station as quickly as possible, gripping my arm and leading me through the doors, without comment or any expression on her face.

We got into the car before she spoke.

'That bloody woman,' she said. 'How are you?' This was certainly not the time to divulge what Nick had told me about Jason.

'It was a set-up,' I said as she drove out of the car park. 'They never thought that I had killed Catherine. They wanted me out of the way so that they could catch some drug smugglers, back in Islay. Hopefully, including the Robinsons. The operation must be over or I wouldn't have been released.'

'Can you imagine how I felt, my husband taken away accused of murder? Now, I discover it is a set-up. Who do they think they are?' Her anger and resentment were palpable. She was gripping the steering wheel tightly, her knuckles white as she worked her way around a one-way system, and I saw that she was taking me back to the Horizon Hotel.

'They have their suspicions about Sally,' I said. 'Seemingly she is on the phone a lot when she takes Ben away.' I saw Jenny frown as she was presented with this additional information

'She has been very friendly. I like her. It's as if I have always known her,' Jenny said, but now with a look of concern. 'Ben is very attached to her – they formed a quick bond.'

'We better be careful, however. We can deal with Sally, later, if necessary. I don't think she is an immediate threat, the two goons bother me more. Let's not complicate things any further,

293

at the moment.'

Jenny agreed. 'They are having breakfast just now I'll let Ben know we are back but we need to talk.'

We got back to the hotel and Jenny glanced in the dining room to check that Ben and Sally were still there and spoke briefly to them, while I waited outside before she whisked me up to our room.

I sat on the edge of the bed and explained most of what Nick had told me, and she listened intently, without comment, standing staring out of the window into the mid-distance, arms folded in front of her. This was not the reaction I had expected.

Finally she spoke. 'Is it over now?'

'We'll find out when we get back to Islay.' I couldn't be more positive, explain that from now on our lives would always be in danger.

'Let's get back, then,' and Jenny left the room. A minute later Ben ran in and jumped on me, hugging me, delighted to see me.

'The bad men let you go,' he said.

'Sort of,' I replied. I noticed Sally standing at the door.

'How are you?' she said. 'Jenny has told me that you are no longer under suspicion.'

'No, I probably never was.' And with that enigmatic statement I turned my attention back to Ben.

Half an hour later we left, hoping to get the evening ferry from Kennacraig.

• • •

As we drove home from the ferry I didn't even ask Jenny which route to take. I turned at the road junction before the Robinson's farm and took the longer route around Loch Gorm. I had had enough of the Robinsons.

Someone had put the metal plate back in its original place, covering the hole in the driveway. What had occurred on Thursday night now seemed dreamlike and I brushed any thoughts of it aside. We were back, even if Jenny still seemed so quiet, hardly speaking. I was getting a little worried about her.

The porch door was locked and it was a huge relief that Robinson and his crowd had not damaged the bungalow in any way.

On the ferry Sally had phoned Brian and he turned up a few minutes later to collect her, with Jonathon returning my car at the same time.

'Hey man,' Brian said 'we had a visit from the police last night. They stopped us from going out for a walk. What's up?'

'Nothing that I said to them,' I replied, and Sally ushered them into their car after giving Jenny and Ben farewell hugs.

As they drove away I looked anxiously at Jenny.

'Let's get Ben to bed and then we can talk,' she said and gave a brief smile, encouraging me to go along with her plan.

Trauma affects everyone differently. It is like living in another dimension, nothing seems the same. I could have told you little of the journey home, since so much of my brain was preoccupied in trying to make sense of recent events. To Jenny this must have been a total nightmare, but she was strong and was dealing with it in her own way.

With lots of hug, kisses and repetition of favourite bedtime stories, Ben eventually settled and I came back to the lounge. Jenny had started the log burner and was sitting on the couch.

I sat beside her and she burst into tears and grabbed me tightly.

'I am sorry,' she said. 'But this has been so hard for all of us. Now tell me everything,' she added, 'and don't leave anything out this time. Promise me!' She twisted my head until I was looking directly into her eyes. 'Everything,' she repeated, and I bit my bottom lip as I started.

Jenny never flinched, God bless her, asking few questions and was stunned to hear about what the Robinsons had got up to. The revelation about Jason visibly shocked her, but she could tell that it was as big a shock to me.

'No wonder Catherine turned to drugs,' she commented when told that Jason had died. 'She didn't have much of a life.'

She was attentive when I repeated what Nick had told me about Sally, but said nothing.

Later, as she went through to the kitchen to switch on the kettle for coffee, the phone rang. We both froze. Then I grabbed the receiver.

'Hello, Peter, Pence Gifford here.'

'I am so sorry that I couldn't make it in on Friday,' I said quickly.

'I hear that there are a few issues,' he went on, 'easier for everyone if you stay at home. Let's say you call in on Wednesday afternoon. Tuesday's the big festival day for our distillery; life will be easier after that. Three thirty?'

'Yes, of course,' I found myself saying, 'and I can explain everything.'

'Of course, I look forward to that.' He hung up.

'Looks like I am at home for the next few days,' I said.

'Good, you could do with a rest.' Jenny's face relaxed. 'And so could I. Last time I am leaving my husband at home. 'I forgot to tell you Jodie had her pups last night. Three dogs and two bitches. Everyone is doing fine.'

'At last good news.'

Before I went to bed I checked that the doors were locked and looked in on Ben, who was sound asleep. We had to think differently now, be more alert, look out for danger. Nick's warning sounded in my head. Something of the peace of Islay had changed, hopefully not forever.

31

Neither of us slept well, perhaps because we were overtired, and Ben also woke early, excited at being back home, to cut short the little sleep that we had managed. After breakfast, Jenny and I took him for a walk along the beach. It was partly curiosity, to see if there was any sign of police activity from the previous Saturday night. I presumed that the drug smugglers would have used the same route as before, but the beach and car park were empty. Ben ran on ahead of us, splashing about in pools of water left by the receding tide, in his favourite red wellingtons, disturbing the birds which were pecking for food in the wet sand, allowing us time to talk about recent events.

We decided to try and have a normal day, whatever that was, partly for Ben's sake, but also to allow us to unwind. Visiting Jodie and her brood of puppies was a priority, then some essential shopping in Bowmore. Breathe in the fresh Islay air and try to relax, forget about the past week. It sounded attractive, but was it doable? I had also arranged to meet Ronnie later at Port Askaig, the ferry terminal for Jura, to return his car. I was going to thank him with a special distillery bottling of fifteen-year old sherry cask Islay, which I knew he would appreciate.

My phone vibrated as we packed the Golf. Fiona from the

Museum of Islay Life had finally got back to me. I sent her a quick text, thanking her, and then got back to preparing for our trip. Jenny had already contacted Susie and, taking our car and Ronnie's, we made our way around by Saligo, past the RSPB visitor centre, and turned up the Ardnave road. Any sense of returning to normality was soon quashed when I saw a police incident trailer parked in the car park and blue police tape stretched across the pathway that lead to the bird hide. Two policemen were standing about looking chilly in their short-sleeved vests; they probably noted our car registrations as we passed. How do you cope with something like the murder of someone you once loved? And who had murdered Catherine? I had lain awake for hours speculating. Now I tried to blank out any images which jumped into my mind, focusing on the road, but it was not easy.

I drove on another mile before turning off the road into Susie's small steading. Jenny, with Ben, was close behind in the Golf. As we parked and got out of the cars Jenny cast me an anxious glance and muttered, 'Okay?' and I replied, 'Yes.' Over the next few weeks there were going to be lots of reminders of what had happened; we would have to get used to it.

Susie rushed out when she saw that we had arrived, still excited by the arrival of the puppies, and ushered us into her kitchen, letting us know that Jodie was tired and a little anxious and that it was probably best not to stay too long. Jenny agreed that made sense and we had a coffee, while we chatted trying to catch up and also thank her for her help. In the excitement about the birth Susie seemed friendlier towards me, or was she still embarrassed by her actions last week?

However, we learnt that, probably out of spite, our pursuers had pushed her ex-husband's van off the pier at Bunnahabhain. Susie was amused, hoping that it would cause him some financial pain, doubting that he was insured.

We really didn't want to talk about last Friday and Susie seemed to respect this, and anyway the chance of meeting Jodie was a great distraction, especially for Ben.

Jodie, looked exhausted but was so pleased to see us, her tail thumping the ground while two of the puppies suckled her, the puppies' eyes still closed. The others were huddled together. Ben stepped into the cage for a moment, and stroked Jodie's head. Jodie was already proving to be a good mum and her puppies were feeding regularly. Susie had even placed two of the puppies already, although it would be a few weeks more before they were picked up. It had been a big ask for us to give up Jodie for a month, but Susie had already repaid us, although in a way that she probably didn't expect, and the eventual income from selling the puppies would help her back on her feet financially.

We left after an hour and drove on to Bowmore, passing by the police again, and collected shopping at the Co-op, wandering through the aisles like any other couple, discussing which item was better value or whether we still had plenty back at the cottage. Usually shopping was rushed, like 'let's get it over quickly', but, today, we took our time, enjoying the process.

Pleased with our morning's efforts, we then drove onto Port Askaig, where Ronnie was already waiting.

'All in one piece,' he said. 'I am surprised and delighted that you have all returned safely. The police spoke to me on Sunday, showed me pictures. I could identify one of our pursuers, creepy individual, the one that ended up in the water. The police say that they are all off the island now, but to keep an eye open just in case. Good company you keep, Peter.'

There was a slight pause and then he added, 'Have they arrested anyone?'

I laughed and Ronnie looked puzzled, but the explanation could wait for another day.

'Not that I know of, but they seem to know some of the suspects very well.'

'It's the talk of the island and I've heard your name mentioned. Just to warn you.'

'I'm in the clear, let people know that,' and before Ronnie could respond Jenny interrupted: 'Ronnie, the last few days have been hell, especially for Peter. He needs to recover, but one thing is for sure – without the help of friends we would not have made it. Thank-you.' She kissed Ronnie on the cheek. 'And please also thank, Maria.' With that, she walked towards our car. Ronnie took the cue and thanked me for the whisky, and then drove to join the queue for the short ferry crossing across the Sound of Islay.

'After what Ronnie did for us, he's entitled to ask questions, but I dread the others who are just nosey. We'll need to learn to cut them off,' Jenny said as she fastened her seatbelt. I knew she was right.

'Like Pence Gifford,' I replied.

'I'm hoping that he will be understanding and if he sends us to Glasgow that might be a good thing.'

It wouldn't help Jenny, however, who used the island as a source of inspiration. To leave was a big sacrifice from one who loved Islay, earned some of her living from the island.

We climbed the steep winding hill out of Port Askaig, and drove back towards Machir Bay, this time passing Robinson's farm, more able to confront the past this morning, curious to see if anything had changed. We slowed down as we reached the farm. A police van was parked outside the house in the farmyard and a forensics' specialist, in white overalls, was walking out of the cavern, its doors now wide open, its mysterious interior now open to inspection. I wondered what secrets would be revealed, but also wondered if I would ever know. Two more policemen were positioned at the entrance. Islay had not seen as much police activity in years, I mused. I hoped that Nick would turn up and fill us in at some point.

I smiled as I drove, probably appearing more optimistic than I felt, but also thinking about the discomfort that the Robinsons would be experiencing. Maybe karma was a good thing.

'So the police are at their farm,' I said to Jenny, not gleefully, more with a sense of relief. 'Hopefully the Robinsons have been arrested,' I added, vocalising my feelings more plainly. 'You begin to hope that the nightmare is reaching an end.'

Jenny abruptly cut short any such thoughts. 'It's not over, Peter. We've got a simple picture, a small part of the tapestry and if you look on the reverse side you will see a lot of tangled threads. The police have only started to cut them.'

She was right, of course. Having felt for over a week that I was drowning the sensation of getting my head above the water was becoming intoxicating and dangerous. I had to remain vigilant.

We arrived back at the house to find a bicycle lying against the outside wall and in the garden, Sally sitting at the picnic bench in a colourful pair of trousers and a white T-shirt. When she saw us, she got up and came over, smiling and waving to Ben, who was pleased to see her.

'My new mode of transport for the next few weeks, while the boys are away,' she said, pointing at the bike. 'A guy called Nick certainly spooked them. They'll return when it is safe. Very kindly they took me to Port Charlotte to hire a bike,' she added with a touch of sarcasm. 'Anyway I need to get fit. Can I get some lunch? Cycling makes me hungry and we need to talk.' Ben was already draping his arms around her, excited to see her.

Jenny opened the gate. 'In you go,' she said, waving Sally into the garden.

'We better tackle Sally now,' said Jenny as we followed her into Mable's Cottage, and I agreed. We had to be honest, make our feelings clear.

Having eaten, the conversation sporadic, and with the dishes washed and put away, we all sat down in the lounge, amusing Ben. When Ben had gone into his bedroom to look for a toy I felt that there was no point in delaying any longer.

'Sally, a couple of things.' Both the women noticed the sharp tone in my voice. 'Easy issue first.' I had their attention, both were now sitting up, Jenny offering silent support as I began. 'Are Brian and Jonathon still looking for the gold or is it now drugs?

Sally blushed slightly.

'When they discovered about the drugs their priorities did change. They thought that it might be an extra opportunity, if there was no gold. They misled you over the reasons for going to the Robinson's farm. I'm sorry.'

'And the drug smugglers now want vengeance for what we did.' I replied. 'They probably think that we alerted the police. They are nasty people, look what they did to Catherine. It's okay for the two of them to leave the island and go into hiding, we have to face up to the consequences. We live here.'

I tried hard not to let my voice sound too harsh, trying not to alarm Ben, who had now reappeared with a toy dinosaur dangling from one hand, looking at me, a puzzled expression on his face. I smiled to reassure him and he went back into the bedroom.

'I'm sorry,' repeated Sally. 'When I planned the trip I needed their backing, especially financially. Brian's father is rich and he was curious about the suggestion that there was still gold on the island. We struck a deal. When we arrived in London, we confirmed the Robinson's involvement from an ex-lady friend of Ryan Loudoun, who Jack Loweski put us in touch with. She works for Janner and Jones and told us that there was still gold arriving from the Robinsons. 'We then hired a private investigator to find out more about the Robinsons. He refused to continue when he found out about the drug smuggling. I think that he was frightened or warned off.'

'Did he find out anything about Jason?' Sally looked puzzled, but I couldn't stop the question; I asked almost without thinking.

'I don't know who you mean,' Sally said, her eyes widening in puzzlement, squashing any faint hope that I had. 'We did speak to a few locals, including a Jim Campbell, a cousin of Charles Robinson who we met in a pub. He lives by himself now, just outside Bowmore, an alcoholic, his wife left him years ago. Very bitter about the Robinsons. It didn't take long to get information, just a cheap bottle of whisky. He told us a lot, mentioned your mum, Jenny.'

'I'm sure that he did,' replied Jenny. 'They knew each other.'

'He also showed us a gold coin, which he claimed to have stolen from the Robinson's farm. We bought it from him for a pittance. I suspect that he will have drunk his way through all the money by now. Brian showed you it the other night.' Sally suddenly looked embarrassed, realising what she had admitted, and wouldn't meet my gaze, her eyes lowered. I saw Jenny moving uneasily on the couch, her eyes now fixed on Sally, her mouth narrowing. 'If the boys' hadn't got distracted by the thought of drugs we might have made more progress.'

That too was unfortunate, Sally, I thought. Their distraction had cost us dear.

'I got a text message this morning,' I said. 'Remember Arthur and Dominic?'

Sally nodded. Jenny already knew, as I had shown her the text.

'Arthur was Private Arthur Lawrence and Dominic was Sergeant Dominic Harris, both of the King's Shropshire Light Infantry, seconded on special duties. They are buried at Kilchiaran graveyard.

Close to the graves is a barn owned by the Robinsons. In the barn is a machine made by Parker and Thomson. They make gold furnaces, I discovered on the internet. Probably the furnace was moved there in the sixties, given how grimy it now is. Other than the furnace the barn is empty, disused. No gold in it now. You are too late, Sally.'

As she thought about what I had said, I threw in the next matter that I wanted to raise with her, hoping to catch her off-balance.

'Why did you break into the cottage? Were you looking for a DNA sample to take to the Lorimar Clinic?'

Sally bit her lip, glancing at Jenny, but Jenny didn't offer any comfort, her face by now fixed.

'That's why I came today. I got the result of the genetic test.' Sally turned to Jenny, knowing that the conversation had not panned out as she expected, but hoping that her revelation would change the tone.

'It's ninety-nine point nine certain that you and I have the same father, Ryan Loudoun III. We're half-sisters, Jenny.'

The two women did not speak; they might have been brought up half a world apart, but they shared a common lineage. While Jenny was stunned, Sally was waiting for a reaction, a response to her claim. She swallowed nervously; it obviously meant a lot to her.

'I have the paperwork here,' she said when there was no immediate response, and she pulled a crumpled letter from the back pocket of her trousers and handed it to Jenny.

Jenny took it, read it, and handed it to me without comment. The letter confirmed the claim. Looking at the two of them, I could see a family resemblance. Sally didn't after all remind me of a TV star from some American soap; the eyes, even the smile were similar to Jenny's. I handed the letter back to Sally.

'Our father slept around a lot, I'm afraid,' Sally said. I felt sorry for Jenny. Now she knew that both her parents weren't exactly paragons of virtue. 'We probably have an extended family around the world, if the stories I hear are correct. He didn't officially acknowledge me, but my mother raised the matter in court, in North Dakota, and he was made to pay for my education. He died not long after. I never met him. Nor did we get any money,' she added.

'I felt that we had something in common.' Jenny spoke quite softly and slowly, trying to control herself. 'But I never imagined this, not even after you told me about the phone calls to the clinic, Peter.'

Sally looked at me.

'I also had a visit from Nick,' I explained.

Jenny's voice was stronger now. 'I should be pleased. I liked you, Sally, hoped for a long-term friendship, saw how well you got on with Ben. Although I believe you used the opportunities when you were alone with him, to make phone calls, which was deceitful. However, you broke into our home, helped to blackmail my husband and put our family at risk. I wanted a bigger family more than you can possibly imagine. You saw the state of Colin and I don't blame him for going away. He did what he could. Now I find that I have a half-sister and look what she has done. Could you please leave, Sally.' Jenny's voice almost broke as she tried to retain control.

'I too wanted a family,' replied Sally, 'and I am sorry for the break-in. Emotion clouded my judgement, I had to know if my suspicions were correct. We got on well. I thought that you would be pleased with the news, but I understand that it was a big mistake to have put Peter and everyone else at risk.'

'I think that you should go, Sally,' I said, and reluctantly she got up, the meeting not having turned out as she hoped. Ben,

306

who was now standing by his bedroom door, rushed forward, but Jenny stopped him getting to Sally and held him close.

I stood up and went to the door and Sally, looking flustered, turned back towards Jenny, wordlessly trying to plead with her, her eyes brimming with tears, but she got no response. After a moment she left.

'I didn't see that coming,' said Jenny, referring to the letter, which Sally had dropped on the floor as she went out. 'And I had so warmed to her, but she has placed us all in great danger; that's unacceptable,' she added firmly.

I watched as Sally mounted her bike and cycled down the driveway.

32

The phone rang later that day and Jenny answered, swapped pleasantries, and handed the phone over to me.

'It's Malcolm,' she said.

'Hi, Peter, how are you, settling back into Islay life?'

'Not really,' I replied. 'We have been trying to be normal for Ben's sake but it's hard to forget what has just happened to us. However, please thank Alison for the drug test, that helped a lot.'

'I am pleased that we could help. A murder, drugs seizure, even car chases are not normal on Islay. Word gets around and the paper will have to comment on events come the weekend, when the new issue is out. The police have been in to talk to us and we are cooperating with them. There is unfinished business, it seems.'

Jenny was watching me, trying to interpret the conversation from how I was responding. I smiled at her, trying to reassure her.

'Peter,' Malcolm continued, 'they have arrested Donald Robinson for the murder of his sister.' I repeated the statement for Jenny's benefit and her eyes widened and her head jerked back involuntarily.

'It's hard to believe,' continued Malcolm, 'but they have the DNA evidence required to charge him. He doesn't seem to deny it; he is so frightened.'

What fear could make someone murder their own sister? My mind went back to that chilling recording that Sally had made in the Celtic House.

'What about drug seizures?' I asked, needing time to grasp the enormity of what he had told me.

'They arrested five people on Saturday night at the Robinson's farm. Donald, Dylan, Andy Johnstone and two others.'

'Andy Johnstone?' I said. 'Not a surprise.'

'A small cog in a big machine, I suspect,' said Malcolm. 'But making sure that nothing came to the attention of the authorities was important and the local police had been corrupted. Catherine blew his cover by saving you. Ironically, he always had a crush on her.'

Another matter jumped into my mind. 'Who else was in the bar when Johnstone spilled the beans about my encounter with Catherine?'

'Why?'

'Someone contacted the police when they thought that nothing was being done. That's why the police were looking for me.

'Let me think,' Malcolm replied. 'There weren't that many people there. Oh, yes, Pence Gifford's PA.'

'Mrs Hall?'

'That's the one.'

'What were the names of the others arrested?' Malcolm had not expected this because he asked for a minute to check.

'A Roy Brown and a Tim O'Rourke.'

The second name meant nothing to me but I hoped that the first name was the guy in the cafe. I would be pleased if he was out of the way.

'They got a number of packages, grade A cocaine, I believe,' said Malcolm, 'and there was more action at sea, off Islay, but there are no details of that at present.'

'I can add nothing,' I said.

'Instructions from Nick?' Malcolm was fishing for information.

'If you like. Is he still around?

'Who knows?'

'Now,' said Malcolm. 'Car chases and vehicles ending up in the sea. The police have put it down to a drunk driver, or at least that is the story they are putting out. We know different, don't we, Peter!'

'Susie took it well,' I replied.

'But not her ex-husband.'

We laughed.

'You will be relieved that it is all over,' said Malcolm, acknowledging that I could add nothing further.

'I hope that it is.' But again I was thinking that an organisation that could order someone to murder his own sister was not one to cross.

'You've had a hard time, old friend. Hopefully we can catch up with you and Jenny soon. Take care.' Malcolm hung up.

I quickly filled Jenny in. Her immediate concern was like mine: where did it all leave us?

'Hopefully Desmond McGrory cuts his loses,' she commented.

'Have you checked that the app Nick placed on your phone is there?' I said.

'Yes,' replied Jenny. 'Have you?' I checked again, hoping that I would never have to use it.

Then I remembered Mrs Hall's involvement.

'I wonder why Mrs Hall went to the police?'

'That's easy,' replied Jenny. 'Mr Hall used to visit my mother.'

• • •

'Interesting times,' said Gifford as I sat down opposite him, and his eyes behind his glasses watched me closely. The familiar smells of the room, the varnish, the sweet scent of the whisky samples, the rows of sample bottles, helped me to settle.

'Glad that you could come in. We missed you last week but I understand that events were out of your control. I had a visitor yesterday.'

'Nick?'

'Yes, if that is his name.' He gave me a knowing look. 'Jenny and Ben, all right?' he asked.

'So far.'

'Peter, I want to implement the plan I suggested last week. Time for Glasgow and lying low. Speak to Jenny, but you could move in a few weeks. By the way, Nick was impressed by how you coped, although my friends at Bunnahabhain may be less so. Start work again next week, if you can.'

'Thanks,' I said. 'And how is the drain blockage doing? Will I still have to divert the tours?'

'Oh no,' said Pence. 'We resolved the issue not long after we spoke. There were several staves blocking the system. We got lucky and were able to remove them. One less issue to worry us.'

'Did you use a company from Larkhall to free the blockage?'

'No,' said Gifford, 'in the end we managed ourselves.'

I told him about the van and the hoses that I had seen last Wednesday as I returned to pick up my car late that evening, after visiting Beattie.

Gifford rose from his seat, agitated, and started pacing the office.

'Tell me more.' His face was thunderous.

I filled in all the details that I could remember.

'Peter, my boy, thank-you!' He ushered me to the doorway and opened the door. Mrs Hall lowered her head, but the distillery manager noticed the movement.

'Peter, thank-you for coming in. I will let it be known that the rumours that have been circulating about you are entirely false and I will take it personally if they are repeated.' And with a large wink that only I could see, he ushered me out.

Mrs Hall kept her head lowered, but I thought that I saw her blush. Gifford was already on the phone, probably to headquarters in Glasgow.

• • •

The seal pack was exposed on a sand bar in the loch as the funeral cortege wound its way down to the small graveyard at Kilnave with its ruined church and historic cross. The funeral director, top hat under his arm, walked slowly, those carrying the coffin a short distance behind maintained a steady pace, the flowers on top safe from falling off. On the far side of the loch, the high sand dunes with their top covering of machir caught the afternoon sun. Cattle munched grass contentedly in front of the ruined farmhouse at Killinallan, with the tall concrete silo to the rear the most prominent of the farm buildings. Between the farm buildings and the low Islay hills, a short distance beyond, was empty moorland. Above Islay's hills the Paps of Jura stood loftily, their peaks covered in mist, several streams sparkling on the slopes, a product of the recent rain. It was as if the hills were joining in the sombre occasion.

Within the small cemetery a grave had been freshly dug. The Rev Walker was waiting to welcome the funeral party. I stood by the cemetery wall, scanning the small group of mourners, all six of them, but didn't recognise anyone. They showed no reaction to our presence.

It struck me how small Catherine's coffin was. As the funeral party entered the graveyard Jenny squeezed my hand more tightly, providing support at a time of high emotion; memories of a happier occasion here and its consequences seared in my mind. I did not, could not, venture near the ruined church. I stared ahead, careful not to catch anyone's eyes, but glad for the company of friends: Malcolm and Alison, Ronnie and Maria, and Susie.

The Rev Walker spoke briefly, looking older, his hair greying, calling on the grace and mercy of Jesus Christ and giving a short Gaelic blessing. Hopefully the blessing in Gaelic could provide a bridge between here and eternity. 'There is always light in the midst of darkness,' he concluded, and I thought how that required faith. I would talk to the minister when all this was over.

As the funeral party left, we remained to place a small wreath of flowers at the graveside, with an added note.

'To Catherine and Jason, love from Peter and Jenny xxx'

If she was looking down, she would get the message.

I saw Alison read the message and her face betrayed her puzzlement, but she said nothing, nudging Malcolm in case he missed it. No doubt there would be a lot of discussion between them later.

House martins flew in and out of the ruins of the church, their activity somehow soothing. Once again nature's display could help calm the troubled soul; life does not pause.

No one spoke as we walked through the field up to the single-track road from the graveyard. As we walked towards our car I became aware of Nick standing by the stone wall. He followed me to the car and motioned me into the back seat.

'It's Nick,' I said to Jenny, who was alarmed by his presence, never having met him before.

'Hello, Mrs Meldrum,' he started. 'Sorry to have alarmed you, but I wanted to provide your husband with an update and remind you about the app on your phone.' His words were a sobering reminder that not everything was over, yet. He had our full attention.

'We have no suspects on the island at the moment, but I wondered if they might try something at the funeral. Thankfully not. Peter, we didn't get Desmond McGrory. He never left the Republic. We did intercept his boat, however, which was carrying drugs, and got a good return, several million pounds, in fact. With the whisky festival on we decided to arrest the Robinsons at the farm, not the beach. I believe that the Islay connection has been severed, and hopefully McGrory will leave it like that. By the way, your two American friends are on their way back, booked on this evening's ferry. Good prospecting,' he said, and a grin played across his face, as he opened the car door and got out.

In some ways the level of surveillance was comforting.

'I hope that it's the only time that I have to meet him,' Jenny said coldly, unimpressed.

33

I waited as the evening CalMac ferry, its red funnel topped with black and a lion inside a yellow circle on its side, manoeuvred into the tight landing slip at Port Ellen, preparing to disgorge its passengers and cars at the ferry terminal. It edged closer, under threatening grey clouds as a weather front moved rapidly in. Already the lighthouse across the bay was partially obscured by mist and what had been a gentle breeze was strengthening, with the first flecks of rain coming down. About forty cars and trucks waited in their allocated lanes, ready to drive onto the ferry, the CalMac staff organising them efficiently in what was a cramped area that needed careful managing. After a few minutes the ferry ramp came down and there was a steady thump as cars cleared the ramp and then drove past to reach the main road in Port Ellen. I saw Brian and Jonathon in their BMW, their faces expressionless, go past, not noticing me as I stood perched by the railing of the war memorial on a small hillock, a good vantage point to scan the foot passengers as they disembarked. I doubted if I would see them again and hoped that I wouldn't. I didn't need them back.

Colin and Mandy were two of the last foot passengers to make their way down the passenger ramp to reach dry ground, Colin, slightly behind Mandy, carrying a couple of cases. I wondered what the chemistry would be like between them. Would Colin still be ordering Mandy about? But the fact that he was lugging the cases was promising and even from a distance Mandy appeared to be excited by her new surroundings.

I waved as soon as I saw them and walked towards them.

'Good to see you both and welcome back to Islay, Colin. Is this your first visit, Mandy?' She shook her head affirmatively as I warmly embraced them, ensuring that they knew that I was pleased to see them; but the signs were already positive, I thought, both seeming relaxed, the body language between them much better than the last time we met.

'Jenny and Ben are back at the house, preparing the meal – well, at least, Jenny is,' I added, 'and Ben will be very pleased to meet you both again. He has been looking out his toys all afternoon, Mandy. Please be patient with him.' Mandy laughed.

We drove out of Port Ellen, and kept to the High Road, which was a little more direct and missed out Bowmore. This wasn't the time for Colin to be reminded of old haunts. The rain had become a downpour by the time we reached the head of Loch Indaal, and it was increasing in intensity, obscuring Bowmore on the eastern side of the loch as we took the Kilchoman road. We drove past Robinson's farm, which seemed deserted, without comment, and reached our cottage. Despite the rain Jenny and Ben came out to greet our guests, accompanied by Jodie.

Colin seemed pleased to see everyone and petted the dog, always a good sign. Mandy was much brighter, more confident, than she had been during our last encounter, although she still said very little.

'I imagine that there is a beautiful outlook from here,' said Colin, and Jenny laughed,

'But being Scotland we like to hide it. The forecast for tomorrow is much better, so you will see the beach, Mandy.'

'That's a nice dinosaur,' said Mandy, as Ben presented his toys for inspection, 'and a big pirate's sword.'

It might have been only a bottle of the Co-op's own Australian Red, but it did the trick. By now the rain was lashing against the windows, but no one cared.

'It does seem strange being back on Islay,' said Colin, finishing his second glass of wine and not refusing a further top-up. I'm glad that I had a further bottle. 'I remember many days like this, but that is Scotland, as Jenny said.' And he smiled affectionally at Jenny.

Was it the wine or the warmth of the welcome? Who cared: a family was making tentative steps at coming together again.

I filled Colin in on recent events, little having been reported in the press, his mouth slackening in amazement as he heard about the fate of the Robinsons, but as carefully as I looked there was no sympathy for them. Both Donald and Dylan faced multiple charges and were on remand. I knew nothing about the fate of the farm, with no one left to run it. The mellowing effect of the wine distanced me, reducing my emotional engagement with the events, but I decided to say nothing about Catherine or Jason. Doing that would only make the evening more taxing for Jenny.

'I wonder where Charles Robinson is now?' Colin pondered and the only response I could think of was that he was in a nursing home, probably with his wife beside him.

'He must be in his eighties by now,' I added.

Hopefully, the discussion would help Colin's journey, promote healing from past grievances. Mandy and Jenny were talking away, no further wine required to lubricate their discussion. The evening went quickly and we showed the couple into our bedroom, which we had given up for them. Ben was already asleep when Jenny joined him in his room, on a bed of cushions. I let Jenny know that our Americans were back on the island before kissing her good night and leaving the room.

I worked my way into a sleeping bag and settled on the couch, Jodie lying down beside me. Once during the night I heard her growling and I put down my hand to quieten her. She soon settled.

The next morning the storm had passed over and the sun was out, the air was fresher and the heat was already intensifying; it was going to be a good day. The first part of the day was spent chatting over a long breakfast before we took Colin and Mandy a tour of Saligo, with a walk along the beach and then onto Bowmore, where we had a coffee. Colin was busy pointing out places to Mandy, more animated than I had expected. We made an obligatory visit to the Islay Distillery shop, where my staff discount was useful in helping to buy a fifteen-year-old bottling, sherry finished of course, having discovered that Colin liked a dram. We collected sausages from the butcher and a disposable BBQ from the Spar, along with rolls and ketchup.

By lunchtime we were back at the cottage planning the barbeque, noticing the first tenuous wisps of a sea mist edging in, not unusual in this part and not something that would us stop us picnicking. It took several trips to gather all the bits and pieces for the barbeque, Colin and Mandy helping out, with Mandy buttering the rolls and Colin gathering tartan rugs to spread over the sand. Finally, I got some bottled beer from the fridge and put the bottles in a cool bag ready for later.

Earlier in the week I had heard from Fiona, at the Islay Folk Museum, with the good news that she had been able to trace John Ferguson's ancestors, so I could finally return the gold watch and chain. I slipped the watch and chain in my pocket to show Colin later, before I posted it. Our two visitors decided to go for a walk to the north end of the beach and we were left with Ben and Jodie.

'This is going perfectly,' Jenny said I feel that I have my

brother back. He helped me so much just by being around when I was young, although he hated my Goth phase.' She laughed. 'I must remind him of that! And I do like Mandy,' she added. 'She is a lovely girl and they are getting on so much better. I had a chance to talk with her while you were in the distillery shop, and Mandy said that Colin was quite different after we visited. I don't think that they would have stayed together for much longer and now they are wanting a baby.' Jenny was happier than I had seen her in weeks, certainly since her return to the island.

'And,' she continued, 'is it not time we thought about another one.' Jenny looked expectantly at me.

'Of course,' I replied, with a big smile. 'I thought the puppy with the mostly black head and one white eye would be perfect, a great companion for Jodie.' I waited for the reaction, a none too playful punch. I held up my hands in mock surrender and Jenny laughed.

It was then that I heard Jodie barking and realised that Ben and she had slipped away. I saw alarm on Jenny's face and in a second I was hurtling down the steep slope of the sand dune towards the beach, my heels digging into the soft sand as I tried to keep my balance. I ran, listening for the direction of the next bark.

'Get Colin!' I shouted back to Jenny, knowing instinctively that something was wrong. Jodie's bark was not a playful one, anxious, repetitive, she was disturbed and trying to alert us.

'Ben!' I shouted, and again, louder. I was rewarded by Jodie's frantic barking, some distance away, but the swirling mist prevented me from seeing where they were. My heart was pumping, my chest heaving. I stopped for a minute to draw breath, calm down, but I still peered anxiously through the mist. There on the sand was one of Ben's red wellington boots, beside sand that had been disturbed; something had happened there.

I shouted Ben's name again. Still no reply. I cursed myself for not watching them, and then I heard footsteps behind me and saw Jenny emerging from the mist.

'Colin is coming,' she gasped and we both picked up pace, continuing to shout. Jodie's frenetic barking spurring us on. Finally, I saw Jodie and she was barking loudly at something ahead of her. She turned briefly but in that way that Border Collies have, she was trying to show us something; our missing child.

We had reached the southern edge of the beach, where there were rocky escarpments, near the path that led up to Granny's Rock and beyond to Kilchiaran Bay. I jumped from rock to rock, not caring when my feet slipped, splashing through deep pools of water.

Then the mist briefly cleared and on a rocky spur ten yards away I saw Charles Robinson, clutching Ben, a knife held at his throat. He was so much older, his face lined and blotched, only a few wisps of hair left on his head, and as I got closer I saw his eyes, cold as ever, red and watering. He wheezed as I approached, his thin raspy voice croaking as he attempted to shout.

'Stop, Meldrum, or I will throw your son off the edge, with his throat slit. An eye for an eye.' I wondered what he meant, but he continued. 'You gave us Jason and we lost him, why should you not suffer a loss? I don't care. I have lost Catherine and you ensured that Donald and Dylan will be in jail for a long time. I have nothing left and only a short time to live. I will take pleasure in what I am going to do. You'll be riddled with guilt, you weren't attentive enough, were you?' He spat out the last few words with contempt, sneering at me.

I couldn't see Ben's face, but saw him struggling. Jenny caught up with me and took in the scene. The mist was finally clearing and I could see that Robinson and Ben were at the end of a rocky spur, about twenty feet above jagged rocks and rock pools. Robinson could react before we could reach him. I felt in my pocket but my phone was back at the barbeque site and I could see that Jenny didn't have her phone with her.

I heard more footsteps and saw that Colin had reached us.

'Oh, this is good,' said Robinson. 'More friends to see Ben die.'

Colin called out. 'Hello father, you don't change, do you?' There was total hatred echoing in his voice, an atavistic outpouring of visceral revulsion.

'I don't recognise you as a son, never have, never will. You were weak, just like your mother, grasping for attention. She was so stupid she didn't realise that I was only interested in carnal pursuits, my pleasure. Yea, she was good at that, a few kind words,' and his voice lingered on the wind, 'and she was anyone's.'

I saw Jenny grasp Colin's arm tightly.

'He's just enjoying winding you up, ' she whispered urgently to him. She transferred her gaze to the old man who was holding her son.

'You killed my father,' said Jenny.

'Oh, the American with a name like a country and western singer who thought that we were too stupid not to recognise his game. Didn't last long, did he?'

I looked beyond Robinson and saw movement on the path leading down from Granny's Rock.

'We need to keep him talking,' I whispered to Jenny, and turned away quickly, not wanting her to question me.

'So Catherine was pregnant when the thugs came and gave you a beating. Gambling away your family, putting your family at risk. But you only ever cared about yourself,' I shouted.

'I was going to stop her seeing you anyway,' he replied. 'She could have done a lot better than a simple island laddie. I was going to have the baby aborted, but they wouldn't let me.' He stopped, realising what he had said.

'Who are they?' I shouted, but he looked down at Ben and I took the chance to move a yard closer, to the end of the rocky spur.

'You were so clever that you let your family be controlled, blackmailed, made to follow orders!' Jenny shouted. 'Pretty useless!' It riled him. I could see that he was tiring too.

Colin chipped in. 'Remember the gold coins that went missing? I stole them, paid for some of my house, thank-you.' Robinson looked up, angry. 'And furthermore I intend to contest your will, make a claim on your farm. After all I'm family.'

Colin had caught my eye, knowing we had to keep talking. Ben was wriggling, shouting for me and Jenny, his face etched with fear. So near, yet we were still powerless.

Suddenly, Sally appeared by our side, out of breath, grasping the situation, holding a leather bag in front of her.

'So you are Mr Robinson, who was responsible for my father's death.'

Robinson looked confused. 'Who the hell are you?

'Ryan Loudoun's daughter.'

'He slept around,' sneered Robinson.

'You can talk,' Sally replied, 'and look at this. Was this what you were here for?' And she emptied the leather bag, gold coins spilling over the ground in front of her, the sunlight, which had broken through the dissipating mist, reflecting off the scattered coins. 'A clever place to hid them, underneath the metal frame of the disused gold furnace. We've taken them all, by the way, part payment for what you did to my family.'

Robinson was tiring, wheezing. He finally put Ben down, still gripping him tightly by the throat, the sharp blade hard against the skin, close to the edge of the rocks, perched above the shore below. Ben had gone mute, his eyes bulging.

I had moved closer each time Robinson looked away, my hand in my pocket grasping the gold watch and chain, waiting for the moment.

I saw a hand appear on the rocky edge behind Robinson and he turned, alerted by the noise, looking down.

I threw the watch, shouting out, 'Pirate's gold!'

Instinctively, he raised his arm to protect himself, unbalancing his body. Jenny released Jodie and she barked loudly as she ran towards him. He started to topple. Brian grabbed Ben by the ankle, the knife falling harmlessly from Robinson's hand.

Robinson toppled slowly at first, shouting out, but the words were lost and he fell to the ground below, hitting the ground and bouncing once. He made a groaning noise, the sound of air being expelled from his body by the force of the impact. He lay spread-eagled at the water's edge, his mouth open, gaping, the incoming tide just reaching him and then retreating. The water around his mouth slowly turned pink, then red as each successive wave briefly filled his mouth. It was as if Machir Bay was cleansing the poison that had polluted it for many years.

We had all rushed forward to push Robinson, aiding his fall, but I was first; looking for redemption for Catherine. Goodness knows we all had enough reason. But at the back of my mind I was thinking: was he acting on his own, an attempt at vengeance for his family's plight, or had he been sent by McGrory? If it was McGrory, would he try again?

Jenny was sobbing as she held Ben tightly. I watched Robinson's body for another minute, not sure if he could ever be killed, if he would arise like a vampire, to seek our blood, haunt us forever. I saw Jonathon go over to his body and kick it. He then looked up at me. 'Dead!' he shouted. I then swung round and grabbed Jenny and Ben in a big collective hug of relief.

For the moment.

Islay

I have visited Islay for over thirty years. I love the island, not just for its malt whiskies but also for its beauty, tranquillity and especially its people. It is a place where you can relax, enjoy the scenery, walk along its many beaches and benefit from a less hectic pace of life. For me it was the natural setting for my story.

I tried to change as little as possible. 'Islay' distillery is, of course, Bowmore distillery but using a fictitious name meant that I was not forced to choose one of the distilleries over the others, something that I would have found difficult. Labelling the distillery 'Islay' also ensured that I could have freedom to create characters and situations to suit my storyline.

The location of the Robinson's farm is critical to the plot and I imagine it to be roughly east of Sunderland farm, which for the sake of the story, I removed. Similarly, there are a few changes at Machir Bay, Kilchiaran Bay and around Coullabus.

There were large transfers of gold bullion across the Atlantic during the Second World War to settle war debts. Initially the British authorities released details of gold sales on the financial markets. The Germans closely followed the financial markets and altered U-boats to look out for ships carrying gold in the days after the sales. It took a while for the British authorities to realise this and not release the details.

I would recommend *Peat, Smoke and Spirit* by Andrew Jefford for anyone wanting to learn more about Islay's history and its whiskies.

Acknowledgements

My special thanks to my wife Christine and son Scott for their support and encouragement, to Gillian Wham for the cover and book design and to Stephen Cashmore for editorial support.

Alasdair Wham
August 2017

Photographs:
Front cover - Machir Bay
Back cover - shipwreck at Machir Bay